# THE AUDIT

## Edward J. McMillan

Harwood Publishing

For

Mazzy

# Acknowledgements

I would like to thank everyone for their encouragement and support during the writing of THE AUDIT, but particularly Anne Jewell, Rosalie Rosetti, Patricia Poupore and especially Eileen Shaw.

Published by

Harwood Publishing
Post Office Box 233
Churchton, MD 20733

ISBN: 1-930270-00-3

Printed in the United States of America

May, 2000

Library of Congress Numbers applied for.

Cover design by Chad Bell

# Chapter One

Hoping to wake from the nightmare, Pat struggled to push open his brown eyes, now dilated and bloodshot. "My legs. I can't feel my legs!" His mind was screaming. "I can't breathe! Why do I ache so much?"

Only he wasn't dreaming.

Patrick Sean McGuire was fighting for his life.

The shock trauma ward at Baltimore's University Hospital was cool, white and sterile. Pat tugged to find his hands strapped to the sides of his bed. Sharp pains seemed to accompany each breath, his lungs held hostage by his broken ribs. A cervical collar enveloped his neck. The tall, well-muscled man's hips and legs lay numb and still. Copper-blond hair tufted out from above the bandage wrapping the top of his head. Mercifully, the pain alternated with a foggy, drug-induced exhaustion as he slipped in and out of consciousness.

Baltimore is a city that shows two distinct faces. In "Balmur", as it is affectionately called by those who live there, it's where you went to high school, not college, that's important. High schools like Loyola, Poly, City, Forest Park, Calvert Hall, Gilman, Dunbar, Patterson, Seton-Keogh, Mount de Sales, Mount St. Joseph are wrapped in tradition and resist change—much like the city itself. Most loom large, with student bodies of over a thousand and are still elite, single-sex schools.

Pat McGuire was raised in a one-bedroom apartment over a liquor store in the western section of the city. His parents worked hard to ensure their only son would get the best possible education, but struggled to make the steep tuition payments to keep Pat enrolled in Mount St. Joseph High School. Pat helped out the best he could by working as a busboy in a Little Italy restaurant and rarely complained.

It was at Saint Joe, as the school was affectionately called, that Pat met Russell Autry who would later become his best friend. Pat and Russell were both starters on the school's football team, the Gaels. Pat excelled both academically and athletically. His grade point average, a solid B plus, was good, and he had exceptional grades in mathematics, but not quite good enough to attract an academic scholarship. He started at linebacker on the highly competitive varsity football team for two years, and was admired for being hard-hitting and aggressive, but his physical stature, six-one and a solid two hundred five pounds, limited his competitiveness on the college level. Russell was considerably larger than Pat at six-foot-four and two hundred thirty pounds, and Pat kidded him constantly about his curly black hair that was so thick and tight Pat felt he didn't need a helmet. Russell, like Pat, accepted that even at his size he would be too small to play tackle in college.

After graduation, accepting the reality of where he was in life and not wanting to be a financial burden on his parents, Pat followed in his father's footsteps and enlisted in the Marine Corps for four years active duty. After completing basic training at Parris Island, South Carolina, and advanced infantry training at Camp LeJeune, North Carolina, Pat received orders to report for duty as a rifleman at Camp Butler on the island of Okinawa. Russell went on to college at the University of Maryland.

Pat enjoyed his tour of duty on Okinawa, played on the regimental football team and started accumulating college credits at night school, taking general study courses, undecided on what his major would be. He continued to correspond with his friend, Russell, who was majoring in accounting and planned to earn his CPA and work for his father's accounting firm in downtown Baltimore.

Pat had served two years when he received a change of duty station and was ordered to report to the Marine Corps Finance Center in Kansas City, Missouri, to be trained as an accountant due to his proficiency in math.

To his surprise, Pat, now a corporal, actually enjoyed accounting. He found it challenging and discovered he possessed a natural talent for it. Continuing his education in Kansas City, he decided to make accounting his major, with the eventual goal of becoming a certified public accountant. Russell was delighted and had hopes they could work together at his father's firm, Autry, Martin & Ramsey.

By the end of his four-year duty, Pat had been promoted to sergeant. Although offered a guarantee of attending officers' candidate school after he earned his degree, he had met a girl, Lynn Gilmore, and they had become serious and he felt that active military life would be difficult on a young couple.

Pat decided not to reenlist, received an honorable discharge and returned to Baltimore, planning to stay with his parents until he found a job and an apartment and then Lynn would move from Kansas City to join him.

Pat quickly renewed his friendship with Russell, who was now a CPA and working for his father's firm. Pat felt almost guilty when Russell told him he had arranged for an interview with his father, Gilbert Autry, for a position as a junior accountant. On one hand Pat didn't want to impose on his friendship with Russell, and on the other hand he realized how fortunate he was to be offered such an opportunity so quickly.

His parents had bought him a conservative navy blue suit for the job interview. It occurred to Pat that this was only the second suit he'd ever owned. His mother had helped him pick out the white button-down shirt and blue-and-red tie. He had polished his black business wing tip shoes to a rich luster. He slid into his old Camaro and drove downtown, noticing the changes in the Baltimore skyline.

The offices of Autry, Martin & Ramsey, CPAs, were located in an office building on Pratt Street, just east of University Hospital. Turning down Greene Street, he passed Edgar Allen Poe's grave, making a right onto Pratt at the Bromo Selzer Tower.

Pat pulled into a parking lot next to the building. The attendant handed him a ticket and directed, "Just pull up behind that bronze Corvette."

He admired the Corvette for a few moments before crossing the street. "Some day," he thought to himself.

He pushed the double glass doors open and crossed the marble floor to search the wall directory. There it was, Room 800. When the elevator doors opened, he stepped directly into the office.

"Wow, they have the whole floor," he whispered to himself.

"May I help you, sir?" The receptionist was a statuesque, pale-blond woman of about sixty.

"Yes, I have an eleven o'clock appointment with Mr. Gilbert Autry. My name is Pat McGuire." He noticed her name plate, Edie Veteck.

"Ann, there's a Pat McGuire here to see Mr. Autry."

A few moments later a tastefully dressed, brunette woman stood before him.

"Mr. McGuire?"

"Yes?"

"I'm Ann Johnson, Mr. Autry's secretary. Please follow me."

The secretary stopped at a large, sun-filled office and tapped on the frame of the open door. Gilbert Autry looked up and rose from his desk. "Pat!" he said cheerfully as he rounded his desk to shake Pat's hand. "Have a seat. Make yourself comfortable. Coffee?"

"Yes, sir."

They sat in comfortable chairs facing each other.

"So tell me, how are you finding civilian life?"

"Well, I've been out for only two weeks, so I can't say I'm used to it yet, sir. It still feels strange not putting on a uniform."

"You'll get used to it. Any exciting adventures?"

"I got engaged."

"I heard. Tell me about your fiancé."

"We met while I was stationed in Kansas City, and we hit it off right away. Her name is Lynn Gilmore. She'll be here next week."

"What does she do?"

"She just graduated from Southeast Missouri State University. She majored in elementary education, and she'll be looking for a teaching job somewhere. We'll be staying with my folks in Catonsville for a couple of days until we can find a place of our own."

"How do your folks feel about all this?"

"Well," Pat sighed, "to be honest with you, I don't think they're exactly thrilled at the prospect of our living together, but they're coming around."

"Russell did the same thing before he got married, so I'm certainly not in a position to comment. I wish you both the best of luck, and I know you'll be fine."

"Thank you, Mr. Autry."

"Now about you," Autry said, "if I remember right, you're finishing up your degree at the University of Baltimore, and you'll be taking a CPA review course."

"Those are my plans, in addition to looking for employment."

"That's why I asked you here. How would you like to work with us? I know a hard worker when I see one, and you'd fit right in. Besides, Russell would really like it if you two were back on the same team."

"I'd like it very much. Can you tell me a little about the position and the firm?"

Studying Pat as he spoke, Gilbert Autry couldn't help but notice Pat's erect posture and the self-confidence in his voice, and was impressed that Pat's first question was about the firm rather than salary and vacation—a refreshing change from most young job candidates.

"Of course. Much as I like you, you'd have to start as a junior accountant and work your way up like everybody else. Our starting salary is competitive, but like most accounting firms, you won't make any serious money until after you pass the CPA exam. The fringe benefits are attractive."

"I understand."

"Our firm specializes in auditing associations. We've built ourselves quite a little niche in this area, and we're getting more audit clients all the time. Most of our clients are in the Baltimore-Washington corridor. We have a few in Northern Virginia, and we're ready to open a satellite office in Chicago. Right now, we have about one hundred-ten professionals on staff, about forty support staff, and ten partners. It's a good place to work. It offers plenty of opportunity for the right person. What do you say?" Autry asked.

"When can I start?" Pat asked, trying to control the surprise in his voice.
"How about a week from today?"

Pat thought for a moment. "Mr. Autry, you've got a deal. I don't know how to thank you."

"We're glad to have you on staff. I promise you'll work for your keep, especially during tax season. Now, follow me, Russell's anxious to see you."

Russell was staring intently at a computer screen when the two entered his office.

"Good news, Russell, it seems you and Pat are on the same team again. I'll let you guys talk. He starts a week from today, Russell. Show him around, take a long lunch, and don't let him pay for anything."

"You've got it, Dad," Russell said.

"Mr. Autry, thanks again," Pat said, and shook the elder Autry's hand.
"Don't mention it."

Gilbert Autry left the office, leaving the two alone.

"This is great, Pat. I can't believe it. Just like old times."

"I'm really looking forward to working here. Can't wait to have my CPA certificate on the wall like you do." Pat said, admiring the impressive document.

"You'll do it, and it's worth it. Come on, I'll show you around. All the junior accountants have their own cubicles. Once you pass the CPA exam, you'll get your own office and a nice raise. I just got my own office, but it really doesn't matter very much. Most of our time is spent in the field, auditing clients at their offices. Hey, are you hungry?"

"Starving," Pat answered, "where do you want to go?"

"Let's walk down to the Inner Harbor."

Pat followed Russell back to the receptionist's desk, where Edie was still working.

"Edie," Russell said, "I'm taking a long lunch with my buddy here. We'll be back in about an hour-and-a-half."

"Have a good time. It was nice meeting you, Mr. McGuire," she said, smiling pleasantly.

"You'll be seeing more of him, Edie. He'll be working here soon," Russell said.

"Wonderful! I'll look forward to your joining us," Edie said.

"Thank you," Pat answered. Russell pushed open the door to the outside. Oppressive heat and humidity had replaced the morning's damp cool. Afternoon smog had already settled its yellow-gray mantle over the city. Squinting into the hazy sunlight, Russell pulled out his sunglasses.

"Jeez—I can feel this sun right through my shoes," said Pat.

"That's Baltimore," laughed Russell.

They talked enthusiastically about old times as they headed down Pratt Street toward the Inner Harbor, passing the new convention center. The

Inner Harbor complex was Baltimore's pride. Almost everyone within walking distance went there or to the Lexington Market for lunch.

At Phillips restaurant, they settled into their chairs, and Pat stared out at *The Constellation* docked in the harbor, barely able to contain his excitement. A crew was busy cleaning the great gun as seagulls wheeled overhead. The blue sky was flecked with white clouds. It was a grand day.

"Care for a drink?" the redheaded waitress asked.

"Two National Premiums," Russell said, " and two crab cake platters. No need to hurry."

They watched her walk away. "Not bad," Pat observed.

"Hey, aren't you engaged?"

Pat lifted his beer. "Engaged, but not dead. Besides I noticed where your eyes were and you're married."

"Touché." Russell grinned.

Pat looked at the National Premium bottle. "What happened to Bud?"

"I'm playing for National Beer's triple-A flag football team," Russell said. "I was hoping you would come out for tryouts next week."

Pat stared at his beer. "It might be too much with me having to finish school."

"It's not that bad. We only practice two nights a week and games are on Sunday mornings. Afterward, the team gets together and we take our families to Snyders' restaurant—National Beer picks up the tab. Come on. It'll be fun. Besides, Lynn will get a chance to meet the wives and make some friends."

"You know, I think I just might. I played some flag ball in the Marines in Kansas City and really enjoyed it. Is the league competitive?'

"Very!" Russell exclaimed. "Tryouts start next Saturday at Slentz's field. Why don't you pick me up?"

"I'll talk it over with Lynn. It sounds good."

After the food arrived, Pat glanced at *The Constellation*. Members of the crew were still cleaning the long guns while the American flag waved over the top deck.

Driving back to his parents' house later that afternoon, Pat felt very optimistic about his future. Sure, accounting wasn't exciting, but it paid well and he was good at it. He couldn't wait to get home and tell his parents and call Lynn with the news.

Pat had no way of knowing how wrong he was. It wouldn't be very long before he would find accounting at the firm of Autry, Martin & Ramsey *very* exciting.

# Chapter Two

Pat was nervous reporting for his first day at work at Autry, Martin & Ramsey.

"Good morning, Miss Veteck," Pat said, stepping into the office.

"Good morning. Are you ready to start work? And by the way, everyone calls me Edie. We're all pretty informal with each other." She smiled, relaxing Pat.

"I'm looking forward to it, Edie. And I prefer Pat."

"Okay, Pat, I'll tell Mr. Autry you're here. Please have a seat."

Pat was glancing through an issue of *Sports Illustrated* when Ann Johnson came up to him.

"It's good to see you again, Mr. McGuire," Ann said, extending her hand. "Let me take you to Mr. Autry's office."

He followed her to the same office where he had met with Gilbert Autry a week earlier.

"Mr. Autry, our newest employee is here."

"Pat! Welcome," he said, grasping Pat's right hand with both of his. "Please sit down. What's happened since I saw you last? Did you and Lynn get settled in?"

"Yes, sir. We got a place in the Town and Country Apartments out on Route 40. Lynn likes it here, and she's hard at work looking for a job. She has her degree in elementary education, but it's from Missouri. I really don't know how it all works; it might be tough for her to find what she really wants until all the paperwork is transferred and she's certified to teach here. It'll all work out though."

"Great. Russell tells me you survived the final cut and that you'll be playing with him on the National Beer team!"

"Yes. I think I'm really going to enjoy it. But I've got to tell you, we had a tough workout; I'm really sore! And our first game is just two weeks away. Do you get to any of the games, Mr. Autry?"

"All of them as long as I'm in town. I enjoy the games. I think it's great that you and Russell are on the same team again."

"Me too. It's going to be fun."

"Well, are you ready to start work?"

"Yes, sir! What do you have in mind for me?"

"Well, you're going to report to Russell for a while. I hope you don't have a problem with that."

"Oh, no. I realize Russell's got his CPA and experience that I don't have yet. Everything will be fine."

"Good attitude. Let's walk down to his office and get you started."

Russell was standing by his door, cup of coffee in hand, talking to another employee about Sunday's Ravens' game.

His father spoke first. "Russell, our newest junior accountant is here."

"Pat," Russell said, "let me introduce you to Mark Levin. Mark, this is the new guy I've been telling you about, Pat McGuire."

They shook hands. "Good to meet you, Pat. Russell's told me a lot about you, and I'm looking forward to working with you."

The older Autry interrupted. "Russell, get Pat started. I've got a meeting with Bob Ramsey."

"Okay, Dad."

"Mark has good news, Pat," Russell said. "He just found out that he passed the CPA exam."

"Congratulations, Mark," Pat said sincerely.

"Thanks. I understand you'll be taking the exam yourself soon."

"Well, I've got a lot of work to do. I've still got one more semester at the University of Baltimore, and then I'm going to take a CPA review course before the exam. Did you take a review course, Mark?"

"Oh, yeah. Lambers."

"Same one I've been thinking about. Did you like it?"

"Yes, I did. Grueling work, but it was worth it. I went three nights a week, four hours a night, and eight hours Saturdays for six months. It still took me three times to pass."

Now it was Russell's turn to interrupt. "Mark, I hate to cut you off, but I've got to talk with Pat for a while to get him started."

"Of course," Mark said. "Good meeting you, Pat. See you around."

"Same here."

"Come on in my office, Pat. I've got some things to go over with you."

He motioned Pat to a chair, as he closed his office door. Carefully lowering himself into his chair, Russell stretched out his arms, closing his hands behind his neck.

"Are you as sore as I am?" he asked.

"Worse. It was all I could do to get out of bed this morning. When I woke up, I felt like I had cinder blocks piled on top of me. Why didn't you tell me practices would be this tough?"

"Coach Annello really wants to take it all this year and beat Glen Burnie. It wasn't nearly as bad last year. Listen, I work out at a health club right across the street. Come on over with me after work as my guest, and we can sit in the whirlpool for a while. That'll help. Hey, why don't you join? We could work out together."

"How much?'

"Fifty-five bucks a month."

"Maybe I will."

"As Dad told you, you'll be starting as a junior accountant working with me. Basically routine stuff until you get some experience and pass the exam. It's not bad."

"What's routine?"

"Bank reconciliations, internal control reports, receivable and pay-able verifications, payroll reviews. Stuff like that. You won't have any problems."

"What's my first assignment?"

"You'll be working with me on the American Nurses Association audit. They just moved to DC from Kansas City, and we got the audit. I'll be in charge of this one. The rest of our guys are there right now. Ready to go and get your feet wet?"

"All set."

"Okay, you drive."

They walked across the street and got in Pat's old Camaro. Pulling out of the lot, Pat pushed in a cassette and the Beatles' "Revolution" came on.

"Still like those Beatles, huh?"

"Yep, they're still the best. I can't get enough of them."

"How in the world did you ever become such a Beatles fan?"

"My mother loves music, and she used to play them all the time when I was a kid. I loved them then and I love them now."

"I've got an idea," Russell said, "let's take the Metro from the New Carrollton Station."

They got off the Metro at the Smithsonian Station and decided to walk the short distance to the American Nurses Association offices on Maryland Avenue.

"Hi, Cheryl," Russell said to the receptionist. "Are my people bothering you?"

"Not me. But I understand the people in accounting can't say the same thing."

"Cheryl, this is Pat McGuire. He's new with the firm. He'll be working here for a while."

"Nice to meet you, Pat," she said smiling. "You can go on back, Russell."

"Our people are working in the finance department," said. Russell. "I'll introduce you to our guys and leave you there. I've got to look in on one of our other jobs so I'll come back for you about four, okay?"

"Fine, you're the boss."

Three other junior accountants with Autry, Martin & Ramsey were working at a large table in the conference room when they walked in.

Even though Russell was a partner's son, he was popular with the other employees because he didn't take himself too seriously. He worked just as hard as everyone else did. His sense of humor allowed everyone to relax.

"This is Pat McGuire. He's new with the firm and he's going to be working with us on this audit. Don't try anything, he's a former Marine."

They all laughed, relaxing Pat.

"Pat, this is Hardy Rauch, Bill Taylor, and Teresa Butler. Teresa is the good-looking one."

Teresa was a tall, polished brunette with all-American good looks. She took the comment well and extended her hand warmly. Laughing, the others, too, shook hands with Pat.

"Listen," said Russell, "I've got to go over to the Automobile Dealers Association for a while. Where do we stand here, Hardy?"

"We're a little behind on the receivable verifications," said the senior accountant. "Can Pat help us there?"

"Sure, get started and I'll see you later."

Unsure of himself, Pat tried to be low-key and informal. It helped that the other three accountants were friendly. By the end of the day he was already feeling more comfortable.

When Russell appeared at the door, Pat noticed that it was already four o'clock. He organized his work to leave as Russell caught up on the audit's status with Hardy. Walking together toward the Metro Station, Russell asked, "So, how did it go?'

"Just fine, no problems at all. I think I'm going to like auditing. Hardy, Bill and Teresa seem good to work with."

They took the Metro back to New Carrollton, and drove together toward Baltimore.

"I'll tell you what," Russell said as the Baltimore skyline became clearer. "Just drop me off so I can get my car. I'll meet you at football practice later. It's already after five. I'll take you over to the health club tomorrow."

After Pat dropped Russell off, he drove west to his new apartment. Lynn, a slender, honey-blonde woman, nestled deep in the couch pillows, was reading the evening paper when he walked in. Her lightly tanned legs were draped over the couch's arm. She swung her legs down to face him better. Using her fingers, she combed a handful of her straight-cropped, shoulder-length hair back away from her face and smiled.

Pat always smiled when he saw Lynn, just as he had the first time he met her in a club in Kansas City. Pat couldn't take his eyes off her. He waited for a slow song to ask her to dance. At last the first notes of the Righteous Brothers' "Unchained Melody" came softly from the speakers. He rarely felt confident asking a pretty young woman to dance and he was relieved when Lynn accepted his invitation.

They danced every dance together that first night and Pat drove her home.

Their courtship was simple and fun. They enjoyed each other's company and liked to do the same things. They were getting serious about their relationship, and Pat asked if she would move to Baltimore when he was discharged. She accepted, knowing her college work would be completed about the same time.

"How did it go, honey?" she asked excitedly.

"Great! The work seems like it will be really interesting. The people seem professional, yet friendly. To be honest, I was a little worried about working directly for Russell, but he couldn't have been better."

"Oh, good," she said. "Let's go out to dinner and celebrate."

"We can't tonight. Football practice, remember? Let's go tomorrow night instead, I promise," he said sincerely.

"Okay, but I won't forget."

"So how was your day?" he asked, as he was getting out of his suit and into his practice uniform.

"Good. I got more unpacking done, and I met some neighbors."

"That's great! See you later, honey, I'm running a little late."

"Have fun," she said. "I'll have dinner ready when you get back."

"Sounds good. Bye."

# Chapter Three

"Have you heard yet, Pat?" Russell asked.

"Nope. I called home and Lynn said the mail hasn't been delivered. I can't understand why it takes so long to get test results out. It's agonizing to take a two-day test in May, and then have to wait until August to find out if I passed."

"Well," Russell said, "everybody has to go through the same thing. Don't worry, you worked hard, I'm sure you did great. Getting credit for what you passed is the trick, and then you won't have to take the whole test the next time. No sense worrying about it, let's get something to eat."

"Okay, where do you want to go?"

"Let's walk up to Lexington Market for a change."

"Okay. Maybe the mail will have come by the time we get back."

Returning an hour later, they took the elevator up to the office.

"Oh, Russell," Edie said. "Mark Levin wants you to give him a call when you get a chance, and Lynn wants you to call her at home, Pat."

Pat and Russell looked at each other.

"Come on, you can use my phone."

"Good luck, buddy." Russell closed the office door to give his friend some privacy.

In Russell's office, Pat eased into Russell's chair, took a deep breath and dialed. He could feel his heart pulsing in his fingertips as he pushed the buttons.

*Busy.*

"Damn," he thought. "Get off the phone, Lynn. She's probably on with her mother again."

He stood up and nervously re-read the diplomas and certificates on Russell's wall, sat down, and pressed the phone's redial function.

The phone rang.

"Hello," he heard after the third ring. It was Lynn's voice.

"Lynn, did the mail get there?"

"A half-hour ago."

"And?" he asked.

"It's here, I think!" she said excitedly. "From the Maryland State Board of Public Accountancy. Shall I open it?"

"Of course," he said, "what does it say?"

"Let's see. *Dear Mr. McGuire, we are pleased to inform you that you have passed the Uniform Certified Public Accountant Examination and have met all qualifications to receive your license to practice public accounting in the state of Maryland!*"

"Yes!" he exclaimed, spinning himself around in the chair.

"We've got to celebrate. Call Tio Pepe's and see if we can get a reservation. It they're booked, try Ruth's Chris. I'm not even going to football practice tonight!"

"Pat, Mom's coming in tonight, remember?"

Pat didn't bother hiding his disappointment, "Don't you think she'd understand if you weren't available until after dinner? This doesn't happen every day. Just leave the door open for her."

"I'm not going to do that. She's flying in and I'm not going to make her take a cab."

"Sweetheart, calm down! I'm sorry—I wasn't thinking. I'm just excited. You know I think your mom is wonderful but, after all, she was just here less than a month ago. "Why don't we all go out together?"

Lynn was quiet as she collected herself. "You should have included her in dinner from the start. What time will you be home?"

"Regular time, I guess. See if you can get reservations for seven-thirty. I've got to go."

"Okay, sweetie, and congratulations," Lynn said sincerely. "I'm very proud of you. I know how hard you worked for this."

"Thanks, Lynn. See you later."

His elbow on the desk, Pat rested his forehead against his hand for a moment. "Damn, I wish it would be just us tonight," he thought, but he didn't let his self-pity last. Remembering that he'd just passed all the parts of the exam at once, he bounded out of his chair.

"Well?" Russell asked, when he saw Pat.

"I passed," Pat said smiling broadly.

"How many parts?'

"All of them."

"Yes!" Russell said and they exchanged high fives.

"Listen up, everybody," Russell said loudly. "Let's hear it for our newest CPA."

Hardy and Mark walked up to congratulate him. Pat had become quite popular with his co-workers, who were clapping and smiling in celebration. They knew how hard he had worked.

"Let's go tell Dad," Russell said. The two walked briskly to the opposite side of the office.

As they turned the corner into his office, Autry looked up from a letter he was reading. "What's up?"

"I just wanted to introduce you to the firm's newest CPA," Russell said.

"Way to go, Pat!" he said as he walked around his desk to shake Pat's hand. "And on the first time at that!"

"Thank you, Mr. Autry," Pat said, finding it hard now to contain his excitement.

"I've been waiting for this. Ann, would you please get that package I asked you to hold?"

"Pat, this is for you," Autry said, handing him the wrapped box.

Pat felt conspicuous as the others watched him open his gift.

Inside the box were three small boxes of odd shapes.

"Open the largest one first," Autry said.

Pat took the lid off a rectangular gray box of business cards, one resting on top of the others.

"PATRICK S. McGUIRE, CPA," it read in large black print, the words "SENIOR ACCOUNTANT" appeared in slightly smaller letters centered under his name.

"Senior Accountant?" he asked, raising his head to look at Gilbert Autry.

"Yes, Pat, effective immediately, and there's a nice raise to go with it."

"Mr. Autry, thank you, that's great. Thank you very, very much," he exclaimed.

"You deserve it, Pat," the older man said shaking Pat's hand sincerely.

"Open the flat one next," Russell said.

Pat picked up the thin package and opened it. A plastic nameplate with white letters against a black background read "PATRICK S. McGUIRE, CPA."

"It fits in the holder on the wall outside your new office."

"My new office?"

"Yep. We can't have one of our best senior accountants in a cubicle, can we?" Gilbert said.

Pat picked up the last box and opened it.

It was a beautiful nameplate, "PATRICK S. McGUIRE, CPA" was engraved on a gold plate against a walnut background.

"Mr. Autry, I don't know what to say."

"You don't have to say anything. Russell, escort Pat to his new office. Pat, take the rest of the day off, and I want you to have dinner on the firm with this.

He handed him a corporate charge card with "Autry, Martin & Ramsey, CPAs" in raised letters above his own name.

"All senior accountants have their own credit cards," he added. "Have fun tonight. I'll see you Monday to get you started with your new responsibilities."

"Thanks, Mr. Autry, but I'll see you Sunday."

"Sunday?"

"Don't forget. That's when we open the season against Catonsville."

"That's right, I'll see you then. Now, get out of here!"

# Chapter Four

Pat had a difficult time over the weekend, curious about what new responsibilities would await him after passing the CPA exam and being promoted. He was glad his team had played on Sunday so he had an outlet to relieve his nervous energy. They won and the team continued the undefeated streak of the previous year.

On Monday morning Russell stuck his head inside Pat's new office. "Let's see what the old man has in store for you. He wants to see both of us."

"You bet. Let's go."

They walked together down the hall to the executive suite.

"Pat, I'm going to put you in charge of a new audit. We just picked up a new client, a Convention and Visitor Bureau out in Alexandria. They're relatively small, about a three million dollar budget, twenty employees, and about five hundred members. Russell will be in charge of the Builders Association audit right down the street from their offices, so he'll be nearby if you need anything. This client has never been audited before and that's the only problem I can foresee."

"I don't understand," said Pat.

"Their executive director, Gordon Banks, feels the board pushed the audit down his throat, and he doesn't like the idea one bit. He thinks an audit is a waste of money, and he isn't all that thrilled about accountants in the first place. You can handle him, he just tends to be rather gruff and vocal."

"That doesn't bother me," Pat said. "When do we start?"

"Late this morning. I'm going over with you to introduce you and get you started."

"I appreciate that. Who else is going to be on the assignment?"

"I was thinking of Teresa Butler and Jim Lewis. What do you think, Russell?"

"Fine. I've just got them doing some prep work for the National Tobacco Federation audit, but they're free."

"Good. Let's meet out front at ten," replied Gilbert.

"I'll tell Teresa and Jim," Russell said, as they walked down the hall. "I'll see you tomorrow night at practice."

Pat turned into his new office; pleased he would be working with Teresa and Jim.

At the Convention and Visitor Bureau the team from Autry, Martin & Ramsey was kept waiting until 11:15 when they were led to a conference room by Gordon Banks' secretary, Susan Bunnell.

"Make yourselves comfortable. Mr. Banks will be right with you."

Five minutes later, the executive director of the bureau, a tall muscular man, walked into the conference room. Gordon Banks' height allowed him to carry a slightly protruding belly. Sharply dressed down to his ivory cufflinks, his auburn hair was graying and thinning, and he sported a handlebar mustache.

Autry walked over and held out his hand. "Gordon, it's good to see you again."

After an awkward moment, Banks shook Autry's hand quickly without saying a word.

"Gordon, I'd like to introduce you to three of our people," Autry said, trying to keep an air of friendliness in his voice.

"This is Pat McGuire. Pat will be in charge of the audit."

Pat extended his hand and said, "Mr. Banks, it's a pleasure."

Again, Banks said nothing, but shook Pat's hand.

"And this is Teresa Butler and Jim Lewis. They'll be working with Pat."

Banks nodded and said, "I'll be up front with you. This audit shit is not my idea of a good time. It's my board that wants it. I think it's a waste of money, and my people have better things to do than to work with a bunch of number punchers. I resent it, and I'm meeting with you only because I have no choice!"

"Gordon, I . . ." Autry said, before he was interrupted.

"As I was saying," Banks continued, "I strongly resent this interruption in our work schedule. If I hear one complaint from any of my people, as far as I'm concerned, the audit will be over. Understand?"

"Of course, Gordon," Autry said. "I assure you . . ."

Banks interrupted again. "Now, our controller will be here in a minute. His name is Dick Loomis, and we've been working together for years. You'll find his work excellent. You work with him, leave me alone, and I don't want to hear any complaints from Dick."

Banks stood and the other four followed his example.

As he was leaving the room, he turned back around.

"By the way," he said, "do you know why they've never had a CPA on a postage stamp?"

"No," Autry said, "why?"

"Because people wouldn't know which side of the stamp to spit on," he replied and left the room, closing the door behind him.

Left alone, the accountants looked at each other with exasperated, wide-eyed expressions.

"What a charmer," Teresa said.

"I know I'm going to enjoy this audit," Jim added.

Autry smiled at Pat and winked at the two junior accountants just as Dick Loomis, the controller came into the room.

Loomis was about forty-five, lean, with shining hair neatly combed straight back. Suited in dark navy with a deep red tie, he was the consummate Washington professional. Walking on the street, most would have guessed him a lawyer or a lobbyist.

"Dick Loomis," he said to Autry, extending his hand.

Gilbert shook his hand and made the introductions.

"Well," Loomis said, sitting at the head of the table, "I understand you've had the pleasure of meeting Gordon Banks." His laughter diffused the tension in the room. "Let's talk about what you guys have in mind."

"Pat will be in charge of the audit on site," Autry said. "Teresa and Jim will be working with him."

"We'll need just a few things to get started," Pat said. "The working trial balance, minutes, and bank reconciliations are all we need for now. We'll start payroll, revenue, and expenses next week."

"Sounds good. I'll have my people get everything for you," Loomis said. "Anything else?"

"Just sign these papers and show us where we'll be working," Pat said, as he pushed the letters toward Loomis.

"What are these?"

"Just routine bank confirmation letters. Basically, you're just telling the bank that our firm is auditing the association. This gives them permission to deal with us."

"No problem," he said, signing the letters and pushing them back. "You'll be working right here, if that's okay."

"Fine," Pat said, adding, "I'm sure everything will be okay."

Loomis sat back in his chair, his hands clasped behind his neck.

"So, how long have you been a CPA, Pat?' he asked, making small talk.

"To be honest with you, Dick, I just passed the exam recently," he answered without hesitation or embarrassment. Gilbert Autry was watching how Pat was handling himself. He looked pleased.

"We're your first audit then?"

"Yes, I'm ready. Mr. Autry is only a phone call away, if I have any problems."

Loomis stood up and stretched.

"I'll leave you guys alone then so you can get to work. I think you'll find this will be a good first audit for you."

The afternoon went by quickly, with Pat supervising the other two under Autry's direction.

Before leaving the offices, Autry asked Pat and his new audit team to gather at the conference table for a few minutes. He explained how he learned more from the mistakes he had made during his career than from his successes. While everyone makes mistakes, he emphasized special care should always be taken to preserve clients' documentation.

"Occasionally you will come into contact with an extremely important document," he said. "Remember how embarrassing it would be to us and to the client, if we somehow misplaced or lost it. It might be a copy of a contract, an IRS letter, a lease, a check or just about anything that seems important or irreplaceable. Be particularly careful about payroll information, of course.

"Now there are no rules on what constitutes an important document and what doesn't. I'm not going to be here most of the time, so I'm entrusting that judgement to each of you. If you come in contact with one of these documents, remember to always, always, make a copy. That way you and the firm will be protected.

"Okay, if everything is locked up, let's go," he concluded.

The ride back to Baltimore was surprisingly jovial. Pat imitated Banks' postage-stamp comment with amazing accuracy. Peals of laughter filled the car, as Jim debated which of the four would be first on the stamp.

# *Chapter Five*

Gilbert was presiding over the weekly Monday morning meeting of partners and senior accountants in the Baltimore office to discuss the week's work schedule.

"So, Pat," he said, "tell us how that Convention and Visitor Bureau audit is progressing. Any problems?"

"No problems with the audit itself. It's been a piece of cake, and we should have all our work done before the end of this week.

"Gordon Banks was right. Dick Loomis, their controller," he explained, looking around the table, "runs a tight ship. Everything we've examined so far has been right on the money. Absolutely perfect records."

"Now that's good news," said Gilbert, "with Gordon's attitude, I'm not sure what we would have done if we had problems with Mr. Loomis.

"By the way, how is Banks treating you and the others?" he asked with a concerned expression.

"He can be pretty short with us, but not nearly as bad as the first day. Basically, he ignores us, and when he does talk, he generally asks us how much longer we'll be."

"What do you have left to do?" asked Bob Ramsey, one of the other partners.

"Just get the required letter from their counsel on any legal issues we should be aware of, check their fixed assets records, and check the year-end checking account reconciliation. Hopefully their final bank statement is here in today's mail, and I can take it with me and wrap everything up."

Gilbert concluded the meeting by reminding everyone that in two weeks, the audit of the firm's biggest client, the National Tobacco Federation, was going to start.

Pat was getting his sports coat out of the closet near the receptionist's desk when Gilbert walked up, "Good game yesterday, Pat. If you guys keep this up, you'll be facing Glen Burnie for the state championship."

"I really hope so. Being undefeated helps. Everyone is up just thinking we could be state champs."

"Listen, you'd better get going, Pat. I want you to get Banks out of the way so you'll be caught up. We'll need you to concentrate on the National Tobacco Federation audit," he said.

"No problem. Any mail for me Edie?"

"Just this," she said, handing Pat a thick brown envelope.

Pat took the envelope and looked at the return address: Virginia National Bank.

"Is that the bank statement you were looking for?" Autry asked.

"Yep. This is it. I'll take it with me and, with this, we should finish the audit by tomorrow."

"Good. Any problems with the bank reconciliations so far?"

"Nope, we've already checked the other eleven months, and everything balances to the penny."

"Good deal. Now get going. I'll see you Wednesday."

Pat drove to Alexandria, listening to his Beatles tapes.

After pulling into the Convention and Visitor Bureau parking lot, he couldn't resist listening to the end of Sergeant Peppers.

"Good morning, Pat," the receptionist greeted him, "your people are in the conference room. Just go on in."

When Pat opened the conference room door, he saw Teresa and Jim with their heads together looking over some papers.

"Hey, guys," Pat said. "What's up?"

"We're just wrapping up here," Teresa said. "The letter from the attorney was in today's mail, and we'll have our work on the fixed assets records done before the end of the day.

"Oh, and Dick Loomis came by a few minutes ago. He said he needs the year-end bank statement right away. Did you bring it with you?"

"Yes, it came in today's mail. I've got it right here," Pat replied, opening the brown leather brief case Lynn had given him for passing the CPA exam.

"Dick's in his office. Do you want me to take it down to him?" Jim asked.

"We should glance through it first and note the beginning and ending balances, and look over a few of the checks."

"You're right," Jim said. "It'll only take us a few minutes to do it right."

Pat tore open the thick envelope, pulling out the five-page bank statement and all the checks. He noted the bank statement's beginning and ending balances and started to review each of the checks in front of him.

A few minutes later, he glanced up at Teresa and Jim.

"What's the matter, Pat?" Jim asked.

"Have there been any large checks made out to Dick Loomis personally?" Pat asked.

"No, why?" Teresa replied.

"Look at this."

Teresa and Jim leaned over Pat to look at the check he was holding.

"Look, a check for three thousand, nine hundred forty-eight dollars and five cents payable to Richard Loomis cleared the bank. Are you sure there haven't been any others?'

"Positive," Jim said. "We looked at every single check for the last eleven months, and everything checked out. Did Dick endorse the back?"

Pat turned the check over, examining it carefully. "Yeah, he endorsed it all right. Look."

"Do me a favor, Teresa," Pat looked up at her, "go over to accounting and get last month's check register. Do you know where it is?"

"Yes. I'll go get it."

"Try not to be obvious, and don't say anything to anyone about this. I don't want to rush to any conclusions."

"What do you think, Pat?" Jim asked.

"Oh, I'm sure it's nothing. He probably had to transfer some money to another account and just acted as an agent."

"You're probably right," Jim said. "But it seems strange and not like Dick."

The conference room door opened and they looked up to see Teresa holding some papers. She closed the door quietly behind her.

"Is that it?" Pat asked.

"This is it. Tell me what to do."

"Okay, is check number seven-eight-four-three-nine on there?"

Pat could see Teresa's index finger running down the check numbers. She stopped midway on the third page.

"I got it."

"Okay, what is the amount of the check?"

She ran her finger across the paper. "Three thousand, nine hundred forty-eight dollars and five cents," she said.

"Good," Pat said. "What account number is it charged to?"

"Account number thirteen-point-zero-zero-one-two," she said.

"What account is that?"

"I'll check," Jim said. "I've got my copy of the chart of accounts right here. What was that number again, Teresa?"

"Thirteen-point-zero-zero-one-two," she repeated.

A few seconds later, Jim said, "Okay, let's see. Here it is. Thirteen-point-zero-zero-one-two, Magazine Postage Expense."

"Okay, that's good," Pat said. "I'm sure there's an explanation for this somewhere. Now, who is the payee, Teresa?"

Teresa still had her index finger on the right spot, moving it to her left. "It was made payable to the *U.S. Postal Service*!" she said, surprised.

"Are you sure?" Pat said.

"Positive," she said. "Check number seven-eight-four-three-nine. It's for three thousand, nine hundred forty-eight dollars and five cents, it's payable to the U.S. Postal Service, and it's charged to account number thirteen-point-zero-zero-one-two."

The three accountants looked at each other, each thinking the same thing. Why wouldn't the name on the check match the name on the check register?

"What do we do now?" Jim asked.

"Remember what Mr. Autry told us the other day about making copies of important documents?" Pat asked. "Well, in my judgment, this is an important document.

"Make a copy of the front and back of this check, Jim. And don't let anyone see you doing it," Pat said, as he handed the check to Jim. Jim put the check in his inside jacket pocket and left the room.

"I don't like this," Pat said as he was putting the other checks back into the brown envelope. "We don't have time now, but we've got to look at every one of these checks very carefully."

Just as Pat was putting the bank statement back in his brief case, Dick Loomis walked into the conference room, wearing his ever-present smile.

"Have you seen last month's bank statement? It's usually here by now, and I'd like to get the checking account reconciled so you guys can get out of here and leave us alone," he said laughing.

"It came in today's mail," Pat answered, "but I forgot to bring it with me."

"What do you mean you forgot to bring it with you? Wasn't it mailed here?" He started to sound agitated.

"No. It was mailed to our Baltimore office," Pat said.

"Why?"

"It's standard procedure. Remember those letters to the bank I asked you to sign on our first day?"

"Yeah."

"That was our standard bank confirmation letter. You gave the bank permission to mail the statement to our office."

"Well, I need it." His voice was getting louder and his tone more agitated.

"I'll bring it out tomorrow morning."

"That's not good enough. I need it today. I think you'd better have a messenger pick it up and get it out here today—at your expense," he said with an unfamiliar hint of anger in his voice. "And remember what Gordon said about not interfering with our work schedule. I'd rather not tell him about this, but I need that statement today. Understand?"

"I understand, Dick. Please calm down. I'll take care of it right now and have the statement sent to you personally."

"You'd better," Loomis replied, and slammed the door behind him as he left the room.

# Chapter Six

Teresa and Jim returned and handed the check copies to Pat, assuring him that no one had noticed.

"What are you going to do, Pat? That envelope has already been torn open. He'll know we've looked at it." Teresa said.

"I've got an idea," Pat said, his mind racing. "I'll be back in about an hour."

Pat put the opened bank statement back into his brief case, and left the conference room. He drove to the nearest Virginia National Bank. Pat stepped through the double-glass doors, into the cool of the blue and beige carpeted office.

"May I help you?" asked one of the loan officers looking up from her desk behind the wooden partition.

"Yes," Pat said. "I'd like to see the manager, please."

"Please come with me." Pat followed her into the manager's office.

"This gentleman would like to see you, Miss Tarun."

A blonde woman stood behind her desk and extended her right hand. "Helen Tarun. How may I help you?"

Pat shook her hand firmly. "Pat McGuire. I'll just need a moment of your time."

"Have a seat, Mr. McGuire."

Pat settled into one of the comfortable brown leather chairs in front of the manager's desk.

"Miss Tarun, I'm a CPA," he said, handing her his business card. "I'm teaching a night course in internal control and banking relationships, and I need a small favor."

"Yes?"

"Tonight's class is on detecting fraud. I want to show the class that a bank's checking account statement can't be opened without tearing the envelope because of the glue you use on the envelope flap. I want the class to try opening the envelope without tearing it, and I was wondering if you could spare a few envelopes? I'd be happy to pay you."

"We'll be happy to help you, Mr. McGuire. How many would you like and what size?"

"Six would be fine, and a couple of different sizes, if you don't mind."

"Here you are. Will these do?"

"Perfect," Pat answered. "What do I owe you?'

"Forget it."

"Thank you very much, Miss Tarun. I really appreciate it."

"Glad I could help. Good luck with your class tonight."

"Thanks, again," Pat said. A pit in his stomach began to dissolve as he left the bank.

Once in his car, he opened his briefcase and took out the client's checking account statement envelope. Next, he took the checks and bank statement pages out of the envelope. He carefully inserted the five-page bank statement into the envelope, making sure the address on the front page could be seen through the glistening plastic window.

He placed the check payable to Richard Loomis in the middle of the other checks. Wrapping the checks with the same rubber band the bank had used, he put them in the envelope and sealed it.

He drove across the street to the Landmark Shopping Center, and walked directly over to the Nationwide Express service center. The clerk was available and asked, "May I help you?"

"Yes, I need one of your envelopes to ship this in," showing the clerk the bank statement envelope.

"Yes, sir," the agent said, handing him an envelope and a shipping label. "Just fill this out, please."

Pat carefully wrote in Autry, Martin & Ramsey's Baltimore address in the "shipper's" box, and the Convention and Visitor Bureau's Alexandria address, attention R. Loomis, in the "ship to" box.

He waited until he was the only customer in the store and walked back up to the clerk.

"Listen," Pat said, "how would you like to earn a quick fifty bucks?"

"What do you mean?"

"Deliver this envelope for me within a half-hour," Pat answered, handing him the addressed envelope.

The clerk took the package and looked at the address. "9995 Stevenson Avenue!" the clerk said, puzzled. He looked at Pat. "That's right across the street!"

"I know. Can you help me or not?" Pat took two twenties and a ten out of his wallet.

"Why don't you take it over yourself?"

"I don't have time to explain right now, but I screwed up. If that package isn't delivered right away, it's my ass. Can you help me or not?"

"All I have to do is drop it off, right?"

"Right. Drive over in your truck, have the receptionist sign for it and drive back. That's it. Do we have a deal?" Pat asked, handing him the money.

"John," the clerk said loudly.

"Yeah?" came a voice from the back.

"I'm taking my break now. Be back in ten minutes. Cover for me?"

"Okay. Bring me back a cup of coffee, will ya?"

"Be right back," the clerk answered.

Pat and the clerk walked toward a white panel truck with Nationwide Express logos painted on each side.

"Damned if I know what's going on," the clerk said as he opened the door to the vehicle, "but it's your money."

"Thanks," Pat said as he heard the van door slam and the engine start.

He waited. Five long minutes later, he saw the same truck pulling back into the shopping center.

"Any problems?"

"Nope, it's there."

"Thanks."

"A pleasure doing business with you," he tapped his wallet, as he walked toward the shopping center.

"One more thing," Pat said.

"Yeah?" the clerk said as he turned back to Pat.

"Don't forget John's coffee!"

# *Chapter Seven*

"Where did you go?" Teresa asked Pat as he shut the conference room door behind him.

"I'll explain over lunch. Has Dick been back in?" he asked.

"Not yet," Jim said.

"Good. Let's grab a bite and I'll fill you in."

As they ate lunch, Pat told his colleagues about the bank and the Nationwide Express delivery. After lunch, they returned to work in the conference room.

Two hours later, Dick Loomis walked into the conference room with the brown bank envelope in his hand.

"Did your bank statement get here yet, Dick?' Pat asked, pretending not to notice the envelope.

"Yes. Nationwide Express dropped it off about three hours ago."

"Here you are," he said, handing McGuire the envelope, "and we've already reconciled the statement." He handed Pat a piece of accounting paper with several figures on it.

"Good," Pat said. "I called the office right after we spoke this morning. I'm glad you got it, and I'm sorry for the inconvenience. I hope you understand."

"There's something strange about this bank statement," Loomis said.

Pat felt himself tense up and, out of the corner of his eye, he noticed that his two colleagues didn't look up after Loomis' remark.

"What?" Pat said, trying to remain calm.

"There's no postmark on the envelope." Loomis said in a matter-of-fact tone, obviously looking at Pat for his reaction.

"Pardon?"

"You heard me, there's no postmark on the outside of the bank envelope. Doesn't that strike you as strange?"

Loomis was now intently studying Pat's reaction to his question.

Pat's mind was racing. He knew then that he had forgotten about a postmark.

"Well?" Loomis asked impatiently.

"No, not at all, Dick," Pat said, still reminding himself to appear calm and trying to buy himself some time to think. Jim and Teresa were now looking up and watching the exchange.

"Can I see the envelope, Dick?" Pat asked.

Loomis dropped the brown envelope in front of Pat without answering.

"Look at the address in the window of the envelope and on the statement."

"I don't have to look. It's ours."

"Listen, Dick. When you signed that letter to the bank I gave you on our first day here you gave the bank permission to mail your bank statement directly to our office in Baltimore."

"So?"

"So the bank just put your statement in another envelope and addressed that envelope to our office. That's the envelope that has the postmark on it, not this one."

The three accountants could see Loomis thinking.

"Oh, oh I get it now!" Loomis said. "Of course they did, I never thought of that."

Pat could feel himself calm down as he watched Loomis' face and gestures.

"Listen," Loomis said, "I apologize. I've been under a lot of stress lately, and I lost my temper. No hard feelings?" he added, extending his hand to Pat.

"No problem," Pat said, shaking his hand. "We'll both know better next time."

"Thanks, I'll let you guys finish up. See you later."

Loomis left the room, shutting the door quietly.

Jim and Teresa both got up after they heard the door shut, and walked to Pat's side of the table where he was taking the checks out of the envelope.

All three pairs of eyes were looking at the check numbers as Pat turned each check over. Halfway into the stack, he came to check number seven-eight-four-three-nine. It was for three thousand, nine hundred forty-eight dollars and five cents.

And it was made payable to the U.S. Postal Service, not Richard Loomis.

The three accountants looked at one another.

"What in the hell?" Teresa was stumped.

"Who endorsed it?" Jim asked.

"Pat turned the check over. The endorsement on the back of the check read:

### For Deposit Only
### U.S. Postal Service

Also on the back of the check were the bank's clearinghouse stamps. And the bottom right front of the check had the bank's encoding information on a piece of white tape.

"I'm dumbfounded," Pat said. "This is not the same check I put back in the statement, but it looks like the post office cashed it.

"I don't understand."

The three were silent for a few moments, each lost in thought and trying to solve the mystery.

Pat interrupted the silence.

"Teresa, do me a favor and get accounting's copy of this check and the back-up receipts, will you, please? And grab a few others so you don't look suspicious."

Absorbed in thought, Pat and Jim waited for Teresa to complete her errand.

She returned a few minutes later with some papers.

"Did you find it?" Jim asked.

"Yeah, it's right here," she said, handing the paperwork to Pat.

The three accountants studied the copy of the check and the receipt. Accounting's copy of the check clearly showed that check number seven-eight-four-three-nine was written out for three thousand, nine hundred forty-eight dollars and five cents. It was made payable to the U.S. Postal Service with an official receipt attached.

A few more moments of silence ensued.

"I think I understand what's going on here," said Pat, getting up from his chair.

"I'd better pay a visit to Mr. Banks."

Pat left the conference room and walked to the executive offices. He saw Gordon Banks sitting at his large mahogany desk. His secretary was away from her desk.

He tapped gently on the office door. "Mr. Banks?" he said.

"What is it?" Banks looked up, annoyed at the interruption.

"I think we have a problem," Pat said.

# Chapter Eight

Pat sat in his new office, days later, intently sorting through a stack of correspondence. He looked up when Ann Johnson knocked on the doorframe.

"Yes, Ann. What is it?" he asked.

"Pat, Mr. Autry wants to see you in the conference room right away."

"What's up?"

"I don't know, but it looks serious. He's in there with some of the other partners and Mr. Banks from that convention group, and they don't look happy."

"You'd better go over there right away."

Pat put on his suit coat, and walked to the conference room.

He took a deep breath before entering, not knowing what to expect.

Gilbert Autry was sitting at the middle of the table, surrounded by his partners. Gordon Banks sat to his right. A single chair was on the other side of the table facing them.

"You wanted to see me, Mr. Autry?" Pat said, trying to hide his nervousness. He sensed that the situation appeared too serious to use first names.

"Yes, Pat, sit down," Autry said, pointing to the lone vacant chair.

Pat sat down and made eye contact with each person sitting across from him, settling with Gilbert Autry, who began the meeting.

"Pat," he said, "this is serious."

"What is it, Mr. Autry?"

"Gordon Banks has informed us of something very disturbing concerning you and the Convention and Visitor Bureau's audit."

"I don't understand, let me assure you . . ."

"Let me finish," Autry said, cutting him off. "You'll have your chance to talk. Do you remember when we first started the audit?"

"Of course," Pat answered. He began to feel beads of sweat forming around his collar. He loosened his tie and unbuttoned his top shirt button, feeling his face flush red. As hard as he tried to maintain his composure, his emotions took over.

"What did Mr. Banks tell us before we started?"

"Well," Pat changed his gaze from Autry to Banks. "He said that if he heard of any problems with us, that as far as he was concerned, the audit was over. He introduced us to Dick Loomis and told us what he thought of CPAs," Pat answered bluntly. "Was there a problem?"

Autry looked stern. "A big one. I think it's better if Mr. Banks tells you how he feels, what the future of our relationship to his organization is now, and what he plans to do with our bill. Gordon," Autry looked to his right.

"Mr. McGuire." Banks stood up. "In no uncertain terms, I told you that there was to be no interference with our work and our people. Am I correct?"

"Yes, sir."

"Well, I think you went just a little bit too far, young man."

"I assure you, Mr. Banks, we were just doing our jobs." Despite the tension in the room, Pat was confident and preparing mentally to defend himself.

"Let Mr. Banks finish," Autry shot a glance at Pat and then turned to the man on his right. "Gordon."

"As I was saying, you and your people went just a little too far."

"In what way?" Pat asked.

"As you told me last Thursday, you took it upon yourself to have the bank statement sent directly from the bank to you and didn't bother informing either me or Dick Loomis, interrupting our work flow.

"And as if that weren't enough, you met with me and rather diplomatically suggested that you felt Dick may be involved in some impropriety. Am I right?"

"Yes, sir," Pat squirmed a little in his seat. He put his hand up to the back of his neck to unobtrusively wipe away a bead of sweat.

Banks walked around the table to where Pat was sitting.

"Would you mind standing up, Mr. McGuire?" he asked.

Pat heard his chair scrape the rug as he stood. He hoped he didn't look foolish in front of this group.

Then Gordon Banks extended his right hand.

"I want to do two things." Suddenly Banks smiled broadly.

"What?" Pat said, taking Banks' hand in his own.

"First, I want to apologize for my remarks and my behavior. I hope I never get so old and so proud that I won't recognize when I'm wrong and admit it.

"And second, I want to tell you that you and your people did nothing short of uncovering a quarter-of-a-million-dollar embezzling scheme that Loomis was involved in."

Pat looked around and saw smiles on the faces of the partners, as they all rose from their chairs. He suddenly felt a lot cooler.

"Mr. Autry started this meeting by saying that I had a few things to say about you, about our association's future relationship with this firm, and about what I intend to do with your bill," Banks said, glancing from Pat to Autry.

"I couldn't be more impressed with you, young man. You worked hard, you did your job, and you uncovered a major crime.

"I intend to give the Board of Directors a full report on my satisfaction with you and your firm, and I'm going to suggest that they approve a five-year retainer. Oh, and one more thing—about your bill, Gilbert . . ."

"Yes, Gordon?"

"I'm telling you, in front of this young man and these partners, that I want you to add five thousand dollars to your final bill."

"*Add* five thousand dollars!" Autry said, feigning surprise.

"Yes, add five thousand dollars. And before you get too excited, it's not for you and your partners. It's a bonus for McGuire here. Understood?"

"Understood," Gilbert Autry smiled and looked at Pat.

"Now I've got to get out of here and back to work. It seems I have some interviews set up for our vacant controller position," Banks said, shaking each partner's hand, ending with Pat's.

"Good job, son. And you tell me if you have any trouble getting your little bonus from Autry here," he said, shaking Pat's hand again and winking at Autry.

"Sit down, everyone, and I'll fill you in," Autry said after Banks had left the room.

Looking around the room, he explained to the other partners how Pat investigated the mysterious check made out to Richard Loomis and how he used the bank and Nationwide Express to get the statement back to the unsuspecting controller.

He told them that Pat had talked privately to Gordon Banks, explaining to him how Loomis had switched the checks before giving the statement back to Pat.

"After Pat left Banks' office, Gordon called me personally and told me that he needed my help. He wanted a fresh pair of eyes to look over what Pat showed him.

"So Russell and I drove down there the same day to meet Gordon. He showed us the check made payable to the post office, and it appeared to have cleared the bank. And sure enough, it was for the same amount and had the same check number as the check that did, in fact, clear the bank with Loomis as the payee. Fortunately, Pat made a copy of the check before Loomis had a chance to destroy it."

"What did you do next?" Bob Ramsey asked. He and the others were mesmerized.

"I asked Gordon to get a few old bank statements for us, and Russell and I pulled out every check payable to the post office, and the three of us went to the bank."

"And?"

"We asked the bank to pull their photocopy of each check that we had payable to the U.S. Postal Service. There was the proof. The bank's copies of several of the checks had the same number and were for the same amount, but had Loomis as the payee."

"But you said that the checks had the same check numbers, and appeared to have cleared the bank. How did he manage to do that?" Ramsey asked again, astonished.

"Actually, it was very simple once it was uncovered. As it turned out, Loomis ordered two sets of identically numbered checks from two different check-printing companies. They looked exactly the same."

"And?"

"He ran checks routinely on his office computer. Every week or so, he would make one check out to the U.S. Postal Service and, of course, not mail it because the post office had nothing to do with it. He'd go home with a copy of the diskette he used to make out the checks in the office. There, he used his name as the payee on that particular check, printed the check on his printer, forged a signature, and cashed the check at a different bank, of course. Because he got the bank statements, he only had to pull out the check he cashed, destroy it, and replace it with the original check from the bank statement, payable to the post office."

"But you said that it looked like the check had been cashed and it had a receipt. How did he manage that?" one of the other partners asked.

"Simple. He had a friend who worked at the post office in on the scheme. His friend endorsed the check with the post office's actual endorsement stamp and then gave him a real post office receipt."

"But how about the bank's encoding information on the bottom right front of the check and their clearinghouse stamps on the back. How in the hell did he fake that?" Bob Ramsey asked, incredulous.

"That wasn't hard," Autry continued, "He had duplicates of clearinghouse stamps made at a rubber stamp company. They'll make just about anything you need. He stamped them himself, and they looked authentic enough to fool anyone."

Ramsey was now shaking his head in disbelief. "But bank encoding is done by a special computer and printer. How did he pull that off?"

"Once again, Bob, simplicity," Autry answered. "What does a bank do when they've made a mistake encoding a check?"

Ramsey answered immediately. "They put a piece of white tape with the correct encoding information over the error and just tape it on."

"Yep," Autry said. "And old Dickie boy would peel off the authentic bank correcting tape from an old check that had already been audited. He taped that on the fraudulent check. I looked at the checks myself and there is no way you would ever know it hadn't been cashed. No way."

"Brilliant," Ramsey added, still shaking his head. "We'll have to tell the rest of our people to look out for this type of thing. And if it weren't for Pat's checking out the bank statement and thinking fast, we never would have uncovered this, would we?" he asked, looking in Pat's direction.

"Nope. It looks like we made the right decision in hiring an ex-Marine after all, huh?"

Everyone smiled.

"Does anyone know what possessed Loomis to do this?" Ramsey asked.

"I talked to Gordon about that after the dust had settled," Autry answered. "He had a gambling problem. Evidently, he got in over his head with some bookie he couldn't pay back, saw a weakness, and took advantage of it."

"Is Banks going to press charges?"

"Oh yeah. This is too big to walk away from. Loomis is in jail waiting for a trial date, as we speak, and so is his cohort who worked at the post office."

Ramsey and the others just shook their heads in disbelief.

"If you guys don't mind, I'd like to meet with Pat alone for a few minutes," Autry said. Gilbert Autry shut the door after the last partner had shaken Pat's hand or slapped his back in congratulations.

"Have a seat." He pulled up a chair for himself directly facing Pat.

"I just wanted to tell you how pleased I am with your work."

"Thank you, Mr. Autry, I'm sorry—Gil, but I was really only doing what we've been trained to do."

"Don't be modest, you did more than just what you had to do, and I'm impressed with how you got the statement in Loomis' hands without his knowing you had seen it first. Good thinking."

"Thank you."

"So what are you going to do with the five-thousand-dollar bonus?"

"Oh, I know exactly what I'll do with it. Put it away and keep it for a deposit on a house."

"I thought for sure you were going to say you would use it for a deposit on a new car."

"Oh, no. The old Camaro runs fine. I love that car."

Autry smiled admiring Pat's practical side.

"Listen, there are a few things I want to go over with you while we're alone. Do you have a few minutes?"

"Sure."

"First, you have a bright future here, and you'll find a nice raise in your next check. It'll help with your house plans."

"Thank you, sir, I really appreciate it."

"Don't say anything, you deserve it after the Gordon Banks deal.

"Second, I want you to take a week off with pay, and use a little bit of that money Banks is giving you for you and Lynn to take a nice vacation. I want you to go to some nice resort, to relax, and to have a good time. Under the circumstances, you deserve it."

"You know, I think we will," Pat said. "We haven't had any real time to ourselves since I started here, and a little vacation at a nice warm resort sounds good." Pat thought for a minute before continuing. "Lynn and I have been having a few problems lately, and some time to ourselves is probably a good idea."

"Anything you care to talk about?"

"Nothing serious. She misses her family and friends in Kansas City. That's all."

Autry nodded knowingly, suspecting there was something more.

"I'd like for you to take your vacation in two weeks," Autry said. "As I told you, you'll be on the National Tobacco Federation audit. We have a week of prep work to do before their fiscal year ends, but then we have to give them some time to close everything out and get ready for us.

"So, really take that vacation! Understand?" Autry's face showed mock seriousness.

"Understood. I can't wait," Pat said smiling.

"There's one condition though."

"Sure, anything."

"Don't do anything foolish and get hurt, and make sure that you're back in time for the big championship game with Glen Burnie. Russell would kill me if you weren't here for the big game."

"Don't worry, I wouldn't miss it. We've worked too hard to come so close and blow it on a vacation. And I promise, I'll stay in shape, too."

"Good. Now about the big audit."

"Yes?" Pat asked.

"I don't want you to take offense, but I can't put you in the position of the accountant in charge. You're doing a super job, but you just don't have the experience yet. This is a very big job compared to what you've just finished. Okay?"

"Sure. I wasn't expecting to be in charge. Who will be, and what are you going to have me do?"

"Russell will be handling it on site and reporting to Bob Ramsey. He did it last year with no problems. What you'll be doing is up to him, but I imagine you'll be auditing revenues or expenses and supervising our people working on that end of it. Bob Ramsey will be making the final decisions though; he'll be the partner overseeing the entire audit. As Russell's father, it wouldn't look good having me review Russell's work."

"Sounds good. When do we start?"

"We're all going to meet here on Monday morning, have a short meeting, and drive on down to their offices in D.C. It's important for you to meet their staff and get organized before you start working there and before you take that week off. Just remember, this is our biggest client, and it means a lot of money to the firm."

"I understand. Is there anything else?"

"Nope. Look, it's after five. Why don't you head on out of here, and I'll see you on Sunday at the Arbutus game."

"Thank you for everything, Gil."

People in the office wondered what Pat was smiling about as he walked toward his office.

He closed the office door, sat on the corner of his desk, picked up the phone, and pushed a speed dial button.

"Hello," came Lynn's voice.

"Hi, honey, it's me."

"Hi. You're late again." She sounded agitated.

"I know but I've got a lot to tell you, and I guarantee you'll like it."

"What?" she asked, her tone changing almost immediately.

"I'll tell you when I get home—I'm heading out now. It's been quite a day."

# Chapter Nine

Gilbert Autry had just adjourned the weekly Monday morning meeting of the partners and senior accountants.

"One more thing," he said, and everyone stopped to look at him as they were leaving the conference room, "Russell and Pat's flag football team finished the regular season yesterday undefeated, and they'll be playing Glen Burnie for the state championship in two weeks."

"I wouldn't mind seeing that game myself," Bob Ramsey said. "Where are they playing?" he looked at Russell and Pat.

"Catonsville High School. One o'clock," said Russell.

"Good. I'm in town. I'll probably be there."

"Try to get there early. There're going to be a lot of people, and parking might be a problem."

"I'll keep that in mind. Good luck, guys," Ramsey said. He then changed the subject. "Pat, I understand Gilbert filled you in that I'll be in charge of the Tobacco Federation audit."

"Yes, sir. I'm looking forward to working with you."

"Thanks, me too. Unfortunately I've got a conflict today. Gilbert will be taking you to their offices, introducing you to everyone, and getting you started.

"Thanks for your help, Gilbert."

"No problem, Bob."

Ramsey picked up his notes and left the room. As he left, Pat was thinking how formal Bob Ramsey always appeared and it did not seem out of character for him not to insist that Pat use his first name, unlike the other partners. Still, Pat was looking forward to working with him, anxious to learn more.

"Pat and Russell, will you two stay a few minutes?" Autry said, sitting back in his chair, " I have a few things to go over with you before we head on over to their offices.

"This is the last time you'll have to hear me say this, but just remember that the National Tobacco Federation is our biggest audit client, and the audit fee means big bucks to us."

"I understand, Gil," Pat said.

"I know you do, Pat. Now a little bit about them. They are a very, very powerful association. Several of their members are Fortune Five Hundred companies. Mega bucks, corporate jets, the whole bit."

Pat was taking it all in and he could tell Autry was very serious.

"Usually, we're pretty relaxed, as you know, but we have to be squeaky clean and professional on this job. Their members are in-and-out of their offices all the time, and that's what they expect."

"What do you want me to do?" Pat asked.

"Just a few things. One, wear a suit every day. I can't even let you wear a sports coat, and no flashy shirts and ties."

"Okay."

"Two, no eating at your desk. Coffee or something else to drink is okay, but no food."

"Okay," Pat said again.

"And three, no fraternization with anyone on their staff. Go out to lunch with our people, and don't eat in their cafeteria.

"Now, don't get me wrong, I want you to be friendly, of course, but I would rather you didn't strike up any friendships with their people. I know it sounds like a bit much, but this is one job we have to play by the rules. Any questions?"

"Who will we be dealing with over there?" Pat asked.

"Primarily their president and their controller."

"And they are?" Pat asked, as he was writing notes on a yellow pad.

"The president is a fellow named Jim Hampson. He's in his early fifties, married, and he's been the boss for five years now. He's the one who brought us in to do the audit. We owe him a lot.

"He's successful and rich, but he's friendly and easy to get along with. In his position, he entertains a good bit out at his place. You'll probably get an invitation to his Christmas party. You won't have any problem with Jim."

"And their controller?"

"Regan Christian—she's a little quiet, but she does a terrific job in accounting. In five years, we've never run across anything serious."

"Good," Pat looked up. "I'm ready."

"Let's meet at Edie's desk at ten. I'll drive," said Russell.

They drove south on the Baltimore Washington Parkway and talked about the audit. Russell turned up the radio, after hearing the first few notes of the Eagles' "Life in the Fast Lane."

"Russell," his father said. "I know I'm getting old, but would you either change that station or turn it off?"

"Sorry, Dad," Russell looked toward the back seat and winked at Pat. "I keep forgetting they didn't have radios when you were our age."

**44**

"Very funny," Autry chuckled. He loved bantering with his son.

"It could be worse, Dad."

"How?"

"We could be riding in Pat's car. All he ever listens to is Beatles music. And I mean that's *all* he ever listens to."

"They're still the best. No apologies."

"Where have you and Lynn decided to go on your vacation next week?" Gilbert Autry asked, changing the subject.

"Believe it or not, I don't know. Lynn's handling the whole thing. All I know is that the plane leaves next Saturday morning. She's packing for me and everything."

"That really sounds like fun," Russell grinned. "Just don't forget to get back in time for the big game."

"And don't get hurt," Gilbert Autry added.

"Don't worry, I'll be back in plenty of time, and I'll keep in shape."

"So, any predictions on where you're going?"

"My guess is somewhere south. The Bahamas is my first guess. Lynn loves the beach."

They were still talking when Russell eased the car onto a public parking lot across the street from the National Tobacco Federation's offices in Northwest Washington, D.C.

"How long will you be?" the parking attendant asked, writing on a numbered ticket.

"All day." Russell answered.

They entered the building and approached the receptionist's desk. "Well, hello, Eileen," Gilbert Autry said.

"Mr. Autry!" she said, "Is it that time already?"

"Sure is, Eileen, let me introduce you to one of our new people. Pat McGuire, this is Eileen Shaw. Eileen, Pat McGuire."

"Nice to meet you." They both said it at the same time, causing everyone to chuckle.

"And you know Russell, of course."

"Hi, Russell."

"Eileen," Russell said, nodding.

"Eileen," Gilbert Autry said, "would you please tell Jim we're here?"

"Of course, I'll buzz Rita," she said.

"She must be away from her desk," Eileen said, putting the telephone down after not getting a response.

"Carol is on her way down to relieve me. I'll just take you up myself."

Pat had been looking at the pictures decorating the lobby. They showed the development of the tobacco industry. The oldest were black and white photos. Some showed tobacco workers hoeing and tending fields of tobacco by hand. One showed Jamestown settlers sitting down for a smoke with Mattaponi Indians. Newer, color photographs showed modern storage and processing, and cigarettes rolling off conveyor belts.

Pat heard the elevator doors open. A young woman walked over to the receptionist.

"Sorry I'm late, Eileen," she said.

"No problem. Are you gentlemen ready?" Eileen asked, looking at the three accountants.

"All set," Gilbert Autry said, and the four of them stepped onto the elevator.

"The executive offices and finance are on the twelfth floor," Russell said, breaking the silence.

"What's on the other floors?" Pat asked.

"They lease a couple of the floors, but government relations, editorial, data processing, and conferences are on other floors. I'll show you around later."

Pat surveyed the offices as he walked. This is the executive level all right, he thought to himself, admiring the furniture, plants, and pictures, all tastefully arranged.

"She's still not back," Eileen said, stopping at a desk with Rita Davies's nameplate on it. "I wonder where she is?"

At that moment, Jim Hampson came out of his office.

"Rita's over at the travel agent's desk getting some tickets for me. Thanks, Eileen."

"You're welcome, Mr. Hampson. It was good to see you again, gentlemen," she said smiling.

"It's great to see you, Jim," Gilbert Autry said, extending his hand toward the president.

"You remember Russell, of course."

"Of course, how are you Russell?" They shook hands.

"Fine, thank you. It's good to be back."

"Jim, I'd like to introduce you to our newest CPA, who will be one of the senior accountants on the audit. This is Pat McGuire."

"It's a pleasure, Mr. Hampson. I've heard a lot about you," Pat said, shaking Hampson's hand.

"It's nice to meet you, Pat, and the name's Jim. Come on into my office, fellas. I'll get you some coffee as soon as Rita gets back."

Pat liked his first impression of Jim Hampson.

He seemed genuinely friendly, not what Pat expected of someone holding such a powerful position. A handsome man, he smiled freely and he shook Pat's hand firmly, a trait Pat always admired. He was taller than Pat expected and looked like a man who worked out regularly. His suit was of the highest quality, and Pat understood why Gilbert Autry insisted on nothing but suits and dresses for everyone on the assignment. His salt-and-pepper hair was parted on the left, his mustache was trimmed neatly, and his fingernails were manicured.

"Please sit down, gentlemen." Hampson motioned toward the corner of his office where there was a plush sofa, over-stuffed chairs, and individual coffee tables made for informal conversation. Pat and Russell sat on the sofa, and Gilbert Autry sat in one of the chairs.

Hampson took another chair that would allow him to face all three men.

Pat noticed the JH monogrammed on Hampson's shirtsleeve, the expensive cufflinks, and his Rolex watch. He had a single-diamond ring on the ring finger of his left hand.

"So," Hampson said, "what's up?"

"Just the usual stuff, Jim," Gilbert Autry said. "We'd like to get set up this week and work with Regan Christian in finance. We'll get together a list of things we'll need to have, and then leave her alone for a couple of weeks to give her time to close out everything and get ready for us."

"Do you need me for anything?" Hampson asked.

"Just a few things. Your signature is required on a few letters to banks and attorneys. We'll be updating you occasionally on how the audit is going. Other than that, we'll pretty much leave you alone. Unless of course, there are any problems we think you should be aware of."

"Sounds good."

"Russell will actually be in charge of the audit on site, and Pat will be one of the senior accountants working with him. Bob Ramsey is the partner in charge, and I understand he told you he has a conflict today."

"Do you have any questions for us, Jim?" Autry asked.

"No. I've been through this before. Are you still playing ball, Russell?" Jim asked, changing the subject.

"Yes, sir," Russell answered. "In fact, we'll be playing Glen Burnie for the state championship in two weeks."

"I read that in the paper. Congratulations."

"Thank you. Pat here is on the team, too. We played high school ball together at Mount Saint Joe in Baltimore."

Hampson turned to Pat.

"Did you go on to college ball, Pat?" he asked.

"No, sir. I went into the service instead."

"What branch?"

"The Marine Corps."

"Oh, we have something in common then," Hampson said. "I'm a former jarhead myself. Semper Fi."

"Semper Fi," Pat returned with a smile on his face, remembering the day when a crusty sergeant major told him how Marines would forever be a brotherhood.

"Oh, I think I just saw Rita," Hampson said.

"Rita, is that you?" he asked in a louder voice.

"Yes, sir. I've got your tickets."

"Good. Would you please come in here for a second? There are a few people I want you to meet."

The four men stood up when Rita Davies entered the room.

"Rita, I know you know Gilbert and Russell Autry, but I'd like to introduce you to Pat McGuire. He'll be working out here on our audit for a while."

"It's nice to meet you, Pat," Rita Davies said. "Please let me know if there's anything I can do for you."

"Thank you, I will. And it's a pleasure to meet you too," Pat said.

Rita Davies was the most stunning-looking woman Pat McGuire had ever met.

# *Chapter Ten*

"Come on, Lynn, where are we going?" Pat asked his fiancé Saturday morning as she drove east on Route 40 toward Catonsville.

"I told you already," she answered, "to your parent's house. Your father's dropping us off at the airport and picking us up next Friday. That way we don't have to pay for parking."

"I know that much," he said, playfully punching her on her right arm. "I mean, where are we really going. I can't stand this."

"If I told you, it wouldn't be a surprise. Now just be patient," she said stubbornly.

As they drove, Pat silently studied Lynn's smiling face. Pat reflected on how fortunate it was that the unexpected money came when it did. They were both trying hard to make it work, but their relationship had become strained. Pat was the one home now, with his friends and his family. Lynn had left everything behind for him—especially her mother, who was always too ready to come out and visit. When things weren't going well between them, Lynn didn't hesitate to remind Pat about the sacrifices she was making. He felt guilty in his happiness to be home again.

He wanted things to get better.

Bud McGuire, Pat's father, was waiting on the sidewalk with a mug of coffee. After waving goodbye to Pat's mother, the three pulled out toward the airport in Pat's car.

Pat's father left the motor running at the passenger drop-off on the upper level of the Baltimore-Washington Airport. He helped Pat pull suitcases from the trunk to the sidewalk baggage check-in.

"Thanks, Dad," Pat said, giving his father an affectionate hug. "We really appreciate it."

"Thanks again for everything," Lynn said, kissing him on the cheek.

"You two just have a good time, and don't worry about anything. Call us when you get there to let us know you arrived safely. We'll call Lynn's mother and dad."

They saw him wave one last time as he made his way back into traffic and drove out of sight around the semi-circular airport drive.

"Now will you tell me?" Pat asked.

"Nope. Wait until we get to the gate, and then I'll tell you everything. Tell you what, I'll check the bags in here at curbside, and you get us a couple of coffees. I'll meet you in the snack bar."

"Okay," he said, faking exasperation, as he walked into the terminal. "But I'll bet its Bermuda. You always said you wanted to go to Bermuda," she heard him say as he walked away.

Lynn checked their luggage in and met Pat at the snack bar. He had a cup of coffee waiting for her, just the way she liked it—a little sugar and almost more cream than coffee.

"Okay, follow me," she said, as she swallowed the last sip of her coffee. "I won't keep you in suspense much longer."

"Okay, I know it's US Airways at least," Pat said after they had passed through security.

They walked hand-in-hand down the concourse until Lynn stopped just before they reached gate D-14.

"Okay. Now close your eyes," she said, "and don't open them until I tell you."

Pat closed his eyes without putting up a fight. He let Lynn lead him about twenty steps.

"Now stop," he heard her say. "Don't open your eyes yet, but turn to your left."

Pat turned to his left, feeling silly; thinking everyone in the airport was looking at him.

"Now you can open your eyes," he heard her say excitedly as she squeezed his upper arm.

Pat looked at the signboard above the agent's head and squinted to read the red words moving from right to left.

"Denver!" he said. "We're going to Denver!"

"Close," she said, "we're flying into Denver and then renting a car, and driving to Keystone, Colorado. There's a big ski resort there."

"You got me, you got me," he said looking at her. "I thought for sure we would be going south."

"I know, but I wanted to do something different."

"But I'm from Baltimore! I don't know how to ski!"

"Neither do I, but I've arranged for private lessons as soon as we get in. Let's sit down, I'll tell you all about it.

"I asked the travel agency to come up with something really special. We fly into Denver and go to Hertz where we have a car reserved. It'll take about an hour-and-a-half to two hours to drive to Keystone Resort. We have a great room that overlooks a big lake, with a fireplace and a Jacuzzi. It'll be very romantic."

"Lynn," Pat said. "It's a great idea, but I've got one small problem."

"What?" she asked.

"When we get to the room this evening, I don't think I'm going to want to go skiing!"

Lynn smiled.

"I told you a little lie," she said.

"What?"

"Ski lessons don't start until tomorrow morning. I've made other plans for tonight!"

They both smiled and Pat put his arm around her shoulders.

# Chapter Eleven

Three days later.

"Are you nervous?" He asked her as they waited at the ski lift for the intermediate slopes. The cold, yet refreshing, Colorado air stung their nostrils slightly.

"Sure," she said. "Don't forget, I've never skied either."

"The instructor said we're ready—let's hope she's right! Let's just try to relax and enjoy it."

In a few minutes, the chair arrived and they headed up the side of the white mountain.

"The scenery alone is worth the trip," said Pat. "This place is just magnificent." Jagged mountain peaks outlined an intensely blue Colorado sky.

"Get ready, this is our stop," said Lynn, as they neared their drop-off point.

They glided off the lift at the same time, and nervously adjusted their equipment.

"Be careful and I'll see you at the bottom," Pat said, kissing Lynn on the cheek and adjusting his goggles.

"Good luck, honey—I'll meet you there!"

Pat pushed off on his ski poles and started gently gliding down the slope, trying to remember everything the instructor had taught him. His nervousness stiffened his body as he negotiated the turns. With every successful turn, he loosened up, feeling his confidence growing.

His first run was exhilarating. He was both sorry and relieved when he saw the end of the run coming.

He came to a stop and turned around looking for Lynn to come down the same path. He recognized her bright yellow jacket on the third skier he saw. Feeling proud, he watched her gracefully use her poles to push off each turn. Feeling she did better than he, he was happy for her.

He smiled as she glided up to him.

"Well, what do you think?" he said.

"Let's do it again. That was wonderful," she answered.

Waiting in line for their fourth run of the day, Lynn noticed Pat staring at the line in front of the "Expert Skiers Only" lift.

"Oh, no," she said. "I know what you're thinking! There is no way you're ready for the expert slopes yet, so don't even think about it."

"No, no, don't worry," he said.

"What's over there then?"

"See the guy fourth in line from the end? Hackman jacket with the red and blue sleeves?"

"Yeah, what about him?"

"I think that's Jim Hampson."

"Who?"

"Jim Hampson—president of the National Tobacco Federation. I told you about him, remember? Nice guy, former Marine and all that?"

"Why don't you go over and say hello?" she asked.

"I should but I don't want to break out of line. I can't really tell if it's him or not with those goggles and ski cap. The last time I saw him, he had on a Hickey Freeman suit. I'll check at the registration desk later."

"Okay. Watch out, here comes the chair," she said.

They had spent a wonderful afternoon together. After a warm shower, Lynn was soundly asleep on the bed. Pat, wearing jeans and the yellow-and-red sweater Lynn had surprised him with, sat quietly in a comfortable chair. Facing a wide window overlooking the snow-covered Colorado landscape, he sipped the last of his gin-and-tonic. Picking up his room key from the dresser and pulling the door closed without a sound, he headed for the registration desk.

"May I help you, sir?" asked the slightly over-weight clerk.

"Yes, my name is Pat McGuire. I'm in room two-fourteen."

"Yes, Mr. McGuire, what can I do for you?"

"Could you please tell me if you have a guest registered by the name of Jim Hampson?"

"Just a moment, I'll check. The clerk hit the keys on the computer keyboard and stared at a screen that Pat couldn't see.

"No, sir. No one here by that name. H-A-M-P-S-O-N right?" he asked Pat.

"Right. Thanks for your trouble."

"No problem. Next?" the clerk said, looking at the woman behind Pat in line.

Lynn rolled over to face the door as Pat entered. "Nope—Hampson's not registered here, honey," Pat said. "It was probably someone who looks just like him."

"Good," she said. "I really don't want to share you with anyone this week."

"I've got to do one thing though, just in case," he said.

"What?"

Pat sat on the edge of the bed, closer to Lynn. "I'm going to call his secretary to see if he's registered at one of the other hotels."

"Oh Pat, come on!" she said, irritated. "This is our vacation! Can't you just leave work back at the office?"

"I know, but if Mr. Autry or Mr. Ramsey found out Mr. Hampson was here and I didn't look him up, they'd have a cow," he said, taking Lynn's hands into his own.

Lynn pulled her hands away. Pat realized they were dangerously close to another argument.

He took a deep breath, weighing his words before speaking.

"Look," he continued. "I don't like this any more than you do, but it's something I just have to do. This is the firm's biggest client we're talking about. Mr. Autry made it clear that we're to handle them with kid gloves. Besides, we wouldn't be here in the first place if it weren't for him."

This time Lynn waited a moment before speaking.

"Oh, go ahead—make your call," she said with resignation. "I'll see where we can eat tonight."

"That's my girl," Pat said, giving her a hug. "I'll be only a minute."

He dialed long distance information for area code two-zero-two while Lynn perused the directory of local restaurants.

"What city, please?" A voice asked.

"Washington, D.C.," he answered.

"How can I help you?"

"I'd like the number for the National Tobacco Federation."

"Please hold for the number."

"Thank you."

"You're welcome, and have a nice day."

Picking up the hotel pen, Pat waited for the familiar computerized voice. "The number you have requested is," it paused . . . "six, two, six, two, seven, zero, two. Please make a note of it." He recorded the number.

Pat quickly dialed the number. He heard a woman's voice after two rings.

"National Tobacco Federation, how may I help you?"

"Rita Davies, please," Pat said.

"Please hold and I'll connect you."

Pat looked over to Lynn and smiled, watching her making notes as she looked over the restaurant guide.

"Mr. Hampson's office."

"Rita Davies, please."

"This is Rita."

"Hi, Rita, this is Pat McGuire of Autry, Martin & Ramsey. Remember me?"

"Sure, Pat, what can I do for you?"

"Listen, Rita, I'm on vacation out here in Colorado."

"Lucky you. I wish I were there."

He hesitated for a moment, remembering how beautiful he thought she was and hoping Lynn didn't read anything in the hesitation of his voice.

"Rita, I saw someone today who looks just like Mr. Hampson. Is there any chance he's here?"

"No," Rita said without hesitating. "He's at an American Society of Association Executives' meeting in Chicago. He'll be gone all week, won't be back until next Monday."

"Thanks," Pat said. "It must be someone else. I just wanted to be sure. I'm really sorry to trouble you."

"It's no trouble at all, Pat. Have a good time, see you soon."

"Thanks again, Rita."

"Bye, bye."

"Bye."

Pat put the telephone down.

"Well?" Lynn asked. "Was it Mr. Hampson?"

"Nope. I just checked with his secretary. He's in Chicago."

"Good," Lynn fell back on the pillow with a relieved smile, and then they discussed the pros and cons of the different restaurants. Later that evening they shared a fabulous dinner.

That evening, in the Rocky Mountain Suite of the same hotel, Jim Hampson sat at the glass dining room table with the Chief Executive Officers of the five largest tobacco companies in the world.

Kerry Barber of Tobacco Exports International, Stewart Cristie of Jamestown Tobacco, Kenneth Chase of Johnston-Morrisson, Duane Byrd of American Brand, and Dave Lovelady of Olde Harbour had flown in from their corporate offices for the three-day meeting. Coming in on different commercial airlines, each had used one alias for the flight and another for the hotel.

No one, other than those in the room, knew that this meeting, like the others before it, was taking place. The men were working to secretly fix tobacco prices and to divide world markets for tobacco in Latin American countries.

"So, we're all in agreement, then?" Jim Hampson asked, as he looked at the executives around the table. "During the week of December fifteenth, each of you staggers a two-percent increase. For January through February each company buys the amount of television advertising in Venezuela and Costa Rica that we've discussed today."

Each executive looked at the other and nodded in agreement.

"Incentives promoting cigarette brands in these countries include only those discussed today. Are we all clear?" It was more of a statement than a question, but each executive nodded.

"Okay, gentlemen, since we're all in agreement, I have two more things to go over with you before dinner gets here," Hampson said, as he opened his brief case and pulled out a small stack of white envelopes.

"Kerry," Jim slid an envelope with the name "Kerry Barber" on it across the glass table to the chief executive of Tobacco Exports International. Barber put the envelope in his pocket.

He repeated the process four more times. Each executive put his en-velope in his jacket pocket without opening it.

"As usual, each of you has a check for fifty thousand dollars with no payee information on it. I've signed the checks and left the payee line blank. You handle it as you see fit from this point on. I don't ever want to know what you do with it after we leave this room.

"Each of you also has a dues assessment invoice in your envelopes for seventy thousand dollars from the National Tobacco Federation. It's billed to each of your companies. I'll need the money before our next meeting so I can have bonus checks for everybody.

"Now, while I hate to repeat myself, please remember that when you approve the invoices for payment, be sure to send them to the post office box on the invoice and in the envelope I've given each of you. They should *not* be sent to the Federation's offices. Understand?"

"Don't worry, Jim," Stewart Cristie said. "We've all done this many times. You'll get the checks on time, and they'll go to the right address."

"I know I sound like a broken record, Stewart," Hampson said. "But if any of your checks finds its way into their offices, I don't know how I'd ex-plain a dues assessment we've never billed for or an invoice we've never used, with an address that isn't ours."

"Jim 's right," Ken Chase added. "We can't be too careful."

"You said there were two things," Duane Byrd said. "What else?"

Hampson hesitated a few seconds before continuing. "We have a little problem, and I've got to discuss it with you."

"What is it?" Kerry Barber asked.

"One of the CPAs auditing the association is here," he said calmly and bluntly. "He's here at this hotel—Pat McGuire. I just met him last week in the office. He was in one of the ski lift lines today."

"Are you sure it's him?" Stewart Cristie asked.

"Positive," Hampson said. "I went down to the registration desk and asked if a Patrick McGuire had checked in yet, and they said he had."

"Did he see you?" Duane Byrd asked.

"Yes," Hampson answered. "But not face-to-face. I'm sure that he thinks he saw someone who just looks like me."

"How would you know that?" Duane Byrd asked again.

"I called the office and my secretary, you know Rita, told me that he had called her to see if I was here."

"And?" Dave Lovelady asked.

"He told her that he saw someone who looks like me, and that he checked with the hotel, but they told him no Jim Hampson was here. He called Rita just to make sure."

"What did Rita tell him?" Lovelady asked again.

"She told him I was attending an American Society of Association Executives' meeting in Chicago. That's where I'm supposed to be."

"I don't like it at all," Lovelady said.

"Neither do I," Hampson said. "That's why I'm telling you."

"Gentlemen, this is serious," Kerry Barber said, and then looked toward the association's executive director. "You've got to get him off the audit, Jim, and I don't care how you do it."

"I don't understand the problem," Stewart Cristie said. "I think he just thinks he saw someone who looks like Jim."

"Listen, Stewart, there's a problem," Kerry Barber continued. "These accountants are detail oriented people. They notice everything. That's what they're trained to do. If he comes across an airline ticket, a hotel receipt, a credit card receipt, or anything else that links anyone in this room to this meeting, he could just put two-and-two together.

"There's a whole lot of money at stake here, and we can't risk having him stumble onto something, as careful as all of us think we've been."

"I agree," Duane Byrd said. "You've got to get him off the audit, Jim."

"How am I supposed to do that?" The tone of his voice suggested he didn't really expect an answer.

"That's your problem. We pay you to handle everything on your end, and this is on your end. Just get him off the audit, and we don't care how. Understand?"

"I understand," Hampson said, "but I don't know what I'm supposed to do about him."

Dave Lovelady spoke next. "I think I can help you, Jim. I'll talk to you after the meeting."

Hampson nodded. A knock on the suite's door broke the tension. "Room service."

"Dinner is served, gentlemen," Jim said.

# Chapter Twelve

The following Sunday.

"Look at all the cars!" said Lynn, as Pat pulled into the Catonsville High School parking lot.

"Well, it's the championship. After *The Sun's* big article, a lot of people probably thought they'd come out and see what a flag football game is all about. Having a great day like this helps too."

"Do you want to put anything in the trunk, hon?" Pat sat on the bumper to put on his rubber cleated athletic shoes.

"Yes. Let me put my purse in there. Are you going to be warm enough with just that jersey on?"

"Oh, yeah, once the game starts, I'll be plenty warm," he said, closing the trunk and taking Lynn's hand. "Here, you take the car keys." She put them in her pocket and wrapped her arm around his waist.

"Darn, it *is* cold," she said, looking up at him and squeezing him tighter.

They walked toward the sidelines where the rest of his team was playing catch, stretching, or jogging slowly around the field to loosen up.

National Beer's team was easy to spot. Their uniforms were distinctive: yellow jerseys, red numbers, and black pants with a yellow and red stripe down the sides.

Across the field, the Glen Burnie team was organizing for pre-game exercises and drills. Their black jerseys with silver numbers reminded Pat of the Raiders' uniforms.

Russell came over when he spotted Pat and Lynn. "Well, the two Olympic skiers!" he said with a smile. "Did you two have a good time?"

"Oh gosh, it was wonderful, " Lynn said, giving him a hug. Pat was glad to see Lynn was finally warming up to his friends.

"How about you, buddy?" Russell asked, "You didn't get hurt, did you?"

"No, I'm fine. Ready to go."

"Did you see my parents here, Russell?" Pat asked. "Lynn wants to sit with them."

"Yeah, they're with my wife and folks—over there." Russell pointed to the center of the stands.

"Well, I'm going to go sit down," Lynn said. "You two have a good game and don't get hurt."

She kissed Pat and hugged Russell again. "Good luck."

Pat looked toward the Glen Burnie side of the field.

"Jesus, they're big!" Pat said.

"You don't win three consecutive state championships by being small," Russell said. "I think we're ready for them this year. At least I hope so."

"My God, look at that number ninety-nine!" Pat said.

"Who?" asked Russell.

"Ninety-nine. The big, blonde-haired guy, what do you think he goes, two-sixty?"

"At least," Russell said. "I'm two-forty and he's got at least twenty pounds on me. Hey, let's go; Coach Annello is starting the drills."

"Okay, fellas, bring it in," Coach Annello said, after the pre-game drills were over. "Same starting line-ups as last week."

Pat started as outside linebacker. Russell played right tackle on offense.

"Who are the refs today, coach?" one of the other players asked.

"It looks like we have four today. Puglisi's head ref."

The teams liked this crew—Puglisi, in particular. He called a good fair game and let the players play. They were lucky to have him today. His schedule as a paramedic for the Baltimore Fire Department sometimes had him working on Sundays.

"Okay, kickoff team on the field. Let's go," the coach said.

The players and the fans from both sides of the field were yelling encouragement when Puglisi's whistle blew, and National Beer kicked off to Glen Burnie.

National Beer held them to one first down on the first series of play, and Glen Burnie had to punt. Pat knew they were up against a good team. They couldn't make any mistakes if they expected to win. Glen Burnie was big, fast, and well-coached.

When National Beer's offense lined up for their first play, number ninety-nine switched from right end to left end and lined up against Russell. When the ball was snapped, he hit Russell on both his shoulders with his open palms, and then grabbed Russell's right shoulder with both hands, pushing him off balance. He grabbed the quarterback's flag before he even got set-up for a ten-yard loss.

The Glen Burnie sidelines were screaming.

"Jesus Christ, Russell, you're going to have to give me more time than that," the quarterback Mickey Pulman, said, looking at Russell and brushing off his jersey.

"That was just the first play, Mickey," Russell said. "Don't worry, I'll get his number."

"It was ninety-nine in case you didn't notice! Now come on!"

On the second play, number ninety-nine did the same thing. When the ball was snapped, he hit Russell hard on both shoulders, then grabbed his right shoulder and tried to push him off balance. He didn't get to the quarterback this time, but he put on enough pressure to force Mickey's throw early, and the ball fell incomplete.

He did the same thing again on the third play and got the quarterback's flag again for another ten-yard loss.

Fourth-and-thirty. National Beer had to punt.

"It's going to be a long day for Russell," Pat told the teammate standing next to him.

"I don't envy him trying to block that guy!" the teammate replied.

Coach Annello met with his offense while the defense took the field after the punt.

"What's the problem, Russell?" the coach asked.

"No problem at all, coach. Give me a few minutes to put on an extra thirty pounds, and I'll be fine," Russell said, exasperated.

"Listen, this is what we've got to do to handle him," the coach said, looking at Russell. "Line up farther to his right so he can't grab your right shoulder so easily."

The coach looked toward Ken Kaminski. "Kenny, we'll have to line you up in back of Russell and a little to his left. That way, if ninety-nine goes outside of Russell, he's got a longer path to get to Mickey. And, if he goes inside, you can help Russell and double team him, okay?"

Kaminski nodded his head.

"Mickey," the coach said, looking at his quarterback, "We're just going to have to run our plays with one less receiver."

"Just give me some time, guys," the quarterback said.

The strategy worked, ninety-nine wasn't as much of a factor when he was double-teamed, but Glen Burnie was ahead by six points at halftime.

"How do you feel, Russell?" Pat asked. Russell was rubbing his right shoulder and had a pained expression on his face.

"I'm okay, but my right shoulder is starting to throb. That son-of-a-bitch grabs it or hits it every play."

"Why don't you say something to the referee?" Pat asked.

"I did, but Puglisi said he's been watching, and ninety-nine isn't doing anything illegal."

"Well, hang in there, buddy. We only have another half to go and the season's over," Pat said.

The National Beer defense held, and the offense scored a touchdown early in the fourth quarter to tie the game.

The defense held again, and National Beer got the ball with two minutes left in the game.

The coach called a time-out before the offense took the field.

Russell went up to his coach.

"You've got to take me out, coach, I can't even raise my right arm," he said, using his left to support his right elbow. "That guy has nailed me on every single play."

"Okay, sit down, Russell. Put some ice on it."

"Pat, come on over here," the coach said to Pat, who was still with his defensive teammates.

"You've got to go in at right tackle for the last series for Russell. Can you handle it?"

"I haven't played offensive line for a while, but I think I can hold my own for a few downs," Pat said, confidently, despite the fact that he would be facing a much larger man.

They heard the referee's whistle signal the end of the time-out, and they went into their huddle.

National Beer had the ball on its own nineteen-yard line, and the quarterback called a pass to the left end. They broke from the huddle, and Pat lined up across from number ninety-nine.

"New meat," he said to Pat from across the scrimmage line. "Get ready to eat some dirt, assface," he added as he got into his defensive stance before the ball was snapped.

Pat was giving away fifty pounds to ninety-nine, but he knew from his high school days at St. Joe how to go against bigger opponents. He had played linebacker and he knew that if he stayed low, attacked the bigger man's legs, and stayed away from his upper body, he could at least slow him down, and give his quarterback some time to throw.

The ball was snapped on two.

Pat lowered his head, raised his arms, and shot out across the line, hitting ninety-nine on the knees, knocking him down, but he fell on top of Pat. He felt an elbow dig deep into his rib cage as the larger man got back on his feet.

The pass was complete for a first down.

In the huddle, Pat said to his quarterback. "This guy's really pissed now, and I know he's going to come after me with all he's got. I think it's time for a screen pass to Kenny on my side. I'll let ninety-nine by, and you just throw it over his head to Kenny, who will be lined up behind me. I'll block down field."

The quarterback looked at Pat. "Okay. Got it Kenny?" Kaminski nodded. "On four," Mickey said, and the team clapped hands and broke from the huddle.

Pat lined up again across from ninety-nine, who looked at Pat. "Try that move again, shit ball, and I'll break your god-damned nose."

The ball was snapped on four, and Pat let ninety-nine hit him as he pretended to block him. Ninety-nine was almost to the quarterback, when Mickey just lobbed it over his head to Kenny Kaminski, who had turned around and was waiting for the ball.

"Go," Kaminski yelled to his lineman, as he caught the ball and followed Pat up the right sideline.

Pat blocked the first Glen Burnie jersey he saw, and Kaminski ran all the way to the Glen Burnie twenty-three yard line before the last defender grabbed his flag.

"Time out!" The coach called and Pat, with his teammates, headed toward the sideline.

"Great call, Mickey. Perfect," the coach said to his quarterback. Mickey looked at Pat and winked.

"Okay, it's down to one play, and it's the one we've worked on but haven't used yet this year," said the coach to his offense. I want the two tackles to line up in the halfbacks' positions in the backfield and the halfbacks to line up on the line. I think this team is in for a surprise.

"When the ball is snapped, I want both halfbacks to run a post pattern, and don't even try to block. Their tackles will be coming right in, but having two linemen in the backfield to block should give Mickey enough time. Mickey, look for Kenny in the end zone. Got it?" The coach finished and the team nodded as they went into their huddle. The whistle signaled the end of the last time-out.

In the huddle, Mickey told the linemen to line up to his left and right and to try to take their men to the outside, so he could step up into the pocket and throw the ball.

"On three," said the quarterback, and they broke out of their huddle.

"What in the hell is this?" Ninety-nine yelled when he saw the linemen in the backfield. He reached across the line and shoved Kaminski, who was lining up across from the much bigger man.

Two referees blew their whistles at the same time and threw their yellow flags.

"Okay ninety-nine, this is your last warning," the head referee, Jim Puglisi said. "That's a legal formation."

Puglisi walked to the twenty-three yard line and picked up the ball. "I've got a personal foul, number ninety-nine on the defense. Ten yards and repeat first down. He then walked to the thirteen-yard line, put the ball down and blew his whistle to resume play.

The teams lined up again, and the ball was centered to Mickey on three.

Kaminski didn't even try to block ninety-nine, and ran his pattern to the middle of the end zone.

Ninety-nine came in unopposed. Pat saw that he was headed to his right. So he bent over low and used ninety-nine's own momentum against him. He pushed him in the same direction he was going, and ninety-nine ran right past the quarterback, who stepped into the pocket and threw a spiral toward Kaminski, close to the goal line.

Everyone's eyes were on the ball: both teams', the officials', and all the fans'.

Pat was watching the ball; his back toward ninety-nine.

Ninety-nine was sprinting toward Pat; all two hundred sixty-five pounds of him hit Pat in the small of his back, driving him to the ground and snapping his head back violently. No one saw what happened.

Lynn screamed when she saw Pat motionless and face down on the field and ran onto the field, with Pat's parents.

Jim Puglisi, the referee and paramedic, grabbed her as she was running toward her unconscious fiancé.

"Don't touch him," Puglisi said loudly and in a voice that commanded authority, as he ran to the injured player.

Mickey Pullman, the quarterback, grabbed Lynn and held her. Lynn was sobbing and Bud McGuire was holding Audrey, Pat's mother, trying to keep her calm.

The paramedic knelt down on one knee near Pat's head. He placed the middle and index fingers of his right hand gently on Pat's exposed neck, feeling his carotid artery for a pulse. He leaned over and put his right ear close to Pat's nose and mouth, listening for breathing.

"Does anyone have a cell phone?" he asked the crowd now gathered on the field.

"I do," one of the spectators said.

The referee dialed nine-one-one.

"Police, fire, or ambulance," a calm voice asked.

"Ambulance," Puglisi said without emotion.

"Baltimore Ambulance—can you tell me what the problem is, please?"

"Dispatcher, this is Captain Jim Puglisi. I'm an off-duty Baltimore paramedic refereeing a football game at the Catonsville High School football field. We need a medivac helicopter from shock trauma at University Hospital. Tell them to expect a possible cervical spine injury, and we'll set up a landing zone right on the center of the field. Do you copy?" His voice was calm and controlled.

"Ten-four captain. The helicopter should be there within ten minutes, over."

"All right, everyone. His pulse and respiration are stable, but I don't want to take any chances. We've got a helicopter coming and I want everyone to go to the sidelines. That pilot will need a clear landing zone."

Seven nervous minutes later, the whine of a helicopter engine could be heard coming from downtown Baltimore. The brown-and-tan Maryland State Police helicopter circled the field once before landing directly in its center.

Two paramedics, one woman and one man, jumped out as soon as the helicopter's skids touched the turf. Carrying a backboard and a medical kit, they ran to the still-unconscious player. The pilot stayed on board and could be seen talking into a radio.

The paramedics, with the help of the referee, expertly rolled Pat onto the backboard while supporting his neck. They quickly put a collar around his neck and taped his head to the backboard so that it wouldn't move. His body was strapped to the backboard, and the three of them carried him to the waiting helicopter. Pat's vital signs were taken and called in to the doctor on duty at University Hospital, telling him what to expect when they arrived.

As the paramedics started to close the door, Lynn broke free and ran to the aircraft.

"Can I come?" she asked desperately.

"No ma'am," the female paramedic said with both compassion and authority. "It's against regulations, and it would be too much weight for this type of helicopter. Believe me, we can't waste time now discussing this. It's best for you to drive to University Hospital."

Without waiting for a response, the paramedic closed the helicopter door.

Lynn turned to see Pat's parents behind her.

Still stunned, they watched as the pilot looked around before lifting his aircraft. Its blades spinning loudly, the helicopter rose up over their heads, drifting away, back toward downtown Baltimore and University Hospital's shock trauma ward.

Patrick Sean McGuire was off the National Tobacco Federation audit.

# *Chapter Thirteen*

The next day. . .

"Pat. Pat, can you hear me?"

Pat tried opening his eyes when he heard the vaguely familiar voice again.

"Pat! Pat, open your eyes if you can hear me."

He tried opening his eyes again but felt they had been glued together. He felt a warm sensation on his face when someone gently wiped his closed eyelids clean.

He tried to reach for his face, but he couldn't move his arms.

He heard the voice again.

"Can you hear me now, Pat? Please try to open your eyes."

This time, his eyes slowly opened. He thought he was a child again, lying helplessly, looking up from the bottom of his crib. His eyes wouldn't focus. All he could see was the thin, white veil covering his crib and a white light in the distance.

"Pat, it's Lynn. Can you see me?" she said, looking down at him.

Her face slowly came into a semi-focus.

"I'm thirsty," Lynn heard him say softly.

A nurse who was standing next to Lynn unwrapped a piece of gauze and dipped the gauze into a pitcher of water. He felt soothing dampness on his dry lips, and tried to suck the moisture into his mouth.

"Better, Pat?" he heard Lynn say.

"Yeah. I can't move."

He then saw another figure lean over him from the other side of his bed.

"Pat, I'm Doctor Whitley," a woman's voice said in a comforting tone. "You can't move because we have your arms and legs strapped down. Don't be frightened."

"Where am I?" Pat whispered.

"You're in University Hospital. You've had an accident," the new voice said again.

"An accident. What happened?" he asked, still trying to focus his eyes on the figures staring down at him, and not yet aware of what happened to him.

"It happened at the football game yesterday, honey. Nobody knows what happened. We just looked and saw you face down on the ground," Lynn continued. "Doctor Whitley has been looking after you."

"Hello, Pat," he heard the voice say again. "Do you feel strong enough to talk to me?"

"I just feel sleepy," he said, his eyes closing again.

Doctor Whitley, a fiery redhead of about forty-five, in a white smock, walked over to Lynn and took her hand.

"Lynn," she said, "I think it's best to let him rest for a while. I'll talk to him later. Why don't you come with me?"

Lynn followed the doctor out of the room.

"Coffee?" the doctor asked.

"Yes. Thank you," Lynn replied.

"I'll be right back. You just sit here and relax."

A few moments later, the doctor came back into the room. Lynn was staring blankly out a window.

"Here, Lynn," the doctor said, handing her a paper cup of coffee. "Please sit down, I need to talk to you."

Lynn took the coffee and sat down.

"Lynn, we're going to have to let Pat rest and get strong enough to talk before we can run some tests to see how badly he's hurt."

Lynn looked straight into the doctor's eyes. "What do you think?" she asked.

"We don't have any idea right now, and we won't know until we can run the tests. With an unconscious patient, it's very hard to tell the extent of injuries involving the spinal cord."

"Best and worst case?" Lynn asked, surprising herself with her calmness.

"We're not worried about the broken ribs. We've taken care of them. We're sure his lungs haven't been pierced. He'll be in some pain, and breathing will be difficult, but he'll be all right."

"Uh-huh," Lynn said. Then waited.

"Pat has definitely had an injury to a vertebrae in the middle of his back. Lumbar four or L-four, we call it. The injury suggests a force from behind, in the small of his back, and his neck snapped back too. Can you tell me what happened?"

"No," Lynn said. "Everybody was following the ball. Nobody saw it happen.

"Everyone thinks this huge guy on the other team hit him, but because nobody actually saw it happen, we're not sure."

"Okay," the doctor continued, "worse case first. He could have damaged his spinal cord where I told you. At that part of his spine, that would mean he'd be paralyzed from the waist down, and there's nothing we could do about it."

"And…" Lynn said, again surprising herself with her own calmness.

"Best case, the spinal cord is only bruised. In this case, he'll have feeling in his legs, but he won't be able to walk without the benefit of time and physical therapy."

"Thank you," Lynn said, digesting what the doctor told her. "Have you talked to Pat's parents?"

"Yes. I talked to them while you were sleeping in the waiting room."

"How are they taking it?"

"His mother is pretty upset, but his father is doing fine. They're very nice people. They're waiting for you downstairs in the lobby. Lynn, I'm going to tell you the same thing I told Pat's parents. You've all been here for almost twenty-four hours, and it's best if you go home to rest."

Lynn shook her head with resignation. Doctor Whitley was glad she didn't have to talk her into it.

"Good. Look, it's eleven now. Why don't you go home, try to get some sleep, and I'll meet you here around five o'clock. How does that sound?" the doctor asked.

"I'd rather stay, but I think you're right," Lynn answered, standing up. "And thank you for your concern, doctor."

"That's my job," the doctor said, taking her hand. "I'll see you at five."

Lynn took the elevator down to the first floor, where Pat's parents were waiting.

"Did they say anything else?" Pat's mother asked nervously as Lynn approached.

"They don't know anything yet. They asked us to come back at five so he can rest before they run some more tests."

Bud and Audrey McGuire and Lynn returned to the McGuire home together. No one got much rest. Audrey put out some milk and sandwiches. Bud and Lynn picked at the food, conversing little. It was a relief when it was time to drive back to the hospital.

At 5:03 P.M., Doctor Whitley opened the door to the neurology department's waiting room. Lynn, Bud, and Audrey were seated, the two women silently staring out the same picture window. Bud looked up toward the doctor, quickly putting aside an unopened *Sports Illustrated.*

"Hello, Mr. McGuire. Hello, Lynn, Mrs. McGuire. I hope you got some rest," she said cheerfully.

"To be honest with you, I'm in a kind of daze, Doctor," Lynn said. "I don't know if I got any rest or not. I'm just here."

Pat's parents were too apprehensive to talk.

"Well, you all come with me. It's time to see how that football player in the other room is doing." She took Lynn's hand and led the three down the hall to Pat's room.

"Lynn, is that you?" she heard Pat say when she looked down at him from the side of the bed.

"It's me, Pat," Lynn replied, encouraged to hear him talking. "I'm here with your mom and dad. How do you feel?"

"It hurts to breathe and I can't move."

"You got hurt in the game yesterday."

"How? I can't remember anything."

"We don't know. Somebody hit you from behind," she continued. Then, thinking Pat might not have remembered waking up the first time, she said, "Pat, this is Doctor Whitley. She's been looking after you."

Pat's eyes moved to the other side of the bed when he saw another figure lean over him.

"Hello, Pat, I'm Kaye Whitley," he heard the other voice say softly. "You've had an accident. Do you feel strong enough to talk to me?"

"I think so. It hurts to breathe, and I can't move," he said again.

"I know. Now don't be scared. It hurts to breathe because you've got a couple of broken ribs. You can't move because we've got you strapped down. Do you understand?"

"I think so," he said. "Why am I strapped down?"

"It's routine procedure in a case like this. I'll explain everything later. First, I just want to ask you a few questions. Okay?"

"Okay," he answered.

"What is your full name?"

"Patrick Sean McGuire."

"Who do you work for, Pat?"

"Autry, Martin & Ramsey."

"And what do you do?"

"I'm a CPA."

"What's a CPA?"

"A Certified Public Accountant."

"And what day is today?"

"Sunday I think."

"Good."

Doctor Whitley looked at Lynn and Pat's parents and smiled, as she pulled a pen from the pocket of her smock.

"What do I have in my hand, Pat?" she asked.

"It's fuzzy, but a pen, I think," he said, looking up.

"Good, now I want you to follow it with your eyes."

The doctor held the pen about twelve inches from Pat's face. First she moved it slowly to her left; her eyes watching Pat's eyes follow the pen. Then she moved it from her left to her right, not taking her eyes off his.

She brought the pen back to the middle, and then moved it slowly up and then down.

"Good," she said, looking at Pat's parents this time.

"Pat, I'm going to see what you can do with your hands and feet now." She exposed his feet and hands from under the white sheets.

First, she put her index and her middle fingers in Pat's left palm.

"Squeeze my fingers, Pat," she said, looking at her patient.

She felt Pat squeeze her fingers in the fist he made with his left hand.

"Good," she said, walking to the other side of the bed and putting the same fingers into his partially closed right hand.

"Now squeeze again," she said.

She felt the fingers of Pat's right hand apply pressure again.

"Very good!

"Now I'm going to the foot of the bed, Pat. You won't be able to see me."

She took the heel of her right hand and rested it against the ball of Pat's left foot and toes and pushed in gently.

"Can you feel me pushing on your foot, Pat?"

"No."

"That's okay. Now I want you to try to move your left foot toward me."

The doctor could not feel any movement from Pat's left foot.

"Pat," she said, "I really want you to concentrate on pushing your left foot toward me, okay?"

"Okay," Pat said.

"Now push," she said.

She didn't feel any pressure against her hand.

"I said push, Pat."

"I can't."

The doctor moved to his right foot and put her hand in the same position.

"Can you feel me pushing on your right foot, Pat?"

"No."

"Just try to move it then."

Once again, the doctor could feel no movement from Pat.

"Okay, Pat, last time," she said. "Try real hard to push your right foot toward me."

"Push, Pat."

Nothing.

"Pat, please try to push."

"I can't," she heard him say again.

She then took an instrument that looked like another pen out of the pocket of her smock.

But this time, she unscrewed the top, and the instrument resembled a carpenter's punch with its sharp point.

Without telling her patient, she held the instrument in her right hand, and ran the point from the heel of Pat's right foot up the middle and stopped at the ball of the foot.

The doctor saw his toes curl before he said, "Ouch! What are you doing?"

The doctor looked toward Lynn, then said, "Could you feel that, Pat?"

"Yes, I could feel that! What are you doing?"

Before answering, she repeated the same sequence on his left foot.

"Ouch! Damn!" he said.

Doctor Whitley looked directly at Pat's parents this time.

"Best case," she said smiling.

"Pat," she said, walking to her patient's side. "We're going to put you through a few more tests, but I feel safe to say that you've got a bruised spinal cord."

"What does that mean?" he said.

"It means you're very lucky," she said. "You'll have to go through some therapy, but I think you're going to be all right."

"I'm ordering that he be transferred from intensive care to the serious-but-stable ward," she said as she wrote. "We'll have to keep him here for a while for observation, but he's going to be okay. Someone will be contacting you from physical therapy soon to set up a schedule. We're going to unstrap his arms, but keep his legs immobile, and that will make him feel better."

She put the chart back on its hook and walked over to Pat's side.

"This is quite a family you've got here, Pat," Doctor Whitley said looking at the others. "I'm going to leave you all alone for a little bit, and come back later. But you still need lots of rest. You'll be okay, but you're not out of the woods yet."

Lynn pulled up a chair next to Pat's side. Pat's parents were on the other side of his bed.

"You sure had everyone worried there, mister," she said smiling, "and you've got a lot of friends."

"What do you mean?" Pat asked.

"Well, you can't see them, but the room is filled with flowers and cards, and everyone has called."

"Who?" Pat asked.

"Everybody. Your teammates, your friends, people you work with, just everybody," she answered.

"So who won the game?" Pat asked. "I don't even know."

"I thought you'd never ask," Lynn said.

Pat's father spoke for the first time. "Just a second, I'll be right back."

"Where are you going, Dad?"

"Just over here to the closet."

Pat heard his father's footsteps. His eyes weren't fully focused but he saw his father's head lean over the bed.

"Here," he said, putting something by his right hand.

"What's that?" he asked.

"The game ball," he answered smiling.

"Kenny Kaminski caught that pass on the last play of the game, and you guys won. Congratulations, champ," he said smiling for the first time in over twenty-four hours. "After the game, the team voted to give you the game ball, and everyone on the team signed it, plus one other person."

"Who?" Pat asked.

"The referee. Jim Puglisi," he answered.

"Why would he sign it?" Pat asked.

"It's a long story. You need some rest so I'll tell you all about it later."

"Okay," they heard him say softly.

"Where's Mom?"

His father put his arm around his wife's shoulder and walked her to Pat's side. She worshiped her only son and her eyes were still puffy and bloodshot from crying.

She leaned over his bed, gently touching his face. As Pat looked at his mother, one of her tears fell on his pillow next to his ear.

"I'm okay, Mom."

He fell deeply asleep.

# Chapter Fourteen

Pat was released from the hospital a week later to the confines of the apartment he shared with Lynn.

He was not a good patient.

He felt depressed and sorry for himself. The first physical therapist assigned to him quit after the second day. Young and inexperienced, he couldn't deal effectively with Pat's emotional state, and he was too slight in stature to handle Pat's larger, more powerful frame. Even though Lynn tended to him, his state of mind had a negative effect on their already fragile relationship. Still, she hung in there and never complained.

The second therapist was a woman much older and experienced than the first. She dealt effectively with Pat both emotionally and physically, and with her help he recuperated quickly. Soon he was well enough to work out of his apartment and a long nine months later he was cleared to drive and go back to work.

He felt awkward driving and even more awkward about reporting to work after being out of the office for so long.

Wearing the same blue suit he wore on the day of his interview, he walked stiffly out of the elevator toward the receptionist's desk. He wondered if he would fit back in. Would they accept him as they had before?

"Hey, Edie, remember me?" he asked the receptionist.

"Pat!" Edie said, as she walked around her station and gave him a hug. "We've all missed you. Welcome back!"

"It's good to be back, Edie."

"I'm not used to telling senior accountants what to do," she said, "but I was told to tell you to come with me."

"Where are we going?"

"To the conference room,"

Edie held on to Pat's arm as they walked together toward the conference room.

Edie opened the closed double doors.

"Surprise!" everyone in the room shouted when they saw Pat.

A big computer banner saying **Welcome Back Pat** hung from the back wall.

Gilbert Autry walked up to Pat and shook his hand.

"From all of us, welcome back, Pat," he said.

"It's good to be back," Pat replied. "I can't tell you how good it feels to be back."

By the end of the day, Pat felt spent, but genuinely happy to be productive and back to work again. On the way home, he sang along to his Beatles music. Somehow, driving seemed easier.

# Chapter Fifteen

Three weeks later.

"Are you sure you feel up to this, Pat?" Lynn asked as she drove the Camaro south on Route 29.

"Are you kidding? Do you think I would miss this party?" he answered. "Besides, I feel fine."

"Why didn't you tell me about this earlier? I would have bought something nicer to wear. If this party's in Potomac, it's probably pretty snazzy." she said.

"You look fine, and it's casual anyway. I didn't tell you because I just found out about it myself. I was leaving the office yesterday when Mr. Autry asked me if I was going to Mr. Hampson's party. I told him I didn't know a thing about it. Apparently, Mr. Hampson has this big open house party every year, and he invites all the partners and senior accountants. Anyway, Mr. Autry had his secretary call and put us on the list, then he gave me directions. Now you know as much as I do," he said, as he smiled at her.

"Okay, you're forgiven, but I wish I had more notice. Here's the Potomac exit; you're navigator from here."

They drove in silence for about five minutes, each wondering how Potomac had earned its reputation as one of the most exclusive sections of the Washington, D.C. area, with service stations and convenience stores lining the street. Once they approached Hampson's subdivision, their minds changed quickly.

"Jeez, Lynn, look at these houses. They all look like something out of *Architectural Digest* or *Better Homes and Gardens*."

"Yeah, I think this area is the place to live, if you're a high-priced lawyer, a lobbyist, or a congressman."

Though less than fifty miles from where Pat grew up, Potomac might just as well be on another planet. There was nothing blue-collar about it.

Winding their way toward Jim Hampson's house, Pat and Lynn talked non-stop. They fantasized about what it must be like to live in such surroundings.

"Look at that house!" Pat whistled as Lynn pulled into the Hampson's driveway. "I'll bet you're glad you came now!"

"Gosh, hon, I don't know if I'd ever feel comfortable with all this." Lynn said uneasily, as she pulled up the long winding driveway until a valet stopped them.

"Good evening, Ma'am," a young man said, opening Lynn's door. "We'll take the car from here. When you leave, it'll be parked in that field over there," he said pointing. "The keys will be in the ignition, and, don't worry, your car will be safe."

"Thank you," Lynn said, unused to such treatment.

"You're welcome. Have a good time," the valet said.

Lynn took Pat's hand as they walked up the cobblestone path leading to the house.

The house was a brick colonial with four white pillars across the front. The grounds were exquisitely landscaped and the lawn manicured. The din of conversation grew louder as they approached the double, teakwood doors. Before they could knock, one of the doors opened, and a woman wearing a blue maid's uniform, small white apron and white hat, greeted them.

"Good evening," she said smiling.

"Hello," Pat said. "We're the McGuire's. We replied to the invitation yesterday."

The maid smiled.

"Have you been here before?" she asked.

"No, this is our first time."

"Please make yourselves comfortable. Beverages and appetizers are being served in the den downstairs. Dinner will be buffet style and will start at nine. Most of the guests are downstairs."

"Thank you," they said together.

The house was huge, elegant, and formal. There were a few people in the kitchen Pat didn't recognize, so he and Lynn walked downstairs to a paneled den. There, about fifty people, gathered in small groups, were involved in lively conversations. A three-piece band, set up in the far corner, provided background music at just the right volume. The room was much less formal than the rest of the house. A pool table, pinball machines, and large-screen television offered guests plenty of entertainment.

"Pat!"

Pat turned and saw Gilbert Autry wearing a bright blue sports shirt and dark blue trousers, walking toward him, with a cocktail in his left hand. Pat found it strange to see Gilbert Autry dressed so casually.

"I'm glad you could make it. Hello, Lynn," he said.

"Hello, Mr. Autry," Lynn said.

"Quite a place, huh?" Autry said. "I've been out here many times, and I'm still impressed.

"Come on over, I want to introduce you two to Jim Hampson's wife, Linda."

They had followed Autry a short distance when Linda Hampson spotted them and moved in their direction.

"Linda," Autry said, touching his hostess on her arm, "I'd like to introduce you to Pat McGuire and his fiancé, Lynn. Pat, this is Jim Hampson's wife, Linda."

"I'm so happy you could come, Lynn," the woman said, extending her hand.

"Thank you for inviting us. You have a lovely home, Mrs. Hampson," Lynn said.

"It's Linda," she said, leaning forward "and thank you. We're both very happy here, and we're going to miss it when it's sold."

"It's for sale?" Pat asked, with surprise in his voice.

"Yes, we just put it on the market. Jim and I aren't getting any younger, and the place is just too big for the two of us."

"Where will you be moving?" Lynn asked.

"We're not sure yet. We'll either get a smaller house or move into a condo or townhouse. Either way, it's going to be near a country club and water. Both Jim and I are avid golfers, and Jim loves to fish and wants to be close to his boat."

"Well, good luck," Lynn said.

"Thank you, Lynn, that's kind of you."

Linda Hampson was a tall woman, nearly five-seven, with short, blunt cut, coal-black hair, clear brown eyes, a beautiful complexion, and a figure that told her admirers that she worked out on a regular basis. Even in casual clothes, she gave the appearance of being formally dressed. Lynn guessed she had probably been a model in her youth.

Linda Hampson was telling them more about the house when her husband, Jim, came over.

"Hello, Mr. Hampson," Pat said when he saw his host approaching, extending his hand. "Remember me?"

"Of course I do," Hampson said, shaking Pat's hand. "Marines never forget each other, right?"

"Right," Pat laughed.

"Mr. Hampson, I'd like you to meet my fiancé, Lynn. Lynn, this is Mr. Jim Hampson," Pat said.

"What a pleasure to meet you, Lynn. I see you've both met my wife."

"Yes," Lynn said, "she's been telling us all about your lovely home."

"I'm a little surprised to see you, Pat," Hampson said, looking at him with concern in his face. "Gilbert told me all about your accident, and I didn't realize you'd recovered to this extent. I'm glad to see you, though; don't get me wrong."

"What accident?" Linda Hampson asked, looking surprised.

"Pat here is a lucky man," Hampson said to his wife. "He got hurt in a football game and could have been paralyzed, the way I understand it. Is that right, Pat?" he asked.

"Yes, sir, I was very lucky. I've just about fully recovered, though, and I've even got the go-ahead to start limited jogging next week. Don't worry, I'll be in better shape for your audit this time around," he said laughing.

"Good," Hampson said. "We're looking forward to having you."

"Thank you," Pat said. "Have you seen Russell Autry by the way?" he asked.

"I don't think he's here yet," Hampson said. "In fact, I've been looking for him myself.

"Listen, we've got a few people we haven't said hello to yet. So, if you two will excuse us," he said, taking his wife's hand. "Please make yourselves at home."

"We will. Thank you; it was nice meeting you both," Lynn said.

"They make a striking couple, don't they?" Pat asked.

"Not bad," Lynn said joking. "How about something to drink?"

"What would you like?"

"How about a rum-and-coke."

"Stay here, I'll be right back."

Pat returned a few minutes later with a beer in one hand and a rum-and-coke in the other.

"Here you are, Hon," Pat said.

"Thanks."

While they were talking, Russell appeared.

"Hey, good to see you guys," Russell said, kissing Lynn and shaking Pat's hand.

"Where's Carol, Russell?" Lynn asked.

"She's not feeling well, and neither are the kids, so she stayed home. I'm a bachelor tonight," he answered.

"Oh, I'm sorry. I was hoping she'd be here. Haven't seen her for awhile," Lynn said.

"Hey, Russell," Pat said. "Do you know where the bathroom is?"

"Sure. There's one over there by the steps and another one upstairs off the music room, next to the living room."

"I'll be right back," Pat said. "Keep Lynn company."

Pat walked to the bathroom by the stairs, but three people waited in front of him, so he walked up the stairs to the next level.

The music room was another huge, paneled room. A black grand piano sat in its center. Its walls were graced by framed paintings of ballerinas. A custom-built bookshelf, two feet deep, occupied one wall. Among the rows of bound books were gold-framed photographs. Pat tried to open the bathroom door, but it was locked. A man's voice from the inside said, "Someone's in here. I'll only be a minute."

"Please take your time," Pat said, embarrassed.

He started walking the length of the bookcase, looking at the photographs. Most were Jim and Linda Hampson together. In some they played tennis, in some, golf; several were shots obviously taken on vacations together. There were a few shots of Hampson on a boat. A closer look showed the boat's name: *The Lady Linda.* As Pat was admiring a photograph in which Jim Hampson and three of his friends were holding up a fish for the camera, he felt his heart pound and a strange sensation come over him.

One of the men in the picture was blond and considerably larger than Hampson. Pat thought he recognized him—number ninety-nine from the Glen Burnie football team.

At that moment, the bathroom door opened, and a man he didn't know said, "All yours. Sorry to keep you waiting."

A few minutes later, Pat walked back down the steps to the den to join Lynn who was still sitting with Russell. They were talking to two other couples.

Pat touched Russell on the arm and said, "Russell, can I see you for a minute?"

"Sure. What's up?"

"Walk over to the bar with me."

When they were away from the others, Pat stopped. "Do me a favor, will you, Russell?"

"Sure, what?"

"Go upstairs to the music room, and look at one of the pictures on the bookshelf. The second row, fourth picture from the left. It's a shot of Mr. Hampson with three men on a boat, they're holding up a fish."

"So?"

"So, I think the guy next to Mr. Hampson is the son-of-a-bitch who took me out in the Glen Burnie game!" Pat said in a hushed tone, but his emotions were making it hard to control the volume of his voice.

"Oh, I don't believe that!" Russell said. "There's got to be some mistake."

"Go up and look for yourself then!"

"Wait here, I'll be right back."

Lynn saw Pat talking to Russell, and walked over to him when Russell left.

"What's going on?" she asked. "Did you two have an argument or something? You look strange."

Pat told her the same story and finished only moments before Russell came back.

"Well?" Pat asked.

"That's not him," Russell said calmly.

"How can you be sure?" Pat asked.

"That's Mr. Hampson's nephew. I'm positive, I know him. His name is Jeff Mellor. He's usually at their parties, and I'm surprised he's not here tonight," Russell answered with certainty in his voice.

"If you say so, I'm sure you're right, but I could swear it's him in that picture," Pat said, looking at his friend.

"Listen," Russell continued. "Don't forget, I played against that guy almost the entire game, and he pounded on my arm the whole time. My arm is still sore. I'd know if it was him." Russell rubbed his arm for effect.

"I guess you're right," Pat said. "I just wanted to be sure."

"Listen," Russell said. "I'll talk to you two later. I've got to see a man about a horse myself."

Russell walked away.

"That was the strangest feeling," Pat said.

"Come on," Lynn said. "They just opened up the buffet line."

They stood in line with several of the other guests and filled their plates with the rich food.

"Come on, Honey, there are a couple of chairs over there," Pat said, pointing to a corner.

They sat down, balancing their plates on their laps, and talked about their own dream house, stealing a few ideas from their hosts.

"Do you mind if I join you two?" a female voice asked.

They both looked up, and Pat saw Rita Davies standing there with a plate of food in her hand. His heart raced when he saw her, and he began to feel a little nervous. She was as beautiful as he remembered her, even though it had been almost a year ago.

"Of course not," Lynn said before Pat could answer. "Please join us."

She sat in a chair next to Lynn, turning it slightly so she could talk to both of them.

"Hi, I'm Rita Davies," she said, sitting down. "I'm Jim Hampson's secretary at the association."

"Hi, I'm Lynn, and this is my fiancé, Pat," Lynn said. "I'm a teacher, and Pat is a CPA working with the firm that audits the association."

"I remember Pat from last year. How are you, Pat?" she asked, smiling.

"I'm fine, Rita. I'm looking forward to the audit," he answered, still nervous.

"I wish we could say the same, but you people can be a pain in the butt," she said laughing.

While Rita and Lynn made small talk, Pat thought about how stunning she was. Rita was about Linda Hampson's height. She wore her slightly curly blonde hair to her shoulders and, like Linda Hampson, she took pride in maintaining her figure. Pat thought her sensuous mouth was even more appealing when she smiled. Her striking blue eyes seemed to sparkle when they made contact.

Pat couldn't take his eyes off her as she and Lynn were talking.

"Don't you just love this house, Rita?" Lynn asked.

"Oh, yes, it's wonderful, and I love the way it's furnished."

"Pat and I are stealing some of their ideas for our own dream house, aren't we, honey?" Lynn said, turning her head toward Pat. She noticed he was staring at Rita, so absorbed that he didn't respond. When he realized Rita was also looking at him, he felt as if he had been caught. He quickly turned toward Lynn, only to see her looking at him too. It was an awkward moment; he felt his face flush.

"I was telling Rita we've been stealing some of the Hampson's decorating ideas for our dream home. Isn't that right?" Lynn was smiling, but he knew her well enough to hear the touch of agitation in her voice.

"Oh, yeah. I can't get over how nice their house is." He forced a smile, but he felt as if he had been caught a second time.

Lynn looked at Pat and then back toward Rita. "Do you know when the Hampsons are going to move, Rita?" she asked, trying to ease the tension.

Rita had a perplexed look on her face. "Who told you they were going to move?"

"Linda Hampson told us as she was showing us around. You seem surprised, didn't you know?"

"Oh, yes. I was just under the impression that they didn't want anyone to know quite yet."

Rita sat there for a moment, obviously thinking, when she suddenly raised her arm and looked at her watch. "Oh, I didn't realize it was this late, I have to be going," she said as she stood up.

"Aren't you going to finish eating, Rita? You just sat down," Lynn asked.

"Please don't think I'm rude, you two, but I've really got to go. It certainly was a pleasure meeting you, Lynn," she said.

Lynn started to get up, but Rita stopped her, saying, "Please don't get up." Rita then turned to Pat and said, "I guess I'll see you in the office, Pat. Goodnight you two."

As she walked away Pat turned toward Lynn and found her glaring at him. "What's wrong?" he said, hoping that he sounded innocent.

"We'll talk about it later," she answered.

"Lynn, I . . ."

"I think it's better if we talk about it later." She was still glaring at him. Feeling guilty, Pat knew enough to be quiet. He was thankful when a couple that they didn't know came up and asked if they could join them.

Rita was walking down the front steps of the Hampsons' house when she heard a male voice behind her. "Rita, where are you going?" She turned around to see Jim Hampson closing the front door behind him. She didn't answer and continued walking. "I asked you where you were going," he said running up to her from behind.

He grabbed her by her upper right arm and turned her around. She shot a look at him, grabbed his wrist with her left hand, and pushed his arm down.

"I have to leave," she said, turning away from him.

He turned her around again and she stopped. He had his hands on his hips and was looking down at her.

"What's wrong with you?" he said, surprised by her reaction.

"I have a date, and I don't want to be late," she said calmly, and then smiled at him.

Hampson looked confused. "You said you would stay. People are going to wonder why you came and left so quickly."

"That's their problem, not mine."

"Please stay."

"I told you I can't."

He reached both hands toward her, and she backed away. "Don't, Jim. I'm leaving." Realizing someone could be watching from the house, he left his arms by his sides. He took a deep breath and looked upward.

"Rita, I don't . . ."

"Jim, is there something wrong?" he heard his wife say, as she walked toward them.

"No, Linda. Rita has to leave, and I was just saying goodbye."

"Leaving so early, Rita? You just got here."

"I'm afraid I have to go, Linda, but thank you for everything."

"Did you get enough to eat?"

"Plenty," she answered. "In fact, I have a dinner date, and I probably ate too much," she laughed, and looked at Jim.

"Anybody I know?" Linda Hampson asked playfully.

"Oh, no. Somebody I've had my eye on finally asked me out. You wouldn't know him."

"Well, have fun, and I hope to see you soon. Come on, Jim, a couple of people are looking for you." She grabbed her husband's hand and turned back toward the house. As he was turning, he exchanged a quick glare with Rita, who turned and walked toward her car.

On the ride home from the party, Lynn looked over at Pat in the passenger's seat. She took a deep breath before speaking, and weighed her words carefully.

"Pat," she said, "there's something I've got to talk to you about."

"What?" he asked, although he suspected what was coming.

"Something has been bothering me, and I can't keep it in any more."

"What is it?" he asked.

"I've tried to be patient and understanding, but I haven't been happy lately. Particularly after tonight's episode."

"I don't understand, what's the problem?"

"You!"

"Me. What did I do?"

"It's both what you've done and what you haven't done, lately."

"Will you please tell me what you're talking about?"

Lynn paused for a long time before answering, gathering her thoughts and trying to maintain control of her emotions.

"It's been nothing but you, you, you, lately. There was a time when you could really make me feel special. But, somehow, I just don't feel important to you any more," she finally said. "I feel like I'm just there to take care of the apartment and make your meals.

"You know, Pat, I encouraged and supported you and typed your papers for you when you went to night school. I spent a lot of lonely nights by myself when you were away then, and what thanks did I get when you graduated?"

"None, Lynn. But that's part of the give and take of a relationship. I would have done the same for you."

"Well, then, our entire social life was put on hold for six months when you were studying for the CPA exam. You didn't give me one thought throughout the whole time. All you did was study, and you never considered how it was affecting me. I know the test is hard, and it's a lot of work, but I really think you could have made at least *some* time for me. When you passed the exam, and don't get me wrong, I'm proud of you, and I know you worked hard, but did you even consider what sacrifices I made toward your efforts? No!"

"Listen, Lynn, I . . ." Pat, said.

"Let me finish," she said, anger building in her voice. "You're living for yourself, Pat. Our ski vacation was so typical. When we were at the resort, you were more interested in finding out if Jim Hampson was there than spending time with me."

"Lynn . . ." Pat said.

"I said, let me finish," she said again, trying to keep her voice down.

"Our lives were interrupted again when you got hurt and went through all that therapy. I helped you and suffered with you the whole time. You never, ever, acknowledged my role in your therapy. You never even said, 'Gee, Lynn, I sure am glad you're here!' I was just like a live-in nurse, taken completely for granted!

"Don't forget, Pat, I left everything I had for you. Family, friends, everything! You've got all your friends and family here."

She paused and Pat didn't interrupt the long silence.

"I don't know, maybe I shouldn't have let all this build up. But tonight was the last straw. I expect you to talk to other people at a party, but that little scene at dinner just did me in."

"What little scene?" Pat asked.

"Oh, please," Lynn continued, "you couldn't take your eyes off that woman, and you know it! I don't think I've ever been more humiliated."

"Can I talk now?" Pat asked.

"Go ahead," Lynn said, without looking at him.

"I didn't realize I'd been hurting you and taking you for granted, I really didn't.

"I apologize, I know I don't show my emotions much. Please, Lynn, I hope you can forgive me." Pat knew his apology lacked sincerity. He knew Lynn would feel it, too.

Lynn drove on without a word.

"Well," Pat finally said. "Can't you say anything?"

"I think I've said all I can say right now. Your apology just doesn't do it, Pat."

"What do you want me to do?" he asked, exasperated.

"It's not what I want you to do. It's time for me to do what I have to do for me."

"What, Lynn?" he asked, not wanting to hear her answer, yet not willing to put up a fight.

"We should just split for a while, Pat. I think it's for the best."

Pat knew he had been wrong. He knew things hadn't been perfect, but he hadn't felt motivated to take the time to figure out just what their problems were. He had always felt things would just work themselves out. He had counted on Lynn. Now it was unsettling to have her so much in control.

She kept her eyes on the road and Pat didn't know what else to say.

It started to rain about five miles from their apartment. They pulled into the parking lot in silence.

Pat couldn't remember feeling worse. Every corner of their once sunny apartment was now permeated with an oppressive, dark cloud. Lynn insisted on sleeping on the sofa, leaving him alone in their bed.

But, still, he couldn't get his mind off Rita Davies.

# Chapter Sixteen

A month later.

The conference room was comfortable. Fourteen plush chairs were arranged around a massive oak table in the rectangular room with its heavy wood paneling and thick, tan carpeting. The huge table allowed everyone the luxury of individual space to spread out their computers, calculators, and work papers. Autry, Martin & Ramsey's audit team was enjoying the assignment.

Bob Ramsey was once again the senior partner in charge of the National Tobacco Federation audit. He usually worked out of the firm's office in Baltimore. Russell was on-site audit manager, and Pat was the assistant on-site audit manager. Another ten accountants were assigned to the audit full time.

One Friday afternoon, after a progress meeting with Ramsey, Russell drove from Baltimore to Washington to check on his crew.

"Hey, how's everything going?" he asked no one in particular, as he opened the conference room door.

No one else answered, so Pat said, "I think we're all just glad it's Friday."

"What's the problem?" Russell asked, pulling up a chair next to his friend.

"Oh, nothing serious. We've had problems with some of the computers, and it's backing everything up."

"Did you drive here?" Russell asked Pat.

"No, I came in with Teresa today, why?"

"Why don't you ride back with me. We can stop at Jasper's on the way home. I'll buy you a brew."

"Didn't you take the Metro?"

"No, I drove for a change."

"I don't know," Pat said. "I think I'll just go home."

Russell looked at his friend and made sure no one was listening. "Listen Pat," he said in a soft voice, "you've got to get out of this funk. You seem depressed all the time, and it shows. I'm sorry about you and Lynn, but you've got a life too. I don't like to pull rank on you, but I'm in charge of this audit on site, and I'm telling you that your next job is to ride along with me and stop for a beer. Understand?"

Pat looked up, smiling weakly.

"Understand?" Russell said again, more forcefully.

"Okay, I'll go. I don't have anything else to do," Pat said, trying to manage a smile.

"Good. Now let's clean up and get moving."

"I'm going to call my parents first," Pat said. "I'm supposed to go over to their house for dinner, and I should tell them I'm going to be late."

As he was dialing their number, Hampson's secretary, Rita, opened the conference room door and walked in.

"Excuse me," she said, "I've got to get something out of the files for Mr. Hampson," and went over to the file cabinets on the opposite wall.

As Pat explained he'd be late for dinner, Rita smiled at him as she headed for the door with a file in her hand. He found it hard to take his eyes off her.

"Sorry for the interruption, guys. Have a nice weekend," she whispered before closing the door.

"Come on, everybody, help me lock everything up so we can get out of here," Russell said to his people. "It's after five, and I want to get out of here before the security system is activated for the weekend."

The office security system was very sophisticated. To get into the office after six o'clock at night and before eight o'clock in the morning and all weekend, you had to punch in a six-number security code within thirty seconds of opening the front door. The code identified the person entering the building, and the security company retained a permanent record of after-hours access. As an additional precaution, if anyone entered the building after hours, the security company dispatched one of its guards to the office to check their identification.

The accountants quickly put their papers and computer disks into file cabinets, and locked them to make sure association employees couldn't disturb the confidential files.

Russell used a key to open the only file cabinet the other auditors didn't have access to. He took from his briefcase a large, sealed white envelope with **"CONFIDENTIAL"** stamped in red across the front and back and put it in the top drawer.

He closed the drawer and pushed in the locking mechanism.

"Okay, everybody, Mr. Ramsey is very satisfied with our work so far, so go on home, relax, and have a good weekend. Things will look better on Monday morning."

After saying good-bye, everyone left but Pat and Russell.

"I didn't want to ask you with everyone else around, Russell, but what's the deal with the envelope?" Pat asked.

"I don't know myself," Russell answered. "Ramsey gave it to me after our meeting on the audit progress. He told me to put it in that particular file and gave me the key. I'm supposed to give the key back to him and him alone next Monday."

"Aren't you curious about what's in it?" Pat asked.

"Sure, but the envelope is sealed, and I know better than to open a sealed envelope a senior partner gives me. I also know some questions are better left unasked. He had a meeting with Hampson earlier this week in the Baltimore office. It's probably just Mr. Hampson's contract with the association that he wants kept confidential. We run into this kind of stuff all the time."

"Okay," Pat said. "Let's go, I'm thirsty." They gathered up their belongings and left the building together. They walked into the crisp Washington air and crossed the street to the Colonial Parking Lot. They were walking toward a brand new, shiny black BMW automobile when Pat stopped.

"What's this?" he asked, confused.

"My new toy," Russell said, smiling and opening the passenger side door. "Come on, get in.

"This is why I drove down here," he said, still smiling. "I had to show you my new chariot."

"Nice," said Pat. He felt the seat and examined the dashboard. "Very nice. But since when can accountants afford cars like this? It's not like we're lawyers!"

"Since I got a nice raise, that's since when," Russell said. "Besides, Dad and the other partners have been on my ass to get a better car to drive clients around in. You know."

"Well, I'm not going to hide it, I'm jealous."

"Hold on," said Russell, as they turned into Connecticut Avenue, "this should be a wild ride."

They drove out of the District of Columbia and headed north toward Crofton, Maryland, talking about the new car the whole way. Russell beamed when he caught other drivers looking at the car.

Having reached the restaurant, Russell parked his new car several spaces away from the nearest car.

"Could you have parked any farther from the restaurant, Russell?" Pat kidded his friend, as they got out of the car and walked toward Jasper's. "I'm not sure I can walk all the way from here." Russell grimaced at Pat.

Jasper's was a popular gathering place. Business people met there for lunch during the day and young professionals gathered there on Friday and Saturday nights to drink, talk, and meet other young professionals.

"I hope Maria is working tonight. She always takes care of us," Russell said, as they pushed open the glass door, looking for an open spot at the bar.

They stood on their tiptoes trying to see over the heads of the people in the crowded lounge. Russell saw Maria waving to him from behind the square, wooden bar in the middle of the room.

"There she is," Russell said.

They worked their way through the crowd to the only two empty bar stools around the bar.

"MARIA DABBONDANZA!" Russell said loudly as he sat down on one of the two stools. "I see you're dressed for tips again, you sexy thing, you."

"Well, a girl's got to make a living, fellas," she said smiling, knowing that each of her new customers, as well as just about every other man at the bar, couldn't help but notice the cleavage she was showing.

"The usual, hon?" she asked.

"What else?" Russell said.

"Why do I bother to ask!"

Pat and Russell watched her walk toward the draft beer dispensers and pour two National Beers into frosted mugs.

"Here you are, guys," she said, putting a mug in front of each of them. "When are you going to take me away from all of this, Russell?" she asked, winking at Pat.

"Oh, you're all talk and you know it," Russell responded.

"You're right," she said, laughing. "I guess my husband and kids wouldn't appreciate it. Let me know if you need anything else, hon," she said, turning to wait on her other customers.

"She really works hard," Russell said to Pat. "Did you know her husband is a county cop?"

"No, I didn't," Pat said, a little surprised.

"Yeah. I've met him several times. Nice guy. They've got five kids."

"Five!" Pat said.

"Yeah, you would never know it looking at her, would you?"

Pat and Russell were talking sports and nursing their second beer, when they heard a female voice behind them.

"So what does a girl have to do to get a gentleman to buy her a drink around here?"

They both spun around on their stools at the same time to see Rita Davies standing there smiling.

"Hello, Rita," Russell said, "What a surprise to see you here!"

"Oh, I come here once in a while. Hi, Pat."

"Hi, Rita," Pat said. "What can I get you?"

"Nothing, I was just kidding. I've got to be going. Oh, this is my girlfriend, Kathleen Schaeffer. Kathy works at American Builders and Contractors in Virginia."

Kathleen Schaeffer was a very attractive brunette with a smooth, olive complexion. She was obviously in a hurry to leave.

"Kathy, this is Russell Autry and Pat McGuire. Russell and Pat are CPAs working on our audit."

"Nice to meet you both," she said, shaking hands, but wanting to leave.

"Would you care for anything, Kathy?" Pat asked.

"No, but thank you. As soon as my boyfriend, Bill, gets here, Rita and I are going out to dinner, and we're late now."

"Well, we won't keep you," Russell said. "Nice to meet you, Kathy. Guess we'll see you on Monday, Rita."

"That's one of the reasons I came over. I'm having some people over to my apartment on Sunday to watch the Redskins-Dallas game. Would you two like to come over?"

Pat and Russell looked at each other.

"I don't have any plans. How about you, Pat?"

"No, I'm free too."

"Good. Kickoff is at one, so try to get there about twelve-thirty. I live at the Four Seasons Apartments in Bethesda. Do you know where that is?"

"Sure, what can we bring?" Russell said, noticing Rita was looking at Pat.

"Just some beer and snacks; and wear jeans or something comfortable," she looked back at Russell. "When you get there, just buzz me on the lobby intercom. It's a secure building, and I'll have to let you in.

"Well, we've got to go. I'll see you guys Sunday, and don't forget to bring your better-halves. I don't want any jealous women on my hands. Bye."

Pat and Russell watched them leave and noticed the glances men were giving them as they passed. When they were out of sight, they turned around on their stools and found Maria putting two more beers in front of them.

"This round is on me, guys. I know you two must be at least a little short of cash." she said.

"Why?" Russell asked.

"Well, I don't know how much, but you two must have paid those two young ladies to talk to you! You're the envy of the bar!" she said smiling.

"What can I say," Russell said. "When you've got it, you've got it."

Maria rolled her eyes and walked away.

Russell sipped his beer and looked at Pat. "I think you've got an admirer there in Rita, old buddy."

"Oh, I don't think so," Pat said. "She's just friendly."

"Yeah, right," Russell said, and they both laughed.

They finished their beers and said good-bye to Maria. They climbed into Russell's new car and pulled out of the parking lot.

Russell was talking about his car, when Pat changed the subject. "Can I ask you something personal, Russell?" Pat asked.

"Sure. Anything," Russell answered, glancing at Pat.

"What would you do if you thought you had a shot at someone who looks like Rita?" Russell glanced at Pat again, surprised.

"This is just between us, right?" Russell asked after a few moments' silence.

Pat nodded.

"To be honest with you, as much as I love my wife, I really don't know if I could turn it down. How about you?"

"I guess I'd feel the same way. I'd really feel guilty though, especially after the way Lynn left."

"Hey, listen, I didn't say I wouldn't feel guilty. I just don't think I could say no."

"I don't think I could either," Pat said. "But it wouldn't be right." Pat gazed out the window.

"I guess I was a real jerk with Lynn," Pat confided. "She must have been unhappy for months, and I never had a clue."

"Hey, man, you know, sometimes these things work out for the best. If you'd both been on the same wave length, you'd probably have read between the lines," replied Russell.

They drove along in the darkness for a few more minutes when Russell spoke.

"I was just thinking," he said.

"What?"

"There is one thing that would hold me back though, even with a woman like Rita."

"What's that?" Pat asked, looking at his friend.

"My old man and the other partners."

"What do you mean?"

"Listen, if my father knew that I was even *thinking* of dipping my pen into a client's ink well, it would be all over for me. He'd let me go in a second, even if he is my father."

"You really think so?" Pat asked, surprised.

"I know it. He's a conservative man, and he takes his ethics and standards of conduct very seriously. No question about it, he'd let me go in a heartbeat. My career with the firm would be over, just like that," he said, snapping the fingers of his right hand. "It just wouldn't be worth it."

They drove along in silence for awhile.

"Did I ever tell you about Mr. Snyder?" Russell asked.

"Who?"

"Mr. Snyder. His first name was Steve."

"No. What about him?"

"He was a senior accountant on the fast track to be a partner in the firm. In fact, I reported to him while I was studying for the CPA exam. All this happened while you were still in the service.

Anyway, as the story goes, Mr. Snyder was married, and everyone suspected he was having an affair with one of the women who worked at a client's offices. She wasn't all that good looking, but then again, neither was he."

Pat chuckled and Russell grinned back.

"She wasn't a Rita, let's put it that way. Anyway, there were rumors flying around about whether or not he was having an affair, and it must have gotten back to the client. I know the boss asked to meet with my father personally, and the next thing you know, Snyder was gone. Just like that."

Russell turned his head toward Pat again, and said, "It taught me a lesson, I can tell you that."

Pat looked at his friend. "I guess you're right. It really wouldn't be worth it when you think about it, particularly after all I've been through to get where I am now, night school and all that."

Russell pulled into the parking lot of Pat's apartment complex.

"Here we are."

"Thanks for the ride. And thanks for the advice," Pat said, getting out of the car.

"What advice?" Russell said, convincing Pat their conversation was just between them.

"Listen, Carol and I will pick you up around noon Sunday. We'll stop on the way for the food and beer."

"Sounds good. See you Sunday," Pat said as he closed the car door and walked toward his apartment.

Russell was backing out of the parking space when Pat jogged over to the driver's side, and tapped on the glass. Russell rolled down the window.

"Yeah?" Russell asked.

"Hey, I almost forgot," Pat said. "I told my dad I'd help him install a new ceiling fan on Sunday morning. I'll just meet you at Rita's house."

"Okay, we'll see you there then." Russell said.

"Russell, one more thing," Pat said.

"What?"

"Great car."

Russell smiled and drove away.

Pat drove to his parents' house for a late dinner. His mother heated up food for him, complaining the whole time. Pat knew that she was only kidding and that she was happy he was home.

Patrick loved and trusted his parents. He could tell them anything.

# Chapter Seventeen

"You watching the game, Dad?" Pat asked. He had just finished helping his father install the ceiling fan.

"Nah, I've lost all interest in pro-football ever since they stole my Colts. I just follow Maryland and Navy now."

Pat nodded. He wouldn't be going except that Russell had talked him into it and an afternoon at Rita's was hard to pass up. Twenty minutes later, Pat pulled up to a red brick guardhouse standing at the entrance to the parking lot.

"Who are you visiting, sir?" The security guard was friendly and polite.

After getting the name, the guard reminded Pat he needed to buzz Rita in the lobby.

Pat parked his car reached in the back seat for the bag of beer and potato chips.

He pushed in the glass door leading to the lobby and walked up to a large directory off to the left. He ran his finger down the long directory until he found *R. Davies* and pushed the button beside her name.

A few seconds later, he heard her voice, "Who is it?"

"Pat McGuire."

"Hi, Pat. When you hear a buzz, open the door. The elevator is across the lobby. Take it to the fifth floor. I'm in apartment five-oh-four."

The buzz sounded before he could answer. As the elevator moved slowly to the fifth floor, Pat thought about how lovely Rita had looked under Jasper's soft amber lights last Friday night. He knocked on her door, feeling anxiety rise inside him.

Russell opened the door and greeted him with a beer in his hand. He was dressed in jeans and a green rugby shirt. "Hey, buddy, you're late, the game has already started."

"What's the score?"

"Seven, zero, Redskins." Russell, eyes still on the game, backed himself into the sofa. Without looking, he plopped down, barely missing his wife's lap.

"Hi, Carol," said Pat, leaning down to kiss the petite redhead.

"Hi, Pat, I'm sorry Lynn's not here. She went back to Kansas City I understand."

"Yeah." He felt uncomfortable and wondered how much Russell had told her. "She's visiting her folks for a while." He didn't like lying, but he didn't want to get into a discussion about Lynn.

Carol gave him a sad, crooked smile. She had always liked Pat and was anxious for him and Lynn to get married and settle in. She had hoped the two couples could "grow up" together, having their kids about the same time, and establishing a comfortable, happy routine as best friends.

Not wanting to discuss the subject at all, Pat quickly said, "Hey, where's Rita?"

"She's in the kitchen on the phone, she'll be right out."

He sat down on the white sofa and looked around.

"What a place," he thought to himself. The center of the apartment had a sunken living room that held an L-shaped sofa, a coffee table, and a big-screen TV. The apartment was full of plants and the framed paintings on the walls coordinated the theme of music and dance.

As he was admiring the living room, Rita walked out of the kitchen dressed in blue jeans and a man's large, white dress shirt that she hadn't tucked in. She had rolled the sleeves up to her elbows. Her blonde hair was tied in a ponytail with a pink ribbon, and she was barefoot.

"Glad you could make it, Pat. What can I get you?" She shot him a smile and leaned down to kiss him on the cheek. He blushed and glanced at his friends, catching Carol's eye. She just smiled and turned back to the game.

"Well, I'll have a beer for now, and here are some reinforcements," he said, reaching to the coffee table for the bag he had brought.

"Thanks, Pat."

"Oh, do you want a glass with that beer?"

"Please."

As she turned back toward the kitchen, he noticed that even a man's large shirt couldn't hide her figure. This time, Russell caught him admiring her and winked. Pat smiled, thinking that he was glad that they had their conversation on Friday night on the way home from the restaurant.

"Here you are," she said a few moments later, handing him a beer and a frosted mug. "The rules of the house are that the hostess gets the first drink and, after that, you're on your own!" She smiled that beautiful smile.

"Thanks." He hoped he wasn't still blushing.

Rita put her own wineglass down on the table and sat cross-legged in a chair next to him. "You accountants sure look more relaxed when you're not in suits," she said, trying to make Pat more comfortable. He smiled.

"You have a beautiful apartment, Rita. How long have you been here?"

"Just over three years. I really like it. May I show you around?"

"I'd like that."

"Take your beer with you," she said, sipping her wine. "You two excuse us. I'm going to show Pat the rest of the place."

Carol looked up and smiled at them, but Russell just waved them on with his hand, not taking his eyes off the television screen.

The large kitchen sported a black-and-white motif, accented by splashes of red. A long white island, surrounded by four tall black leather stools, graced its center. Rita had tastefully decorated with bronze pans, kitchen utensils, onions, garlic, and plants. Pat admired her taste—simple, yet dramatic and elegant—just like she was.

"Very nice, I've always liked large kitchens. Do you like to cook?"

"I really do, I find it relaxing after a hard day. How about you?"

"I can't really say I'm good, but I do like to cook. Most of my cooking is on the grill though." He shrugged, grinning and finally relaxing a little.

Rita laughed as she poured herself another glass of wine. "Are you ready for another beer?"

"I will be in just a second," he said, raising his mug and swallowing the last little bit of beer.

She opened the refrigerator and handed him another beer.

"Here you go. Let me show you the bedroom."

They walked across the hall into the master bedroom.

It was huge, with a queen-size bed under the two windows on the far wall. The near wall had two closed doors. She opened both of them, revealing a walk-in closet and a private bathroom with a Jacuzzi tub, shower, and two sinks.

He looked around, feigning interest in the apartment to be polite. Standing beside her like this distracted him. He couldn't keep his eyes off her, and he hoped he wasn't being too obvious.

"By the way, where is everybody else?"

"The only other people I invited were Kathy Schaeffer and her boyfriend, Bill. You met Kathy last Friday evening at Jasper's."

"I remember. Pretty girl."

"She sure is. We've been friends for a long time. She and Bill must have had an argument. She called me this morning and said they couldn't make it. By the way, where is your girlfriend I met at the party? It's Lynn, isn't it?"

"Yes, well, that's a long story, but we decided that it was best to split for awhile. She's with her parents in Kansas City."

"Oh, I didn't know. I'm sorry. I wasn't trying to be personal."

"That's okay, how could you know?" He took a sip of his beer. "If you don't mind my being personal, are you seeing anyone?"

"I've had a relationship with someone for a couple of years. He couldn't make it today," she answered, avoiding his eyes, staring instead out the window.

"I'm sorry, I'm sure I would have enjoyed meeting him."

She paused a moment, then looked directly into his brown eyes. "I'm not," she said bluntly, continuing to hold his gaze.

They stood inches apart, facing each other. He could smell her perfume—something like lilacs. "My God," he thought to himself, "she's breathtaking!" He breathed her aroma in again before a sudden thought hit him. "What am I doing? I can't do this." Suddenly, he began to feel awkward, not knowing what to say.

"Damn!" They both heard Russell yell from the other room. Pat was thankful for the interruption.

"Come on, let's see what's going on with the game. I guess we'll have to be each other's date today." Rita reached for Pat's hand, and they walked out of her bedroom toward the living room, holding hands. Though he loved the feel of her light touch, he felt relieved when she let go before Russell and Carol noticed.

"What's going on?" Pat asked.

"The Skins just fumbled on their own eight. Dallas has the ball, first and goal," Russell answered with exasperation, never turning from the screen.

As soon as Pat and Rita sat down, the Cowboys scored a touchdown on their first play from scrimmage.

"Shit," Russell said, standing up. "Here we go again. Time for another beer," and he walked to the kitchen.

The four sat talking, drinking, and snacking their way through the first half of the game. Russell and Carol followed the game intently, while Pat and Rita didn't even keep track of the score.

The light conversation put Pat at ease with Rita. Talk came naturally as they compared notes about growing up in Baltimore. Rita was genuinely impressed that he was a veteran and had earned his degree the hard way by going to night school. As they continued talking, Pat began to realize there was a lort more to Rita than her appearance. She was intelligent, personable and fun to spend time with.

When the first half was over, Russell stood up and stretched. "Oh well, this game is getting out of hand. It's just as well, though." He looked down at his wife still sitting on the sofa. "Carol, we have to get going. Don't forget my parents are coming over for dinner tonight, and we haven't even thought about what we're going to eat."

Carol glanced at her watch. "Oh wow, you're right! Thanks for everything, Rita. We had such a good time. Can I help you clean up?" She started gathering mugs and bowls that were strewn on the coffee table, but Rita stopped her.

"I'm sorry you have to go already. Just leave everything. I'll clean up later."

Russell and Carol said their good-byes in a flurry of "thank-yous," "see-you-tomorrows," hugs, and handshakes, leaving Pat alone with Rita. For a fleeting moment, he thought he should follow his friends, but something seemed to hold him.

Rita closed the door after them and turned back into the living room. Her turn was sudden, and she didn't expect Pat to be so close. For a moment, neither of them could look away. Then, Rita broke the tension. She put her hands on his arms and said, "Pat, go on in and relax, and I'll get our drinks."

Her voice was calm and Pat had no way of knowing she was forcing back the shakiness she felt. He was busy trying to keep his own emotions in check. After taking a deep breath, he picked up the remote control to distract himself. He was changing channels when she came back with another beer.

"I'm just channel surfing. This game is already over."

"Why don't we turn it off and listen to some music instead."

Rita walked to her stereo system on the other side of the room.

"What do you like?" she asked, looking through a stack of compact disks and cassettes.

"The Beatles are my favorite. Do you have any of their CDs?"

"You know, I've got to get some Beatles. Hey, how about the Platters?"

"Fine, anything but disco or rap," he grinned, and she laughed.

Pat could see her putting in the compact disk and pushing some buttons. The Platters started singing, "Smoke Gets in Your Eyes" as she walked back toward him. She sat down on the sofa close to him, holding her wine.

"This is nice," he said. "I don't usually take time to relax." He took a long sip of his beer. "You have a really beautiful apartment." He tried for small talk, hoping he didn't sound awkward.

"Thanks. I'm very happy here." She put her glass on the coffee table in front of her.

"I think I pulled this ponytail too tight." She reached behind her to take off the pink ribbon and shook her head, freeing her long blonde hair, which fell around her shoulders. "I was getting a headache, and I don't know if it's my hair, or too much wine," she laughed.

He was struck by her every movement—her fingers as they moved through her wavy hair, her head as she tossed it back to laugh. His emotions were building up again. Then, "Remember When" started playing.

She stood up and held her hands out to him.

"Come on, let's dance, I love this song." She pulled him to his feet.

He reached over and dimmed the light on the table next to him, satisfied that he was creating a romantic mood.

"That's better," he said as he led her to the middle of the room. Before they got there he stopped and reached down, taking off his shoes. The last thing he wanted to do was to step on her bare feet. She was waiting for him with her arms outstretched when he put his right arm around her waist and held her right hand in his outstretched left hand. She placed her left hand on his shoulder and they turned slowly to the music.

He was surprised at how comfortable he felt. He had missed Lynn, but, right now, he wasn't even thinking about her. He focused on this moment, on this woman, on this dance. He pulled her body a little closer, wondering what her reaction would be and hoping he hadn't misread her signals.

Without hesitating, she moved her hand from his shoulder to the back of his neck. She leaned her head back slightly, glancing at him before resting her head on his shoulder. They danced through two more songs, neither of them saying a word. Time had stopped for them. Nothing else existed except the feel of their bodies, moving close together.

After the last beat of "The Great Pretender," Rita half-whispered, "Let's sit down." She led him by the hand back to the sofa.

Pat put an arm around her shoulder and a hand under her chin. "She is so beautiful," he thought. When she closed her eyes, he leaned down and kissed her full lips. She accepted his tongue and caressed it gently with her own. His hands slipped to her waist as he drew her to him.

Their first kiss was long and sweet, and he didn't want it to end, but Rita pulled away and stood up. He wondered if he had gone too far, when she suddenly straddled his legs, sitting on his knees and putting both of her hands around his neck.

"Just relax, and don't say a word," she whispered again and pulled his face to hers, kissing him much harder than before.

Pat reached behind her, putting his hands under her shirt. Her skin was silky smooth. She kissed him more passionately as his hands made their way slowly up her back, toward her bra. She didn't try to stop him as his fingers fumbled with the clasp. Finally, it gave.

He felt himself growing more excited with every move. Patrick had never felt like this, ever.

He inched forward on the sofa, and she sat back on his knees, slowly unbuttoning each button of her shirt. She let it and her bra slip to the floor. He took her head in his hands and studied every feature before kissing each one—her eyes, her nose, her chin. He brushed her neck softly with his lips before kissing her throat. She took his hands and slowly slid them down to her breasts.

He was about to move her to the deep-pile carpet in front of the sofa when, abruptly, three loud buzzing sounds came from the kitchen.

"No, no, no." She moaned.

"What's that?"

"The intercom; someone is downstairs buzzing me. I have to get it."

"No, don't answer it, please. They'll go away. Rita, I want you so much."

"Pat, I can't." She sounded as though she might cry, as she slowly pulled herself away from him, reached for her shirt, and quickly slipped it back on as she walked toward the kitchen.

The interruption hurt Pat and destroyed the mood. He eased himself back into the cushions on the sofa. "Why does she feel so compelled to answer the buzzer?" he wondered. He strained to hear her voice.

"Who is it?" She spoke in a muffled tone.

Pat could hear a muffled male voice, "What do you mean, who is it? I gave the signal. Let me in."

"You said you couldn't come over today!"

"Well, I did. Now open the door, will you?"

"Okay, just a second."

Pat could see Rita's shadow from the kitchen light. She leaned against the wall with one hand, her head bent. Then, a moment later, he heard, "Pat, I feel terrible about this, but I'm going to have to ask you to leave now."

Dumbfounded, Pat couldn't move right away.

"Rita, I don't understand…."

"Please, Pat, leave now. I'll call you later and explain everything." There was an urgency in her voice that he knew he couldn't fight.

He had no choice.

"Alright," he said as calmly as he could. Feeling uncomfortable, he put on his shoes. He grabbed his jacket and started for the door. But he wasn't moving fast enough for Rita.

"Please hurry and it's best if you take the steps. They're on your right at the end of the hall."

"This is incredible," he thought. But all he could say was, "Okay, I guess I'll talk to you later." The hurt and disappointment were welling up in his throat.

"Thanks, Pat. I'm so sorry." She was obviously embarrassed. "I'll call you later tonight, I promise." She closed the door behind him.

Suddenly, Rita remembered that her next visitor sometimes took the steps for exercise, and she started to panic. They couldn't run into each other.

She opened the door again and could see Pat's back, as he neared the end of the hall.

"Pat," she called.

He turned around.

"Do me a favor. Walk up a level, and wait in the hall for about five minutes before leaving, will you?"

This was too much! He looked at her with a questioning expression.

"Please, Pat." Her voice had a tone of desperation. "Please."

He nodded to her, opened the stairwell door, walked up a flight to the sixth floor, opened that door, and stood there in the hallway, thankful he was alone.

He walked a few steps to the window at the end of the hall, crossed his arms and peered outside. There was no movement in the parking lot below, and the only thing he noticed was that his car was still there. He glanced at his watch and for the next five minutes he thought of the range of emotions he had experienced over the past three hours; anxiety and exhilaration to disappointment and humiliation.

Suddenly his thoughts were interrupted when the apartment door to his left opened. Turning, Pat's motion startled the elderly woman in her bathrobe as she reached down to pick up the Sunday newspaper lying in front of her door. She pulled the top of her robe tight against her neck, glanced at Pat with a hint of confusion in her eyes and quickly shut her door without saying a word. Pat could hear her turn the deadbolt lock.

Fear that she might call building security sobered Pat. He quickly opened the door to the stairwell, ran down the six flights of concrete steps to the lobby and walked as inconspicuously as he could to his car. He got in, started the engine and drove out of the apartment complex, relieved to see the same guard who questioned him earlier simply smile and wave him through.

He drove two blocks and pulled the car into a convenience store parking lot. He didn't have a taste for coffee at the moment, but felt the caffeine would do him good under the circumstances. He poured himself a black coffee, paid the clerk and sat back in the driver's seat. As he was blowing on the steaming liquid he began to think.

"Is this what it would be like to have a relationship with Rita?"

"Who was on the intercom?"

# Chapter Eighteen

Driving home, Pat felt he had sunk to the bottom of a very deep well. At the same time, he felt embarrassed, hurt, angry, confused, and frustrated. Driving in silence, he tried to put all the pieces of this afternoon in place.

He wanted to be with someone he could count on. Turning left, he headed for his parents' house and parked outside.

His mother answered the door, surprised to see him.

"Pat! What are you doing here? Come on in," giving him a tight hug.

"Hi, Mom, sorry I didn't call, but I was in the neighborhood. I bet you never thought I'd visit you and Dad twice in one day, did you?" He hugged her back, hoping he sounded lighthearted.

"Well, come on in. I'll heat up tonight's leftovers. Your Dad's taking a nap. Want a beer or anything?"

"Yes, I'll get it," Pat said, as they walked toward the kitchen. "Do you want one, Mom?" he asked, as he opened the refrigerator door.

"Okay, sure." After pouring the beers, he sat at the kitchen table across from his mother.

"Have you heard from Lynn?" his mother asked, sipping her beer.

"Not since last week."

"You miss her, don't you, Pat?"

"Yeah, but . . ." he stopped himself.

Pat explained to his mother about how guilty he felt about his role in bringing Lynn all the way to Baltimore, and then not following through on his promises to her. He knew how he would have felt if the situation had been reversed and he had disrupted his life for Lynn.

His mother, in her unique way, agreed with him, yet—at the same time—she made him feel better. She echoed Russell's comment of the night before: Things usually happen for a reason. Pat's mother served him leftover dinner, and they talked while he ate. After Pat finished, he put his dishes in the sink, poured himself another beer, and sat down.

"Pat."

"What, Mom?"

"What's wrong?"

"What do you mean?"

"You're not yourself tonight. Is something else bothering you?"

"No, really, I'm fine. Nothing's bothering me." Again, he tried for a cheerful tone, but knew he wasn't fooling her.

"You were fine this morning, but there's something wrong now, isn't there? Come on, I know you."

Pat gave his mother that familiar "I'm telling the truth, and how do you know it's not the truth" look.

She waited a few seconds before continuing. "You can talk to me, you know."

"I know Mom, and I appreciate it."

They sat in silence for a few minutes, then his mother reached over and touched his hands. Her maternal intuition told her not to press the point at this time.

"I'm here if you need me, son, always remember that. And I'm a good listener."

Pat leaned down to kiss her hand, and said, "Thanks, Mom. Thanks for everything."

"Well," she sighed, standing up. "I'd better get the old fellow up. He'd be mad at me if he found out you were here and I didn't wake him."

As she was walking toward her bedroom, Pat called to her.

"Mom."

"Yes, Pat?"

"Thanks, and I'll remember what you said."

His mother nodded and went upstairs to wake her husband.

Later that night, as Pat drove back to his apartment, he felt better, glad that he had spent some time with his parents. He pulled into his usual parking spot, locked the car, and walked to his apartment. It felt strange walking into a dark, empty apartment after everything that had happened that day. He turned on lights as he walked into his bedroom. The red number two was blinking on the answering machine. A queasy feeling started growing in the pit of his stomach. He sat down on the bed and pushed the MESSAGES button. He heard the tape rewind, stop, and click before the familiar, computerized voice said, "Hello, you have two messages. Message number one."

Lynn's voice came from the machine. Mixed feelings. Lynn wasn't Rita.

"Hi, Pat, it's me. Sorry you're not there. You're probably with Russell watching a game or something. It's hard, Pat, but I'm not ready to talk. I just wanted you to know that I'm okay." He could hear her sob. "Good bye, Pat, I'll always love you." He heard her hang up the receiver.

He pushed the machine PAUSE button. Tears welled up in his eyes. He picked up the framed picture of the two of them. They were smiling and happy.

He remembered the picnic they had had that day. It was a spontaneous outing, something Pat rarely did. On an urge, he had stopped at the Italian Deli on the way to their apartment. He had bought bread, cheese, grapes, and wine. Lynn was so surprised. He smiled as he thought about the way she rushed around finding a picnic basket, a tablecloth, and candles in gold holders. It was a perfect day.

A former Marine and an athlete, Pat knew people often assumed he was macho and unemotional. Generally, he worked to fight this image and to show others how he felt—he really didn't like men who seemed hard. No one saw him today, though, as he buried his face in his hands.

After he had composed himself, he sat down and pushed the PLAY button. Another female voice came from the speaker.

"Pat, it's Rita. I just wanted to tell you how badly I feel about today. I'd like to meet you for breakfast tomorrow morning so I can explain a few things. I'll meet you at seven-thirty at the Denny's Restaurant near the Landover Metro Station, if that's okay.

"If there's a problem, call me. If not, I'll see you tomorrow morning. Thanks, Pat. Good night." It was all he could do, but, finally, he pushed in the ERASE button. It was the last time he would ever hear Lynn's voice.

He set the alarm for six o'clock, took off his clothes, and crawled under the covers to sleep.

# *Chapter Nineteen*

$P$at had trouble sleeping and got up in the morning before the alarm went off. Despite his mood, he did seventy-five push-ups and fifty sit-ups before showering and shaving, as he did every morning.

He drove in silence through a misty rain to the Landover Metro. He wanted to allow plenty of time for his breakfast with Rita. The drive seemed to take longer than usual.

Pat tried out different openings to greet her. "Hi, Rita, long time, no see." No, that was too trite. "Good morning, Rita, how are you?" No, too formal. He wondered how the conversation would go. But, really, he had no idea what to expect.

When he arrived at Denny's, he saw her sitting in the last booth on the right, drinking coffee. She was wearing sunglasses, despite the weather.

He was walking toward her booth when he heard a female voice behind him say, "Pardon me, sir, can I help you?" He turned to see a hostess standing behind him, smiling, with a menu in her hand. "Oh, I'm sorry," Pat said, noticing the sign that said PLEASE WAIT TO BE SEATED. "I'm meeting someone; she's already here."

"Good morning," he said as cheerfully as he could, taking off his suit coat and hanging it on a hook before sitting down.

"Hi," Rita said. "I guess you got my message."

"Yes, I did, and I'm glad you called."

They gazed at each other, Pat wishing he could see her beautiful eyes behind the sunglasses. Pat finally spoke first.

"Rita, I want to make this as easy as I can for both of us," he said as he sat on the bench across from her.

She just looked at him from behind her sunglasses.

Pat took a deep breath and was about to speak when a waitress came to their table.

"Good morning. Would you care for coffee?"

"Yes," Pat said, and she poured the steaming black liquid into his cup.

"Would you like a few minutes before ordering?" she asked.

"No, I only want coffee this morning, thank you. How about you Rita?"

"Nothing else, thank you."

The waitress walked away from their booth.

Pat welcomed the interruption to gather his thoughts. He managed a small smile.

"Rita, about yesterday afternoon," he said, taking another deep breath. "First, I want to say that I think you are an exceptionally beautiful woman, and I'd be a liar if I said that I wasn't attracted to you."

"Thanks," she said. "You're not bad yourself," adding a slight smile of her own.

"But Rita."

He paused.

"When I was at your apartment yesterday, I was thrilled being so close to you, touching you, holding you. You are so beautiful, Rita, and I'm only human. You know what I mean."

"Uh huh." She looked down.

"Yesterday was something that I'll never forget, and I want you to know that you are very special to me and you always will be."

"Pat, there's something I have to say too," she said.

"Can I say one more thing first?" he asked.

"Sure."

"Russell and I were talking last Friday night on the drive home after we saw you at Jasper's. You know the way guys talk sometimes."

Rita smiled.

"Well, we were talking about what we would do, as men, if we had the chance to be with a beautiful woman like you. Both of us agreed that it would be hard to say no to some women, married or not. But a few minutes later, Russell said that he didn't think he could have a relationship with a client, no matter how he felt. He knew that if he were somehow caught, he would be fired and his entire career would be in jeopardy. He said no one is worth that amount of risk." He leaned closer to her.

"Rita, I have to tell you that, even after all that happened, you were worth the risk, no matter what the consequences of being caught were."

This time, he smiled at her. He meant every word. They looked at each other for a few moments before she said, "My turn?"

"Yeah." He sank back in the booth, feeling a sense of relief. He had been honest about his feelings and had surprised himself with the words he had chosen to tell Rita how he felt about her.

"Pat," she said, taking a deep sigh of her own. "I have never felt worse about anything in my life than I did yesterday—when I had to ask you to leave and wait upstairs. I'm a little surprised you're here. I wouldn't have blamed you if you hadn't come and if you had never spoken to me again. But I'm glad you are here, and I'd like to ask you to forgive me. I was rude, but I want you to know that I didn't have any choice under the circumstances."

Her voice softened. "Do you hate me?"

"No, of course not. No," he said, nearly whispering. "I couldn't hate you."

She closed her eyes, obviously relieved.

"Thank you." I don't know what I'd have done if you didn't forgive me. And I want you to know that I don't go around inviting guys to come up to my apartment."

"I never even considered that."

"We do have a little something else in common, you know?"

"What?"

"I didn't go into it, but I've had a long relationship with someone, too. He's married, and I'm not saying that's right, but I think I love him, just like you thought you loved your girlfriend, and I don't want to spoil this relationship. I'm so sorry, Pat. Friends?" She slid her hand across the table to him.

"Friends," he answered, as he took her hand in his. They held each other's hands gently.

"Rita?" Pat asked, breaking the silence.

"Yes?"

"We had a moment, didn't we?"

She smiled.

"Yes, Pat, we had a moment"

He didn't want to let go of her, but reality set in. He stood up, "Well, I guess we'd better get to work before we're both fired anyway!" he said, trying to end on a humorous note. "Ready?"

"You go on ahead," she said. "I'm not going into the office today. I have a hair appointment this morning, and I'm getting my nails done this afternoon. I'm taking a day off for myself."

After Pat put on his suit coat, he leaned over the booth, putting both of his hands on the table.

"Rita, one last thing."

"Yes, Pat?"

"I just want you to know that you can trust me. Everything we've done or said and everything we will ever do or say is between us."

"Thanks, Pat. I know you mean it, and I appreciate your saying that."

She watched him pay for the coffee and hand the waitress a tip at the counter. Rita then watched him walk across the parking lot and get into the Camaro. Her hand thoughtfully tucked under her chin, she wished the other man in her life had some of Pat's qualities and she wished she had met Pat long ago. Pat was honest with her about making a mistake. He was courteous—he didn't embarrass her with too many questions about whom it was he might have run into or about the sunglasses.

She knew she could trust Patrick Sean McGuire.

# *Chapter Twenty*

Five weeks later . . .

The team of auditors from Autry, Martin & Ramsey had been working seven days a week on the audit of the National Tobacco Federation. Each person in the room was busy, engrossed in their own particular assignment, when Bob Ramsey walked into the conference room.

"Good morning, everyone," he said.

"Good morning, Mr. Ramsey," they said, almost in unison, looking up from their computers and smiling.

The team was wrapping things up. A partner in a CPA firm often spent more time at the client's office at this stage of an audit. Ramsey sat down at the head of the conference table.

"Russell and Pat, I'd like to talk with you two for a minute," he said.

They each took a chair on either side of Ramsey.

"Well, fill me in," he said.

Russell did most of the talking.

"Everything is going fine, Bob. Pat has been supervising the audit of the revenues and assets side of the balance sheet, and I've been working on expenses and liabilities."

"Any problems I should be aware of?"

"Not really. Just routine problems that one expects on an audit of this size."

"So, where do we stand now?"

"I think we'll have everything wrapped up here before the end of the week. We'll have the financial statements ready for your review next week at the latest."

Ramsey nodded.

"We have to get Mr. Hampson to sign the management representation letter and we're still waiting for the required letter from their attorney about any pending litigation, but other than that, we're almost done." Pat added.

"Good," Ramsey said. "I'll leave you two then. I'll be at the office if you need me."

An hour later, Pat was standing over the conference table, organizing a stack of files. He looked over his shoulder as Russell approached him. "Hey, what's up?"

"Hey, Pat. Do you think you can take this down to Hampson's office? I think we're ready to get his signature."

"Sure."

Pat left the conference room and walked toward the executive suites. He was glad that he and Rita had talked at Denny's. It was important because they ran into each other so often in the office. They had established an easy relationship—even when they were alone.

The more he thought about it, the more he felt Russell was right. It would have been terribly foolish to have an affair with a client. One mistake could ruin everything he had worked so hard for. He didn't regret anything though. He was happy that he and Rita had "shared a moment."


Rita was glad to see Pat approaching the office. She finished the notes she was making on a yellow pad as he walked up to her desk outside Hampson's closed door.

"Morning, Rita," he said.

She looked up at him, and they both smiled, knowing each was thinking the same thoughts.

"Is Mr. Hampson in? I need him to sign this letter for us."

Rita looked at the buttons on her telephone. "He was on the phone, but he's off now. Let me tell him you're here." She picked up the receiver and placed her index finger on the dark button beside the words, "MR. HAMPSON". "He's leaving soon for an appointment out of the office."

"Oh, wait a second," Pat said, as he was thumbing through the papers in his hand. "Russell forgot to give me the signature page. I'll be right back."

"I'd better tell Jim they'll need him before he leaves," Rita thought. She didn't notice that the button under her index finger had lit up before she pushed it in to tell him.

As she put the receiver to her ear, she was surprised to hear Jim 's voice. About to hang up, she recognized the other voice as Linda Hampson's. She kept the receiver to her ear, covering the mouthpiece of her phone with the palm of her hand. She knew she couldn't be heard, but she still tried to breathe softly.

"I just got off the phone with the real estate agent," Linda Hampson said. "Settlement is next Monday at one. The agent said we'll come away from the table with a cashier's check."

"Good," Hampson said. "How are you doing with selling everything?"

"Very well," she answered. "That Mr. Peasley I told you about will buy all the furniture in one lot, and the car dealer is coming by tonight to look at the cars."

"Good," he said again. "What about the clothes and everything else?"

"I think it's best if we just take what we need and leave everything else for charity. What do you think?"

"I think you're right. We'll just buy new stuff when we get there. Less baggage will make things a lot easier."

"That's what I was hoping you would say," she laughed. "So, how are things on your end?"

"I'll pick up the box at the bank next Tuesday, and I'm meeting with our friend that afternoon to pick up our ID's, leave the box with him, and go over everything. Then on Thursday morning, I fly to Vegas for our little meeting. I'll give them the word on Friday after the meeting and go right to the airport. You've got our tickets?"

"Right here," Rita heard Linda Hampson answer. "Did you transfer the money yet?"

"I'm taking care of that this afternoon." There was a pause. "Listen, I've got a lot of things to wrap up here, so I've got to go. See you tonight."

"It won't be long now, will it?

"Nope. By next Friday, it'll all be over."

"I can't wait. But I have to tell you, we've never done anything like this before—I'm pretty nervous."

"It'll be worth it, honey. Don't worry. We've planned this for a long time. All our bases are covered. I've got to go, now."

"One more thing."

"Yeah?"

"Aren't you worried about how they're going to react?"

"Nope. In fact I can't wait. I'm sick of being their boy, and I'm even sicker of their self-righteous, condescending attitudes. After all I've done for them, you would think they're doing me a big favor."

He stopped talking, knowing his emotions were getting the best of him. He knew he needed a clear head and no distractions for the few days ahead.

"Good-bye, Darling, I love you," Linda Hampson said, seizing an opportunity.

"Bye, Honey. I'll see you tonight."

Rita heard the sound of two phones hanging up. She waited for a dial tone before hanging up her own phone softly. She could feel her heart pounding and her face flushing in anger.

"That son-of-a-bitch!" she thought. Her jaw clenched, she was staring at her blank computer screen when Pat walked back to her desk.

Pat noticed Rita's strange look. She seemed to be looking at nothing. He snapped his fingers near her face and said, "Earth to Rita. Earth to Rita. Do you hear me?" He was smiling.

Rita seemed startled as she looked up at Pat. In a serious tone, he said, "Rita, are you all right?" Still looking up at him, she said, "I'm sorry, Pat. I must have gone into a trance. I'm okay."

"Are you sure?" Pat asked with more concern this time.

"Yeah, positive," Rita said. "Did you get what you need?" She was smiling again.

"Yeah, I've got everything I need this time. Is Mr. Hampson free?"

"Yes, he's in his office, just go on in."

Pat began to walk toward Hampson's office door when he felt Rita touch his arm to stop him.

"Pat."

"Yeah, Rita?"

"Can I ask a big favor of you?"

"Sure. What can I do for you?"

"Remember we were talking about music at my apartment?"

"Sure," he answered, smiling.

"I remember you said that the Beatles were your favorite."

"Yep, they're the best."

"Would you mind lending me your tapes so I can make copies of them?"

"Sure." He felt flattered that she wanted to listen to "his" music. "They're right outside in my car. I'll get them for you before I leave today."

"Don't forget," she said smiling.

"Oh, I won't," he said, and he walked into Hampson's office to get his signature. After a short discussion, Pat left the office and headed back to the conference room with the signed document.

He was surprised that Rita wasn't sitting at her desk as he walked by.

A little while later Pat went to his car to get his Beatles tapes. He put them in a large manila envelope. Walking back to the federation's offices, he was hoping he and Rita would have time to talk about which particular tapes he liked best. He walked to her desk and was disappointed to find she still wasn't there. He left the tapes on her chair.

He walked to her desk one final time before leaving, but she still wasn't there.

Pat noticed that the envelope he had put on her chair was gone.

# Chapter Twenty–One

The following Tuesday, Hampson pulled his white Mercedes into the parking lot of Bank of America's Upper Marlboro branch. Removing his safe deposit box key from his key ring, he walked into the bank's lobby. He was standing by the counter that separated the lobby from the work area when one of the clerks, Joan Tezak, got up from her desk and walked up to him.

"May I help you, Mr. Hampson?"

"Yes Joan, I would like to get something out of my safe deposit box please."

"Of course," she said, "please follow me. I just need your key and for you to sign the access record."

Hampson signed the form, handed her his key and followed her into the bank vault where the safe deposit boxes were located. After having him sign the access card, she put his key into one of the locks on the safe deposit box door and inserted a key from her key ring into the other lock and then turned them both. The door to safe deposit box number seven-forty-three opened.

The bank clerk removed the long, white container and asked him if he wanted privacy. He said he didn't. After removing a white metal box about the size of a cigar box, Hampson handed the larger container back to the clerk, who slid it back into place.

After making sure the contents were intact, Hampson left the bank with his box and headed west on Interstate Seventy toward Shady Grove and the law firm of Hardesty, Poupore, and Hardesty.

When he walked into the lobby area, no one was sitting at the receptionist's desk. He stood alone for a few moments before a woman opened the door leading to the offices. "Sorry to keep you waiting," she said. "May I help you?"

"Yes, I'm Jim Hampson, and I have an appointment with Ralph Poupore."

"Oh, Mr. Hampson," she said. "Mr. Poupore is expecting you. He asked me to take you to his office. Please follow me."

Ralph Poupore, attorney at law, was sitting in a black leather chair behind a walnut desk. He looked up blankly when he heard the receptionist. His expression changed when he saw Jim Hampson.

"Jim, please come in," he said, as he slid his chair back, stood up, and extended his right hand. "Thank you, Beverly. Please shut the door."

Ralph Poupore was in his mid-forties. He was tall, but his poor posture made him appear stoop-shouldered. He had combed long strands of his thinning hair from one side of his head to the other, in a poor attempt to cover his baldness. His beard wasn't full enough for his face to be attractive. He was impeccably dressed and wore an expensive watch and jewelry, but his lackluster shoes told the real story. The paneled oak walls displayed several framed diplomas and licenses from law schools no one would recognize.

Hampson carefully placed the white metal box on the edge of the attorney's desk.

"I got your message. You've finished preparing my will?"

"Yes, I have." Poupore opened the center drawer of his desk and removed a large brown envelope. "And we can talk freely in here, these walls are soundproof. But first, let me see what you have for me."

Hampson reached into his suit coat, pulled out a white envelope, and slid it across the desk. Poupore put the envelope in his own suit pocket.

"You're not going to open it?" Hampson said, with a slight element of surprise in his voice.

"No, Mr. Hampson, I trust my clients. I'd be very surprised if there were not exactly twenty thousand dollars in cash in that envelope.

"But there are a few things I need to go over with you." He opened the large brown envelope and carefully spread out the contents on his desk.

"Your new names will be Jim and Linda Sanchez. A common Spanish surname works well under the circumstances; it'll be much harder for anyone to track you down. I have found through experience that it's better to keep your own first names. It's much more natural when you and your wife talk in public, especially as long as you two have been married."

Hampson shook his head, agreeing with the logic, and happy that he had decided on this particular lawyer.

"You have everything you need in this envelope. Passports, Maryland driver's licenses, voter registration cards, birth certificates, immigration certificates, and social security cards. I've even included library cards and a few check-cashing approval cards, just for a nice touch."

Poupore's half-sneer, half-smile, was his best attempt to add levity to the transaction. Something about it made Hampson long to turn the clock back five years. For a moment, the churn in his stomach made him wish he had never seen this place.

Hampson examined the identification cards and looked up. "I'm impressed; they look authentic."

"Mr. Hampson, they are authentic." Poupore smiled again.

"How in the world do you do this?"

"Let's just say that I have friends in all the right places." He smiled again.

The knot in Hampson's stomach was starting to relax, though he thought to himself that Poupore should divert some of the money he was spending on his wardrobe for a good dentist.

"Anything else?"

"Yes," the attorney said, and he reached back into his top drawer, taking out another envelope and shaking out more cards.

"I thought you might appreciate it if I opened both a bank account and a travelers' check account for you. The statements will be sent to your new address." He handed the cards to his client, smiling again.

"Mr. Poupore, it seems that you've covered all the bases," Hampson said, as he put the identification cards back into the brown envelope, and put everything in his suit coat pocket.

"You have something else that you would like to go over with me?" the attorney asked, looking at the white metal box on the corner of his desk.

"Yes, I was wondering if you would be interested in earning an additional fifty thousand?"

"I love it when you talk dirty." Poupore sank back in his chair, folding his hands in his lap.

Not smiling, Hampson slid the metal box across the desk in front of him and opened it.

"Mr. Poupore, the contents of this box are important to me, and it's extremely important to me that it be kept safe."

"I understand." The lawyer leaned forward in the chair.

Hampson removed a white envelope from his other breast pocket, opened it, and spread several stacks of hundred dollar bills on the desk.

"There are fifty thousand dollars in cash here," he said as he gathered the bills together, put them back into the envelope, licked the flap, and sealed it.

He slid the envelope across the desk.

"Mr. Poupore, please get your pen, and write something on the envelope for me."

Poupore looked suspiciously at his client before opening his desk drawer and removing a fancy black case. He carefully took out a Mont Blanc pen.

"Just write the words, 'The contents of this envelope are the personal property of Ralph Poupore,' and sign it, please."

The attorney did as he was asked and put the top back on his pen.

"May I have the envelope back, please?"

Poupore slid the envelope back across the desk, watching curiously as Hampson put the envelope into the white metal box.

"Mr. Poupore, as I said, the contents of this box are extremely important to me and several other people, and this is what I would like you to do."

"I'm listening."

"I would like you to keep this box safe for me. As you know, I've planned carefully, and I'm certain I haven't overlooked anything. I'll pay you a visit in a few years when the statute of limitations expires on my activities. Then I'll get the box, and I'll give you the fifty grand for keeping it for me. Interested?"

"Of course, is that it?"

"Not quite, but almost." Hampson opened his billfold. He removed a rectangular piece of white paper about the size of a large bandage.

He put the paper on the desk, pulled out his own pen, and wrote *Jim Hampson* across its center.

"Mr. Poupore, this piece of paper is a seal similar to the type the FBI uses to seal file cabinets and the like when they seize documents." Poupore watched him lock the box, remove the backing from the white paper, and affix the seal on the front of the white metal box, thereby covering the lock and connecting the hinged lid to the lower part of the box. "You see, it's impossible to open the box without breaking the seal, and I will keep the key."

"I see." Poupore watched intently.

"As I was saying, we're almost there. You are to give the box to me or to my wife, and only to me or to my wife. In the highly unlikely event that something should happen to us, you are to take the box to the district attorney's office. There you explain who gave you the box and under what conditions you were to take the box to authorities. You are to open the box in the district attorney's presence, remove the envelope with your property in it, and give everything else to the DA. He'll have everything he needs to handle it from that point on. Understand?"

"Yes. Do you mind if I ask what is in the box?"

"I would prefer that you didn't. Let's just say that you'll know in due time, when the box is opened. I assume you can be patient. Do we have a deal?"

"Of course," the attorney said, moving the white metal box to his side of the desk.

Hampson stood up and held out his right hand. "It's been a pleasure dealing with you, Mr. Poupore, and I'll see you in a few years. You know where to get in touch with me in case of an emergency, and I certainly know where you will be."

Poupore returned the handshake.

As he was leaving, Hampson turned around.

"Mr. Poupore, there is one thing I forgot to tell you."

"What's that?"

"I play hardball. When I come back for the box, the seal had better be intact, or you're going to have quite a price to pay. Am I making myself clear?"

"Crystal," came the response.

"I thought so. If you don't think I'm serious, use your resources to find out what happened to a young accountant named Pat McGuire, who was working on the National Tobacco Federation audit last year, and all he was guilty of was being in the wrong place at the wrong time. Have a good day, Mr. Poupore; I'll show myself out."

Poupore sat in his chair after Hampson left, staring at the white metal box on the desk. Then, he closed the office door and took one of his framed diplomas off the wall, revealing a gray wall safe. He spun the dial a few times, opened the door, put the box into the safe, locked it, and put the framed diploma back in place.

Poupore sat back in his chair and reached for his daily calendar. He glanced down at the page where his secretary had written the day's appointments. Next to three o'clock, his secretary had written *Jim Hampson*. With his Mont Blanc pen, he made a notation: *Pat McGuire*, accountant, National Tobacco Federation audit.

# Chapter Twenty-Two

The following Thursday, Hampson flew first class from the Baltimore-Washington International airport to Las Vegas for his scheduled meeting. Arriving at the Mirage Hotel on Thursday evening, he dined with Dave Lovelady of Olde Harbour, who had also arrived early.

Together they enjoyed gambling at the casino and took in a show later in the evening. Hampson was more comfortable with Lovelady than other members of the secret group and as the only member of the clandestine group who was a National Tobacco Federation board member, Lovelady had a regular working relationship with Hampson.

Hampson's past dealings with Lovelady had been upbeat; Lovelady didn't put on the airs of his colleagues, who would be joining them in the morning. Hampson guessed Lovelady had worked hard to get where he was.

Since the McGuire football injury, Hampson was getting to know a new side of Lovelady. He had been surprised by Lovelady's access to unlawful contacts.

Lovelady was handsome and olive-skinned, and Hampson guessed that he was a second-generation Italian. The self-confident Alabama native had a slight southern drawl that didn't fit his executive image. A sharp dresser, unlike Ralph Poupore, he knew enough to keep his shoes shined.

Lovelady's black, thinning hair looked sophisticated, combed straight back. His well-groomed moustache was curious—one side was as black as his hair, the other side was peppered with gray.

The other four Chief Executive Officers arrived early the next morning. The meeting began at one o'clock in the afternoon, in the presidential suite.

The suite, on the top floor of the Mirage Hotel, commanded a view of the Las Vegas strip with the Nevada mountains forming an impressive backdrop. It overlooked a fountain in front of the hotel that turned into a volcano every night, erupting with brilliant red spotlights and lasers.

The meeting moved quickly, proceeding with little argument or discussion. The increase in prices they had agreed on at their last meeting had gone generally unreported by the media. Even National Tobacco Federation's board members, who usually questioned why other companies were finding increasing prices necessary, had few questions at the last board meeting held a few weeks earlier.

At the end of the meeting, they agreed again to increase prices slightly. This increase was to be blamed on a truckers' strike. The only other important business they had to discuss was the strategy on how to keep Dave Lovelady on the Federation's Board of Directors. Everyone knew the importance of having an insider.

Dinner was scheduled for delivery to the suite at six o'clock. When the business decisions of the meeting were wrapped up by five, Ken Chase, the only person attending the meeting dressed in shorts and a tee shirt, suggested that they adjourn for cocktails. The men tossed appreciative comments toward Ken and began rising out of their chairs, anxious to relax and enjoy the evening.

Hampson stood, raising his voice, "Gentlemen, there are a couple of other items. I promise you, I'll take only a few more minutes."

Exaggerated groans were interrupted by Lovelady who said, "Gentlemen, gentlemen, don't forget, Mr. Hampson here hasn't given us our little bonus envelopes yet. Please, let's not be in *too* much of a hurry."

They laughed, settling down with smiles and anticipation.

"Thank you, Dave. That's one of the things I find it necessary to go over with you."

"Don't think we forgot, Jim," Lovelady said again. Although laughs were quieter this time, all eyes were on Hampson. He bent over, placing both his hands on the long conference table.

"Gentlemen, please excuse me, but, again, I promise I won't take long."

He paused dramatically.

"My first announcement is going to take you by surprise, but, after a lot of thought, I've decided that it's in my best interest to resign my position as the executive director of the National Tobacco Federation. So, today is my last day. Of course, I'll be unable to meet with this group in the future."

He paused again. "I know I should have given you a little more notice, but time got away from me." Looking around the room, he added, "I'm sure you understand."

The room was totally silent. He continued.

"I gave my official notice of resignation to a small office supply store here in town, and they are going to fax my letter of resignation to each member of Federation's board of directors at ten o'clock Monday morning, Nevada time."

He waited again.

"There are a few other things of which I want you to be aware.

"First," he said, looking directly at Dave Lovelady, "about the matter of the little bonus checks I know you are expecting. I received your company checks for our 'special' dues assessment billings, and, as usual, everything went perfectly well. I compliment you, once again, for your thoroughness and attention to detail.

"But," he paused, "this time, I kept your checks myself. You see, I'm just a little short on what I need for my plans and, knowing all of you the way I do, I'm sure you would want the best for me. In any event, I'll be keeping the entire three hundred-fifty thousand."

No one took their eyes off Jim Hampson, and his audience grew more tense with every passing minute. He folded his arms before adding, "Just one or two more items." He took a deep breath.

Lovelady bolted out of his chair. He pointed his right index finger toward him and shouted, "What the fuck are you saying, you god-dammed piss ant! You wouldn't be anywhere without us, and you know it."

Hampson looked at Lovelady, and spoke in a calm, almost condescending voice. "You know there is one thing I've learned in my life. Temper tantrums don't work. People who lose their tempers lose control. I can say that most of the bad decisions I've made in my life came when I was angry."

Hampson's tone conveyed to everyone in the room that *he*, not them for a change, was in charge of the situation. Lovelady sat down after someone else said, "I think we'd better let him talk, Dave."

Hampson smiled before he continued, "You should also know that I transferred eleven million dollars in Federation funds to an account I opened at a bank in Switzerland. Of course, I opened the account under an assumed name and, because there is no way to get information from a Swiss bank, I feel comfortable telling you this."

Hampson smiled and then began to walk around the conference room. All eyes followed him.

"Now, though I hate to repeat myself, I know that all of you want the best for me, so I'm sure you all agree with what I did." His voice dripped sarcasm.

"While I know it's not necessary for me to say this," he added, "but, just in case anyone is tempted to go to the authorities with this, I don't think that would be a very good idea. You see, gentlemen," he said, as he pulled a padded envelope from the breast pocket of his suit, and threw it onto the middle of the table, "I've recorded all of these meetings."

The room was eerily quiet as he continued to walk around the conference table.

"You see," he said, "I have a little insurance policy. If the authorities approach me, I will have absolutely no problem releasing the tapes to them for a reduction, or possible elimination, of any sentence I might face." He swept the room with his hand. "Collectively, you represent bigger fish to fry than I do, individually. I don't think I have to remind you what kind of a prison sentence violating the Sherman Anti-Trust Act for price-fixing brings. I *definitely* will not go down alone."

Hampson stopped between Ken Chase and Dave Lovelady. He put a hand on each of their shoulders, then moved his hands deliberately to their necks and squeezed. He smiled again; then -in a quick movement— he fixed his eyes on the padded brown envelope still sitting untouched on the shiny surface of the mahogany table.

He nodded toward the envelope.

"That's a souvenir tape of our meeting in Colorado, in case you think I might be bluffing you. You can keep the tape; I won't charge you for it," he said smiling.

No one looked at the envelope. They were mesmerized by this man they thought they knew and felt they could control.

"One final thing and I'll let you go. I also find it necessary to recommend that you not get cute and come after me personally—not that any of you would participate in that type of thing," he said, reminding them silently about Patrick McGuire.

"You see, I've entrusted the original tapes to a colleague of mine. He knows exactly who to go to in the justice department with the tapes in my absence. Now, you know as well as I do how much they would love to get their hands on those tapes."

He walked to the door, putting his hand on the brass knob. Thinking for a moment, he turned back toward the silent group at the table.

"I guess I'd better not forget my equipment. You're probably wondering how I managed to record these meetings without your knowing it, anyway."

He walked back to the head of the table, reached under it, and pulled out a hand-held tape recorder with two pieces of packing tape attached to it.

"You see, all I did was tape a recorder under the table. Simple, don't you think?"

He pulled off the two pieces of tape, rolled them into a ball, and threw it across the room into a black, plastic trashcan. "Two points," he said.

He pushed the REWIND button on the recorder and held it for a few seconds. He pushed the PLAY button, and they heard " . . .under the table. Simple, don't you think? Two points." Jim Hampson laughed as he ejected the tape and put it into his pocket. He slid the recorder across the table, where it stopped next to the envelope with the Colorado meeting tape in it.

"Don't for a minute think I forgot about *this* tape," he said, tapping his breast pocket. "I'm destroying this baby, for obvious reasons." He smiled again and walked back to the door.

"Please excuse my rudeness for not joining you good people for dinner, but I'm afraid my limo is here." He looked at his watch. "I don't want to keep the driver waiting. I do have a plane to catch.

"Have a good evening, gentlemen." He was chuckling to himself as he rode down the elevator to the lobby. Now *he* was in control.

"May I call you a taxi, sir?" the bellman asked Hampson as he stepped into the bright Nevada sun from the dark hotel lobby.

"No, I ordered a limousine. I think it should be here."

"Are you Mr. Hampson?"

"Yes."

"Your limousine is right over here, sir. Let me show you the way."

"Just a moment, please. I'll be right with you. I need to use the men's room first."

"Right over there, Mr. Hampson."

Hampson walked across the lobby into the restroom. It was empty. He went into one of the stalls, locking the door behind him. He took out the tape of the "final" meeting, dropped it on the floor, crushed it with the heel of his foot, picked up the flattened cassette and pulled the brown tape from its plastic casing. He ripped the tape several times, dropped the pieces into the toilet, and flushed them. He waited for the bowl to fill with clean water, and flushed again, just to be sure that the tape was gone forever. He washed his hands and checked his hair. As he was walking out of the men's room, he threw the broken plastic casing into the trashcan and headed back to the hotel entrance.

"I'm sorry to keep you waiting," he said to the bellman.

"No problem, sir. Please follow me."

Hampson followed the bellman, who held the door of the white stretch limousine for him.

He handed the bellman a fifty-dollar bill and smiled, feeling generous and satisfied with himself. "Thank you, *sir*!" the bellman said with sincere appreciation.

"Thank you for calling Lucky Limousines," the driver said, turning and looking at Jim Hampson.

"To the airport, Mr. Hampson?"

"Yes."

"Which airline, sir?" the driver asked, as he pulled onto Las Vegas Boulevard.

"The International Terminal, please."

"Yes sir. I hope you enjoyed your stay in our little town."

"Yes, I did."

"Did you have any luck, sir?"

He chuckled to himself at the irony of question. "Yes," he answered. "I had a very lucky day indeed."

# Chapter Twenty–Three

The following Monday afternoon, Pat sat at his desk at the headquarters of Autry, Martin & Ramsey, reviewing a tax return for one of the other accountants. Russell stepped into his office, adjusting his tie, and talking fast.

"Drop whatever you're doing, Pat, and come with me to the conference room. Dad wants to see us both right now."

"What's going on, Russell?" Pat asked, adjusting his own tie.

"You know as much as I do, but it's got to be good. The last time Dad sounded this excited was when there was a fire in the computer room. Come on."

The two friends walked briskly through the halls. They didn't even bother to knock on the closed conference room door before opening it. Pat followed Russell into the room, where Gilbert Autry and Bob Ramsey sat in chairs next to one another, deep in conversation.

"What's going on, Dad?" Russell interrupted them.

"Sit down, both of you. We just received some extremely important information."

They sat directly across from the two partners, both looking quizzical.

The older Autry folded his arms and put both of his elbows on the table. His gaze switched back-and-forth between his son and Pat.

"I just got a call from Ira Gagnon."

"Who?" Russell asked.

"Ira Gagnon—he's the elected chairman of the board for the National Tobacco Federation. His office is in Atlanta, and I doubt if you've ever met him, but he's their top dog."

"What's the problem," Pat asked this time.

"It seems Jim Hampson just resigned as the Federation's president. Bob and I were just discussing it," he said, looking at his partner and then back to the other two.

Pat and Russell looked at each other, raising their eyebrows in surprise.

"When is he leaving?" Pat asked.

"It seems he's already left," Ramsey said, adding his voice to the conversation. "He faxed in his letter of resignation to the board from Las Vegas about an hour ago. No notice, no nothing. He just sent a fax to everybody on the board saying that he resigned his position and that this past Friday was his last day."

Russell whistled softly.

Gilbert Autry continued. "I just got off the phone with Ira. He's called an emergency meeting of the board at the Federation's office tonight at six. He wants the four of us to be at the meeting. Initially he just wanted to talk to Bob and me, as you might expect. But I convinced him to include you two, since you did all of the detail work on site. At this point, you know as much as I do. Look, it's already pushing five. Just call home if you have to, and tell them it's going to be a long night. We'll meet at the receptionist's desk in ten minutes."


Conversation didn't flow easily with Ramsey. Staid and proper, he generally kept his personal thoughts and feelings to himself. He was a family man who kept clear of after-hours staff gatherings and avoided office politics. Business was business with Bob and, during his long tenure with the firm, his objectivity and fairness had won him the staff's respect.

Ramsey rested his head back against the seat, stretching out his long legs in front of him. Apparently deep in thought, he stared at the ceiling of the car, occasionally turning his head of thick, salt-and-pepper gray hair to face the window. Pat, assuming Ramsey was mentally preparing for the meeting, didn't dare to interrupt the senior partner's thoughts.

Pat was relieved when Russell found parking across the street from the Federation's offices.

Rita sat at the receptionist's desk in the lobby waiting for them. She stood up. "Follow me, gentlemen," she said, without her usual pleasantries. "Mr. Gagnon and the rest of the board are in the conference room." Rita avoided eye contact with Pat, as he did with her.

The doors were shut, and Rita tapped lightly on one of them before opening it. The seven members of the National Tobacco Federation board were gathered at one end of the conference room table. They looked up from their yellow legal pads when the new group entered the room.

The only other person in the room was the federation's outside counsel, Henry Goodman. The accountants knew Goodman; they had worked often with him over the years, whenever any legal questions arose during the course of the audit.

Gagnon, who was sitting at the head of the table, stood up to shake Gilbert Autry's hand. "Thank you for coming so quickly and without notice,

Gilbert, but you know I wouldn't have asked you and your people to come if it weren't important."

"I understand, Ira."

Ira Gagnon didn't fit Pat's image of a Chairman of the Board. He appeared to be about sixty. He was bald, except for the hair on the sides and back of his head. A short man, about twenty-five pounds overweight, he was dressed in jeans and a sport shirt. Looking around the table, Pat noticed that most of the other board members were also dressed casually—not what he'd expected. Goodman, the attorney, was wearing a suit, but he had removed both his tie and jacket. He was especially surprised to see that two of the seven members of the board were women. Until this point, all the directors and managers he had come into contact with were men.

Gagnon was still talking to Gilbert. "Let me introduce you quickly to the other members of the board, and I apologize for the lack of social conversation."

As he was speaking, Pat realized why Gagnon was chairman. His voice was confident and, despite the situation, friendly. It was obvious that he commanded respect and gave it to everyone around him. Pat noticed the other board members' deference to him.

The chairman introduced each board member to the group, beginning first with the women. Then, Gilbert introduced himself and the three members of his team.

"Please sit down, gentlemen," the chairman said. "We have several things to go over with you. First, I'm sure you know Mr. Goodman here, our outside counsel." All four nodded in Goodman's direction and nodded back. "Obviously we need legal advice, and Mr. Goodman agreed that we also need our auditors under the circumstances."

As the four accountants were taking their seats, Rita walked to the conference room door.

"Will that be all, Mr. Gagnon?" she asked, her hand on one of the doorknobs.

"Yes, thank you, Rita; please close the door."

"Mr. Chairman?" It was one of the female board members who spoke.

"Yes, Sue?"

"Under the circumstances, I think it's a good idea if Miss Davies stays. She may have some information we need." She paused. "I would like to make a motion that we invite Rita Davies, the president's administrative assistant, to be included as a guest in this executive session."

"You have heard the motion. Is there a second?" the chairman asked.

"Seconded," Dave Lovelady answered.

"You have heard the motion and the second. Is there any discussion?"

One of the male board members in attendance raised his hand and was recognized by the chairman.

"Mr. Chairman, I certainly don't have any problem inviting Miss Davies, but I just want some assurance from our auditors and counsel that this is proper."

The chairman looked at Goodman, "Henry, what do you think?"

Goodman cleared his throat, " Mr. Chairman, not-for-profit organizations typically enter into executive session for one of two reasons: one, to discuss personnel matters and two, to discuss current or pending litigation. It is my opinion that this particular situation embraces both reasons and that inviting the president's secretary is allowable under the circumstances. My only caveat is to advise everyone that the minutes reflect titles rather than any individual's name."

The chair continued, " You have heard our counsel's opinion and advice. Is there any further discussion?"

The other female board member raised her hand.

"Karen?"

"I agree with counsel, but I would also benefit from the opinion of our auditors."

The chairman turned to Gilbert Autry, "Gilbert?"

As Gilbert Autry was preparing to reply, Pat watched and listened to him intently, knowing that he may be in the same position one day.

"Obviously we can't give legal advice, but I agree with counsel, Mr. Chairman. If you direct us to help this body resolve the issue, we will need staff contact and the inclusion of the president's secretary would be very important to us."

"Is there any further discussion?"

The other six members of the board looked at their chairman in silence.

"Hearing no discussion, the motion is that we invite the administrative assistant of the executive director as a guest. All in favor, signify so by saying "Aye.""

"Aye," came a chorus of replies.

"Those against the motion, same sign," the chairman said, continuing his responsibility as chair, according to Robert's Rules of Order.

Silence.

"The motion carries."

The maker of the motion excused herself and stepped out into the hall. She returned in a few moments with Rita. "Miss Davies, please join our group, and welcome," the chairman said, smiling at her.

Rita closed the door and sat in the chair next to Pat. This time, they did make eye contact, but quickly looked back to the head of the table.

"Let me bring all of our guests up to date," Ira Gagnon continued. "As chairman, I called an emergency meeting of this board. After convening the meeting about an hour ago, we immediately went into an executive session. You should be reminded there will be no names mentioned in the minutes while we are in executive session, so everyone should feel free to join our discussions openly and honestly, taking into consideration the comments from our counsel."

The five new guests looked at the chairman without speaking.

"And for the benefit of our guests, I have a responsibility to advise you that nothing we discuss behind those closed doors," he turned his head briefly in the direction of the conference room doors, "and I mean *nothing*, is to leave this room."

Pat was impressed that the chairman didn't add the "Is that understood?" closing he expected. Ira Gagnon treated others with too much respect to state the obvious.

"I appreciate your interrupting your plans and schedules, but this meeting could not be delayed." He paused and took a deep breath.

"At ten A.M. Las Vegas time, each member of the board received a fax from Jim Hampson announcing his resignation as president, effective last Friday. Obviously, this action took everyone by surprise. When I called each member of the board personally I told them that I thought we needed our lawyer and our auditing firm here and they all agreed."

Pat noticed the other members of the board glancing in Gilbert Autry's direction and nodding.

"The faith and confidence of this association's members in its leadership and stability are paramount. All of our decisions are to take that fact into consideration.

"In any event, we have decided to issue a press release announcing that Jim Hampson has resigned his position as president and that a member of the Board of Directors has been appointed interim president. This person will assume full responsibility for managing the day-to-day operations of the Federation until a search committee has been formed and a successor named."

Ira Gagnon looked in Rita's direction. "Rita, you will probably get most of the calls about what's going on."

She nodded her head knowingly.

"We all feel that you should simply acknowledge the fact that Jim is no longer with the association. You can refer callers to the interim president. What do you think?"

"That's fine with me, Mr. Gagnon. I'll be sure to tell the receptionist and the rest of the staff what they should do, in case they get any calls."

"Thank you, Rita. And I want you to know that we all appreciate the position you'll be in."

Gagnon turned his gaze toward Gilbert Autry. "And now for our accounting guests."

"How can we help you, Ira?" Gilbert said.

Gagnon sat back in his chair and thought for a moment before answering.

"Gilbert," he said, pausing again and searching for just the right words. "Understandably, this is a very unusual situation. People in Jim Hampson's position don't just up and quit without notice. All of us here hope we're wrong, but the possibility exists that Jim may have done something foolish with the Federation's assets."

"Such as?"

"Such as stealing our money," he answered bluntly, this time without pausing. "And we need you and your people to find out if he did. If he did, we need to know how much."

"Understood." Gilbert had guessed at the answers to both questions, but decided not to steal any of the chairman's thunder. "We'll start a cash audit first thing in the morning and get back to you as soon as we find anything, but that's only the start."

"What else do you suggest we do?"

As he spoke, Gilbert was making notes on the yellow tablet in front of him, "A few things."

Pat and Russell were also taking notes of Autry's comments and Bob Ramsey was listening intently.

"I suggest that you arrange to have Hampson's name removed as a signer on all the bank accounts, that you contact the credit card companies to void his credit cards, telephone cards, gas cards, and so forth, call the security company to ensure he has no further access to the building, and if there are any checks payable to him that are still outstanding, issue stop payments."

The chairman was nodding his head in agreement.

"Anything else?"

"Not from our side, but I would like to know if counsel has any further suggestions."

The chairman switched his gaze, "Henry?"

"I don't have anything to add at this point. I think we all have to wait for the accountants to finish. If there are additional problems, and I hope there aren't, I'll do what I can to tie up his personal property and so forth."

"Thank you, Henry."

"I guess it's back to you, Gilbert; what do you need from us?"

"We just need someone to let us in tomorrow morning, a letter from you to show the security people that we're okay, and a couple of letters to the bank authorizing us to check things out. I think that's it to get us started," he answered, looking at Ramsey, who nodded.

"Rita," Gagnon said, "it looks like you're going to have to cancel your plans for this weekend."

"I understand, Mr. Gagnon," she said. "I'll be downstairs to let everybody in at eight tomorrow, if that's okay. I'll get those letters you need right away, before you leave." Everyone was looking in her direction.

"Thank you, Rita, I knew we could count on you. Is there anything else before we adjourn? It's been quite a day."

The group looked at each other, shaking their heads "no" when Gilbert spoke. A motion was made and seconded to adjourn the meeting. The "Aye" vote was unanimous.

"This executive session stands adjourned."

Everyone was rising from their chairs and gathering their belongings, when Gilbert got Ira's attention.

"Ira, there is one more thing."

"Yes, Gilbert."

"If you don't mind, who is the interim executive director?"

"Oh, I almost forgot," he said, surprised by his own forgetfulness. "I've asked someone I have the utmost confidence in, and he has graciously agreed to help us. Our interim president will be Dave Lovelady."

# Chapter Twenty–Four

Pat and Russell worked at the Federation's headquarters around the clock for the entire week. Every record was checked for signs of unexplained dealings and the two young accountants reviewed their findings with Bob Ramsey. Now, along with Bob, they updated Gilbert Autry in his office in Baltimore.

"Now, look," Gilbert Autry said, "we have to present our findings to both Ira Gagnon and Dave Lovelady in just a couple of hours. Bob, are you absolutely sure about all of this?"

"Positive, Gilbert," Ramsey answered, "eleven million dollars in CDs were wire-transferred from the association's bank to a bank in Switzerland last Thursday. We have copies of all of the documentation."

"Who signed the transfer slips?" Gilbert asked. The three of them looked at each other knowing that the answer to that question would surprise him.

"Ira Gagnon and Dave Lovelady. Two signatures were required to transfer funds and sign checks."

Gilbert looked astonished.

"So, you're telling me that I have the pleasure of telling Ira and Dave that their signatures are on the transfer slips!"

"There's no way around it, Gilbert." Ramsey handed him the paperwork, saying, "Look for yourself."

He put on his reading glasses and examined each paper carefully. When he was satisfied, he handed the papers back.

"So what do you three think?"

Pat spoke up. "We're not handwriting experts, but you can bet these are forgeries. Jim Hampson probably forged the signatures, took the paperwork to the bank, and transferred the money to an account in Switzerland."

"Did you contact the Swiss bank to find out the name or account number that it was transferred to?" The question was directed to the group. Russell answered.

"We contacted the Swiss bank, of course, Dad, but we ran into a brick wall."

"How's that?"

"They acknowledged that the money was transferred, but they won't give us any more information than that. It's their policy. The only people they'll release any information to at all are the holders of the account. They won't budge."

"How about the Federation's bank here in the states, what do they have to say?"

Ramsey answered, "They couldn't be any more cooperative, but there's not much they can tell us that we didn't already know."

"Humor me. What did they tell you?"

"Just that Jim Hampson asked to speak to the manager and went through him to transfer the money. He said it was unusual, but Hampson has the authority to facilitate banking relationships. He had all the necessary paperwork and signatures. He even told us that after Hampson left, he checked Lovelady's and Gagnon's signatures on the paperwork against the original signature cards on file at the bank. Everything seemed fine as far as the bank was concerned."

The older Autry sat back in his chair and stared blankly at the ceiling, thinking about everything he had been told. After about two minutes, he looked at the others and stood up.

"Okay, gentlemen, if that's what we've got, that's what we've got. One thing I don't like about this work is delivering news like this, but I guess that's what they pay us for.

"Let's go then. Gagnon and Lovelady are waiting for us downtown."

Driving to the Federation's headquarters, the four accountants debated on how they might be able to find out the name or account number the money had been transferred to in Switzerland. The conversation released tension more than anything else. They all knew their chances of finding more information were almost non-existent.

As they walked through the offices toward Lovelady's new suite, Pat noticed that none of the employees would make direct eye contact. He realized they knew that what these outsiders had to report could affect their future and he tried to imagine the stress they were going through as they attempted to concentrate on work.

The four of them passed Rita's desk, but instead of exchanging the usual pleasantries, they simply nodded. It occurred to Pat that they hadn't spoken at all since their meeting with Gagnon and Lovelady earlier in the week.

As he was taking his seat with the others around the coffee table, Pat felt that, for the first time in his career, he didn't like what he was doing for a living. Up to now, working with numbers had been fun, and except for the embezzlement that he and the others had uncovered, it never affected people's lives. But as the meeting began, Gilbert's words about being the messenger took on a new meaning.

"So that sums it up. Eleven million dollars from the Federation's account were transferred to a Swiss bank by Jim Hampson last Thursday. The bank's records show that the paperwork was signed jointly by both of you. Considering that neither of you has even been in town for over four months, it's obvious that the signatures were forged.

"And," he said, pausing for a breath, "unfortunately, there is no way of knowing what happened to the money once it was transferred to Switzerland."

As Gilbert was speaking, Gagnon and Lovelady exchanged long, unspoken glances.

They each asked a few questions and, when they were satisfied that they knew all there was to know, Gagnon stood up and walked across the office to the window. He put his hands on his hips and stared at the street below without saying a word.

When he turned around, he addressed the silently waiting group.

"Gentlemen," he said, with a self-assurance and calmness in his voice that surprised Pat, who was expecting outrage and indignation. His voice grew slightly louder with each sentence. "First, no one person is going to destroy this Federation that so many people have worked so hard to build, not even someone who has apparently stolen the bulk of our resources. Whatever comes of this unfortunate set of circumstances, this association will survive.

"Despite what we all think, none of us in this room really knows what happened, and I can't let an unknown quantity cause panic among the members and the staff. I'm going to personally call each member of the board and other influential members and tell them what we think happened. I will ask them for their assurance that this information be kept confidential until we can repair the rudder that let this ship go off course."

No one took their eyes off him.

"I'm going to ask each of them to consider lending the Federation enough funds to get us through this. That will give us a little breathing room.

"Second, I'm going to meet personally with the staff, answer any questions they may have, and assure them that their jobs are not in jeopardy. If anyone has a right to know what's going on, it's the staff. I won't allow them to suffer.

"And finally, I think that too many hands in this stew aren't good for anything."

He turned toward Lovelady.

"I'm going to exercise executive privilege and tell the board and the staff that Dave Lovelady, and only Dave Lovelady, is empowered in his position as acting president to handle the investigation, in order to uncover what has apparently taken place. Dave will be responsible for contacting the appropriate authorities.

"Dave?"

"You can count on me, Ira. I won't trouble you or the other board members, unless I feel it's necessary, if that's okay with you" Lovelady sounded confident.

"Thank you, Dave."

"Gilbert, do you or any of your people have anything to say before I leave?"

"No, Ira," he answered, "we're here to help you any way we can, but I really don't know how much more we can do without going to the authorities, and that decision is up to you, not us."

"I'm not sure I know what you mean, Gilbert."

"Ira, the relationship between your organization and us, us being your independent CPA firm, is similar to the relationship between you and your lawyer."

The chairman was listening intently.

Gilbert continued, "What I'm trying to say is that the conversations between you and your accountant are confidential and very much like attorney-client privilege. We can't go anywhere with this information without your approval, even if we uncover something in the course of our audit."

"I never knew that." Gagnon was obviously surprised. "So tell me, what would you do if you, on your own, uncovered fraud or something?"

"We would take it to the highest level possible within the organization for correction."

"And if it's not corrected?"

"We withdraw from the engagement but we don't go to the authorities."

As Pat and Russell observed the exchange, each of them realized that the principles they had been taught about professional conduct and ethics were coming alive in front of them. Even though they were fully licensed CPAs themselves, they were as taken in by the discussion as the Chairman of the Board obviously was.

"Is there anything else then?" Gagnon directed the question to the group.

He turned to each one. When they indicated that there was nothing else to discuss, he looked at Lovelady.

"Okay then, I've got a few phone calls to make, so the ball's in your court, Dave."

He shook each person's hand before leaving the room. Lovelady walked him to the door, then asked the group to sit down again. He wanted to discuss his plans.

While walking back to his seat, he pulled a piece of paper from his breast pocket, looked at it, then tucked it back in before looking at the four accountants.

"First, I want to know if any one of you knows anything I don't know. I'm a fair man, but I lose patience when I'm kept in the dark."

Gilbert answered for the group, "You know as much as we do, Dave. We've told you everything." Surprised by the question, he kept his expression passive.

Lovelady shook his head slowly and turned his eyes toward Ramsey.

"Bob, you've been quiet through all of this. What do you have to say?"

Ramsey looked at Gilbert before answering " Gilbert is right, Dave. We don't know any more about all of this than we have already told you."

Lovelady waited a few moments before continuing.

"All right, then. So let me tell you what I have in mind. I've decided that I'm going to do my own little investigation before going to the authorities. I've already had a locksmith change all the locks on the file cabinets. I'm going to review files personally, just to double check to see if Hampson might have gotten careless and left something unusual that could give us a clue about where he is. I want to get our money back. It's possible that I may need your firm's help going through the files. I assume I can count on you, if I need help?"

"Of course, Dave," Gilbert said. "We'll be there when you need us. Because Bob Ramsey was the partner in charge of the audit, I would be grateful if you would contact Bob directly. He's much more involved with the situation than I am." He paused. "We give you our assurance that we realize how important this matter is to you and the Federation, and you will continue to be our highest priority."

"Thanks, Gilbert, I appreciate your cooperation. First, I want to go through some of the files myself. But, if I find anything, I'll call you right away. I'm sure it'll be a couple of days, so your people can plan on other work.

"Is that acceptable to you, Bob?"

"Sure, Dave. I know you said you've changed the locks on the file cabinets, but how about the alarm system. Are you going to change the access codes?"

"I've thought about that, Bob, but I don't think that's necessary. You need a code to get into the building, and there's an electronic record of everyone who comes in after hours. I also found out that the security company automatically sends someone to the office, after hours, to check out IDs of everyone in the building—to make sure they're employees. That's pretty tight.

"Besides, I can't imagine Hampson involving an employee in this. He's too smart to involve anyone who might talk. I think the security situation is fine, particularly considering Hampson's own access code was terminated."

Lovelady twirled his pen in his hand a few seconds before continuing.

"I think that's about it for right now, gentlemen," he said as he stood

"Good luck, Dave," Gilbert Autry said. "I know you have a lot to do, so we'll leave you alone."

# Chapter Twenty–Five

It was close to five o'clock the following Wednesday when Bob Ramsey knocked on the frame of Pat's open office door.

"Pat, sorry to interrupt you."

Pat stood up as soon as he saw him.

"Yes, Mr. Ramsey?"

"Pat, I just got a call from Dave Lovelady. He's wants to see me right away, so I'm going to have to head on down there."

"Can I help you with anything?"

"No, he just wants to see me. I've already told Gilbert and Russell that I would probably be gone the rest of the afternoon. Do you need anything from me before I leave?"

"No, I'm fine, Mr. Ramsey. I'm just getting things ready for Gordon Banks' audit over at the Convention and Visitor Bureau."

"Oh yeah, that was your baby, wasn't it?"

"Yes sir, but I just got lucky. I was fortunate to have Teresa and Hardy there to help me."

"Don't be modest. What ever happened to their CEO? What was his name?"

"Dick Loomis."

"Loomis. Right. Whatever happened to him?"

"Oh, they pressed charges. He was convicted. He's doing time right now."

"Good. Listen, I'll call you from the Federation's office if I need anything. Otherwise, I'll see you tomorrow morning and fill you in."

"I'll be here," Pat smiled and looked down at the pile of papers on his desk. "I've got plenty to keep me busy."

"Okay then, Pat. See you tomorrow."

Ramsey took the Baltimore Beltway instead of the Baltimore-Washington Parkway, after hearing on the radio that an accident around Laurel had blocked the Parkway southbound. He decided that the fastest route would be Interstate ninety-five. He didn't want to keep Lovelady waiting. Lovelady had asked him to drive all the way to Washington, D.C., with no notice, and after five o'clock. Something important was up. Ramsey had a growing sense of uneasiness as he drove toward Washington.

Pulling on the lobby door of the Federation's office building, he found it was locked. At first, he was surprised, but then he realized that it must be after six o'clock. The doors automatically locked after six.

He turned around, looking for a pay phone, when he heard knocking from the other side of the glass door. Looking back, he saw Rita turning the lock and opening the door for him.

She led him to the executive suite.

"Mr. Ramsey is here, Mr. Lovelady," she said, standing in the doorway.

Lovelady looked up with his eyes without raising his head and silently stared at Ramsey for a few moments.

"I came here as fast as I could, Dave," Ramsey said. "It took me a little longer than usual because of an accident on the parkway. I had to take ninety-five."

Lovelady was still staring at him, but he spoke to Rita. "Rita, you can go home now. I appreciate your staying late to let Mr. Ramsey in." He continued his stare, unblinking.

"That's my job, Mr. Lovelady. Are you sure you don't want me to stay? I have plenty to do."

"No. Go home and relax. You've been working hard and deserve a night off. Mr. Ramsey and I will be here for a little while, and we'll let ourselves out. I'll see you tomorrow morning."

Lovelady kept his eyes on Ramsey while Rita turned off her computer, picked up her coat, and placed her purse strap on her shoulder.

"Good night, Mr. Lovelady, I'll see you in the morning," she said, standing behind Ramsey.

"Thanks again for staying."

"Good night, Mr. Ramsey."

He turned in her direction. "Good night, Rita. Thanks again for letting me in."

Ramsey turned back only to meet Lovelady's still unblinking stare.

"Is there something wrong, Dave?" Ramsey said.

Lovelady waited a few moments. "Let's continue this discussion in the conference room. We'll have a little more room to spread out in there."

"Whatever you say, Dave," Ramsey said, feeling his uneasiness grow.

Lovelady slid his chair back and walked toward Ramsey, who was now standing in the office doorway. Lovelady stopped when their faces were just inches apart. "Follow me, Bob," he said curtly.

Ramsey followed Lovelady to the conference room. "Please have a seat. I'll be with you in just a moment."

Ramsey watched Lovelady walk away. He had no idea why he had been called to this meeting. His heart raced as he sat in the conference room alone. *Whatever's making him unhappy seems personal,* he thought.

It was five long minutes later when Lovelady walked back into the room a large white envelope with the word **CONFIDENTIAL** stamped in red ink under his arm. He seated himself in a chair on the opposite side of the long conference table and he dropped the envelope on the table in front of him.

Putting his left elbow on the table, he cupped his chin in his open palm, smiling across the table at the uneasy Ramsey.

"You're making me uncomfortable, Dave," Ramsey blurted out. "Would you please tell me what's going on?"

Lovelady took his time responding, and never changed position. It may have been only a few seconds or more, but to Ramsey, it seemed like an eternity. He pulled his hand away from his face, crossed his arms on the table in front of him, and finally broke the silence in a voice louder than necessary in the room.

"Andy, you can come in now," he said, keeping eye contact with Ramsey.

Ramsey watched a tall, muscular, blonde man walk into the conference room on cue. The young man wore a dark blue sport coat, a white crew neck tee shirt, blue jeans, and white tennis shoes. He pulled out the chair next to Lovelady, and sat down, smiling at Ramsey.

"And this, Andy," Lovelady said, gesturing toward the accountant still seated across from him, "is Bob Ramsey."

Ramsey moved his chair back and started to rise to introduce himself to the newcomer when Lovelady interrupted him. "Sit down, Bob, formal introductions aren't exactly necessary under the circumstances."

"Would you please tell me what in the world is going on here, Dave?" he said. Now, there was a tone of agitation in *his* voice. As a professional, he wasn't used to this type of treatment.

Lovelady said, "Here's what's going on, Bob." He quickly slid the white envelope across the shiny surface of the conference table to Ramsey, hitting him in the chest before he could react. The envelope fell into his lap.

Ramsey picked it up, placing it on the table.

"What's this, Dave?"

"Open it. I think a lot of your questions will be answered."

Ramsey switched his gaze from Lovelady to the envelope in front of him. He slowly picked it up and pulled out the contents. When he looked at the papers, he dropped them feebly on the table and swallowed hard. He reached up to loosen his tie and unbutton the top button of his white shirt that had suddenly become too tight. He looked up at Lovelady.

"Where did you get this?"

"Oh, it wasn't hard. I found it late last night in one of the file cabinets. I must say that I'm very disappointed in you, Bob."

"Dave, I assure you that I can explain everything." Lovelady was now sitting back in his chair with his hands clasped behind his neck. The newcomer continued to smile blankly.

"No explanations are necessary, Mr. Ramsey. It's all quite obvious to me." Lovelady unclasped his hands in a large gesture before getting out of his chair and walking around the conference table to where Ramsey was sitting. He sat on the edge of the table next to him and folded his arms before speaking again.

"Like I said a few days ago, I'm a patient man, but I don't like to be kept in the dark."

"Dave, I," Ramsey began, but was cut off quickly.

"Shut up, I'll do the talking." Lovelady's face turned suddenly serious.

"So, Bob, why don't you tell me about your role in all of this?" Lovelady switched his gaze from Ramsey to the newcomer in the room, and back to Ramsey, "and don't worry about Andy here. You have my assurance that you can speak freely in front of him. Now talk."

Ramsey took in a deep breath and sighed loudly. "About four years ago, when I was in the Federation's offices going over some audit work with our people, Jim Hampson asked if I could meet with him for a few minutes. We were alone in his office, and he was asking me some strange questions."

"Such as?"

"Well, he was asking me how it might be possible for some members to send in checks to the Federation without the staff or anyone else being aware of it."

"Didn't that seem strange to you?"

Ramsey fidgeted in his chair. "A little, but Jim said he was concerned about internal control and cash flow. He said a few members wanted to make contributions to the Federation's treasury without anyone else being aware of it."

"Interesting."

"I explained to him that there was no way to keep it from his own accounting department. I told him that, even if he were able to swear them to secrecy, we—we being the auditors—would uncover their contributions in the course of our audit, and had an obligation to report our findings of any irregularity to the Federation board in our management letter."

"And?"

"I explained to him that we had to report a situation like that to the board because it would appear as if these companies might be trying to buy Federation influence and favor. If we didn't report it, and the contributions surfaced later, we would undoubtedly lose the Federation account, and its board could even report *us* to the Board of Public Accountancy. If they did that, we could lose our license to practice public accounting."

"And?"

"Jim said that he understood and asked that I keep the conversation confidential. I really didn't think much more about it until I got a letter from Jim about a week or so later."

"What happened then?"

"His letter thanked me for my time. There was a money order in the envelope for a thousand dollars payable to me."

"What did you do then?"

"I called him and told him I couldn't accept the money."

"Why not."

"It would have been unethical, and if the other partners found out I was accepting money from a client personally and not advising them, I would lose everything I had invested in the firm."

"What did Hampson say?"

"He said that he understood, that he hoped I hadn't taken offense, and he invited me to meet him for dinner that night."

"What did you do?"

"We met that evening."

"What happened at dinner?"

"I gave him the money order back, and we had a casual conversation. He asked me how things were going with me personally, and I told him how expensive it was having two kids in college at the same time."

"Go on."

"I told him that I was laying out about thirty grand a year for tuition, and things were pretty tight financially."

"And?"

Ramsey breathed deeply again before continuing.

"Later on in the conversation, he asked me if I would be interested in earning enough on the side to pay for my kids' tuition."

"What did you say?"

"Obviously, I was curious about what he had in mind, so I asked him about it. He told me he had a business going on the side and needed accounting help. I told him again that it still wasn't worth it because if the other partners found out, my career with the firm would be over.

"He told me that he understood my position perfectly and that he respected my ethics and loyalty to the firm."

"What happened next?"

"We had a nice dinner, and he said that if I had a change of circum-stances to please let him know, or else he would have to look for some-one else, and he wanted me to have first shot at the account."

"Then what happened?"

Ramsey wished he had a glass of water; his throat was drying up. He swallowed hard, trying to moisten it.

"Well, about two weeks later, my wife got laid off from her job. She was working as a legal secretary and making good money, but the firm she was working for lost a big client and a major suit that they were counting on, and had to let a lot of people go. She had been working there almost fifteen years, and all she got was two weeks' s everance."

"And . . ."

"Well, about the same time she was let go, we got the two tuition bills at once, and we had to lay out almost fifteen thousand to keep the kids in school. We didn't know how we were going to make the tuition payments. Then, I remembered Jim telling me that if my circumstances were to change, to contact him right away."

Ramsey put his hand to his forehead and massaged it slowly before continuing.

"Dave, the last thing I wanted to do was hold back from my partners, but I was desperate. I love my kids and I wanted to keep them in college, so I called Hampson and told him that my circumstances had changed and that if he still needed an accountant, I would like to talk about it."

"What did he say?"

"He told me that he was glad I called, that he understood my position, and that he wanted to meet me for a confidential conversation."

"What did you do?"

"I met him that night at the same restaurant where we had met before. In fact, Jim was sitting at the same table. He stood and shook my hand and eased my mind that the conversation was confidential and that I could change my mind at any time."

"What did he tell you?"

"He asked me how it was that I changed my mind, and I told him about my wife's getting laid off and the financial problems we were going through. After listening to me, he leaned forward and asked if he had my absolute confidence, regardless of the circumstances."

"And you said . . ."

"I said, 'of course,' and that's when he pulled an envelope out of his coat pocket and handed it to me. He said that there was twenty five hundred in cash in the envelope and that I could expect the same every month if I would help him with the accounting problem he had. I told him I was very interested." He swallowed hard again, sucking his tongue, trying to generate more saliva.

"He told me the whole story. He said that a group of influential Federation members had gotten together and worked out a scheme to bill their companies for extra Federation dues, but he didn't know how to open up a Federation bank account without anyone else knowing about it. He said that he didn't know how to keep it from the staff accountants and from us, as auditors, and that he needed an accountant on the inside. He made it clear that he was willing to pay generously for the help."

"What did you say?"

"I told him how it could be done."

"How?"

"I told him how to open a bogus Federation bank account in a bank the association wasn't using by going to the bank with a completed, falsified corporate resolution, with the Federation's seal on it and depositing the checks he already had. I told him we could get a new post office box and put the address on the bogus dues statements we were going to have printed.

"I told him how I could get the bank statement, reconcile it for him, and meet with him once a month to tell him what to do. It was all very simple. We had fake Federation dues bills made up, his people had checks mailed in, and he deposited the money. I told him how much he could pay everyone in on the scam and I kept all the records."

"Why did he need you then?"

"He knew our people might run across something during the course of our audit. If they did, he needed someone on the inside to take care of it. As the partner in charge of the audit, that would logically be me."

Ramsey looked at Lovelady with sadness and humiliation in his eyes.

"He caught me in a weak moment and I did it, Dave."

"Why didn't you come straight with me, when you had the chance a few weeks ago?"

"When I found out that Hampson had split, I thought it was all over and, frankly, I was glad it was."

"You were?"

"Like I said, Hampson caught me in a weak moment, and I found myself involved in something I didn't want to be involved in any more."

"Why didn't you get out before this?"

"I tried to, but I couldn't."

"Why not?"

"He told me that I was in too deep, and I knew too much for him to let me out. And he reminded me about what happened to Pat McGuire when he got a little too close to this scheme and it scared me. You have to believe me, Dave. That's all I know."

Lovelady thought for a minute after Ramsey had finished and stood up. He walked back to his seat and stood behind the chair. "It's interesting that you mentioned Pat McGuire."

"Why is that, Dave?"

Lovelady put his hand on the shoulder of the man sitting next to him. When he did, Ramsey realized that he had gotten so involved in his confession that he had forgotten about the third person in the room.

"Forgive me for not formally introducing you," Dave said smiling, "but you two know someone in common."

"Who?" Ramsey had a puzzled look on his face.

"Pat McGuire."

"Pat McGuire?"

"Yeah," Lovelady continued. "It seems your Pat McGuire and Andy here both played football and met on the field once. If my memory serves me correctly, it was the game that McGuire was injured in. Am I right, Andy?"

Lovelady looked at the muscular blonde man still seated next to him. "That's right, Mr. Lovelady. McGuire wasn't a bad ballplayer. Too bad he got hurt. I understand he needed physical therapy and everything." His smile lacked even a hint of compassion.

"Yes, that was too bad, Andy. I think he had to be taken off the Federation audit that year."

Lovelady then walked back to where Ramsey was sitting, pulled out the chair next to him, and sat down.

"So tell me what you know." He leaned in as he asked the question.

Ramsey pulled a handkerchief out of his pocket and wiped his hands before talking again.

"Dave, I swear, all I did was take care of the money and make sure our people didn't stumble onto anything. I met Hampson every month and gave him an envelope like this one with notes on what to do."

Ramsey turned the envelope in his hand. "I even remember sealing this envelope and giving it to Russell Autry to bring here one day. Hampson wasn't in town. I told Russell to put it in a certain filing cabinet that Hampson and I used for occasions like this. Look, Dave, all it is are instructions on what to do, I swear." Ramsey slid the envelope toward Lovelady.

"Don't bother, you can be sure I've already read it. I guess Hampson got sloppy and forgot to get rid of the envelope, huh?"

"I guess so." Ramsey said, resignation in his voice.

"What else do you know?"

"Nothing, Dave, I swear. I know who was involved, of course, but I've protected all of you for over three years now. Please believe me." Ramsey's voice turned from resignation to desperation.

Lovelady absorbed and thought about what Ramsey had told him and paused momentarily before continuing.

"What do you know about tapes of meetings?" He gauged Ramsey's response carefully.

"What tapes? I've never heard anything about any tapes." Ramsey had a surprised look on his face as he answered.

They stared at each other a few moments.

"It seems that Mr. Hampson left some tapes with a confidant of his that I'm very interested in. What do you know about them?"

"Nothing, Dave, I swear. Please believe me! I don't know what meetings you're talking about either!"

Lovelady stood up.

"I wish I could believe you, Mr. Ramsey, but I'm afraid I can't."

"Why not? I swear I told you everything."

Lovelady suddenly struck the conference table with his fist. Ramsey winced, startled. "Listen, Ramsey. You've already lied to me once about not knowing anything. I had to look through almost every fucking file in this place before I found this envelope. I'm convinced you know more than you're telling me, to protect yourself from Hampson. Now, where are the fucking tapes?" The last question approached a scream.

"Dave, I swear I never heard of any tapes."

Lovelady became calm as quickly as he had become enraged. "I can see this is getting us no where. Now, you listen to me. You have the tapes or you know who does. I'm trying to be patient and I'm trying to be reasonable, but I'm getting upset." He paused, leaned down, and put his face directly in front of Ramsey's. He spoke calmly.

"Here's the deal. You call me by four o'clock tomorrow afternoon and tell me what I want to hear, or . . ." and Lovelady glanced at the other person in the room, "or you'll pay dearly."

He looked back at Ramsey. "I hope I'm making myself clear. Am I?"

"Dave I . . ." Ramsey started to speak, desperately groping for words. "Dave, I don't know what to do. I swear I don't know what you're talking about."

"Then I think it's in your best interest to find out," Lovelady said as he walked toward the door. "You have until four tomorrow afternoon. Now, out."

Ramsey stood, gathered his belongings and walked toward Lovelady who was holding the door. He stopped at the doorway. "Dave, listen, I swear I don't know what you're talking about," he implored.

Lovelady folded his arms across his chest and leaned against the doorway. "Four o'clock. I'll be waiting for your call. Let yourself out, Bob," Lovelady said, smiling coldly.

Lovelady watched Ramsey go down the hall and get into the elevator before turning to Andy Lombardo, who was still seated at the table.

"What do you want me to do, Mr. Lovelady?"

"Go ahead as we discussed. Be sure to call me at four-thirty. You'll know what to do then. Understand?"

Lombardo stood up. "I understand, sir. You'll hear from me at exactly four-thirty tomorrow."

Bob Ramsey stood by his car but had difficulty inserting his key in the lock. He couldn't stop his hand from shaking. When the door finally opened, he sunk into the driver's seat, slowly pulled the door shut, and started the engine. Before putting the car in gear, he folded his arms across the steering wheel, rested his forehead on his crossed arms, and began to cry. His world was coming apart fast.

# Chapter Twenty-Six

The following morning, Pat and Russell met for breakfast at the Double-T Diner on Route Forty West and Rolling Road. They tried to meet at least every other week to catch up on each other's lives away from the accounting firm and they looked forward to these meetings.

After breakfast, since they were both working in the Baltimore office all day, they decided to ride into the office together. Russell drove because he didn't want to leave his new BMW on the Double-T Diner parking lot all day.

On the way in, the conversation revolved around Jim Hampson. Pat and Russell speculated about what Hampson might have done with the eleven million dollars, with which he had absconded. They wondered where he might have gone without leaving a trace, and they doubted that anyone would be able to find him. He had been so careful, so clever, that his plan seemed flawless. As friends do, they admitted to each other that it was exciting being on the "inside" of this one.

After parking and locking Pat's car, they stood on the corner, waiting for traffic to clear. Pat exclaimed, "Jesus Christ, Russell, look at that guy!"

"Who?"

"On the corner outside our building. Look at him!"

Marching in a circle directly in front of the door to their building was the strangest looking person either of the two friends had ever seen in a city that wasn't lacking strange-looking people. Crossing the street and approaching their building, they assessed the curious-looking individual.

He was tall, at least six-feet-four. His long, tangled, dirty hair fell almost to his shoulders, and his black beard was coarse and untrimmed. A brown cloth, hooded robe with a rope belt and wooden cross tied to one end dangled at his left side. He wore high-top tennis shoes with no laces. The only thing that didn't seem to fit the picture was the expensive Revo sunglasses, that reflected a brilliant shade of blue.

His hands were in the robe pockets. A cardboard sign with handwritten lettering that said VENGEANCE IS MINE SAYETH THE LORD hung from his neck by two shoelaces tied together.

"Where in the hell did he come from?" Russell said, "Have you ever seen him before, Pat?"

"No, and I'm sure I'd recognize him. Maybe he's one of the new accountants your father recruited from the University of Maryland." Pat chuckled.

"Very funny."

They passed the man without incident and entered the building. When they reached their floor, they found Edie Veteck talking on the telephone. She looked up at Gilbert Autry who was standing over her desk, listening intently to her conversation. When she hung up, Gilbert anxiously asked, "What did they say?"

Edie kept her calm. "They said there's nothing we can do as long as he isn't creating a nuisance. He has the right to walk anywhere on a public street. As long as he isn't bothering people or blocking the entrance to the building, there's nothing we can do."

"That's it?" Gilbert's tone had an unusual edge.

"They just said to call back if he becomes a nuisance, and they'll take care of it. The only other thing they said was to try not to worry about it because people like that have a tendency to move on if nobody pays attention to them."

The older Autry caught sight of his son and Pat.

"Can you believe this?"

"What, Dad?"

"Is that idiot still out in front of our building?"

"Yep. Can't miss him. What's the problem?"

"We called the authorities and there's nothing we can do about him unless he starts bothering people. Great timing for him to show up today— we've got reps from two prospective big clients coming over in about an hour. What are they going to think?"

"I wouldn't worry about it, Mr. Autry, I'm sorry—Gil." Pat still had trouble adjusting to addressing Mr. Autry by his first name. "You see those people everywhere, particularly in D.C. He's not going to bother anybody, and if he does, I'm sure they'll be able to handle it."

"I guess you're right. I just wish he'd picked another day." Gilbert shook his head and walked back toward his office, obviously irritated.

"Do us a favor, Edie," Russell said. "If that guy starts acting up, just call Pat or me, and we'll take care of it. Don't get Dad involved."

"Okay. We've got to open up the switchboard. I'll call you two, if I hear of any problems."

The morning passed and Edie never had to call. Around noon, Russell popped into Pat's office to see if he was free for lunch.

"I really should pass, Russell. I've got a ton of work to do, and I have to get it done before I leave tonight."

"Come on, *I'll* buy, and I promise to keep it short. I have to talk to you about something."

Pat looked at his watch and then back at his friend. "Okay, but I've got to get back in half-an-hour."

The two friends passed through the circle the strangely-dressed man was walking. He seemed intent on his mission, but he wasn't bothering anyone.

They each bought a kosher hot dog, a bag of chips, and a soda from a street vendor. They sat on a bench under a shade tree in a small park.

"So what did you want to see me about? " asked Pat, as he took a bite of his hot dog.

"Have you talked to Bob Ramsey today?" Russell watched Pat's face for a reaction.

"No, why?"

"You probably will. He's really acting strange."

"What do you mean?"

"He's really hyper and not acting like himself."

"In what way?"

"He asked to talk to me alone about the Federation situation and Jim Hampson."

"What did he say?"

"Do you remember the day I met you down at the Federation's offices when I brought an envelope with me marked **CONFIDENTIAL**?"

"Yeah. Why?"

"He kept asking me if I'd opened it and if I was sure I'd put it in the right filing cabinet. He wouldn't let up, and I had to repeat the story about twenty times."

"What did you tell him?"

"I told him the truth. I told him I did what he asked. He'll probably ask you about it, and I need you to confirm my story."

"Sure. What's up with the envelope?"

"I don't know, he wouldn't tell me. You know as much as I do."

"Strange. Doesn't sound like Ramsey."

"It gets stranger."

"What else?"

"Then he started asking me if I knew anything about some tapes."

Pat looked puzzled. "What tapes?"

"I don't have the slightest idea. All I can tell you is that Ramsey came back to talk to me three times about some tapes. He kept going on and on about whether I knew anything about some missing tapes. He wanted to know if I saw anybody carrying tapes around and whether I ran across any in the file cabinets in the office. He even asked me if I had heard of any-one at the Federation's office ever talking about some tapes. Strange."

"What did you tell him?"

"Like I said before, I told him the truth. I told him I didn't know anything about them. In fact, I told him the only tapes I know about at all are your stupid Beatles tapes that you're gonna wear out. And I can't wait, by the way. Anyway, he's probably going to talk to you later today; so I thought I'd warn you."

"Thanks, but I don't know anything about any tapes either. Did he tell you why?"

"Not a word, and as hyper and out-of-character as he was, I didn't think I should ask him."

As they expected, the strange person was still in front of the building when they returned.

About an hour later, Pat was working at a computer terminal in his office when he looked up to see Bob Ramsey standing in front of his desk. Pat was startled, even though he was expecting him. The formal Bob Ramsey would normally knock.

"Pat, can I see you for a few minutes?" Ramsey was already closing the office door.

"Sure, Mr. Ramsey, what can I do for you?"

He was obviously nervous and not himself.

"Pat, I need to talk to you about the Federation audit."

"Yes. What can I help you with?"

"I want you to be honest with me."

"Of course."

"Do you know anything about any Federation tapes? Anything at all?"

"No, Mr. Ramsey. Doesn't ring any bells at all. I'm sure."

"Think hard. Did you happen to open any file cabinets or desk drawers and happen to notice any tapes?"

"No. Positive."

"How about in conversations. Did you ever hear Jim Hampson or any of the Federation people, for that matter, talking about any tapes?"

"No. I'm sure."

Ramsey took a deep breath and closed his eyes for a few seconds.

"Pat, are you absolutely certain? I can't tell you more, but this is extremely important. Russell said something to me this morning about your having Beatles tapes or something. What is that all about?"

"Well, yeah, I have all the Beatles albums on tape, and I keep them in my car, but they don't have anything to do with the Federation," Pat said, remembering as he said it that he had loaned them to Rita Davies. He decided not to mention this to Ramsey in the state he was in, particularly considering that Rita still had them.

Ramsey grimaced and then continued, "How about Teresa or Hardy? Do you think they know anything about any tapes?"

"I doubt it. I'm sure they would have mentioned it to Russell or me if they had. Have you talked to them about it?"

"No. Where are they, by the way?"

"They're working on the Nurses Association audit today in D.C. Do you want me to call to see if they know anything?"

"No, don't bother. I'll call them myself." He stood up and left Pat's office without another word. Pat quickly picked up his telephone and dialed Russell's extension.

"Autry here."

"Russell, it's me. Ramsey just left my office."

"And?"

"Same conversation he had with you. Weird."

"I told you."

"Listen, what time are we leaving today? Don't forget you're my ride."

"About five. Okay?"

"See you at five."

At exactly four o'clock, Ramsey closed his office door, picked up his telephone, and nervously dialed Lovelady's direct line in Washington. He heard someone on the other end of the line pick up the phone halfway through the first ring.

"Right on time. What have you got?" It was Lovelady's voice.

"Nothing, Dave. I swear I don't know anything about any tapes, and neither does anyone in this office. You've got to believe me." After a few long, silent seconds, Ramsey said, "Dave, can you hear me?"

"I hear you."

"Do you believe me?"

Lovelady's voice was calm. "Yes. I believe you."

Ramsey closed his eyes and exhaled, "Thank God. Thank you, Dave." He breathed a long sigh of relief. Then Lovelady said, "Listen, Ramsey, tell you what. I need your help."

"Anything."

"Meet me next Monday at six after work in my office. Are you free?"

"If I'm not, I will be."

"See you then." Lovelady hung up the telephone before Ramsey could say anything else. Ramsey hung up his own phone and felt a wave of relief like he had never experienced before. He made a note on his calendar to meet Lovelady at six the following Monday and to cancel another appointment earlier in the day.

At exactly four-thirty, the telephone on Lovelady's desk rang again. He let it ring twice before picking up the receiver and hanging it up again immediately.

"One if by land and two if by sea," the person who dialed the number said to himself, after counting the rings. He was smiling as he hung up the receiver.

Pat and Russell stopped by Ramsey's office on their way to the front door. "Mr. Ramsey, is there anything else you need from us before we go?"

"No, thanks, guys." For the first time that day, he had a smile on his face. "Hey, listen, I'm sorry I had to impose on you two today. I know I must have sounded strange, but it was important."

"No problem," they said together. "Let us know if you need us for anything else."

"Get out of here. Thanks for your help. I'll see you both tomorrow."

As they left, they heard Ramsey whistling.

"This has to be the most bizarre day on record," said Russell, and the two of them left the building talking about the day's happenings.

Around six-thirty, Ramsey put on his coat and dialed his home.

"Hello." It was his wife, Jimmie.

"Hi, honey, it's me. Listen, drop what you're doing, and get ready to go out somewhere for dinner."

"Okay," he heard her uncertainty. "Are you sure you're all right, honey? You sure were preoccupied last night and this morning."

"Couldn't be better. See you in about a half-hour."

"Okay, I'll get ready. Bye."

"Bye," he said cheerfully. He picked up his briefcase and took the elevator down to the first floor.

He walked out the front door into the cool Baltimore air and put his briefcase on the sidewalk, while he buttoned his jacket. Before he could finish, the man who had been marching in circles all day walked up to him. No one else was close to them.

"Do you accept Jesus in your life?" the stranger asked.

"Actually I do," Ramsey said, smiling and pulling his wallet from his hip pocket. "And I'm feeling generous today." He smiled and pulled a ten-dollar bill from his wallet and put the wallet back into his pocket.

"Do you repent for your sins?" the stranger asked, not taking the money.

"Listen, do you want the money or not? I don't have time for all of this."

"I said do you repent for your sins?"

Ramsey looked at him curiously.

"Do I know you from somewhere?"

Behind his sunglasses the stranger looked first to his left and then to his right. Suddenly, he pulled a pistol from the pocket of his robe, and fired five quick shots through the cardboard sign across his chest and into

Ramsey's chest. Ramsey was knocked backwards violently and fell to the concrete sidewalk, face up, motionless.

The man in the robe walked quickly around the corner and got in the back seat of a waiting Cadillac. The driver pulled into the still-heavy traffic on westbound Pratt Street.

As they drove, he pulled off the wig, uncovering neatly-cut blonde hair. He peeled off his beard, and put the wig and beard into a plastic bag.

Next, he folded the cardboard sign, took off the robe and tennis shoes, and put them in the plastic bag. He now wore running shorts and a tee shirt.

The driver turned left into an alley three blocks from where he had picked up his passenger and immediately lowered the back window as he slowed down to ten miles an hour.

"Now," the driver said, and the blonde man held the plastic bag out the window. A man walking down the alley took it, tossed it into an open trash-can and continued walking.

The driver rolled the tinted window up, picked up speed, and turned right at the end of the alley onto Lombard Street.

He drove another four blocks on Lombard Street, and turned right into another alley and stopped. Checking his left and right, he said, "Go," and his passenger left the car.

The blonde man walked the few steps to Lombard Street, and opened the back door to a waiting white Lincoln. As soon as he heard the door shut, the driver of the Lincoln drove off.

After a few turns, the Lincoln headed east on Baltimore Street. His passenger had put on the slacks, dress shoes, shirt, and sport coat waiting for him on the back seat. The passenger slid over to the right side of the car.

They were crossing a bridge over the Baltimore Inner Harbor when the rear passenger window next to the passenger slid down.

"Now," the passenger heard, and he threw the pistol out the window, but he couldn't hear the splash as the weapon hit the dark Baltimore harbor water.

A few seconds later, the passenger said his first words to either driver, "While we're in this part of town, take me to Little Italy for dinner. I'm starving."

"Any particular restaurant?" he heard.

"Vellegia's will be fine. Drop me off at the front door, and I'll take a cab home."

# *Chapter Twenty–Seven*

Three days later, Pat sat next to Russell and his wife, Carol, at Bob Ramsey's funeral. It was held at St. Agnes Church in West Baltimore, the same church Pat and his family attended when Pat was a little boy.

The mood was somber. Everyone on the staff of Autry, Martin & Ramsey was there, along with most of their spouses. The murder had received a great deal of media attention, and artists' drawings of the white Rastafarian were being shown on all of the local TV channels. As Father Zeller was delivering the eulogy, Pat noticed that many of the firm's clients were represented. Ramsey was well liked, and his violent death touched everyone who knew him.

His wife and children rode in a limousine, following the hearse to the cemetery, just a few miles from the church. After the gravesite service, as Pat walked back to his car, he saw Rita get into her car and drive away. He had noticed her at the church, and they had made eye contact as they were walking out, but they didn't exchange words. He was glad she didn't speak. He didn't feel like making idle conversation.

Pat drove back to his apartment complex in silence.

The next morning it was difficult for the accounting office to get back to business as usual. They had lost a popular partner and friend. A stranger would notice nothing unusual, considering it was a CPA firm. It was supposed to be quiet and stiff. No casual conversation, everyone serious—typical accountants.

Police were interviewing employees for any possible clues. There were none. A partner had died, leaving behind a wife and two children.

This evening everyone went home on time, even the partners.

Pat had left the building and was opening the door to his Camaro. "Pat! Wait a minute."

He turned around and saw Russell coming toward him, holding a small brown bag. "Here, I almost forgot to give you this."

"What is it?"

"Yesterday at the funeral, Rita Davies gave it to me and asked me to give it to you."

Pat opened the stapled top and looked inside. He smiled for the first time in quite a while.

"What is it?" Russell peered into the top of the bag.

"One of my Beatles tapes. I loaned them to her so she could copy them. I wonder why she didn't return them all. I guess maybe she's had a chance to copy only one. Thanks, Russell."

"No problem. Want to stop somewhere on the way home for a brew? I think we could both use one."

"You know, that's not a bad idea. Where do you want to go?"

"Let's just walk down to the Inner Harbor. How does that sound?"

"Fine, but I don't want to stay late."

"Me, either."

They walked the three short blocks to Phillips Restaurant and sat at the bar. Ordinarily, they would have been joking and kidding, but this conversation was serious. Why was Bob Ramsey singled out from the hundreds of people walking in and out of the office building that day? Had his strange mood on the day of the murder had anything to do with the situation? They decided it did.

They continued to talk in a serious vein, a rare happening for them. When they went back to their cars, they tried to assure each other that everything was going to be okay.

Pat was driving west on Route Forty toward home, listening to the news on the car radio. *Slow news day,* he thought, listening to the radio. Turning off the radio, he reached for the brown bag Rita had given Russell. He needed some music to cheer him up.

Fumbling with the cassette cover, eyes still on the road ahead, he forced it open and glanced at the label before inserting it into the cassette player.

"Sergeant Peppers! Perfect!" he said out loud, as he pushed in the cassette, side A up.

Hearing the hiss at the beginning of the tape, he waited for the familiar notes of George Harrison's guitar. It was taking longer than he remembered for the music to start when, instead of the first notes of *Sergeant Pepper's Lonely Hearts Club Band*, came a male voice. He was about to push in the eject button to see whether, somehow, Rita had mixed up a self-study tape or something with his precious Beatles music, when he suddenly realized that the voice was Jim Hampson's. He pushed the rewind button, waited for the whirring sound to stop, and turned up the volume while he continued driving.

After a few seconds, he heard . . .

*My name is Jim Hampson, and I am the executive director of the National Tobacco Federation. The date is November the tenth, and I am recording this tape from the Rocky Mountain Suite of the Keystone Resort in Colorado.*

*In approximately one hour, I will be present at a secret meeting involving the Chief Executive Officers of five of the largest tobacco companies in the world. The purpose of the meeting will be to fix the price of tobacco on the international market.*

*This tape is a record of the eleventh consecutive meeting we have been involved in over the past few years. The other meetings have also been recorded and are in my safe deposit box.*

*Those attending this meeting, including their names, positions with their companies, flight arrangements, room assignments, and the aliases used to book their flight arrangements and room assignments are as follows:*

*I flew into the Denver International Airport on American Airlines, flight number eight-one-four from Baltimore under the alias of Jay Leahy. I took the Rocky Mountain Shuttle from the airport to the Keystone Resort. I registered at the hotel under the name of Daryl Montgomery and stayed in the Rocky Mountain Suite.*

*Dave Lovelady, the only National Tobacco Federation board member involved in the secret meetings, is the Chief Executive Officer of Olde Harbour. Dave Lovelady flew from Atlanta to Colorado Springs on United Airlines, flight number eighteen-sixteen under the alias of Kevin Harr. He registered at the hotel under the alias of Robert Nelson, and stayed in room number five-oh-four.*

Glancing into his rear view mirror, Pat pulled into an almost empty 'Park and Ride' lot off Social Security Boulevard in Woodlawn, Maryland. He turned the motor off to give his full attention to the tape.

He heard exactly how each of the chief executive officers of some of the largest tobacco companies in the world conspired to fix prices. Hampson gave the effective dates for the new prices would go into effect and the excuses that would be used for the increases. Pat listened as Hampson explained to the group how they were to continue to send payments for bogus dues invoices, so that they could receive their "bonus" checks.

At the end of the tape, he heard Hampson tell them that one of the CPAs auditing the National Tobacco Federation happened to be at the resort. And, after a short discussion, he heard a voice tell Hampson to "take care of it."

He heard the off button click when Hampson announced that dinner had arrived; then, immediately after the pause, the tape resumed.

Hampson described how each of those in attendance had arranged for the trip home the next day, including details about aliases and flight numbers.

When the tape was over, Pat pushed in the eject button, took out the tape and put it back into its case.

He sat in silence, eyes closed, forehead resting on the palm of his hand. He had no idea what he was going to do next.

He took out the appointment book he carried everywhere, looked up a name in the address section, wrote down a telephone number and walked across the dark lot to a pay telephone. He deposited several coins and dialed a number. Before the call went through, he heard a voice say, "Please deposit an additional one dollar and seventy-five cents." The voice was a strange combination of a female voice and computer pauses. He reached into his pocket and was relieved to see several quarters. He deposited seven into the slot and heard each one drop.

The dial tone came on again, and after the second ring, he heard a familiar voice say, "Hello."

"Rita?"

"Pat. I've been waiting for you to call."

"Would you please . . ."

She interrupted.

"I'll explain everything. I need to see you right away."

"When?"

"Tonight."

"Okay, where? At your place?"

"No, I don't think we should. There's a Mexican restaurant called La Gringada on Route One just south of Laurel. Do you know the area?"

"Yes, I've been there before."

"It's seven-ten now. I'll meet you there at eight."

She waited a moment for him to respond, but before he did, she said, "I've got to go. See you at eight."

It was just about eight o'clock when he opened the door of the restaurant and walked toward the cash register stand. A young Italian woman picked up a menu and smiled at him. "One for dinner?" she asked.

"No, actually I'm here to meet someone"

"Are you Mr. McGuire?"

"Yes."

"Please follow me. Your party is waiting for you."

Pat spotted Rita sitting alone at the last booth on the right. She had a coffee cup sitting in front of her, but no food. She looked up when she saw him, but didn't smile.

"Here you are, Mr. McGuire. Will you be having dinner tonight?"

"Just coffee, please." He sat down across from Rita.

They looked at each other in silence until the waitress returned with the coffee.

"Thank you," he said, not taking his eyes off Rita.

Rita finally said, "I guess you're wondering what's going on." He leaned toward her. "You might say that, particularly considering that Bob Ramsey may have been murdered for the tape I have in my car right now."

"You have a *copy* of the tape," she said.

"What do you mean, a copy? Would you please tell me what's going on?"

Rita heard the urgency in his voice, but she still took time for a deep breath. "First, you have to promise me something, and then I'll explain everything."

"What?" His voice rose a little louder than he wanted.

"You have to promise me that this conversation stays between us."

"I don't know if I can do that. I think those tapes are connected to Bob Ramsey's murder." He was trying to keep his voice down.

She reached across the table and covered his hands with her own. "Pat, this is serious. You've got to promise me you won't tell anyone, at least for a couple of days. I'm so afraid of what might happen to me, and I don't have anybody else to go to. Please promise me! I need your help!"

Pat heard the desperation in her voice and saw it in her eyes. He took a deep breath before responding.

"What do you need my help for? What did you do? Don't tell me you're involved in this!"

"No, no, listen. You'll understand after I tell you. And if you don't, then you've got to do what you've got to do." She reached for a tissue in her purse to wipe away a tear.

"But Rita, I've got to tell Mr. Autry and Russell about this. I don't have any choice."

"I don't think that's a good idea."

"Why not?"

"Pat, I'm not sure, but I think they may be involved in this."

"What!" he said, incredulously.

"Pat, I could be wrong, but I think you've got to be careful."

"With Mr. Autry and Russell?" This was something he couldn't even imagine.

"I don't have proof of anything, but I do know that Jim and Mr. Autry were very good friends and met with each other all the time."

"Shit," he said and looked away.

He looked up at the ceiling, closed his eyes for a moment, sighed, then said, "Okay, you have my word—I won't do anything right away. Now will you please tell me what is going on here?"

She composed herself and said, "I don't know where to start, Pat."

"Why don't you start from the beginning?" he said gently. "I'm a good listener." He leaned back in the booth.

"Okay." She waited a moment, collecting her thoughts and began her story. "I've been having an affair with Jim Hampson for over two years." She looked up for his reaction. Pat said nothing, but a change came over his face; she couldn't tell whether he felt anger or disappointment.

"I know it'll be hard for you to believe me after what I have to tell you but, believe it or not, I was in love with him. It all began a little while after I started working at the Federation. As Jim 's secretary, we were at a convention together and found ourselves alone one night. I was recently divorced and vulnerable, and Jim had me convinced that he was unhappy in his marriage and was in the process of leaving his wife."

Pat's expression softened, and Rita sat farther back in the booth, gradually relaxing as she told her story to Pat.

"Anyhow, one thing led to another, and the next thing I knew, Jim and I were seeing each other as much as we could. I fell in love with him, and he took care of me."

"What do you mean he took care of you?" There was a hint of jealous anger in his voice.

"In every way. We were in love, and he supported me financially. How do you think I was able to afford my apartment?"

"I did wonder about that."

"Anyway, he said he wanted to marry me, and we started making big plans for the future. He was going to retire from the Federation in about two years. He convinced me that then he would have the financial resources to lead a good life with me. We both agreed that it would be best for both of us to wait until he left the Federation before going ahead with our plans."

Pouring herself another cup of coffee, she continued, "Then, one day, he told me he needed my help with something."

"Help with what?"

"He needed me to help arrange some Federation trips he was planning, but he said the trips were secret."

"Secret? Didn't that seem strange?"

"Yes, but I didn't question him, and you've got to remember that I was in love with him. I'd have done anything for him. *And* he was still my boss."

"Okay."

"Anyway, he'd give me names, and I would book airline flights and rooms for them. I always gave the tickets and other details, like room confirmation numbers, to him."

"Weren't you curious about what was going on?"

"Sure, and one day I confronted him."

"What did he say?"

"He told me some things, but obviously not everything. He told me the names he gave me were assumed names for important people and that the meetings had to be secret."

"How could you do it, Rita? Price-fixing is serious. People go to prison for a long time for that."

"What did I know, Pat? I didn't know anything about price-fixing. All I knew was that I was in love with him, and I'd do anything for him. He could be very charming, and he had me *convinced* that what they were doing wasn't bad. Besides, no one was getting hurt, so I continued helping him by handling all the travel arrangements. Then, before I knew it, I knew everything."

"Like what?"

"Like the tapes."

"Tell me about the tapes."

"One night, Jim was at my apartment and he said he needed more help from me. That's when he told me that he'd been taping the meetings."

"Uh huh."

"He told me he was doing it for us."

"What? What do you mean for 'us'?" Pat seemed annoyed.

"He told me that if he ever got caught, that he would turn the tapes over to the authorities to plea bargain for a lighter sentence for himself, and we could go on with our plans."

"What were you supposed to do with the tapes?"

"After he returned from each meeting, he would give me the tape, and I'd put it into a safe deposit box at a bank. He and I had the only keys, and I was supposed to get the tapes to him, if he were ever arrested.

"It went on like this for a long time. I made the arrangements, gave him the tickets and reservation numbers and everything else, and he went to the meetings. When he came back, he gave me the tape, and I put it in the safe deposit box. Simple. We kept seeing each other and making our plans."

"So what happened? Where is Hampson now, and how did Bob Ramsey ever get involved in all of this, and where do I fit in? I don't understand!" Pat gestured with his hands in the air, palms opened.

"Listen for a few minutes more, and you'll know. It all started coming apart when you got hurt playing football."

"What do you know about that?" He was curious to hear her response, especially after hearing the Colorado tape.

"You heard me, it all started coming apart when you got hurt.

"Jim and the rest of them were meeting in Keystone, Colorado, at the same time you were there. Do you remember calling me to ask if Jim was there?"

"Yes, but you said he wasn't."

"I lied, Pat! I can't tell you how sorry I am, but you've got to believe me—I had no idea you were going to get hurt. Otherwise, I never would have said anything to Jim."

"What did you say to him?" he asked, still puzzled and anxious to pull together all the loose ends.

"Jim called me later that same day and asked if I knew that you were staying at the same hotel in Keystone."

"How did he know I was there?"

"He saw you on the slopes and checked at the registration desk. He called me just to be certain."

"What did you tell him?"

"I told him the truth. I told him you had called to see if he was there. I told him that I covered for him by saying he was at an American Society of Association Executives meeting somewhere else. I didn't think anything more about it. He got back from his trip, gave me the tape as usual, and I put it in the safe deposit box." She stopped. "And then you got hurt."

"Are you telling me Jim Hampson was involved in my getting hurt at that football game?" He already knew the answer, having listened to the Colorado meeting tape on his Sergeant Pepper cassette.

"He never admitted it, but I'm sure he was. Pat, I'm so sorry!" She reached for his hands again.

"After you got hurt, I was suspicious, and I asked him about it one day."

"What did he say?"

"He said that the rest of the group was concerned that you had seen them at the resort. They were afraid you could tie them there together and they told him to get you off the audit. He told me he refused, but I didn't believe him then, and I surely don't now."

"What next?" Pat asked, expecting anything now.

"We broke up for a while. I told him I didn't want anything to do with him anymore, and the night after we broke up, I ran into you and Russell at Jasper's. "

She reached across the table, taking his hand again.

"Pat, I've always thought you were a special person, and I've always been attracted to you. I wanted to see you, and that's why I invited you over to my place that Sunday to watch the Redskins game. I *really* wanted to see you again. At the time, I thought that Jim and I were through. It seemed like you and your girlfriend were having problems too."

Pat smiled a faint smile, for only the second time in several days. "Why do you think I came over? And I had to think twice about it."

Rita returned Pat's faint smile with one of her own.

"It was Jim on the intercom, wasn't it?"

"Yes. I didn't expect him, he just showed up."

"Well, that explains it."

"Explains what?"

"Why you were so upset and why you made me wait upstairs. You didn't want us to run into each other, did you?"

"No, Pat, I didn't. Who knows what would have happened if you two had met?"

"Since we're being honest, can I ask you something now?" Pat asked.

"Sure."

"Remember meeting for breakfast the next morning?"

"Sure."

"Why the sunglasses? I've always wondered."

Rita tightened her grip on his hands and bit her lip before answering.

"After you left, Jim came up to my apartment."

"Yeah?"

She answered quickly and wasn't the least bit embarrassed. She surprised herself. "Jim had had a little too much to drink. He noticed the glasses in the sink and asked me if another man had been there."

"What did you say?"

"I didn't know how he would react and I lied. I told him my girlfriend, Kathy, had been there. He didn't believe me. He grabbed me by the shoulders and shook me. Then he slapped me. I was really upset and afraid. I had never seen him that way."

"I'm sorry." Pat frowned as she was talking. His voice was full of compassion for this woman and he felt a growing hatred for the man who mistreated her.

"It's okay, I'm over it now. Anyway, after he slapped me, I ran into my bedroom and locked the door. He kept knocking on the door, asking me to let him in and telling me how sorry he was."

"What did you do?"

"I stayed in there and wouldn't let him in. After a while he stopped knocking, and I must have dozed off." Rita swallowed some coffee. "Anyway, I finally got up, and I thought he had left. I went to the kitchen to fix myself a cup of tea, and he was sitting at the kitchen table drinking coffee. He had sobered up by this time. He stood up when he saw me. I knew he had been drinking earlier, but both of us had calmed down by then and we just hugged each other for a while. He told me he couldn't live without me. He said he was still going to leave the Federation and his wife so we could be together."

"I believed him, Pat, and my love for him was as strong as ever."

Pat marveled at how worldly she seemed yet, how naive she really was.

"Anyway, the next morning, you and I met for breakfast. I can't tell you how much I admired you for making that meeting so easy on both of us and not asking me about the sunglasses. You're quite a guy, Mr. McGuire." She flashed a full, beautiful smile this time.

Pat smiled, too, flattered by her remark about him.

"What happened next?"

"You were in the office one day and needed to get Jim 's signature, remember?"

"Yes"

"Well, I was going to buzz him when you walked away, and I overheard the last part of a conversation he was having with his wife. They were talking about going away together, leaving right after the Las Vegas meeting I had set up for him."

"What did you do?"

"At that moment, I knew he'd been lying to me all along. He had been *using* me. I thought about it, and I realized that if this whole scheme were uncovered, that I was as involved in it as everyone else. So I did what I had to do to protect myself."

"Which was?"

"That's when I borrowed your Beatles tapes. I didn't have much time, so I went to the bank that afternoon and removed the tapes of the meetings. All I did that evening was copy the meeting tapes over your Beatles tapes in my apartment. I put the meeting tapes back in the safe deposit box the first thing the next morning, before Jim got back from his trip. I didn't have enough time to go to the store to buy blanks, and I knew I had your Beatles tapes, so that's what I did."

"Does Jim know what you did?"

"No, there's no way he could."

"How do you know?"

"I went back to the bank a week later—just out of curiosity. Jim had closed out the safe deposit box and taken everything with him. There's no way he would have known, and if he had, you and I both know he would have confronted me."

Pat sat back in his seat, thinking.

"Where are the rest of the tapes," he finally asked.

"I have them locked for safekeeping, in a safe deposit box at a bank."

"How many are there?"

"Thirteen—I'm afraid I copied over all your tapes, Pat."

"I'm not worried about that, Rita—but why didn't you give me copies of all of them?"

"I just didn't have time. Believe me when I tell you that I'm not holding anything back from you any more."

"So, Rita, what did Bob Ramsey have to do with all of this?"

"Nothing that I know of. Why?"

"I know he met with Dave Lovelady the day before he was murdered."

"That's right. I was at the office, and let him in before leaving."

"Well, on the day he was shot, he kept asking everyone connected with the Federation audit if they knew anything about any tapes. He sounded desperate."

"Really?" She seemed surprised this time, and her face began to flush.

"Yes, he kept pressuring everyone to see if they knew anything about any tapes, and the next thing you know, he's dead. And I've got a copy of one of the tapes he was looking for in my car! Christ!"

He rolled his eyes.

"And so, Dave Lovelady, CEO of one of the largest tobacco companies in the world and a member of the Federation's board, has actually been involved in a price-fixing scheme of world proportions and is probably involved in Bob Ramsey's murder! And if that's not enough, now he's running the show from the inside! Holy Christ!" He looked away and then back at her. "What are we going to do?"

"Nothing right now." Tears were pooling in her reddening eyes. "Right now, *I* need your help! Pat, I'm really scared. If you can help me, I'll be leaving as soon as possible. Then it will have to be, what are *you* going to do, not what are *we* going to do."

"Why do you need me—or should I be afraid to ask?" Pat asked, already resigned to helping her.

"Pat, you're the only one I can trust."

"What are you scared of?"

She paused to keep her voice from quavering. "Listen, Lovelady had all of the file cabinets locked!"

"So what? What does that have to do with you?"

She paused again.

"He's going through all the cabinets one-by-one looking for things. That's probably what happened to Ramsey."

"What?"

"Ramsey was probably tied into this in some way we'll never know, and Lovelady must have come across something."

"And?"

Rita put her face into her hands, wiping her eyes before answering.

"There's something in the files that implicates me with Hampson, and Lovelady is going to find it."

"What is it?"

Rita took a deep breath before beginning. "Remember, Pat, I was a *good* secretary. When I made travel plans, I took notes. Jim specifically told me not to, but I did anyway, just in case something went wrong. So, every time I took notes, I put them in a sealed envelope in my personnel folder, and I destroyed them after each trip."

"So, what's the problem?"

"So, I took notes for the Las Vegas trip and put them in my file before all of this happened. Lovelady came in and had all of the file cabinets locked before I could get my notes. I'm afraid he's going to find them and put two-and-two together, and the same thing that happened to Ramsey is going to happen to me! These are nasty people, Pat. You've got to help me. I don't have anyone else I can turn to!

"I know you can't think much of me, Pat, but I'm desperate."

She was wrong. He would have done anything she asked.

"Why don't you just have the personnel manager get your file for you?"

"I tried, but even she can't get into the files." Her voice wavered again.

Pat leaned forward, surprised at how calm he felt. "I'll help you, Rita. Don't ask me how, but I will."

A relieved smile came over her face. "Thanks, Pat, somehow I knew I could count on you."

After thinking a few minutes, he continued, "Maybe you're right. Maybe it is better if we do wait a little bit to sort things out and try to get you situated."

"We can't just break into the file cabinet during the day and the security company has the place tight as a drum at night. I don't know how we'll get those notes." Rita's expression was desperate.

"Give me a while. I'll think of something." He turned from her, tapping his fingers on the table, absorbed in thought. Finally he looked at her.

"Listen, where does Lovelady keep the keys to the file cabinets? Maybe we can have a copy made."

"I've thought of that. I've been watching him as carefully and discreetly as I can. He keeps a big key ring in his brief case, and the key is probably on that ring. Two days ago, he had to go to a meeting outside the office, and he left his briefcase. I went into his office and shut the door, but his briefcase has a locking mechanism, and he had locked it."

She buried her face in her hands and shook her head. "I don't know what I'm going to do, Pat!"

Pat drummed his fingers again on the table. He finally spoke. "Listen, do you know any locksmiths or anyone who could help us out?"

Rita looked relieved when Pat used the word "us." She sighed, "No, nobody. Do you?"

"Nope." He took a deep breath. "It was a dumb question anyway. Even if I did, I don't think I could ask anyone to break into a locked file cabinet. It's too dangerous, and it wouldn't be worth the risk for anyone."

They both sat silently.

Finally, he pulled a five-dollar bill from his wallet, and put it on the table while they put on their jackets. Pat walked her to her car and opened the door. She threw her purse across the seat and turned, putting her arms around his neck and her head on his shoulder. Softly she said, "Thanks, Pat. It helps just to know I can count on you."

Pat felt a familiar sensation surge through his body, rekindling the feelings he had had for her that night. Now, somehow, they were mixed with a strong desire to protect her.

He waited a second before saying, "I promise to do what I can, and I'll call you as soon as I think of something. But I'll be damned if I know what it is."

# Chapter Twenty–Eight

An hour later, alone in his apartment, Pat sat on the living room couch, staring out a large picture window and searching his mind for ways to get into that file cabinet. Something had to be done quickly—Lovelady couldn't be too far from opening Rita's file.

Pat rose as he picked up his keys to put them in their customary place—a hook he had attached to the side of the refrigerator. As he fumbled with his keys, he remembered a time when they had been lost. He had been unable to use his car—his father kept his spare and had gone on vacation, so Pat had called a locksmith. When he explained his situation, the locksmith had told him there wasn't anything he could do without the key number. He was able to get the number and the locksmith made him a new key.

Did the file cabinet have a key number?

He dialed Rita's telephone number, and she answered after the first ring.

"Hello."

"Rita, this is Pat."

"Pat! Have you thought of something?"

"I hope so."

"What?"

"Do you know if the locking mechanism on the file cabinet had a number on it?"

"I don't know. Why?"

"This is important. When you go to work tomorrow, see if the file cabinet has a number on the lock. If it does, write it down, and also write down the name of the manufacturer of the cabinet, its model name, and who made the lock, if you can."

"Why?"

"It's a long shot, but maybe I can have a key made at one of those key places. I did it before when I lost my car keys."

"Oh, Pat, I knew you would think of something!"

"Don't get excited yet; we don't know if this will work."

He heard Rita breathe a sigh of relief.

"Rita, listen."

"Yes, Pat?"

"We've still got a long way to go. What time can you get to the office in the morning, without arousing suspicion?"

"Around seven, I guess. What do you want me to do?"

"Just get to work and it's business as usual. As soon as you can, get me that information. I'll see what I can do about getting a key."

"Where should I call you?"

"At home. I'm not going to work in the morning."

He heard Rita breathe deeply again, and he didn't interrupt her thoughts. After a few long seconds—

"Pat."

"Yes, Rita?"

"Do you think this will work?"

He realized he had no idea. "Yes, Rita," he tried to sound convincing. "I'm sure it will work."

Both Pat and Rita had difficulty sleeping. Both woke early and wanted to call the other, but each decided not to. Rita left for work around six and, about the same time, Pat picked up his telephone and dialed Russell Autry's home. After just two rings, Pat heard Carol's voice.

"Hello."

"Carol?"

"Yes, is this Pat?"

"Yes, Carol, sorry to call so early. Is Russell there?"

"Pat, it is early. Are you okay?"

"Yes, I'm fine, but I do have to talk to Russell for a minute. I'm sorry."

"Don't worry, we've both been up for a while. Hold on and I'll get him."

Pat heard her put the receiver down and heard her footsteps fade as she walked from the phone. Soon he heard the sounds of heavier steps.

"Hey, what's up, Pat?" he heard Russell ask.

"Russell, I need to take the day off. Can you cover for me?"

"Sure. What's going on anyway?"

Pat hesitated.

"I can't tell you now." He was sorry he had to keep his friend wondering, and he was relieved when Russell didn't press him.

"Okay," Russell stretched out the word. "I guess I'll see you whenever."

Pat closed his eyes for a moment.

"Russell?"

"Yes?"

"I promise I'll tell you everything, but I can't right now."

"It's okay, Pat. I'll see you tomorrow."

The next hour seemed like forever to Pat as he waited for Rita's call. Finally, at 7:10 A.M., he jumped as the phone next to his bed rang.

"Rita?"

"It's me. I think I have what you need."

Pat reached for the paper and pen he had put next to the telephone hours before.

"Yeah?"

"The number on the lock is 5481. The manufacturer is Hardy-Built, and the model is Fire Chief. Is that all you need?"

"Okay, let me repeat it: 5481, Hardy Built and Fire Chief. Right?"

"Right."

"I'm leaving right now and I'll call you as soon as I can."

"Where are you going?"

"To a hardware store to see if I can get this key made."

"Pat, I'm scared of doing this all alone."

"What do you mean?"

"I mean I need your help. I'm too scared to do this all by myself. I'll have to get into that filing cabinet by getting around security after hours, and I would feel so much better if you would go with me."

Pat thought for a moment. He would do all he could to help her, but he didn't think he should go to her office and risk being seen.

"Rita, I'll do all I can for you, but I don't know if that's a good idea. I'll do what I can to get you the key, but there's no reason for me to be down there. If Lovelady sees me, he's going to wonder what's up."

Rita thought for a moment and realized that Pat was right.

"Okay, what now?"

"You stay there, and I'll see what I can do about getting the key."

"I'll be here, Pat."

"Okay, I'll call you as soon as I can."


Pat put on jeans and a shirt and ran to his car. He drove too fast, yet it seemed to take too long to get to the hardware store. His car created a gray cloud of dust as he pulled into the gravel parking lot. He didn't wait for the dust to settle before getting out and jogging toward the front door. He saw the store clerk alone and looking bored when he entered.

"How can I help you?" she asked cheerfully.

"I need a key made," he stated, taking the information Rita had given him from the pocket of his blue jeans.

"What kind of key is this?" she asked as she put on her eyeglasses and studied Pat's note.

"It's for a file cabinet."

"Oh no," she said, taking off her glasses. "The only keys we can make are car keys and door locks. I'm afraid I can't help you."

As Pat heard the words, he visualized Rita waiting nervously by her phone for his call.

"Can you suggest a place I might go for this type of key?"

"You're going to need a locksmith. We're just a hardware store."

"Do you have any suggestions?"

"Oh my! I don't have any idea. I know there's not one around here."

Disappointed, he reminded himself he had known that it wouldn't be easy.

"Do you have a phone book?" he asked.

"Sure," she said. She reached under her desk. "It might be a little old, though."

She put a dog-eared telephone book on the counter, and he looked for locksmiths. Pat glanced through the few listings. The closest locksmith was in Catonsville, in West Baltimore. He jotted down the store information, thanked the store clerk for her time and left.

The drive toward Catonsville in the morning work traffic seemed to take much longer than usual. Pat didn't even turn on his radio, too absorbed in thought. He finally saw the Frederick Avenue exit. His spirit lifted when he located the locksmith store and, once again, he saw that he was the only customer in the store. An older gentleman sitting behind the counter smiled at him as he walked in.

"And how can I help you on this beautiful day, young man?"

"Do you make keys for filing cabinets?" he asked. Pat felt guilty that his tone wasn't friendlier, considering the man's demeanor.

"Sure. What have you got?"

Pat pulled out the information Rita had given him.

"Can you help me?" he asked, sliding the note toward the clerk. The man picked up the paper and took off his glasses. "I'm not like most people my age," he said. "I need glasses for distance but not for reading! Isn't that funny?" He laughed, looking at Pat.

Pat just grinned.

"Okay, let's see what you've got here," the store attendant said, studying the information.

Pat looked carefully as the man read the note and then took a large, spiral-bound notebook off the shelf behind him and opened it. He flipped through a few pages, found what he was looking for, and ran his left index finger down two columns of information that Pat couldn't decipher upside down.

"Let's see. Hardy Built—their locks are made by Schaffer. I should be able to help you."

Pat put both of his hands on the counter, exhaling in relief as the man spun around a rack of keys. Pat could see the man scrunch up his face as he looked for the right key.

"I might not be able to help you today, my friend. Oh, no, wait—here it is, it wasn't in the right spot. I should have this ready for you in just one minute. Do you need just one key?"

Pat heaved a sigh of relief. "Let's go ahead and make it two, just to be safe," Pat replied.

After the third ring, Pat heard Rita's voice.

"Hello."

"Rita, it's Pat."

"Pat! Where are you?"

"I'm home. Can you talk?"

Rita looked around. "Yes, but not long. Lovelady went to the restroom or something."

"Listen, I've got the key."

"Really? Oh, that's great!"

"Look, you're going to need to figure out how we're going to get by security to get into the building after hours."

"You know I will. I'll think of something, and I'll call you right after work. I need to go, now." Rita hung up abruptly.

At six-thirty that evening, Rita called Pat at his apartment.

"Pat, it's me."

"What have you figured out?"

"Can you meet me at one o'clock Friday morning in front of the Federation's office."

"One A.M.?"

"Yes. One hour after midnight Friday morning."

"Okay."

"Pat, bring your ID and a couple of framed pictures of your family. I'll take care of the rest. Oh, yeah, and wear jeans."

"What in the world are you planning?"

"Just do everything I said, and leave the rest up to me. I'll see you Friday at one. I've got to go."

# Chapter Twenty–Nine

Pat arrived at the Federation's office ten minutes early. He sat in the dark car in silence, waiting for Rita. He had not contacted her since their telephone conversation, and he was anxious for her safety.

At exactly one A.M., Pat saw her car approaching. She parked next to him and they got out of their cars at the same time. Not engaging in light chatter, they walked together across the street to the Federation's front door. Pat noticed that she was carrying a Nordstrom's shopping bag and that she actually appeared calm. She inserted the key into the door and opened it. Once they were in, she locked the door from the inside and led the way to the security panel by the elevators.

The security panel's red light was blinking. She quickly pushed a series of numbers on the keypad, and a green light came on in its place.

"Hurry, we have only a few minutes before the security company gets here to check up on us. Let's take the stairs; they're faster than the elevator."

Pat followed her into the stairwell, and they took the steps two at a time to the twelfth floor. Out of breath, Rita pulled the heavy door leading to the Federation's lobby. She pushed in the elevator button as she passed it, then hurried down the hallway. Before Pat could say anything, she said, "The security people always take the elevator. We need all the time we can get—at least the elevator will be on this floor and will have to go back down to pick them up."

She stopped at an office halfway down the hall. On the wall outside the office door was a metal sign holder. The gray sign read STEVEN STEURER. Rita slid the sign out and put it in her shopping bag. She pulled out another sign that read PATRICK McGUIRE, and slid it into the metal holder. She walked into the office and picked up Steven Steurer's business-card holder, put it in her bag, pulled out another holder, and placed it on the desk. Pat took one of the cards from the holder, and was surprised to see official Federation business cards with PATRICK McGUIRE, PAYROLL MANAGER in bold raised letters on the front of the card.

Rita moved to the credenza behind the desk. She took the framed pictures of Steve Steurer's family and thrust them into the shopping bag.

"Quick, Pat, put your pictures on the credenza."

Pat did as he was told. When the switch had been completed, Rita didn't have to tell him to follow her to her desk. She turned on her computer and hid her shopping bag under the desk.

"We don't have much time. Just pull up a chair to my desk."

Again, Pat did as he was told. Rita gave him a pad of paper and a pen. "The security company will be here any second. They'll want to see our ID's and ask what we're doing here. We'll say we've got to run payroll, and we're having a computer problem, okay? Just act like you're busy, and try to be natural. I hope the guard is somebody I know."

Before they had time to say anything, they heard the sound of the elevator's chime and footsteps walking toward them. They looked up to see a tall, muscular security guard.

"Well, hello, Rita, long time no see. Burning the old midnight oil again?"

"Hi, Jeff. I was hoping you'd be working tonight. Sorry to bother you so late."

"It's my job, no bother. Rita, I hate to ask you, but you know the rules. I have to check your ID."

"I know, Jeff, here you are." She handed him her driver's license and her business card.

The security guard looked at the license and the card, and gave them both back to her. "Thanks, Rita, I appreciate your understanding. I don't believe I've met this gentleman."

"Jeff, this is Pat McGuire. He's pretty new."

They shook hands. "What brings you out so late?"

"Payroll," Rita answered. "We've got a computer problem, and tomorrow is pay day. We don't want an uprising on our hands if checks aren't ready."

The guard laughed and said, "Okay, no problem. I'm sorry though, Mr. McGuire, I'm going to have to ask you to show me some ID."

Pat reached for his wallet, pulled out his driver's license, and handed it to the guard, who examined it carefully.

"Do you mind showing me your office?" he asked, clipping Pat's license into his clipboard. "It's just a formality."

"Sure," he said. Pat stood up and began to walk down the hall. Rita went to follow them when the guard said, "Don't bother, Rita, I know you've got a lot to do. I'm sure he knows where he works." He smiled at her. She returned his smile and sat back down at her desk, pretending to work on her computer.

They came to Pat's office and the guard looked at the nameplate outside the door. He walked into the office, picked up one of the business cards from the holder on the desk and compared it to Pat's license before putting it back. He then walked to the back of the desk, looked at the pictures on the credenza, occasionally switching from the pictures to the license.

"Sorry to inconvenience you, Mr. McGuire. You've got a good-looking family there."

"Thanks," Pat said, feeling uneasy and trying to act natural.

The guard apologized again for disturbing them and headed toward the elevators. Abruptly, the guard turned around.

"Mr. McGuire, I think you forgot one thing."

"What's that?" Pat asked, hoping he didn't look as uneasy as he felt.

The guard then held up something in his left hand. "Your license—you'll probably need this again." He laughed at the look on Pat's face.

When the elevator doors closed, Pat leaned against the wall and breathed a sigh of relief. He hurried back to Rita's desk.

"Any problems?" she asked. "You were gone a while."

"He had my attention for a minute, but he's gone now," Pat said. "Let's move."

"Okay, well, security shouldn't be back. Let's go ahead and switch the name plates and everything back so we can get out of here as quickly as possible, once we have those notes."

Rita and Pat scrambled to take the pictures off the credenza and put them back into her shopping bag. Rita dusted off the top of Steurer's credenza before replacing the pictures of the Steurer family. She then wrote a note with her left hand that said, "I CLEANED YOUR DESK. SORRY IF I DIDN'T PUT THE PICTHURES BACK RIGHT. AMANDA." She put the note on Steurer's desk.

"I never noticed you were left-handed before, Rita."

"I'm not." She showed him the misspelled note and smiled. Pat was impressed. She had thought of everything.

Once again they caught each other stealing glances. Simultaneously they reached forward and held hands very gently.

Rita dropped Pat's hand suddenly. "Did you hear something?"

Pat listened carefully for a moment. "No, did you?"

"It's the elevator. I can hear it coming up. Someone else is in the building!"

"Shit!" Pat said. "Where can I hide?" he asked desperately.

Rita frantically looked around. "Just get in here." She ushered Pat into an open office. "Lock the door from the inside and be quiet." The name-plate outside the office said RHONDA JOHNSON.

She took a deep breath to try to calm herself, when she heard the elevator doors open. Rita was praying it was Jeff from the security company again, when she realized she was nowhere near her desk. Instinctively, she walked to the office lunchroom, opened the refrigerator door and peered inside.

She could hear heavy footsteps coming toward her. Her heart was pounding and she was too frightened to look up. She heard the light switch click and immediately the room was flooded with bright light. She picked up an unopened can of soda, turned in the direction of the light switch, and saw a male figure standing in the shadows of the doorway.

"Ahhhh!" she yelled when she saw Dave Lovelady. She dropped the soda can and fell back against the open refrigerator door, knocking several items onto the floor. "I thought I was alone; you scared me to death!"

Lovelady looked confused and somewhat startled himself.

"Rita! What are you doing here at this hour?"

"I have to sit down a minute and calm down." She went to one of the tables, sat down and covered her heart with her right hand. Her breath was shaky.

"I'm sorry, Mr. Lovelady, I thought I was the only one here."

"I didn't mean to startle you, but I thought I heard something. I saw the refrigerator light come on. What are you doing here anyway?"

"I'm so far behind with everything that's going on, I had to come in to try to catch up."

"I didn't realize I was putting that much on your plate."

She managed a grin. "Well, I'm here."

"I'm not coming into the office tomorrow and I want to get a few things to work on over the weekend. Are you staying much later?"

"No, sir."

Lovelady looked at her with just a hint of suspicion on his face, turned, and walked toward his office on the other side of the floor.

Rita's mind was racing. She opened the can of soda, shut the refrigerator door, and walked back to her desk outside of Lovelady's office. She was thankful she had turned her computer on earlier. She sat down and began typing.

Five minutes later Lovelady turned out the lights to his office. He was adjusting some papers under his arm when Rita looked up.

"I've got all I need. Are you leaving now?"

"No sir. Now that I'm here, I want to finish up."

"Well, don't stay too late."

"I won't. Have a good evening, Mr. Lovelady."

Lovelady looked down at her without smiling and stared a second or two longer, then walked toward the elevators.

She closed her eyes when he was out of sight, whispering "Thank God."

Lovelady seemed to magically reappear in front of her desk, surprising her again. "Why is Rhonda Johnson's office locked?"

"Pardon me?"

"I said, why is Rhonda Johnson's office locked?"

Rita's mind was racing. She hadn't prepared for this and hoped she sounded businesslike.

"I don't know, Mr. Lovelady."

"I was walking down the hall and everybody's office was open except hers. Her door is shut and locked. Do you know why?"

"No."

"Come with me."

She followed him to Rhoda Johnson's office.

"You try it."

She grabbed the doorknob, trying to turn it.

"See? I want to know why this is the only door locked."

Inside the office, Pat could hear the exchange in the dark. His handkerchief covered his nose and mouth to muffle his breathing. Light came from under the door, broken by moving shadows created by four legs.

Pat prayed quietly.

"Oh, I know why!" Rita said.

"Why?" Lovelady was studying her.

"Tomorrow is pay day. She's probably got payroll information on her desk and doesn't want anyone to see it. She's very good about confidentiality."

"Do you have a key?"

"Oh, no."

"Who has it then?"

"Mr. Lovelady, I really don't know. Mr. Hampson was very serious about keeping payroll secret. Someone obviously has a key besides Rhonda, but I know I don't."

Lovelady continued his gaze. "Okay Rita, I'm leaving now. Just do me a favor and check with Rhonda in the morning to make sure everything's okay."

"Yes, sir."

Lovelady walked back to the elevator, and Rita headed back to her desk. She went to a window, making sure she wasn't seen, and watched Lovelady drive off in his car. Satisfied they were alone, she went back to Rhonda Johnson's office and tapped lightly on the locked door. "It's Rita. You can come out now."

She saw the doorknob turn and heard a click before the door opened. Pat's face was ashen, and Rita knew better than to say anything.

The two moved more quickly as Pat followed Rita to the association's Human Resources Department. She put her hand on a file cabinet marked PERSONNEL FILE, A-M. "This is it," she said excitedly.

Pat pulled a key from his pocket. He carefully inserted it into the lock—a muffled click—and the lock popped open.

Rita put her palm up to her mouth, closed her eyes, and exhaled. "Let's just hope my notes are still here."

She fingered through the file drawer for a moment, pulling out the Rita Davies file.

Pat smiled when she said, "Yes!" She found the envelope still sealed.

She slid the file back in the drawer, minus the notes, making sure the cabinet was locked. She put her notes into the shopping bag, then gave Pat a tight hug. "I'll repay you for this someday, Pat. I don't know how, but I will."

He smiled down at her. "You can repay me right now by getting me the hell out of here."

They double-checked the office and left the building. Rita reset the alarm system. As they approached their cars, Rita put the shopping bag down and turned to put her arms around Pat. Hugging him warmly, she started to cry. She wiped away the tears with the back of her hand, before Pat gave her his handkerchief. "Don't worry, it's clean," he said, trying to make her smile.

"Well, we should get moving," said Pat, gently pushing the hair from her eyes. Reluctantly, he let go of her hand and they parted.

Pat was opening his car door as Rita called to him. "Oh Pat, I almost forgot to tell you."

"Yeah?"

"I'm leaving town next week. Sooner than I thought. I'll write explaining everything."

Pat's heart sank. Before he could answer, Rita got into her car, turned on the ignition and lights, and drove off. He watched her leave the lot.

Driving back to his apartment, Pat wondered when he would hear from Rita again and what he should do now.

# Chapter Thirty

Ten days later, Pat sat at his desk, going through a stack of backed-up mail. He had spent the past week at a client's office.

The mood in the office had improved over the past several weeks since Bob Ramsey's death, and life was slowly returning to normal for the staff, but Pat couldn't get Rita off his mind. He worried about her and was frustrated that he couldn't contact her. He also realized that he missed her more than he had a right to. He still didn't know what to do or whom to trust.

Most of the mail was routine: IRS notices, letters from clients, and seminar brochures. He was separating the mail into piles when he came across an envelope with a handwritten address. On the bottom left-hand corner was written, "Personal and Confidential. To be opened by P. McGuire only." The letter was postmarked Irving, Texas, and the name on the return address read *R. Herrera*. He got up from his desk, walked across the room, and closed the door. Sitting down, he picked up the envelope. It was sealed with tape and stapled across the top. He removed the staples but still had to use scissors to open it. He pulled out a short letter written on yellow legal paper, and began to read.

> *My Dear Pat,*
>
> *What can I say? I owe you so much, and I don't know how I'll ever express how grateful I am, much less repay you. But I'll try to do both somehow, someday.*
>
> *I owe it to you to tell you what's going on and where I am, if you need me. I resigned the Monday morning after we retrieved the papers I was worried about. I told Mr. Lovelady that I had to resign on doctor's orders, because I was headed for a nervous breakdown if I didn't get away from all the stress. Lovelady said he understood, thanked me for all my hard work, and wished me luck. That Monday was my last day.*
>
> *I decided to move back to the Dallas area to live with my sister for a while, and I'm using my maiden name, Herrera, to make it harder for*

*anyone to track me down. You're the only one who can contact me. My sister's name is Lisa.*

*If you need to contact me, the number is (214) 741-1814.*

*My thoughts are with you. Please be careful, Pat; these are not nice people.*

*Until next time.*

*Rita*

After reading the letter three more times, he wrote down "Lisa and Rita Herrera" and their phone number in his address book and ripped up the letter. He turned around in his chair and stared out the window.

He was twenty-nine years old, and he was in the middle of something that he didn't want to be involved in. He was still depressed and torn over losing Lynn, he missed Rita and was worried about her. He didn't know what to do, whom to trust, or where to go.

And then he met Ralph Poupore, attorney-at-law.

The next week, Pat pulled into the Double-T Diner to meet Russell for breakfast. They hadn't met for several weeks following Bob Ramsey's death, and Russell thought it was time for them to get back to their routine.

Breakfast wasn't the same as it had always been. Instead of casual conversation about the Orioles or reminiscing about their football days together, talk seemed stiff. Pat couldn't seem to shake Rita's admonition about not trusting anyone, and Russell couldn't dent Pat's wall, as hard as he tried. Neither of them noticed the man sitting in the next booth across from them. Neither took notice when he left.

"Come on, Pat, we've both got to get over this. We can't let this affect our friendship." Russell was pleading with him.

Pat took another sip of coffee, put the cup back on the saucer, and looked his friend in the eyes. The time had come.

"Russell, something has been bothering me, and I've got to get it off my chest."

"What is it," Russell said, showing concern. "You know you can tell me anything."

"It's about that picture in Jim Hampson's room."

"What picture?" Russell had a sincerely puzzled look on his face.

"You know what picture! The one in the music room with Jim Hampson on his boat. I still think the guy in the picture is the son-of-a-bitch that took me out in that game. I don't think you're being up-front with me!" As he spoke, Pat's voice began to rise, and several people sitting at the counter turned in their direction.

"Calm down, will you, Pat! People are staring!" Russell looked around, feeling embarrassed.

Pat felt the flush in his face and tried to hide his emotions. He folded his arms on the table and looked toward the window without seeing anything in particular.

"Come on, let's go outside and talk," Russell said, after a few minutes of uncomfortable silence.

Pat didn't move or reply right away, still looking out the window.

"Come on, Pat!" Russell said again.

Finally he looked back at him. "Okay, let's go, you're right."

They both reached into their pockets at the same time when Russell said, "Put your money away. This one's on me, you can get it next time." He threw a ten-dollar bill on the table.

Pat knew he didn't have to say thanks.

When they reached the car, Russell put his hand on Pat's arm. "Okay. Now will you tell me what's bothering you?"

"You heard what I said. I don't know if I can trust you, Russell! I think that guy was a ringer to get me off the Federation audit, and I think you know who he is!"

"Listen to me, Pat," Russell said, now grabbing his friend's arms, "I swear I don't know what the hell you're talking about. Like I told you before, I know for a fact that the guy in the picture is Hampson's nephew—Jeff Mellor. He's definitely not the ass hole who set you up. I was up against that guy for most of the game! Don't you think I'd recognize him? You're getting paranoid. Why don't you believe me?" This time, it was Russell's voice that was beginning to rise.

Pat raised his arms, his hands were shoulder height and his palms were open. He was upset and he didn't care who saw them arguing.

"I don't know who to believe anymore, Russell. All I know is that I got hurt, Hampson stole eleven million dollars and left the country, and a partner has been murdered in the process, so don't call me paranoid! I think I have a right to be suspicious!"

They were arguing back and forth, oblivious to the strangers in the parking lot.

"Listen to me. Pat, I swear I didn't have anything to do with this. I know my father didn't, and I'd be surprised if Ramsey did either. I can understand your suspicions but you've got to believe me and, after all these years, you've got to trust me!"

Russell lowered his voice. "Pat, listen! High school, playing ball together, working together, sharing stuff we would never share with anyone else! Do you really believe I would do anything to hurt you after all we've been through?"

Pat was listening. After hearing the words and the sincerity in Russell's voice, he realized he had been wrong not to trust him. After a few seconds of looking at each other, Pat looked down at the ground, then back at Russell.

"I don't know why," he said, shaking his head, "but I do believe you."

They shook hands firmly, then spontaneously hugged each other in the way only good friends do, slapping each other on the back.

Finally, Russell said, "I think we've got to talk, and I think you're carrying a load that you don't want to carry alone. Am I right?"

Pat felt a comfort level that he hadn't experienced for several weeks. "You're right, but I can't talk right now. There're a few things I've got to sort out on my own first."

"Anytime you're ready, buddy. Come on, we've got to get to work or we'll both be looking for other jobs." Pat realized that he had said almost the same words to Rita when they met for breakfast after the incident in her apartment weeks earlier.

Russell opened the door to his BMW, jumped in and fastened his seat belt. Then Pat heard the crunch of gravel as Russell pulled off the lot and onto Rolling Road. He walked back to his old Camaro.

He got into his car but, before putting the key into the ignition, he noticed a piece of paper under the windshield wiper on the driver's side.

"Damn," he thought to himself, "probably some stupid ad." It turned out to be a napkin with writing on it. He used his body as a shield from the bright sun to read:

*Dear Mr. McGuire,*

*If you're interested in knowing where Jim Hampson is, meet me at Kibby's Restaurant tonight at seven.*
*Don't bring anyone with you, sit at the bar and put your jacket on the stool next to you, as if you're saving it for someone.*

*A Friend*

Re-reading the note several times, he looked around the parking lot, hoping to see someone watching him, but he couldn't detect anything. Thinking it best to get rid of the note, he tore the napkin into little pieces. Walking over to a trashcan, he threw it away and drove back to work in silence.

Russell left Pat alone all day, asking him questions only when they had to do with business. He knew his friend well and knew when not to push him. They had come a long way, and he wasn't going to blow it.

At six-thirty, Pat got up from his desk, folded his jacket over his arm and walked toward the elevators. As he passed Russell's office, he was relieved to see he had gone. At the same time, he appreciated Russell's friendship. He believed his friend didn't know anything more than he said he knew.

He drove west on Wilkins Avenue toward Kibby's restaurant, which he knew very well. It was across the street from Saint Agnes Hospital, the same hospital where his parents used to take him as a child, and it wasn't too far from Mount Saint Joe. Kibby's had built a reputation for the best shrimp salad in town.

Pat drove in silence, thinking, and soon found himself in the restaurant. A short young host greeted him, "Good evening, sir, one for dinner?"

"No, two," Pat answered. "A friend will be joining me."

"Please, follow me," the waiter said, as he turned and started to walk toward the dining room.

"Do you mind if we sit at the bar?"

"No, not at all, just make yourself comfortable," and the host led him to the bar in another room.

Pat took a seat at the bar. Taking off his jacket, he put it on the stool next to him and ordered a coke from the barmaid.

He looked at his watch. Six-fifty-two.

As he sipped his coke, he glanced unobtrusively at the few people sitting at the bar.

"Thanks for waiting for me, my friend," Pat heard a voice behind him say. He turned to face a tall, gaunt man with stooped shoulders and a beard too thin to ever be attractive. The man picked up Pat's jacket, sat down, and folded the jacket carefully on the empty stool next to him.

The barmaid walked over again. "What can I get for you?" she asked.

"I'd like to order two shrimp salad platters for my friend here and me, and bring us a couple of drafts, please."

"Okay," the barmaid said. "It'll be about ten minutes for the food." She came back immediately with two draft beers in frosted mugs.

Pat took a sip from his mug and turned to his left. "Who the hell are you?" he asked directly.

The stranger was looking at him. "In due time. I have to be sure I can trust you first."

"And you know where Jim Hampson is?"

"Yes."

"Where?"

"Again, in due time. Let's get to know each other first."

"Where did you get my name?"

The stranger changed the subject.

"I have an idea. Why don't we get a booth so we can talk in private? Miss!" he said, getting the barmaid's attention. "We're going to sit at that booth. Can you send the food over there?"

"Sure," she said.

The two dinner partners carried their beer to a booth in a far corner of the restaurant. Ralph Poupore started to speak as soon as they sat down.

"I'll tell you everything I can for now, and then we'll get together again to see if we can help each other out.

"I've been doing business with Jim Hampson for years. Without his having to tell me, I've put two-and-two together, and I think I know what's going on, and I definitely know where he is."

Pat sat in the corner of the booth, listening intently and observing that his host refused to make eye contact—a habit that irritated Pat.

His dinner companion told him that he was an attorney and that he did most of Hampson's personal legal work. And, after gaining his confidence, Hampson had approached him about the possibility of getting fraudulent identification for him and his wife, as they had plans to leave the country and establish new lives elsewhere. He told Hampson that it could be arranged and that, in fact, he could provide them with everything they would need: passports, drivers' licenses, credit cards, and the like, and that they would be authentic and untraceable. He said that he had done just that. Jim and Linda Hampson couldn't be tracked down without knowing their present names and where they were living.

"How do I fit into all of this, and how did you track me down?" Pat asked.

"Your name came up in a conversation I had with Hampson before he left."

"How?"

"Well, Hampson didn't mince his words. He told me that if I ever violated our agreement there'd be a price to pay. You were his example. After he left, I wrote your name down. I like to cover my bases. You never know when you'll need that kind of information."

"And?"

"Well, after Hampson left, a few weeks ago, I read about Ramsey's murder."

"And?"

"The paper said he was a partner at Autry, Martin & Ramsey. For some reason, I thought there might be some connection with you, so I called the office. I asked for you and when the receptionist said you were on another line, I knew I had my man. Finding you was easy."

"What's in this for you, particularly considering Hampson is dangerous?"

"At this point, let's just say I'm an impatient man. It's in my best interest, if he somehow finds it necessary to cut his little vacation short."

The two of them stopped talking when the waiter arrived with their food. They ate in silence.

Dinner was almost over, when the stranger spoke.

"I think we can help each other, Mr. McGuire." Poupore pushed a smile across his face, exposing tobacco-stained teeth. Cocking his head, he looked at Pat directly for the first time. "We'd both like to see Hampson back here—for different reasons—but we both want him back. I know who he is and where he is. If you can come up with a plan to get him back here, I'll tell you everything I know. What do you think? I need you and you need me."

Hesitating before answering, Pat cringed inside. "I might be able to come up with something, but I'm going to need some time and help."

"How much time?"

"Give me a week."

"How much help?"

"I'm not sure yet. I'll let you know after I've decided what we can do. When will I hear from you again?"

"I'll call you at exactly seven o'clock next Friday evening at your office. If I like what you've got to say, we've got a deal. If I don't like your plan, it's been a pleasure, and you got a free meal. Fair?"

"Fair," Pat answered. His dinner host asked him to leave first. A few minutes later, after watching Pat drive down Wilkens Avenue, he drove off in the opposite direction.

# Chapter Thirty–One

Later that evening.

"Hello?" It was Russell's voice.

"Russell, it's Pat."

"Hi, Pat."

"Do you have a few minutes?"

"Sure, what's up?"

"Do you think there's any chance you and I can get tomorrow off? I need to talk to you about something, and I think it'll take most of the day."

Without hesitating, and anxious to get their friendship back to normal, Russell said, "I don't see why not. We've both got a lot of comp time coming, and there's nothing all that important going on at the office."

"Good, let's meet at my apartment. It'll need to be private."

"So what's going on?"

"I can't tell you right now. I've still got a little thinking to do. But I will tell you it has to do with Jim Hampson."

"What!" Russell almost shouted.

"I don't want to talk about it on the phone. See you tomorrow about eight. I've got to go."

"Okay, but I want you to know I'm going to be thinking about this all night. I'm probably not going to get any sleep."

"It'll be worth it. See you tomorrow morning."

"Okay, Buddy."

"And, Russell."

"Yeah."

"I do believe you."

"Good."

They both hung up.

Russell pulled into Pat's apartment complex at seven forty-five the next morning. Russell took the steps two-at-a-time and Pat opened the door before he had the chance to knock.

"Come on in, Russell. I think I've got a plan that might interest you, but I'll need your help to thrash out some details."

Russell followed him into the kitchen and sat down at the table. Pat brought a cup of coffee for each of them.

"It's going to be a long day, Russell," Pat said.

It was five-thirty that evening when Pat asked, "Well, what do you think?"

Russell thought before answering. "I think we can do it. Will Rita go along with it?"

"Well, she owes me. I think she just might."

"Okay, what do you want me to do now?"

"I want you to think over everything we've talked about and patch up any holes in the plan. I'll call Rita tonight and, if she agrees, I'm going to go over everything with—whoever in the hell that guy is—on Friday, to see if he'll buy it, and I guess we go from there."

"Okay, when will I hear from you?"

"Probably sometime Friday night. I'll call you one way or the other. Listen, I've got a lot to do yet, so why don't you get out of here."

"Okay," Russell said, standing and stretching. "I'll see myself out."

Taking a deep breath, Pat picked up the wall phone and dialed the Texas number.

"Hello," came a female voice from the receiver.

"Is this the Herrera residence?"

"Yes, this is Lisa."

"Is Rita there, Lisa?"

"Yes, who's calling?"

"This is Pat McGuire."

"Hold on, Pat, I'll get her."

A few moments later.

"Hello?"

"Rita?"

"Yes, Pat, this is Rita."

"Rita, is this a good time?"

"As good as any, I guess."

"Well grab a chair, then, this is going to take a while."

Rita Herrera Davies put down the receiver, got a chair, and came back to the phone.

Half-an-hour later.

"Well, what do you think?" Pat asked.

"You've thought of everything, haven't you?"

"I really think we have. Will you help us then?"

"Oh, Pat, I don't know. It sounds like it could be dangerous. I don't know if I want to get involved in this."

"I understand, and I won't pressure you."

"When do you have to know?"

"By Thursday night. He's going to call me Friday at seven in the evening."

"Let me think about it, and I'll call you at your office on Thursday. Okay?"

"Okay."

"Good bye, Pat."

"Good bye, Rita. And Rita?"

"Yes?"

"Thanks."

On Thursday afternoon, Pat was sitting at his desk with the door closed, when his telephone rang.

"Pat McGuire speaking," he said in his business voice.

"Pat, this is Rita."

"Hello, Rita. Have you thought things over?" he asked, not bothering with small talk.

"Yes, I have."

"And?"

She hesitated before answering. "Count me in," she said, adding, "but it's only because I owe you."

"Good." Despite his uncertainty over the last few days, he somehow expected Rita's answer.

"Where do we go from here?"

"I'm not sure. I really won't know until I talk to our friend tomorrow evening. I'll call you as soon as I know anything."

"Okay. I'll wait to hear from you." She hung up before he could say anything else.

Friday evening, at exactly seven, Pat's telephone rang.

"Hello, Pat McGuire speaking."

"Hello, Pat. This is your friend. Have you come up with anything?"

"Yes. Let me shut my door."

An hour later, Pat finished talking the plan over with the man.

"Well, that's about it. What do you think?"

"I like it. I like it a lot, and I think I can arrange everything."

"What do we do now?"

"The four of us have to get together."

"When?"

"ASAP. When can you get your people together?"

"Next week, I guess."

"Good. Let's plan on meeting at seven next Friday evening."

"Okay" Pat answered. "But only under one condition."

"What's that?"

"You have to tell me who you are now—or no meeting." His voice rang with authority and confidence. After a few moments of silence, Pat said, "Well?"

"Fair enough. My name is Ralph Poupore. I'm a lawyer, and I have a Baltimore office in the professional building on Wilkens Avenue next to Saint Agnes Hospital. Do you know where that is?"

"Yes. Why don't we meet there next Friday at seven?" Pat was taking notes as they spoke.

"Okay."

Pat put his finger on the telephone cradle, waited a second for the dial tone, then punched in Rita's number in Texas.

"Hello."

"Rita, this is Pat."

"Yes, Pat. What's the story?"

"All systems are go."

"I was afraid you were going to say that."

"You'll need to fly back east next Friday for a meeting. Fly into the Baltimore airport, try to get in around six, and I'll pick you up."

"Okay, I'll see what I can do and call you later with my flight information. Anything else?"

"Not right now. I've got to go. Just call me with your arrangements."

"Okay.

He walked down the hall to Russell's office. The door was open, and he looked up before Pat had a chance to knock.

"And?" he asked.

"It's a go. We're all meeting next week at our new friend's office in Baltimore."

Pat closed Russell's door and told him everything he knew.

The next Friday evening, Russell drove Pat to the airport to pick up Rita. They drove to the upper part of the terminal, and Pat spotted her standing outside under the American Airlines, sign just as she said she would be. She was right on time and looked more beautiful than he remembered. He jumped out of the car and they squeezed so tightly, a passerby might have thought they were lovers. He opened the car door and both of them got into the back seat. He turned while Rita was saying hello to Russell. They were young and nervous and about to put an exciting, but dangerous, plan into action. They could manage only small talk on the drive to Ralph Poupore's office. On the way, Pat and Rita's hands touched.

When they pulled into the parking lot, Pat spotted Poupore waiting for him outside the front door.

"That's him."

The three of them walked toward the front door. Poupore met them halfway. "I assume this is Russell Autry and Rita Herrera?" he asked, without shaking hands or exchanging pleasantries.

"Yes," Pat answered, "and this is Ralph Poupore."

"Follow me," Poupore said. "The receptionist and everyone else has left. I didn't think it would be a good idea to be seen together. That's why I scheduled this meeting on a Friday night."

Pat, Russell, and Rita followed him into his office. He closed the door, "You can talk in here. My office is soundproof."

They sat in front of his desk, and the meeting lasted over two hours. Near the end, Poupore pulled a brown envelope out of his lap drawer, opened it, and spread the contents on his desk.

"These are exact duplicates of Linda Hampson's new identification," he said, handing several items to Rita. "Her passport, driver's license and credit card all have her picture on them. What are you going to do?"

Rita studied the passport photograph of Linda Hampson. "I think I can pull it off," she said. "I know a hairdresser and cosmetologist in Dallas who can do wonders." She continued to study the ID. "Fortunately, we're about the same height and weight. Our eyes are different colors, but any optometrist can fix that with colored contact lenses. It'll take a little time, but I think it can be done."

Pat and Russell were impressed with Rita's confidence.

As she took notes, she continued. "In the meantime, I'll memorize everything on this ID and practice her signature." She could see that they were curious, so she looked around and said, "I just made a note to myself. Linda Hampson wears an engagement ring and a wedding band. I'll get my old wedding rings and wear them on the trip." She looked up at Pat and Russell before glancing at Poupore. "Don't worry, I think I have everything I need except one thing."

"What's that?" Poupore asked.

"Money."

"How much do you need?"

"Let me think. Round trip airfare from Dallas to Spain and Switzerland, back to Baltimore, clothes like Linda Hampson would wear or, should I say

Linda Sanchez would wear, hotel, meals and food. I think I'll need about three thousand."

Poupore immediately opened his bottom right-hand drawer, and took out his checkbook and another small brown envelope. He put them on his desk and began to write. When he was finished, he tore out the check and handed it to Rita.

"I made it out for four thousand, just in case." Then, he opened the little brown envelope, squeezing it so she could see inside. "I've already exchanged fifty dollars for pesetas. You'll need Spanish money for cab fare and tips." She shot him a quick smile.

While Rita was putting her new ID, the check, and the pesetas into one envelope, Poupore turned to Pat.

"When are you two leaving for Chicago, and how much do you need?"

Pat answered, "Only about a thousand, and we'll leave for Chicago next week. Assuming we have enough on him to convince our man, Hampson should be receiving a few surprise guests about the same time Rita leaves Spain."

"You mean Linda," Rita corrected Pat.

"Right, Linda."

Everyone smiled.

"Anything else?" Poupore asked.

"Are you absolutely sure about their bank and the account number?" Rita asked.

"Perfectly. If nothing else, I'm thorough." He reached into his middle-left drawer again, and pulled out another brown envelope. He slid the envelope across his desk to Rita. As she was opening it, he continued.

"What you have is a photocopy of a check they made payable to me for some money they owed me. You'll notice it's drawn on a Spanish bank. You can get the address of the bank once you're in Madrid. I had another associate of mine print exact duplicates of these checks. They're in the envelope, too."

Rita glanced at Pat and Russell before turning back to Poupore. "I don't believe you."

"You don't have to believe me. Just believe what you see in front of you."

"What about his other account numbers?" Pat asked. "Surely he doesn't have the whole eleven mill in a checking account!"

"Hampson and I discussed this, and I suggested that he make a series of transfers from Switzerland. I'd be surprised if it weren't all there by now.

"I'm sure you're right, but I don't think Rita, or rather Linda, should have any problem getting the other account information with the ID she has."

"Right," Russell added. "All she has to do is to get the account history from the bank manager or someone else at the bank. I have a few international clients, and I've dealt with Spanish banks lots of times. I don't see any problems."

The others nodded in agreement. When they looked back at Poupore, he was sliding business cards toward them with his right hand. "Call me at the hand-written number on this card, if any of you need me or if anything goes wrong." Pat and Russell each put a card into his wallet, and Rita put one in her purse.

After a few moments, Poupore broke the silence. "Anything else, then?"

They looked at each other in silence.

"Okay, then," Poupore said as he was getting out of his chair, "the ball's in your court, and it's up to you three now. I'll have to let you out."

They left the building from the rear entrance. Poupore was the last to leave.

"You never know who might be watching," he said, "so just get in your car, drive straight to the airport, and then home. I'll go in the opposite direction. Good luck, and I guess I'll be seeing you all again in a few weeks."

They rode back to BWI airport in silence, but this time Rita and Pat held hands firmly.

# Chapter Thirty-Two

The next day.

"Hello, Rita. How are you?" Rita Herrera Davies heard as she opened the door to the hairdressing salon.

"Hey, Sandy! Good morning. Are you ready for me? I'm a little early!"

"All set, Sweetie. Sit down here. So what are you here for today?"

"Something different," she said, opening her purse and pulling out a picture of Linda Hampson. "I want you to do my hair exactly like this."

The hairdresser took the picture, looked at it and glanced at Rita quizzically. "Why on earth would you want to do that?"

"It's a long story. This is a picture of my best friend, Linda, back east. She's getting married, and a couple of us girls are going to play a trick on her and show up at her shower looking exactly like her. It'll be a real hoot," she said, laughing.

"You're kidding."

"Nope. Serious as a heart attack. She's a practical jokester and she deserves it. Don't worry, we're not going to the wedding that way!" She laughed.

"And you want me to color that beautiful hair black?" she asked, doubtfully.

"Yep, and then I want you to cut it and style it just like hers."

"Okay, it's your head, but I don't think that color and style are you."

"Oh Sandy, where's your sense of adventure? Besides, I've always wanted to know what I'd look like as a brunette."

"Okay, Darling, but we're going to be here a while." She taped the picture of Linda Hampson to the mirror in front of Rita.

"As long as you're finished by six," she said.

"Why, hot date tonight?" she asked playfully.

"No, Nordstrom's at the Galleria closes at eight."

She was finished with her hair appointment at five forty-five and drove to the Galleria. While driving, she found herself glancing in the mirror on the sun visor, trying to get used to the change in her appearance.

At six-fifteen, she walked up to a beautiful young woman at the Lancôme cosmetics booth. Her nametag said "Donna Flournoy."

"Donna?" Rita asked.

"Yes," she answered, "and you must be Rita."

"Yes. Are you ready for me?"

"All set. Do you have the picture you were telling me about?"

"It's right here in my purse." She pulled out Linda Hampson's picture.

"Do you think you can help me match her colors and look?"

The woman studied the picture. "No problem, just sit tight while I get my color charts."

Forty-five minutes later, Rita left the Galleria Nordstrom's cosmetics department with a bag full of Lancôme cosmetics and a different face. She found her way to the women's clothing department, carefully selecting three expensive outfits that she thought Linda Hampson would have purchased for herself. Taking her time, Rita stopped to pick up coordinated shoes and accessories before leaving, laden with shopping bags.

Two days later, Rita was at the optometrist's office early.

"I'm going to have to take some measurements," the optometrist said. "Contacts need to fit just right."

"How long will this take, doctor?" she asked.

"The exam and measurements should take about half-an-hour. If everything is okay, we should have your new lenses here by Wednesday. Friday, if you want color."

"I've always wanted to try brown."

"Okay, Rita, let's go then." He turned down the lights in the examination room. "You'd look good with brown eyes."

Finished with the optometrist, Rita found her car and headed toward the address of a travel agency she had found in the telephone book. The ad highlighted the agency's specialty: international travel.

"Can I help you, Miss?" the travel agent asked Rita, as she walked up to her desk.

"Yes, I'd like to make some flight arrangements. I'm Linda Sanchez. I called you earlier."

"Please sit down while I make a few notes. By the way, hi, I'm Doris.

"What airport will you be leaving from?" the agent asked, smiling.

"Dallas—Fort Worth."

"And the date of departure?"

"Next Monday, the ninth."

"And your destination?"

"Madrid, Spain."

"What time would you like to depart?"

"You'll have to help me with that," she answered. "I'd like to arrive in Spain early in the morning. Seven or eight, their time, is preferable."

"Okay." The agent was taking notes and looking up at her occasionally. "And when will you be returning?"

"Well, I'm assuming that if I fly out Monday, I'll get to Madrid Tuesday. I'd like to leave Madrid later that day. Early in the afternoon is best."

"You're leaving the same day?" she asked, looking up curiously.

"Sort of, it's just a quick business trip. Actually, I'm not returning directly to the U.S. I want to go from Madrid to Zurich."

"Okay," said the agent, taking more notes. "That's no problem. And when will you be leaving Switzerland?"

"Around mid-day, the morning after I arrive." The travel agent looked up at Rita again, surprised.

"Listen," Rita said, wanting to avoid personal questions. "I know this sounds very unusual, but it's an emergency trip, and I really don't have much time. Maybe it would be better if I wrote down travel plans for you and let you work on it alone. They're very complicated. I'll give you my credit card number now and call you later. If the times are all right, you can just charge it and have a courier deliver the tickets to my apartment. How would that be?"

"Fine," the woman said, feeling a little embarrassed that she might have offended her customer.

"What time do you close tonight?"

"Eight. But I'll be here only until six."

"Okay, I'll call you before six."

Rita jotted down travel preferences and credit card numbers on the legal tablet the woman gave her. The agent gave Rita her business card, and Rita left the agency.

At five-thirty that night, Rita called the travel agent.

"World Wide Travel, may I help you?"

"Yeah, this is Linda Sanchez calling. I'd like to speak with Doris, please."

"Oh, good evening, Mrs. Sanchez, this is Doris. I have all the information you need. Are you ready?"

"Ready." Rita said, cradling the telephone receiver between her left ear and shoulder, making notes as the woman spoke. After about four minutes of taking notes about airlines, cities, flight numbers, and departure times, Rita put down her pen and studied the travel plans.

"How does that look, Mrs. Sanchez?"

"I think this will be fine."

"Okay, do you want me to charge both sets of tickets on your credit card?"

"Yes."

"Okay, then, I have your address, and I'll have a courier deliver them tomorrow morning. How will that be?"

"That'll be fine."

"Oh, I forgot to ask you. Will this be first class or coach?"

"First class."

"I think that's all I need, Mrs. Sanchez, and I want to thank you for your business."

"You're welcome."

"Oh, and Mrs. Sanchez."

"Yes?"

"I want to apologize for this afternoon. I should have known better."

"It's no problem, really. I understand."

"Thanks again, and don't forget us in your plans the next time."

"I won't."

"Good-bye, and don't forget your passport!" the woman said cheerfully before hanging up.

At ten forty-five the next morning, a courier handed Rita an envelope with airline tickets inside. After checking the dates and times, she put them in her purse. She was glad the travel agent had mentioned her passport.

At about the same time, Pat and Russell were walking into the Internal Revenue Service district office in Chicago.

# Chapter Thirty–Three

The next Monday. . .

"Hello, this is Pat McGuire," Rita heard him say.

"Pat, this is Rita. I'm in New York at La Guardia. My next plane leaves in twenty minutes."

"How did everything go with security and the airlines?"

"No real problems. There was absolutely no problem with the passport and the other IDs Poupore got me. He's amazing. The customs agent looked at the picture of Linda and then looked at me and asked a couple of questions but that was it. Thank God you can get colored contact lenses now, or I don't think I could have pulled this off."

"How about luggage?"

"I'm only taking one suitcase with two changes of clothes and some personal items. The agent opened it and closed it right back up. He did ask why it was such a quick trip, and I said it was emergency business. That's all he said."

"That's all?"

"That's all. How are things on your end?"

"Great," he answered. "It couldn't have gone better in Chicago. My friend took all the information that Russell and I gave him and said he'd call us back on Wednesday."

"And?"

"And he called back. The Hampsons should be getting unexpected visitors the day after you leave Spain, probably not until just before noon on Wednesday."

"Perfect. Listen, I've got to go."

"Rita?"

"Yes?"

"One more thing. When do you get back to Baltimore?"

She pulled some notes from her purse and looked at them. "Let's see, here it is. I return on Wednesday, United flight two-fourteen. I'm scheduled to arrive at six-thirty P.M., Baltimore time."

"I'll be there, and then you can fill me in on your trip."

"Fine." After a moment. "Pat, I can't wait until this is over."

"Don't worry," he said, trying to convince himself as well. He wrote a note in his desk calendar: "6:30 BWI, United Airlines flight #214."

"Thanks."

"And Rita."

"Yes?"

He wanted to say so much to her, but all he could manage was, "We couldn't have done it without you." They hung up at the same time. His heart dropped at what he couldn't say.

Rita leaned against the wall next to the telephone. She closed her eyes and bit her lip, hoping she was doing the right thing. Picking up her purse, she walked to her gate. The ticket agent at the gate was already announcing boarding procedures for the Madrid flight.

Rita Herrera Davies boarded the plane and settled into her first-class seat, relieved that no one sat in the seat next to her. She wanted more time to memorize everything on her new identification cards and to practice Linda Sanchez's signature. From the moment the plane left the boarding gate, Rita felt nervous and self-conscious. At dinner, when the flight attendant handed her a ginger ale, she clumsily tipped it as she received it, spilling a few drops in her lap. She felt that the flight attendant was staring at her at times. Her mind raced when she noticed the flight attendant talking softly into the first class galley telephone.

"Why am I doing this?" she thought.

# Chapter Thirty-Four

Almost nine hours later. . .

Rita, feeling shaky and exhausted, was one of the first passengers off the plane when it landed at Madrid's busy international terminal. Travelers rushed here and there, ready for the start of the business day, though it was still just after 1:00 AM in Dallas.

Rita went directly to the baggage claim area. As she picked up her bag and waited her turn in line at customs, adrenaline pumped through her body, pushing down her exhaustion. Finally, her bag was opened and Spanish officials examined the contents. Satisfied that she wasn't carrying any contraband, they asked for her passport and other identification. The agent examined the picture in the passport, glancing up at her several times and making her nervous.

"What brings you to Madrid, Mrs. Sanchez?" the agent asked in English, surprising her.

"A business trip."

"And how long will you be staying in Madrid?"

"Just a few hours. I leave later this evening for Zurich."

"What is your destination in Madrid?"

"I have a meeting at the Bank of Spain this morning."

"It must be an important meeting to fly all the way here for just a few hours."

"Yes, it is," she answered without emotion or offering further explanation.

"Okay, Mrs. Sanchez," the agent finally said. "Everything appears to be in order." He handed back her passport and other papers.

She asked him where the TWA counter was located, and he told her to go to the main lobby.

She walked briskly to the main lobby and waited in a short line in front of the TWA counter, until a ticket agent waved her up to the counter. She smiled at Rita and said, "How can I help you?" in Spanish.

"Do you speak English?" Rita asked.

"Yes, of course."

"I just have a small favor."

"Yes, how may I help you?"

"May I trouble you for an envelope to put this in?" She held up her ticket from Madrid to Switzerland. "I lost the ticket jacket and the envelope this came in, and I'm afraid I'm going to lose this ticket."

The woman took the ticket, looked at it briefly, and said, "Of course," as she pulled out a ticket jacket and envelope from a side drawer. "Would you like me to get you your boarding pass while you're here?"

"Yes, that would be nice," she said as the woman entered some information into the computer. A few seconds later the printer churned out a boarding pass, and the agent stapled it to the original ticket and put them into a new ticket jacket, which she put into an envelope with the TWA logo and local address in the upper left hand corner.

"There you are, Mrs. Sanchez," the woman said, handing the envelope to her. "Will there be anything else today?"

"Yes, I need to go downtown. Where can I catch a taxi?"

"No problem. Just go downstairs to the baggage claim area and go out any door."

"Thank you for your trouble. You've been very helpful."

"You're welcome. Have a nice flight to Switzerland."

Rita put the envelope in her purse and hurried to the escalator leading to the baggage claim area. Once on the ground floor, she stopped in a women's restroom.

Pulling her bags into the largest stall she could find, Rita quickly pulled out fresh clothing and high heels. Leaving the stall, she splashed her face with cold water and touched up her makeup. Pulling out Linda Sanchez's identification, she tried to brush and fluff her hair into shape. Not sure it would make the grade after the long night on the plane, she pulled it back into a tight knot, fastening it in the back with an elegant clip. She screwed on the Dior earrings and colored her lips coral red. She stood back, pleased with her appearance, made a face in the mirror as she tucked in a stray piece of hair, then grabbed up her bag and headed out the door.

The early morning fresh air felt good as she stepped outside. Finding a taxi stand, she stood in line behind three other people. After waiting a few minutes, Rita climbed into a cab.

"Where to Señora?" the driver asked in Spanish.

"Do you speak English?" Rita asked.

"Yes, Señora," he answered in English with a noticeable accent, adding, "Where can I take you?"

"The Bank of Spain, please, the main branch."

Rita climbed into the back seat of the cab while the driver put her bag into the trunk. "Si," the driver said, and pulled out into traffic.

Rita allowed herself to settle back into the taxi's worn seat and to relax and feel the weight of her tiredness during the short drive to the bank. She contemplated her situation. Here she was—in a foreign country with identification that was not hers. She couldn't even speak Spanish. Her real identification and passport were hidden in a pocket she had sewn on the inside of her dress. She began to wonder what would happen to her if she were somehow caught. Absorbed in thought, she didn't even notice the taxicab pulling to a stop at the curb.

"Señora, Señora!" she heard. Startled she looked up to see the driver turned around in his seat, facing her.

"We are here, Señora."

"I'm sorry. It's been a long trip." As the words came out of her mouth, she realized that this was the only small talk in which she had engaged since leaving Dallas the day before.

The driver took her luggage from the trunk and opened her door. She pressed a hefty tip into his hand.

"Gracias, Señora!"

Suddenly, Rita realized that walking into a bank to close out a sizeable account with luggage would look very suspicious. Despite all the planning she had done with Pat, Russell, and Poupore, no one thought about her luggage. She was sorry she hadn't left it in a locker at the airport.

She thought for a moment, then called to the driver, who was opening his car door, "Sir?"

"Yes?"

"My appointment shouldn't take too long. Would you please wait here for me and take me back to the airport? I'll make it worth your while."

"How long will you be, Señora?"

"I can't imagine this taking longer than an hour."

"I will wait right here for you," he said, extending one of his hands. "Would you like for me to watch your luggage?"

"Yes, please." She handed him her bag, which he put back into the trunk. He returned to the driver's seat, turned off the illuminated light on the cab's roof, and opened a book.

After assuring herself that the driver would wait, Rita walked slowly toward the front door of the Bank of Madrid's main branch. Pushing the glass doors open, she walked into the lobby, approaching the first available teller.

"May I help you, Señora," the teller asked in Spanish.

"Do you speak English?"

"Yes, how may I help you?"

"I need to speak to someone in the wire-transfer department." Rita's heart was pounding, but her voice was calm and steady.

"Yes, Señora, please have a seat. Someone will be right with you."

She eased herself into one of the over-stuffed chairs against the wall, crossed her legs, and picked up a magazine from the table. She began to glance through it, even though it was written in Spanish.

After a few minutes, a tall well-dressed man walked up to her.

"May I help you?" he asked in perfect English.

"Yes," Rita said as she stood up and put the magazine back on the table. "My name is Linda Sanchez, and I need to speak to someone about transferring funds. Are you the right person?"

"Yes," he answered. "My name is Jose Travino. I am the bank's wire-transfer specialist. Please come into my office." He turned and walked slowly down a hallway toward his office. Rita followed him, too nervous to notice her surroundings, her heart still pounding.

"Please have a seat, Mrs. Sanchez." He gestured to a chair across from a large wooden desk. As she was taking her seat, he closed his door, walked behind his desk, and sat down. All his movements seemed studied, deliberate, and formal. He moved some papers to one side, put his elbows on the desk, clasped his fingers, looked up to her, and said, "Now then, what may I do for you."

Rita took another deep breath, hoping he wouldn't notice how nervous she was. "I need to close out the accounts that my husband and I have here at your bank, Mr. Travino, and wire transfer the balance to a new account that we would like to open in Switzerland."

"Fine, Mrs. Sanchez. May I trouble you for some information?" he asked, as he pulled a pen and paper from his desk drawer.

"Of course," Rita answered, bracing herself, hoping to remember all of the details.

"What is your full name?"

"Linda Sanchez."

"Any middle name?" he asked while he was writing.

"No," she answered. She knew that no middle name for Linda Sanchez appeared in any of the identification papers that Poupore had furnished her. She secretly prayed that Linda hadn't used a middle name to open the bank account.

"And your husband's name?" he asked.

"Jim Sanchez."

"The account number?" he asked, still writing and not looking up.

She reached into her purse, pulling out one of the duplicated checks Poupore had printed for her.

"Here is one of our checks, if that will help," she said, handing it to the banker.

"Thank you," he said, taking the check from her.

"Just a moment while I bring it up on my computer screen." He turned in his chair and entered the account number from the check on his keyboard. Rita could tell immediately that he had been trained not to remark on the size of a balance when it appeared.

"Mrs. Sanchez, you and your husband have four accounts at the bank. Do you wish to close out only the checking account?"

"No, all of them, please."

"You would like to close out all of the accounts and transfer all of the balances?"

"Yes. I would like to transfer the money to an account I'd like you to open for me in Switzerland."

"Which bank in Switzerland?" he asked.

"The Trust Bank of Switzerland," she answered. "It's in Zurich."

"And you say that you don't have an account there now?"

"That's correct. Is there a problem?"

The bank officer turned toward her and hesitated a moment before answering. "Mrs. Sanchez, I'm afraid I'm going to have to get my supervisor."

"Why?" she asked, feeling her heart beginning to pound again.

"The total of the accounts is beyond my authority to transfer. The available balance is over ten million U.S. dollars."

"I realize that."

The bank officer stood up and said, "Mrs. Sanchez, if you wouldn't mind waiting here, I should be only a few minutes. Would you care for a coffee or anything while you wait?"

"No, I'm fine, but thank you."

He smiled and walked out of the office, closing the door behind him.

When she was alone, she realized the magnitude of what she was trying to do, and her anxiety level rose. Her head started to ache and, as the minutes passed, she began to have doubts.

*What if he's calling Jim Hampson?* she thought to herself. *What if this is some kind of elaborate set up?* She thought of walking out of the bank and taking the cab back to the airport.

When the door finally opened, she was startled to see the bank officer come in with an older man and a uniformed police officer.

"Mrs. Sanchez?" the older man said.

"Yes, I'm Linda Sanchez."

"Mrs. Sanchez, my name is Roberto Lopez, and I'm the senior vice-president of the bank, and I'm going to have to ask you to come with me."

"Where are we going?" Her mind was racing now. She repeated the phrase *keep calm* over-and-over to herself.

"Just to my office. There's no reason to be concerned. It's just that we'll have more room in there. Please follow me." The tone of his voice was serious but kind.

"Before we go, what is the police officer for?" she asked.

"Just for security. It's not every day that people close out accounts of this size. I'm sure you understand that it's for your protection and the bank's security. Please follow me."

The four of them walked down the paneled hall to the senior vice-president's office. The vice-president extended his left arm, to allow Rita in first. He closed the office door behind him and asked everyone to have a seat.

"Mrs. Sanchez, before we can help you, we're going to have to ask you a few questions, if you don't mind, of course."

Rita concentrated on staying composed despite her nervousness and looked Mr. Lopez directly in the eye. She knew she didn't have any choice but to answer his questions.

"No, I don't mind," she said, unruffled, while repeating the only words she could think of—*keep calm*—to herself.

"Why are you transferring your funds?" he asked.

"My husband is an international business man, and he has been transferred to Switzerland. He moves like this often."

"I see. Where is your husband now?"

"He is already en route. I'm leaving for Switzerland right after I leave here to meet him."

"Can I trouble you to see your airline ticket, then?" he asked with a smile.

"Certainly." She calmly reached into her purse and pulled out the envelope that the ticket agent had given her at the airport earlier. "Here you are," she said, as she handed him the envelope with the TWA logo on it and the Madrid, Spain, return address.

"Thank you." He opened the envelope and pulled out the ticket jacket. He looked at the ticket for a moment, examining the address on the envelope, as well as the name and destination noted on the ticket. He put the ticket back into the envelope, but kept it.

"Is everything in order?" she asked.

"It's fine. Thank you. May we trouble you for your identification, please?"

Rita opened her purse again, pulling out the identification papers Poupore had given her. The bank executive laid the documents on the desk in front of him. Examining each document carefully, particularly the passport and the driver's license, he looked up occasionally to compare the photographs to the face of the woman sitting in front of him.

After he finished his examination, he handed the documents to the police officer who repeated the procedure. The officer took longer than the bank executive, but finally handed them back to him without saying a word. He slowly nodded.

Then the bank executive pulled a form from his drawer, and slid it across the table to Linda Sanchez. Pulling a pen from his pocket, he handed it to her.

"Would you please sign this document in our presence, Mrs. Sanchez? We'll fill in the information later."

Wordless, she looked for the signature line, pushed in the tip of the ball point pen and, confidently and without hesitating, signed *Linda Sanchez*. As she was handing the document and pen back to the executive, she was thinking how grateful she was to have had the long hours on the flight to Madrid to practice Linda Sanchez's signature.

The bank executive took the form and compared the signature to those on the passport and driver's license. He then handed the documents back to the police officer to examine them. The officer returned them, and the two men looked at each other again, without saying a word. The bank executive turned back in his chair.

"We have only one more thing to do, Mrs. Sanchez."

"What's that?"

"We're going to ask the branch that services the account to send over a copy of the original signature cards by facsimile."

"Fine," she said.

"Mr. Travino," he said, addressing the wire-transfer specialist, "would you please contact the branch for a copy of their signature cards?"

"Yes, sir, it will take only a moment," Jose Travino said as he left.

"So, Mrs. Sanchez," the bank executive said, trying to make small talk while they waited, "you and your husband are moving to Switzerland?"

"Yes," she said quietly. "Unfortunately, we find ourselves moving quite often. We have to go where the business is. I'm sure you understand."

"Of course," he said. "And what type of business is your husband in?"

Before answering, she thought for a moment. Poupore had prepared her for this question.

"He is a security consultant. Very technical and confidential, I'm afraid."

"I see. And where will you be living in Switzerland? I spent some time there myself."

Her mind raced again before she answered this one. She wasn't prepared for this question. "We're not sure yet. We're going to stay in a hotel for a while until I find a place for us to live."

"I see."

Jose Travino walked through the door at that moment and handed the bank executive a piece of paper. "Here they are, sir."

The bank executive and police officer huddled over the documents together, carefully studying the signatures on the bank slip, the passport, the driver's license, and now, the bank's signature cards. After a few minutes of silence, the police officer looked at the bank executive, again nodding. Already, Rita Herrera Davies, alias Linda Sanchez, was feeling relieved.

"Everything seems to be in order, Mrs. Sanchez," he said. He stood up, extending his hand across the desk to her. "Please accept my apology for the trouble we have caused you. Please do not take our precautions personally."

"Of course not, Mr. Lopez. I understand perfectly."

"Thank you. All we have to do now is to make copies of your identification for our files and we can honor your request." He then turned to the wire-transfer agent. "Mr. Travino, you may go ahead with this. We'll need copies of Mrs. Sanchez's identification for our files." He handed everything to the younger man.

"Yes, sir," he said. "Mrs. Sanchez, please come with me."

The two of them were walking back to his office when he said, "And where did you say we would be transferring your funds?"

"The Trust Bank of Switzerland."

"Good. We work with them all the time."

Fifteen minutes later, he gave her a receipt for the transfer of funds, her ticket, and all of her identification. She put them in a zippered compartment in her purse and left the bank.

She was relieved to see her cab still waiting. She opened the rear passenger door, startling the driver, who had fallen asleep over his open book. "Sorry, Señora," he said, turning toward her. "I didn't notice you."

"That's okay," she said, closing the door. "Thank you for waiting for me."

"And you would like me to take you back to the airport now?"

"Yes, the TWA terminal, please."

As the airport came into sight, she reached into her purse to pull out money to pay the driver. She was feeling generous, and the time that the driver spent waiting for her was worth much more than his regular fee.

Neither Rita nor the driver had noticed a car with a male driver and woman passenger following them from the airport. It had parked only two spaces behind them at the bank.

When Rita had entered the bank, a young, curly-headed woman had been close behind her, unobtrusively observing her movements. Then the car followed the taxi back to the airport, where the woman was dropped off in front of the terminal.

In less than an hour, Rita passed through security and was boarding a twelve-thirty flight for Zurich.

The woman who had been following Rita was now sitting three seats behind her. The woman noted that, after getting comfortable in her seat, Rita asked the flight attendant for paper and an envelope. The attendant found paper, but not an envelope. Rita wrote busily during the short flight.

Back in Baltimore, Pat worried about Rita and couldn't get her off his mind.

# Chapter Thirty-Five

By four in the afternoon, Rita was tucking herself into bed in her Zurich hotel room. She had indulged herself with a late lunch in her room, and now, her body spent, she planned to sleep as long as she could before her Wednesday morning bank meeting.

At the same time, Dave Lovelady sat alone in his office at the National Tobacco Federation's headquarters in Washington, D.C. His door was locked, even though he was sure he was alone. Waiting for the phone to ring, he absentmindedly tapped the point of a pencil on the top of his coffee mug. Startling him, the phone finally rang. "Lovelady here," he said.

"Mr. Dave Lovelady?" a male voice asked.

"Yes, this is Dave Lovelady."

"Mr. Lovelady, I'm an operator with ESI telephone service, and I'm co-ordinating an international conference call. Will you please stand by while I ensure that all parties are properly connected?"

"Yes."

"Mr. Lovelady has just been connected to the conference call, gentlemen. Mr. Barber, are you still on the line?"

"Yes," Kerry Barber answered.

"Mr. Cristie, are you still on the line?"

"Yes," Stewart Cristie replied.

"Mr. Chase, are you still connected?"

"Here," Ken Chase answered.

"Mr. Byrd, are you still there?"

"I'm here," Duane Byrd said.

"Gentlemen, all parties are connected and on the line," the operator said. "I'll excuse myself now so you can have a private conversation. Is that acceptable to all parties?"

Five voices answered.

"Thank you for choosing ESI," the operator said. "After I disconnect, your charges will start."

Everyone heard the click and Lovelady began.

"Gentlemen, I thought it would be a good idea to give you a status report on what has happened since our meeting in Vegas when Hampson split. Unless I hear otherwise, I assume each of us is alone and that this conversation is confidential."

Silence.

"Okay, then." Lovelady leaned back in his chair, looking up at the ceiling as he spoke.

"As we all know, Hampson did exactly what he said he was going to do. He faxed in his resignation to the Federation board the following Monday. As a board member, I got a call from Ira Gagnon that afternoon."

"Who's Ira Gagnon?" Stewart Cristie asked.

"The Federation's chairman," Ken Chase said, answering for Lovelady.

"Anyway," Lovelady continued, a little annoyed that Ken Chase had answered for him, "Gagnon called an emergency board meeting at the Federation's offices and, of course, I was there."

"And what happened?" Duane Byrd asked.

"Listen," Lovelady said, sitting up right in his chair and letting his agitation come through the phone. "Listen, let's hold the questions or we'll be here all night! Please let me get through this, and then I'll field questions. Does anyone have a problem with that?"

When no one answered, he smiled, pleased with himself for asserting his new authority.

He continued telling them about the meeting, explaining that four members of the CPA firm who had audited them were there, as was Rita Davies and the Federation's attorney.

He told them again about the eleven million dollars Hampson had transferred to a Swiss Bank. He explained that he had put all new locks on the filing cabinets so only he had access. He then explained how he personally handled every piece of paper in every file, hoping Hampson had gotten careless somehow and left a clue. Finally, he told them that Hampson had left one clue, a file implicating one of the CPA firm's partners.

"He was helping Hampson with the little slush fund that we set up with the fake dues invoices; a fellow by the name of Ramsey."

"What did you do about that?" one of the five asked.

"I confronted him. I thought that, since he was in bed with Hampson on the slush fund bit and didn't tell me, he was probably the guy Hampson told us about who was keeping those fucking tapes for him."

"How did Ramsey react?" Barber asked.

"At first, he denied any involvement at all, of course, but when I showed him what I had, he came around and told me everything he knew about the money. I pushed him real hard about the tapes, even threatening him, but he swore he didn't know anything about any tapes."

"And?" someone else asked.

"And," Lovelady sighed, "I believed him."

"So, what did you do?"

"I had to get rid of him. He knew way too much at that point, and I didn't have any choice."

"What do you mean *you got rid of him*?" Ken Chase asked.

"I mean his body is now at room temperature, Ken," Lovelady said sarcastically. "He's dead, what else do you think 'I had to get rid of him' could mean? Shit!"

"Christ, Dave," Duane Byrd said. "Was that necessary? I never thought we would be getting into anything like this!"

"Listen," Lovelady said loudly, reasserting his authority. "I didn't have any choice, and you know it, Duane! Do you people want to go to prison? Engaging in price-fixing is serious shit! What if Ramsey had put two-and-two together, gotten frightened, and gone to the authorities? He was just an accountant for God's sake!"

Silence.

Finally, one of them asked, "How did you do it? Since we're all involved now, I think we have a right to know."

Lovelady waited a few moments before answering. "Do you remember when we were in Colorado and Hampson told us that one of the accountants auditing the Federation was there?"

"Yeah."

"Well, if you recall, we all directed Hampson to get him off the audit, and I was the one who said I knew someone who could take care of it, right?"

"Yeah, and . . ."

"I used the same guy! Simple."

"What happened."

"He shot him. Very clever how he did it. Anyway, Ramsey is no longer a factor, I assure you," Lovelady said calmly.

Another silence.

"Listen, everybody," Duane Byrd said, breaking the silence. "I don't want any part of this. I want out! All of this is too much for me."

"Now, you listen, Duane," Lovelady commanded, suddenly standing, though no one else was in the room. "You're up to your ass in this, just like the rest of us, and you can't get out. We're way beyond the point of no-return on this. Understand?" he asked, not expecting an answer. "Anyway, Ramsey is no longer an issue."

"What else?" Byrd asked.

"That's all I could find, and believe me, I went through every piece of paper in the place."

Lovelady was calm and in control again.

"Where do you think Hampson is?" someone asked.

"Absolutely no idea," Lovelady answered. "There is no trace of him or his wife, and I've checked everything. All we know is that he is gone, he's got a lot of Federation money, and even if we do find him, I don't know what we could do!"

"Why?" Barber asked.

"Don't forget, somebody else has those tapes. I don't think Hampson is bluffing either. If anything happens to him, his little confidante is going to the authorities at the Department of Justice with those tapes, and we're up shit's creek anyway!"

A long silence.

Finally, someone said, "Do you think anyone else could be involved with Hampson, Dave? You know, women or anything like that?"

"The only other one that could be involved might be his secretary, Rita Davies."

"Well?"

"She resigned shortly after I took over, but I got to tell you, she worked her ass off for me while she was here, and if there was any involvement, she was pretty cool about it."

"What do you think?"

"At this point, I don't think so, or Hampson would have taken care of her or taken her with him. I looked at her personnel file and it was clean."

"Why did she leave then?"

"She said stress, and I believed her."

"You believed Ramsey, too," Cristie said. "The only people who know what she knows are she and Hampson. I don't think we can let her off the hook just yet."

"I agree," Barber said.

"Same," Chase said.

Pause.

"What about you, Duane?" Lovelady said. "Don't forget you're in this as much as the rest of us, whether you agree or not."

Silence.

"Well?" Lovelady asked, in a louder voice.

"I guess I don't have any choice," Duane Byrd said, after a sigh.

"Good," Lovelady said.

"What do you think we should do, Dave?" Chase asked.

"I'm not sure yet," he answered. "Give me some time to sort this out, but I'll take care of her."

Pause.

"Well gentlemen, I guess that's it for now," Lovelady said. "You know as much as I do at this point, and I know what I've got to do."

"Not quite, Dave," Barber said. "There is one last little matter."

"What?"

"What about that accountant who saw Hampson in Colorado? What's the story with him?"

"Oh, I'm sure he's not involved," Lovelady answered. "Hampson took care of him after Colorado. If anything was going on with him, I'm sure he would have tipped his hand by now. He's not an issue."

"Don't be so sure, Dave," Cristie said. "He saw Hampson in Colorado, a lot of money is missing, and his boss was murdered, not to mention Hampson's skipping. I think we've got a little more to discuss here."

"I agree," Barber said. "I'm not telling you what to do, Dave, but I'm afraid this young man is a big concern, and I'm not comfortable. The way I see it, both he and the woman are a problem."

This time Lovelady sighed. "What do you think I should do?"

Silence.

"Anyone?" Lovelady asked.

"Let me tell you what I think," Kerry Barber said. "Another hit is out of the question. Listen, we've got a murder, the feds are suspicious about to-bacco prices and, on top of that, we've got a major embezzlement. Another hit and the bullshit is going to be at high tide, and we all know it. We've got to get rid of both of them, but a hit is not the way."

"What do you think we should do then, Kerry?" someone asked.

"An accident. Or two accidents, maybe," Barber answered. "Who knows, a hit and run, a drug overdose, a fire, who knows. Anything, but not an obvious hit."

Another pause.

"I hate to tell you, but I agree," Duane Byrd said. "There's too much at stake here to take a chance."

Lovelady was listening to the conversation, nervously drumming his fingers on the table.

Finally someone said, "Can you take care of it, Dave?"

Lovelady answered slowly. "Yes, I can take care of it. I guess I'm going to have another meeting with our friend to discuss our options."

"Okay, then, when do we meet again?"

"I don't know just yet," Lovelady answered. "Let me handle the other problems, and I'll get back to you.

Unless anyone has anything else, let's call it a day. I've got a lot to do."

"Dave," Christie said.

"Yes?"

"Give it some time. I don't think Ramsey's murder should be too closely connected."

"Just do it," someone else said.

Lovelady heard four clicks before hanging up his own phone. He took a deep breath, picked up the receiver and dialed another number.

After two rings, he heard a male voice say, "Yeah?"

"Is this Lombardo?"

"Yeah. Who's this?"

"Dave Lovelady."

"What do you need, Dave? I didn't think I was going to hear from you again."

Lovelady hesitated a moment before beginning, taken aback by Lombardo's sudden informality.

"Dave? What do you mean 'Dave'? Whatever happened to Mr. Lovelady? After all I am still the boss here, right?"

This time Lombardo hesitated, "Let's just say I'm more comfortable with Dave. I hope you don't have a problem with my calling you by your first name."

Lovelady was taken aback once more and knew Lombardo's question was really a statement. Was Lombardo somehow establishing some sort of power over him? He wanted to get the issue settled but came to the conclusion that he would be wasting valuable time on something trivial. He decided to take care of the matter later.

"Are you interested in more work?"

"Always. What you got?"

"Not on the phone. We've got to meet in person."

"When and where?"

Consulting his desk calendar, Lovelady thought for a moment.

"Well, let's make it for the end of the month. This is important, and I want to be sure you're free to handle it. How about the evening of October 26th at eight?"

"Where?"

"How about Blackies' in Washington?"

"I'd rather go to Ruth's Chris."

Once again Lovelady was surprised but felt it wise to settle the situation at another time.

"Baltimore or D.C.?"

"The new one in Annapolis. No one has ever seen us together there."

"I'll be there."

Lovelady heard the dial tone and spent the next half-hour deep in thought, wondering why he was suddenly feeling so uneasy.

# Chapter Thirty-Six

Rita stood downstairs at the hotel, showered, refreshed, and looking lovely. An elegant brown-and-orange scarf gracefully draped the collar of her tailored, taupe-colored dress. A porter rushed to take her bag, escorting her to the downtown taxi stand.

Within minutes, Rita was sitting in the lobby of the Trust Bank of Switzerland. A tall, blonde woman approached her, speaking German. Rita smiled at the woman. "Do you speak English?"

"Yes, of course." Her English was perfect. "My name is Elsa. How may I help you?"

"I've just transferred money here from an account in Madrid. I'd like to discuss my options with someone."

"I'm sure I can help you. Please come with me, madam."

Rita followed Elsa to her office and sat down. Elsa closed the door, pushed a stack of papers to one side, and courteously waited for Rita to settle herself.

"Now, what may I do for you, madam?" she inquired.

Rita opened her purse and took out a piece of paper, handing it to the woman. "This is a receipt for funds I transferred here yesterday from Spain."

The woman took the paper, studied it, and started typing information into her computer. A few seconds later, she said, "Yes, it's here. Now, what would you like to do?"

Closing her eyes for a moment, trying to conceal a surge of relief, she said, "I'm leaving soon, and I need to discuss what my options are."

"Yes, madam."

"I want to withdraw some funds now, in American dollars, and leave the balance of the funds here, until I've had an opportunity to open another account—somewhere else. Is that possible?"

"Of course, madam. How much would you like?"

"Twenty-five thousand dollars," Rita hoped she appeared calm—even nonchalant.

Elsa seemed a little taken aback. "All in cash, Mrs. Sanchez?"

"I don't understand."

"Most of our customers who make major withdrawals prefer traveler's checks. Perhaps take three thousand in cash and the rest in traveler's checks? It would be much safer that way."

"I think you're right. Why don't you give me five thousand in cash and twenty thousand in traveler's checks?"

"I do hope I haven't offended you, madam."

"Not at all. I appreciate your concern."

Elsa pulled a withdrawal slip and checked the computer screen several times as she filled out the form. "Please sign here, if you will."

Rita carefully signed "Linda Sanchez" in Linda Hampson's handwriting. Elsa scanned the withdrawal slip and then looked up at Rita. "I don't believe it!"

Rita felt herself flushing, feeling the same sensations she experienced in Spain when she transferred the funds.

"What's the problem?" Once again, she concentrated on remaining calm.

"I should've asked you to sign the bank's signature cards and other paperwork first. I'm so sorry."

"I understand," Rita swallowed to stop the thumping in her throat. "I make mistakes too."

"I apologize," the woman said, reaching back into her desk drawer. "This should take only a few minutes."

Rita waited patiently as Elsa typed in account numbers and other information on several bank forms.

"Would you sign each form, madam?" She pointed to signature lines. When Rita had finished signing, Elsa separated the papers into two stacks, folding one stack neatly and putting it into an envelope. "These are your copies. Obviously, they're very important, and I'd suggest putting them in a safe deposit box or some place secure when you return. Here is a set of blank cards. I suggest you add someone else on the account in the event of an emergency. What you're signing now will be sufficient for you to make transactions, though, until these are returned with additional signatures."

"Thank you." She put the envelope into her purse, making a mental note to add it to the identification papers already in her concealed dress pocket.

Elsa stood up. "Please make yourself comfortable while I process your traveler's checks and obtain your cash. May I get you a refreshment while you are waiting?"

"No, thank you, I'm fine." At last, she was alone with a little time to collect herself.

About five minutes later, Elsa returned. With a card dealer's skill, she carefully counted out five thousand American dollars and twenty thousand in traveler's checks. She placed the cash into an envelope and the checks into a flat, plastic wallet that Rita slid safely into her purse. Elsa handed Rita copies of the traveler's checks in a separate envelope.

"You can cash the original checks anywhere in the world, and I suggest that you keep your copies in a safe place, but not with the originals. That way, if the originals are ever lost or stolen, you'll have a record of the numbers, and you can file a claim at almost any bank for the lost checks. They'll take care of you. Have I made it clear?" she smiled.

"Thank you, I'll be sure to do that."

"Now what else can I do for you, Madam?"

Immediately, Rita said, "I'm going to leave the balance of my account here until I've had an opportunity to open another bank account elsewhere."

"You wish to leave the funds here?" the woman asked without expression or emotion.

"Yes, you have attractive rates, and it's my understanding that I can benefit from the exchange rate and tax laws if interest is earned here. Is that correct?"

"Yes, and we will send you monthly statements. Our policy is not to violate the confidentiality of your account by reporting information to anyone but the account holder."

"That's fine. What do I have to do?"

"Well," the woman said, "the account has already been opened in your name, and funds are available. You have a receipt for your account balance and instructions on how to transfer funds to your bank elsewhere. It's very simple as long as the other bank has an agreement with us, and most banks do." The woman smiled.

"Please relax while I get you a listing of the reciprocal banks we use in other countries. I should be only a few minutes."

Rita sat back in her chair after she heard the woman close the office door. A slight smile crossed her face when she realized how much easier it was to open an account than it was to close one.

A few minutes later, she heard the office door open and she turned in her chair. She was surprised to see Elsa standing there with another, older woman.

"Mrs. Sanchez?" the older woman asked.

"Yes?" Rita said, feeling the familiar pounding in her heart once again.

"Please don't get up. My name is Gretchen Leboff. I'm a senior vice-president, and Elsa here just informed me that you were the person who transferred the money yesterday."

"Yes. Is there anything wrong?"

"Oh, no," the woman said. "I just like to introduce myself to our major accounts. I want you to feel free to contact me if there is anything I can do for you," she said smiling.

"Thank you, Miss Leboff," Rita said, taking her card and putting it in her purse. "I appreciate your courtesy. Elsa has been very helpful to me."

Her business finished, Rita started walking toward the door when she stopped and turned around. "I almost forgot, Elsa, may I ask a favor of you?"

"Of course."

"May I trouble you for an envelope?"

"That's no trouble at all. I'll get one right away."

As the woman was walking away, Rita opened her purse and searched for a pen. She pulled out the letter she had written on the plane and folded it neatly.

Elsa returned with a white envelope. "I assume you would prefer one without the bank's return address."

"Perfect." Rita said, impressed with the woman's perception. She wrote an address on the envelope, put in her letter, and sealed it.

"Would you like me to mail that for you, Madam?"

"Would you, please? I'm afraid I'm tight on time, and I don't have any Swiss stamps." Before handing the envelope back, Rita opened her purse to give her some money. Elsa told her not to bother, assuring her that it would be in the mail that day.

Rita thought for a moment, reaching back into her purse and taking out a one-hundred-dollar bill. "Elsa, I have a very big favor to ask."

"Of course, anything."

"I insist that you take this money and use it to mail that letter today, overseas priority. It's very important."

"I'll be happy to, Madam, but it won't cost nearly this much." She tried to return the money but Rita had already closed her purse and slipped the strap over her shoulder.

"I insist and I won't take no for an answer. I appreciate the favor and you keep the difference." Rita smiled.

The woman smiled back at Rita with a somewhat frustrated look, but she saw that her new customer meant what she said.

Four minutes later, Rita was in a taxi on her way to the Zurich airport. Shortly she would be on the way to her destination.

As in Spain, all of her movements were being carefully observed without her knowledge.

# Chapter Thirty-Seven

Late the same morning, two Spanish police cars were parked on the top of a hill with a view of Jim and Linda Hampson's leased villa. In each car were two Spanish police officers and one U.S. marshal. An officer in each car was looking at the villa through binoculars.

"That's our man," one of the officers said.

"Are you sure?" his partner asked.

"Positive. Look for yourself." The other officer trained the binoculars on the man now walking down his front steps and toward a new BMW parked in the driveway. After squinting through the eyepiece for a few moments, he put the binoculars in his lap and looked at the photograph that lay between them on the front seat.

He handed the binoculars to the marshal, who, after observing Hampson for a few seconds, handed them back and said, "That's him." The marshal didn't have to look at the picture.

"Any sign of his wife?" the first officer asked.

"No. He must be going somewhere alone."

"Good. It's better this way. Why don't we escort Mr. Hampson and have our friends in the other car call on Mrs. Hampson. What do you think?"

"Fine," the second officer said, as he picked up the hand-held Motorola radio and spoke into it.

"Sixty-five, this is two-fourteen, do you copy? Over."

"Go ahead, two-fourteen," came the response from the small speaker inside the radio.

"Hampson left alone. We're going to follow him while you visit Mrs. Hampson and wait for us to come back. Do you copy?"

"We copy. Should we proceed with the paperwork?"

"Affirmative. Watch the house for about five minutes to be sure she doesn't duck out the back door or something."

"We copy."

The first car followed Hampson's BMW inconspicuously as he drove downtown alone. Five minutes later, the police officer in the second car drove up to the Hampson's villa, parking the cruiser in the driveway beside the house.

Two officers and the second marshal got out of their car and walked to the front door. The marshal rapped the circular brass door knocker several times, while the police officers stood by each side of the door, with their hands on their service revolvers.

"Senora Sanchez, the door—ah, someone to see you," a young, olive-complexioned maid called out the open patio French doors to Linda Hampson.

Linda, surprised and uneasy, got up from her poolside lounge chair. Pushing her feet into her white clogs, she quickly slipped a terry wrap over her swimsuit. Jim and Linda had barely acknowledged their neighbors since their arrival; she wasn't sure she'd even recognize them. Who could be visiting? Linda anxiously wished Jim would get back. Catching a clog on a hallway rug and almost tripping, she headed nervously toward the open front door.

No, she did not recognize the strangers standing on her porch. She glanced over to the police car.

"Yes, may I help you? Is there anything wrong?" she asked with a puzzled look on her face.

"Are you Linda Hampson?" the marshal asked.

"I'm Linda Sanchez," she answered, feeling her face flush as she told the lie that she somehow knew was unraveling.

"Mrs. Sanchez," the officer said, "I'm afraid we have to ask you a few questions. May we come in?"

"I'd rather you waited until my husband returns," she said tersely.

"Where is your husband now?"

"He just went to the bank. He'll be back in less than half-an-hour."

"I'm sorry, but this can't wait. May we come in?" he asked again.

"No. You'll have to wait until he's back."

The marshal reached into his breast pocket, pulled out a piece of paper, and handed it to her.

"Mrs. Sanchez," he said, "this is an order of deportation which mandates that we to take you and your husband with us."

Taking the paper from him she began to read but, after glancing at the first few lines, she handed the paper back to the marshal.

"I'm sorry, but you'll have to wait for my husband." Growing more and more anxious, she wanted to slam the door and run inside to the safety of the house.

"Mrs. Sanchez, you don't understand. These are our orders to take you and your husband with us."

"Why?" Her voice was curt and sharp. "We haven't done anything wrong. Why in the world do we have to go with you?"

"Let's put it this way. A warrant has been issued for your arrest, and because you are American citizens on Spanish soil, we make the arrest with Spanish authorities. Officials at the American embassy will explain the rest to you. Now, may we come in?"

Feeling trapped and scared, she choked down the tears that were welling-up and opened the door. She led the men to the living room, where they sat on the sofa and she perched on the edge of a leather chair.

"What do we do now?" she asked.

"Please just sit with us until your husband returns from the bank," the marshal said.

"Do you mind if I smoke?" she asked, pulling back into her seat.

"Go right ahead." The marshal patted his breast pocket for a book of matches, but she had already reached for the lighter on the table beside her. "We have just one more question," he said.

"Yes?" Her fingers were shaking, as she lit her cigarette and inhaled deeply.

"Are there any weapons in the house?"

"Yes. My husband has a pistol he keeps in the nightstand next to our bed upstairs."

"Does your husband carry a weapon with him?"

"No."

"Are you sure?"

"I'm positive."

After exchanging glances, one of the officers stood up and looked toward the stairs. He walked up to the bedroom to retrieve the pistol.

At about the same time the officer was taking the bullets out of Hampson's pistol, the other police car was parking outside a branch of the Bank of Spain. The officers and U.S. marshal watched through binoculars as Hampson walked through the doors.

"Good afternoon, Mr. Sanchez," the bank manager said enthusiastically as he approached his best customer. He had noticed Hampson filling out a bank form at the stand in the middle of the lobby.

"Hola, Felipe," he said cheerfully, "Como estas?"

"Bien, gracias—so kind of you to ask. More importantly, how are you? And what may I do to help you?"

Hampson looked at the well-dressed bank manager. "Mrs. Sanchez and I are going to take a vacation, and we need a little cash."

"How much will you need?"

"Five thousand U.S. dollars in American Express traveler's checks, please."

"If you don't mind, why don't you give me the withdrawal slip, and I'll take care of the transaction for you, while you make yourself comfortable in my office. The line is rather long, and it would be my pleasure to help you."

"Gracias, Felipe." Hampson handed him the signed withdrawal slip.

The manager showed Hampson to his office, and brought him a cup of coffee. After making sure that his client was comfortable, he walked around to the back entrance leading to the teller windows. He walked up to one of the tellers, who had just completed a transaction.

"Marguerite, would you please take care of this transaction for me. It's for Mr. Sanchez."

The teller, knowing how important Mr. Sanchez was to the bank, wasn't surprised by the interruption. She looked at the withdrawal slip he handed her and began to enter the account numbers into the computer's keyboard in front of her.

"He would like the funds in U.S. dollars in American Express Traveler's checks," the bank manager added, smiling and nodding to another customer he knew who was standing in line.

After waiting a few moments for the transaction to process, the disconcerted teller looked up at the manager. "Mr. Guitterez, this account has been closed out," she said in an urgent whisper.

"What!" he said, trying to keep his voice low? "That's impossible! Check again."

The teller put the bank slip in front of her, and, again, carefully pushed in the numbers on her keyboard and waited. A few seconds later, she turned the computer screen to her manager so he could see.

"Look," she said, "closed out yesterday—not just that account, but all of them. Mr. and Mrs. James Sanchez. Available balances zero. Would you like a printout?" she asked.

"Yes," he said, unable to fathom what he was seeing. He searched his mind to prepare some explanation for Mr. Sanchez. The teller tore paper off the printer and handed it to the manager.

"Do you know anything about this?" he asked.

"No," she said, "See, it was closed out at the main branch. Look at the code on the receipt." She pointed to the last line on the paper.

He frowned as he looked.

"Mr. Sanchez must have transferred the funds to another account and forgotten about it," he said, walking away from the teller, who motioned for the next person in line to come up.

The manager thought for a moment, choosing his words carefully. He walked back to his office, where Hampson was waiting. Hampson turned to him and smiled.

"Mr. Sanchez, did you, by chance, transfer your funds to another account?"

"No," Hampson answered. "Why? Is there a problem?"

"Oh, no." The manager spoke calmly, although his stomach had started to churn. "We just have a little computer glitch. I'm sorry, but it's going to take me a few minutes. Can I get you another cup of coffee while you're waiting?"

"No, thank you, Felipe, I'll just wait here," Hampson said, "but please hurry. My wife and I are leaving soon."

"I promise you I'll be only a few minutes," he said, apologetically. He went directly to the assistant manager's office; he walked in without knocking, shoved the door closed with his back and leaned against it. The assistant manager looked up.

"Vera, do you know anything about Mr. Sanchez's closing out his accounts?"

"No," she said with surprise in her voice, "if he did, I would think that he would have gone through you."

"Look," he said, handing her the receipt the teller had given him. "It looks as if he closed out his accounts yesterday at the main branch."

The assistant manager studied the receipt carefully and looked up. The expression on her face said more than she could put into words.

"Get Roberto Lopez from the main branch on the phone for me."

The assistant manager picked up the receiver and speed-dialed the bank vice-president's number.

A few seconds later, she said, "Mr. Lopez, this is Vera Bonilla, would you please hold for Mr. Guitterez?" She handed the receiver to the bank manager, who was now standing beside her.

"Roberto, this is Felipe. Listen, I have something important here. Do you know anything about Mr. and Mrs. Sanchez closing out their accounts?"

The younger woman watched her manager's facial expressions and body language. She handed him a pad of paper and a pen, when he motioned with his hand. He took notes as he listened.

Several minutes later, and after giving the assistant manager a few very surprised looks, he said, "I see. Can you have someone fax the identification you have and a copy of the transfer slip with her signature on it? Fine, I'll go over to our fax machine, and I'll wait for it myself." He hung up the phone without exchanging the usual pleasantries. He looked at his assistant manager. "Come with me."

When they reached the fax machine, she said, "Would you please tell me what's going on?"

The manager spoke in a soft tone while they were waiting. "It seems that *Mrs.* Sanchez closed out the accounts yesterday and transferred the funds to a Swiss bank. I don't think Mr. Sanchez knows anything about it!"

"What!" she said, her eyes wide with surprise.

"*Verdad!* She went to the main branch yesterday to close out the accounts! Lopez said he handled the transaction himself because of the size of the accounts. He even had a police security specialist there to make sure her identification and signature were authentic."

"And?"

"They were. He's sending me copies of the ID and transfer papers now!"

"And you don't think Mr. Sanchez knows anything about it?" The young woman thought this little piece of gossip was too good to be true. She hung on his every word.

"I'm sure he doesn't or he wouldn't be here trying to take money out!"

"Who's going to tell him?"

"Lopez told me to tell him."

As he finished speaking, the fax machine started printing copies of the passport, driver's license, bank transfer slip, and other documents. He studied each one carefully, handing them to his assistant, one by one.

"That's her all right," she said, handing the documents back to her manager, and smiling. "I've seen her in here many times."

"So have I," he said, "and the signatures match too."

They were still looking at the documents, when they were startled by Hampson's voice coming from the manager's office.

"What's taking so long, Guitterez? I told you I don't have all day!"

The two officials glanced at each other for a moment, smiling wide-eyed, as if in on a secret conspiracy. The manager gathered and shuffled the papers into a neat stack and walked nervously back to his office. Hampson, still in his chair, looked up as Guitterez quietly closed his office door and took a deep breath before speaking.

"Mr. Sanchez, I'm sorry but I have to talk to you."

"What is it?" Hampson said, in an annoyed tone.

"Mr. Sanchez, please calm down. I have to tell you something."

"Now, what in the hell is going on here?" Hampson said, not attempting or caring about keeping his voice down.

"Mr. Sanchez," Guitterez said, swallowing hard, "your accounts have been closed out."

"What! What are you talking about?" Hampson jumped out of his chair, facing the bank manager.

"Your accounts were closed out yesterday at the main branch."

"That's impossible!" Hampson said loudly, now with anger in his voice. "When this is straightened out, I'll be dealing with another bank, and several heads are going to roll for this."

"Please calm down, and I'll try to tell you what happened."

"I don't want to calm down. Just get this straightened out."

"There's nothing to straighten out. Your wife closed out the accounts yesterday and transferred the funds to the Trust Bank of Switzerland."

"My *wife*? Get the hell out of here!" Hampson pushed the manager hard, opened the door, and stepped out of his office. Guitterez grabbed the arm of the chair to stop himself from falling and then started after Hampson.

"Get me the bank's president on the phone, and get him *now*! And I don't care what he's doing, interrupt him." Everyone in the bank had stopped what they were doing to stare at Jim Hampson.

"That won't do any good, Mr. Sanchez," the manager said, talking in low tones. "The accounts were closed, and the bank did everything to ensure that the transfer was authorized."

Hampson gave the bank manager an angry look and pushed him aside again. He walked briskly toward the front door of the bank when he stopped and turned, pointed his finger, and yelled, "I'm going to have your job for this, Guitterez."

Desperate, the bank manager said in a voice one pitch louder than Hampson's, "Mr. Sanchez, is this your wife's identification?"

He got Hampson's attention. "Let me see that," he said as he walked back into the lobby and tore the papers from Mr. Guitterez's hand. As he was looking wide-eyed at the papers, Guitterez said, "That is a copy of the identification used to close the accounts. Is that Mrs. Sanchez's license and passport?"

He stared at the papers in disbelief. Slowly, he realized that he was looking at copies of his wife's identification, purchased from Poupore several months earlier. The manager held another paper toward him. He took it, not asking what it was.

"That's a copy of the transfer-of-funds slip. As you can see, the signatures match."

Hampson examined the paperwork carefully. "Where does it say the money was transferred to?" he asked, not looking up.

Guitterez pointed to one of the lines. "As you can see, the funds were transferred to Switzerland."

Despite his state of mind, Hampson tried desperately to comprehend what he was being shown. "Which bank?"

"The Trust Bank of Switzerland."

"Where is the account number?"

"We don't have it. Swiss banks won't release that information."

"Where did she sign?"

"On the back."

Hampson looked up after studying the signature himself, "She closed out the accounts!" he said softly. Then his voice rose, "That bitch closed out the goddamned accounts!" Appearing disoriented, he turned and hurried toward the front door, the papers still in his hand. Shoving the door hard as he moved through it, he knocked back a woman who had been entering the other side of the door.

Without stopping to help, he ran down the steps and crossed the road to his car. He didn't hear the manager calling his name. All he knew was that his wife had closed out the accounts, and he had left her home alone to pack.

# Chapter Thirty–Eight

Hampson drove wildly through traffic toward the villa, failing to notice the police car following him. Making a right into his circular driveway, he was bewildered to see a Spanish police car parked there. Stepping on the brakes, he brought the car to a stop and ran to the house, without shutting the car door. The police car that followed him pulled up, blocking his car in. The officers quickly got out, service revolvers drawn. One waited by Hampson's car while the other went with the U.S. marshal to the front door.

Hampson burst into the living room, shouting, "Linda! Linda, where in the hell are you?"

"I'm right here, Jim," he heard his wife say in a soft voice. He turned to see her sitting on the sofa, a uniformed police officer standing by her side. His hand was on his pistol. A man in a suit was on her other side, hands on hips, moving his jacket just enough to expose a shoulder holster.

"What in the hell is going on here?" Hampson raved, his voice angry and puzzled.

"Are you James Hampson?" asked the marshal calmly.

Hampson looked at the marshal. "I'm Jim Sanchez," he said. "Who the hell are you, and what are you doing in my house?"

"We have reason to believe that you are really James Hampson. We have orders to take you and your wife into custody."

"What are you talking about?" Hampson said in a loud voice.

"We're U.S. marshals," the officer said. "Please put your hands up where I can see them."

"I'll be goddamned if . . ." Hampson said, stopping when he heard another voice behind him say, "Just raise your hands, please. Don't make any fast movements." As he heard the words, he turned to see another marshal with his pistol pointed at the ceiling. "Now just raise your hands slowly."

Hampson raised his hands. Suddenly his left wrist was grabbed, pulled down and across his back. He heard the click of handcuffs. His right wrist was drawn behind him. Another click.

After they searched him for weapons, he discovered his wife was standing with her hands behind her back too. "I wish you'd never talked me into this," she said.

"What did you do with the money?" Hampson temporarily ignored the situation they were facing.

"What are you talking about?"

"You know *exactly* what I'm talking about. You knew this was coming. You were going to get out and leave me here to face the music alone, weren't you?"

"I still don't know what you mean!" she murmured softly.

"You bitch! You thought you could get away with this, didn't you?"

"It's the truth, Jim. I don't know what you're talking about!"

Hampson looked at her contemptuously and turned around. "I want a lawyer," he said, "and I want one right now."

"That's going to have to wait," said one of the marshals. "We've got to take you with us. But first I'm required to read you your rights." Pulling a small card from the pocket of his suit coat, the marshal started reading from it. "You have the right to remain silent. . ."

The two other Spanish officers came through the front door.

"Is everything okay in here?"

"Yes, you two can take the woman, and we'll take him."

# Chapter Thirty-Nine

It was Wednesday, October 11th, 5:25 P.M., Eastern Standard Time.

"Come on, clock," Pat said out loud, waiting in his office with Russell.

"What time do you have, Russell?"

"It's the same time over here as it is on your side of the desk!" He was trying to be lighthearted to calm Pat's nervousness. "I know you're worried about Rita, but I'm sure everything went fine and she's okay."

"I know, but I can't help worrying about her."

"You really like her, don't you?"

Pat jerked his head. "What's not to like?" Now he was smiling.

As they talked, Russell saw the digital clock on the credenza behind Pat's desk turn from five twenty-nine to five-thirty. Russell pointed at it, and Pat turned around.

"Finally," he said, slipping on his sports coat. "Let's go."

Rita's United Airlines flight from New York was due to touch down at the Baltimore-Washington International Airport at 6:30 P.M. Pat and Russell pulled out of the parking lot across from the office at 5:40 P.M., for the short drive south on route 295 to the airport.

Pat parked in the hourly parking lot, and they walked hurriedly across to the international terminal. Once inside, they quickly checked the arrivals monitor for concourse and gate information. The flight information was on screen, but Pat's heart sank as he spotted the word DELAYED blinking next to the flight information. The ticket counter was crowded with passengers checking in, so they went directly to the gate to see if they could get more information.

Both were quiet as they passed through security and walked to the gate. A gate agent was busy entering information into a computer as they walked up to him.

"May I help you?"

"Yes. Can you please give us an update on the flight due in from New York? The screen says it's been delayed," Pat said.

"Su—re," he said, stretching out the word as he punched some keys. He looked at the information and then looked up. "It's probably weather. Seems like it's been storming all day in New York. Everything coming in from there seems to be off. No—that flight actually had to change planes—looks like they had a mechanical problem right before takeoff. It's going to be quite delayed. The latest information we have from the control tower is that they should be here right around ten-thirty." He smiled. "Don't be concerned, I'm positive everything's fine."

Pat and Russell looked at each other, impatience showing on their faces.

"Could you please tell me if Linda Sanchez is on the plane?" asked Pat.

Apologetically, the gate agent said, "I'm sorry, but I'm not allowed to give out that information."

"All we'd like to know is whether or not she's on the plane," stated Russell a little more forcefully.

"I understand, sir, and I really wish I could help you, but you have to understand that rules are rules." The gate agent's voice was both sympathetic and firm. "Why don't you two go and have something to eat and come back around ten-thirty?"

Both Pat and Russell resigned themselves to the situation and walked away from the ticket counter.

"What now?" Pat asked.

"Come on. Let's go on over to the lounge. I'll buy you a crab cake." Russell squeezed Pat's shoulder and led him away.

After they ordered their food, Russell was surprised that he was actually able to change the subject and talk about upcoming sports events. Considering the circumstances, the time passed quickly. At 10:20 P.M., Pat checked his watch and said, "Let's go see what's up."

The same gate agent was behind the counter. He saw them walking toward him and before they could ask he said, "The plane's pulling up right now."

They walked over to the windows next to the gate and saw the plane pulling up slowly toward the jet ramp. They heard the ramp's alarm as someone positioned the jet-way against the plane's middle door. As they watched the field crew ready the airplane, the gate agent opened the gate door for the arriving passengers.

"She should be one of the first off. She had a first class ticket," said Pat.

The first few tired passengers entered the terminal. Smiling, some greeted families and loved ones. Others rushed off to pick up baggage, anxious to end long business trips. Pat and Russell strained their necks to look down the jet-way ramp for Rita. Not seeing her, Pat began to feel his stomach churn. Tense, he and Pat looked at each other but didn't speak.

They stood in the gate area waiting as over three hundred passengers slowly entered the terminal. Rita wasn't among them. Finally, the airplane's crew appeared at the door pulling their luggage. One of the flight attendants shut the door, locking it behind him.

"Oh, my God," Russell said. "Could she have missed the flight?" Pat and Russell looked at each other, perplexed, when suddenly Pat walked up to the crew. "Is everyone off the plane?" he asked desperately.

"Yes. May I help you?" the attendant who had locked the door asked.

"We're waiting for someone who was supposed to be on the plane."

"What's the passenger's name?"

"Rita Davies," he said, immediately realizing his mistake. "I'm sorry, it's Linda Sanchez." He hoped his voice sounded confident.

"What was that name again?" another crewmember asked.

"Linda Sanchez. Do you know anything about her?"

The other crewmembers continued walking, leaving Pat and Russell with the flight attendant. The woman waited a few moments until the rest of the crew was out of earshot before answering. "What's the problem?" she asked.

"We're here to pick her up, and she's not on the plane." Pat looked worried. "Can you help us?"

The uniformed flight attendant looked around. "Look, I'm not supposed to give out this information. Do you understand?"

"Yes. I swear this conversation is just between us, but I've got to know what's going on. This is extremely important."

She looked around again. "She missed the plane. When she didn't check in, we had her paged but she never showed up. We waited as long as we could, but we finally had to cancel her reservation and give it to a stand-by passenger."

"Did she book another flight?"

"That I don't know. Even if I did, I couldn't tell you. I really shouldn't have told you what I did. Look, I'm sure she just missed the flight for some reason. She'll probably be on the next plane."

"Do you know when it'll be in?"

"Well, the next flight coming into New York from Zurich wouldn't be arriving until early in the morning. You probably wouldn't see her until the 9:00 A.M. flight in from La Guardia.'

"Is there any way at all we can find out if she's coming in on that flight?"

"No, I'm really sorry, but there's no way for you to find that out."

"How about if we call the reservations center?"

"You can try, but I doubt if they'll be able to help you. I'm really sorry."

"Well, what do we do now, Pal?" asked Russell.

Dismayed, Pat finally said, "Look, it's already after eleven. If we drive back home, we're only going to get a couple of hours' sleep before heading back here again, particularly with the morning traffic. Why don't we just get a room around here?"

"Good idea. I'll call home."

They checked into a hotel near the airport. As soon as they were in the room, Pat picked up the telephone.

"Who are you calling?"

"United Airlines."

"What for?"

"Maybe they'll give us some information."

"You heard what the flight attendant and gate agent said."

"I know, but I still want to give it a try."

Pat did everything he could but, yes, rules were rules. The airlines could not help and every other call was to no avail, frustrating both of them.

Pat lay restlessly in his bed, facing the window. A security light outside penetrated the room's heavy shades. Hearing Russell get up for water, he said, "Hey, are you sleeping?"

"Nope, not a wink."

"I can't help thinking that I've put Rita in terrible danger."

"Let's hope for the best, Pat. I don't have a clue what to do next, if she's not on that flight."

Russell climbed back into bed at precisely the same time as the flight attendant on Rita's plane announced the flight's final approach before landing. Rita pushed in the button on her armrest, and brought her seat to an upright position.

# Chapter Forty

The light in the hall outside Pat and Russell's room at the airport hotel dimmed, as the pale orange sun became visible through the morning's gray haze. Pat unwrapped a pre-measured, complimentary coffee packet and sleepily filled the small-sized coffee maker with water and plugged it in. Exhausted, Russell rolled over as the smell of brewing coffee reached the bed.

Sleep had eluded Pat and Russell, and the night had been a long one. Today they were spent, nervous, and worried. As they prepared for the day ahead, neither said much but each knew what the other was thinking. The possibilities of what could have gone wrong seemed endless.

They breakfasted quietly together in the hotel restaurant. Their meal was almost devoid of conversation; they had exhausted the subject the night before. Before leaving, they called Poupore at home, the only other person in the world who might be able to help them. The call patched over to a recording—Poupore's home number was now unlisted, further frustrating them.

Pat and Russell arrived at Baltimore Washington International Airport fifteen minutes before the next flight from New York was due. Walking toward the gate, they passed the flight attendant who had helped them the evening before. She smiled and, as she passed, wished them luck. They checked the arrivals monitor on the way to the gate. They were relieved that the screen noted ON TIME next to the flight information.

As the plane pulled up to the gate, Pat prayed silently that she was a passenger. She wasn't.

Neither Russell nor Pat had noticed the tired young woman dressed in smart business clothes, who had deplaned right after the first-class passengers. The woman ran her hand through her short, curly, light-brown hair as she turned in a slow circle, looking around the terminal for someone she knew.

Neither Pat nor Russell could hide his anxiety as the last of the flight crew locked the jet-way door. Lost in thought, Pat jumped when he felt tapping on his left shoulder. He turned.

"Are you Pat McGuire?" the curly-headed woman asked.

"I'm McGuire," he said, with a touch of surprise as he looked curiously at the woman. "Who are you?"

"I'm Agent Hackman with the FBI. I'm the one Agent Karl told you about." Hackman held out her hand to the men.

For a petite woman, Charlene Hackman had a firm grip. She didn't meet Pat's idea of a female FBI agent, though. He was expecting a much taller woman with a rasping voice complementing her features. Hackman was only about five-two, she was slender, and she had a very appealing face. Pat hadn't noticed that Russell looked as surprised as he was.

Pat's anxiety over Rita and her safety sobered his thought processes. "Where's Rita?" he asked abruptly.

Agent Hackman took a deep breath, put her hands on her hips, and looked to her right before turning her head toward him. She answered honestly, "I lost her."

"What do you mean, you 'lost her'? How could that happen after what we were promised?" Now Pat's hands were on his hips. He stared at her, waiting for her answer.

"All I can tell you is that everything went as we expected—up to the last minute."

"Go on."

"I was with her all the way in Spain. I sat right behind her on the trip to Switzerland."

"And?"

"Once we got to Zurich, I stayed in the same hotel, and I followed her directly from the Swiss bank to the airport. We got on the same plane together to come back here. And that's when I lost her."

"How could you possibly lose someone when you were on the same plane? You people assured us you were the professionals!"

A few passersby in the terminal turned to see the exchange between them. Agent Hackman waited for them to lose interest and walk away before continuing.

She spoke quietly. "Pat, I know you're upset. You have a right to be, but you have to calm down. Let's find a quiet place to talk."

Russell, who had remained silent during their conversation, spoke calmly, trying to diffuse the tension. "Let's head over to that bench—there's no one over there."

The bench was centered against a long stretch of corridor wall decorated with posters of tropical destinations. As they sat, Russell asked the agent to tell them what had happened next.

"Listen," she said, with both compassion and firmness. "I was sitting a few rows behind her on the aisle, trying not to look obvious, when this couple told me they had the center and window seats. I got up to let them in, the plane was really crowded, and when we finally got settled, I noticed she wasn't in her seat." Hackman paused.

"I thought she had gotten up to go the lavatory. I got up to check, and the lavatory occupied sign wasn't lit." This time, her demeanor spoke frustration.

"She wasn't on the plane. I asked one of the flight attendants if she had noticed anything, and he told me she had suddenly gotten up from her seat and left. Immediately, I ran down the jet-way as fast as I could, but she was gone. I did everything I could. I even had her paged and got airport security to help me, but I couldn't find her! Pat, believe me, I tried!"

"Why didn't you, or someone else, contact us last night? Do you know what we went through when she wasn't on that plane?"

"I called the agent-in-charge—Karl—and filled him in. He may have been too busy trying to locate her himself after I talked to him. That would have been his first priority."

Hackman's calm voice and professional manner settled Pat. He surprised himself when he asked calmly, "So what do we do now?"

"I think you should go back to your office and wait for Agent Karl to contact you. Once I get my bags, I'll be heading to his office. I'll let him know you're waiting on a call from him." Pat and Russell accepted their only course of action, which was now clear. They would have to go back to their office and just wait for someone to contact them to tell them what to do next.

They didn't take time to stop to change clothes on the drive to Baltimore. Every sentence they spoke seemed to start with "if only," or "I wish." During the uncomfortable ride, they decided that, once they got to the office, they would contact Poupore at his office to see what he might know.

It was eleven o'clock when they got off the elevator.

"Good morning to both of you," the receptionist said cheerfully. "You're a little late today." As they walked toward her, they could see the curious look on her face. She had never seen them unshaven and in rumpled clothing. "If you two need money for razors and the laundry, I'll be happy to lend you some," she said, attempting to coax smiles onto their serious faces.

When they didn't react to her comment, Edie turned serious. "What in the world is going on?" She put down the stack of mail she was working on to give them her undivided attention.

They both liked Edie very much and, even now, they were concerned for her feelings. "Edie," Pat said, "please don't be offended, but this just isn't a good time and, believe me, this has nothing in the world to do with you."

Edie's sympathetic look told both of them that she understood.

"We're going to be in Pat's office for awhile, Edie. We'd appreciate it if you would screen our calls and not put anything through unless it's an emergency."

"Okay. I'll cover for you," she said, as they turned to walk down the hall. "I'm not one to break tradition," Russell said. "Let's start some coffee brewing." They were walking toward the office kitchen when Russell put his hand on Pat's shoulder. "I don't know why or how, but everything is going to be all right." Pat couldn't manage a smile.

In the kitchen, they saw that Edie had already made coffee and she had two Baltimore Orioles coffee mugs in hand. She smiled, handed them their mugs and left the room, respecting their silence.

Alone in Pat's office, they just looked at each other, not knowing what their next step should be. "What did you say to your father?"

"I told him we needed to see him today."

"What time?"

"One. That's a little over an hour from now."

Still looking at Russell, Pat reached over and picked up his telephone and began dialing.

"Who are you calling?" Russell asked.

"Poupore. He should be in his office by now."

When he finished dialing, Pat pushed in the speakerphone button so that Russell could hear the conversation. They looked at each other intently before the call went through.

"Law offices," they heard a male voice say.

Looking at Russell, Pat asked to speak to Ralph Poupore.

"I'm sorry, but Mr. Poupore is not here."

"May I leave a message for him to return my call, please?"

"Certainly, but I don't know when he'll be able to call you back; he's on vacation for the next few weeks."

"Did he leave a number where he can be reached?"

Russell could see the mounting frustration on Pat' face.

"No, I'm sorry. Would you like for me to take your number?"

Pat's sigh could be heard through the phone line.

"No, thanks. I'll call back in a couple of weeks."

Pat hung up the phone, ran his hands through his hair, rested the side of his face in his left hand and looked across the desk to Russell, whose expression was surprisingly impassive. Neither spoke for over a minute.

"Well, you heard." Pat said.

Russell suddenly stood up, heading for the door. "I'll get you just before one." Without waiting for Pat's response, he left.

Pat was too upset to face any of the other employees but, as he closed his door, Edie stopped him. "This is yesterday afternoon's mail. I'm trying to get a head start for the day." He simply said, "Thank you," and Edie kindly walked away. He put the mail in his in-box.

He sat for a while, replaying everything in his mind. He was hoping that he could think of something else to do or someone else to call. He couldn't.

At twelve-thirty, knowing that the last thing he needed was a cup of coffee, he got up to get one anyhow. As he walked toward the kitchen, he noticed the surprised looks on several faces, when they took in his disheveled appearance. He was glad no one else was in the kitchen, not wanting to talk or answer questions.

Back in his office, he figured that the mail might keep him occupied before meeting with Gilbert Autry. He flipped through it quickly until he came to an overseas priority envelope addressed to him with no return address. On the bottom left corner of the envelope was written: "Personal and Confidential." It was sealed with packing tape.

He fumbled in his desk drawer for his scissors and clipped off the right edge of the envelope. His heart was pounding as he pulled out the letter. He put on his glasses and began to read

> *My Dear Pat,*
>
> *I debated whether I should write you this letter, but I just couldn't let you and Russell worry. We've all been through so much.*
> *I can't tell you where I am right now, but both my sister, Lisa, and I are safe and it would be very difficult for anyone to track us down.*
> *I'll try to fill you in on everything that has happened since I left.*
> *I arrived in Spain safely and I was able to transfer the money to a Swiss bank. I was nervous and there were a few tense moments, but I pulled it off. I left Madrid for Zurich and I'm on that plane right now, writing this letter. I'm not sure how I'll get this to you, but I'll figure out something.*
> *When I was getting ready to go to Spain and Switzerland, reality began to set in, and I know that returning to the States right away would be too dangerous. I know you understand.*
> *Who knows what Lovelady might find out or what he already knows, and we both know what he is capable of. Also, what might Hampson do once he finds out what I did with the tapes?*
> *I hope this letter finds you safe. I'll never be able to repay you and Russell, especially you, for all your help.*

> *When everything calms down and I have time to sort things out, I'll contact you.*
>
> *Until then, all my love,*
>
> *Rita*
>
> *P.S. I just wish things between us could have been different—I think of you often.*

Pat read Rita's letter again before asking Russell to come to his office. After Russell read the letter, they both sat in silence, taking everything in. Finally Russell looked at his watch and said, "It's almost one. I told my old man that we'd be in the conference room."

Pat put on his jacket and placed Rita's letter in his pocket. "I believe I'll go freshen up. See you at one."

Just as he was leaving his office, the telephone on Pat's desk rang, startling him. He picked up the receiver and, before he could speak, Edie said, "Pat, there is an Agent Karl with the FBI on the line. He said it was urgent. Do you want me to put him through?"

"Yes. Thanks, Edie."

For the next several minutes, FBI Agent Malcolm Karl updated Pat on everything. Pat called Russell immediately and advised him before their one o'clock meeting with Gilbert Autry.

# Chapter Forty–One

At one o'clock, Pat entered the conference room, with Russell where they found Gilbert Autry waiting. The two younger men glanced at each other, taking deep breaths.

"You'd better have Anne cancel your appointments for today, Dad, this is going to take a while." Gilbert Autry gave his son a look of confused surprise as Pat settled into his chair. He could tell by the looks on their faces this was important and he told his secretary he was not to be interrupted.

Russell started. As the older Autry sat across from his son and Pat, he listened, interrupting only occasionally, as they unfolded their story.

They told him everything. They explained about Rita, the secret meetings, the cash-skimming scam, the tapes, Lovelady, Poupore, Hampson, and their fears about Bob Ramsey.

When they were finished, Autry sat back in his chair, folding his arms across his chest. His face was a strange mixture of astonishment, pride, and hurt for not being informed. "My turn?" he said.

They both nodded.

"Tell me again about the FBI."

"Well," Pat said, taking a sip of water. "As I said, I didn't know who to trust. I saw that picture of Hampson and his nephew on the boat, and I could have sworn that he was the one who took me out in the football game. Even when Russell tried to tell me different, I just wasn't convinced. And then, after Mr. Ramsey's murder, Rita warned me not to trust anyone and she reminded me about your friendship with Jim Hampson. I didn't know what to do!"

"I'm very disappointed you didn't come to me, Pat," Autry said, sitting back in his chair.

"Mr. Autry, I can't tell you how sorry I am, and I really don't blame you for being disappointed, after all you've done for me, but I didn't know what to do. All I can ask is that you imagine yourself in my shoes at the time. Here I was, seriously hurt, and I find out that the executive director of the firm's biggest client had something to do with it, and then a partner was murdered on top of it! I am sorry, Mr. Autry." Gilbert Autry was like a second father to Pat, and the look of pain that crossed his face touched Pat. He hadn't wanted to leave him out. When Autry heard the apology and saw the remorse on Pat's face, he swallowed his pain, and smiled as he gave a patriarchal nod.

"So that's when you went to the FBI?" he asked.

Hoping the nod meant forgiveness, Pat said, "Yes. We went to their Baltimore office near Social Security Boulevard."

"Run it by me again, what they said."

"Well, we told them everything and gave them the tape, and they said they would get back to us within a week."

"And?"

"And, in three days, they said they wanted to see us, and we went back to their office. Like I said, we told them everything once, and we told them everything again from beginning to end. Then they started questioning me carefully, and I guess I convinced them that I was the real deal."

Autry was looking at Pat intently, taking in every word.

"They said they wanted to go after Jim Hampson first because, if they got him, that would throw off the rest of the group for a while. Initially, they concentrated on the slush fund checks that had been distributed at each meeting. They thought that if they could prove Hampson had a substantial amount of income that he didn't report on his tax returns, they might be able to extradite him back to the states on a tax-evasion charge."

"Tax evasion?"

"Yes, they said if they had enough to get him back here on a tax charge, that would give them time to tie him to the embezzlement and, eventually, to Ramsey's murder; not to mention the time they needed to move in on the entire group's involvement in price-fixing."

"Amazing," Autry muttered, never looking away from him.

"Well," he was breathing hard and paused before he spoke, "I told the Feds that the only other person I'd confided in was Russell," and he smiled at Russell. "I told them the truth, and they flew us to the IRS and FBI district offices in Chicago."

"I see."

"They chose Chicago because of our satellite office there. They thought our going wouldn't present any suspicions if we were being followed. Anyway, at the IRS office we met with the district director, some of her deputies, and the same FBI people we were dealing with in Baltimore."

"What did they say?"

"That they checked out the tape and conducted a confidential review of Hampson's bank records."

"And?"

"They were very thorough. They told us they had talked to Hampson's banker and found out that he'd set up a business account using the Federation's federal identification number, instead of his own social security number. He had run the slush fund through those accounts."

"Didn't the bank manager suspect anything?"

"No, the bank manager told the agents there was nothing to suspect. Hampson was the Federation's executive director. He came in with completed corporate resolution cards and signature cards for the account and opened it. He certainly had authority to open up bank accounts for his own organization and, considering the Federation was one of the bank's biggest accounts, it's understandable that nobody questioned him."

Gilbert Autry nodded. "I guess so."

"The IRS would never have known about the money-laundering if we hadn't gone to the FBI," continued Russell.

Pat chimed in. "So, after reviewing the bank records against Hampson's tax returns, the IRS knew he wasn't reporting income. Then they had enough on him to work through the FBI for extradition to the U.S. for income tax evasion."

"How did they know where he was?"

"We told them what Ralph Poupore told us. They checked it and found out that Poupore was right."

"Why would Poupore turn in his own client?"

"All he said to us was that he wanted him back, too, but for a different reason."

"Why?"

"He never did tell us, but our guess is that it probably had something to do with money, knowing Poupore."

Autry rolled his eyes and looked at the ceiling. "I've heard of sleazy attorneys before, but this son-of-a-bitch takes the cake." He shook his head again.

It occurred to Pat that this was the first time he had ever heard Gilbert Autry curse. He saw the surprise in Russell's face too.

"So the Feds brought Hampson back on a tax charge?"

"At this point, all they would tell us is that they arrested him without incident."

"But I still don't understand. Why was I kept out of the loop—I mean—after you went to the FBI?"

"Mr. Autry, the FBI made us swear we wouldn't tell anyone anything."

"Why not?" Autry said, appearing a little hurt again.

"They said the best thing we could do under the circumstances was 'business as usual,' and the fewer people who knew, the better—for them and for us, and they swore us to secrecy. They wouldn't even let us tell Rita! Rita went to Europe not knowing what we had done, and they assured us she would be in their sights at all times and safe." He paused, "Of course, that's before they lost her in Switzerland."

"You've got to believe us, Dad!" Russell said. "It wasn't our idea. We didn't like it either, but don't forget that Lovelady is still in charge over at the Federation and his little price-fixing party is still out there too."

"What about whoever murdered Bob Ramsey?"

"They don't know. That's another reason they need Hampson and the rest, but right now they don't know," Pat said.

Autry's eyes widened, as he began to understand the danger he might have been in, and the danger his son and Pat faced. Then he said, "But, I am in on it now."

"Yes," Pat said, "you are."

"So what do I have to do?" His voice was calm.

"Our contact at the FBI thought it would be better for the two of us to fill you in, instead of them. The special agent in charge from the Baltimore office, Malcolm Karl, will be here to talk to you tomorrow morning at ten. We've been told you don't have to do anything if you don't want to, in which case they would just swear you to secrecy."

"You have all night to think it over, Dad," Russell said.

"Nothing to think over," he said in a matter-of-fact tone. "I'll cooperate fully. Bob Ramsey was a long-standing, good friend of mine. We all have our weak moments, but Bob couldn't have done anything serious enough to be murdered for. Anything I can do to help them prosecute Lovelady and the rest of that bunch is fine with me."

"How is Mrs. Ramsey doing by the way, Dad?"

"Not good. I understand Bob didn't carry nearly as much insurance on himself as he should have, and things are pretty tight for her and the kids. It's a real shame."

After a brief silence, Autry said, "So, where do we go from here?"

Russell turned to Pat for a response. "Well, with your permission, the FBI has asked us to help them from our office here. The firm would be compensated for my time, of course."

Gilbert Autry sat back in his chair and relaxed. "So, what would we be doing?"

"First, they need me to help them out as they target Lovelady and the others. They don't want to waste time."

"Makes sense."

"They want to make a tight case on the price-fixing angle. They figure if they get them on that, it will lead them to Bob Ramsey's murderer and everything else."

Pat leaned forward, looking serious. "They want an iron-clad case on this group, and they say the tape alone isn't enough."

"Why not?"

"Well, by itself, the tape can't bring in a conviction, and the FBI doesn't want to lose this opportunity. They've suspected something was going on for a long time, but they couldn't identify all the players. Rita gave me only the one tape. I turned it over to the FBI and, after analysis, they have two problems."

"Which are?"

"One, it's not an original tape, and that's a problem, and two, they need the rest of the tapes to really nail down Lovelady and that crowd."

Gilbert Autry thought for a moment. "So, that's why they may be willing to cut a deal with Hampson?"

"Right. They want more information—and fast. They know Rita has the original tapes, but now they don't know where she is and when they'll find her."

"Okay, what now?" Gilbert Autry asked.

"That's where Pat comes in, Dad."

"It seems I'm the only one who knew everyone involved, without a scorecard, so they think I'm the logical one to help them gather other solid evidence."

"Ahh—sounds like real detective stuff. What kind of evidence do you mean?"

Pat grinned at the analogy. "Well, the tape gives lots of information about airlines, hotels, and aliases. So they want me to work with the airlines and hotels, getting copies of tickets, signatures on hotel registration cards—things like that."

Pat took another sip of water and continued.

"After I gather all of that, they'll see if everything lines up with what's on the tape. Assuming it does, they'll have the handwriting samples analyzed. If they can match the handwriting with the handwriting on other documents bearing their names, they'll make their move against the whole group, subpoena their personal calendars, time and attendance records and the like and, hopefully, prosecute."

"May I ask a couple more questions?"

"Sure, Mr. Autry," Pat said.

"What are the Feds going to do about Poupore?"

The two younger men exchanged a knowing glance. Russell said, "Right now, we're not exactly sure, but I think it's going to be a long, interesting story."

"Why?"

"Well, like I said, they were adamant that the fewer people who knew what was going on the better. When we initially came up with the plan it was obviously very exciting, but once we started the ball rolling, we realized we were getting involved in something that not only was over our heads to begin with, but was also illegal on *our* part. That's when we went to the FBI the first time. They let us contact Poupore for two reasons: one, they needed him because he was the key to Hampson and the money and two, they want Poupore almost as bad as Hampson because of his little fake ID operation, which is a very serious offense itself. If they had proof of his issuing fake ID to Rita, they had what they needed to move in on him also."

Pat took another sip of water, "But now Poupore is gone too."

Gilbert Autry whistled. "The plot thickens. Where do you think he is?"

"No idea. We just found out when we tried to call him, he's on vacation and his home telephone number is unlisted."

"What about Rita?"

Pat and Russell exchanged glances.

Autry shook his head in continued fascination.

"No one knows where she is either."

"And she has the money and the original tapes?"

"Yep."

They went over the story one final time. Gilbert Autry was now as involved as Pat and Russell, and all they could do was wait to meet Malcolm Karl, the FBI agent in charge of the investigation.

# Chapter Forty–Two

It was early in the morning on Friday, the thirteenth of October. Jim awoke, wondering whether he had just had a nightmare. Breakfast trays noisily clattered through the hallway of the jail compound in the basement of the U.S. embassy. Jim suddenly remembered where he was. He remembered his outrage of the night before—he had demanded to see an attorney and the ambassador, but to no avail.

By noon, Hampson was pacing in his cell when he heard the sound of a metal door opening and closing. In the distance, he saw the silhouette of a U.S. Marine guard walking toward him. When the guard walked into the light, Hampson could see that he was accompanied by a man of about forty, dressed in a blue suit with a white shirt and red tie. He was carrying a briefcase and a gray sweater.

"That's him," the marine said when the two stopped in front of Hampson's cell. The other man pulled a photograph from his coat pocket, glanced at it, and then at Hampson.

"Are you James Hampson, also known as Jim Sanchez?" he asked.

"I'm Jim Sanchez," Hampson answered in a confident voice, though slowly, secretly, he was accepting the futility of keeping up the charade.

"Sir," the man said, "My name is James Vensel and I'm a United States marshal." He pulled another paper from his breast pocket and held it up for Hampson to read. "As you can see, I am under orders to escort you back to the United States. I'll be turning you over to authorities who will meet us at Kennedy Airport in New York."

"What am I being charged with?" Hampson asked.

"All I can tell you, and all I know, is that it has something to do with income tax evasion," the marshal said. "Do you understand?"

"Income tax evasion! You've got to be shitting me!" Hampson said excitedly. "You people don't go through all of this on a tax case, and you know it! What's going on?"

The marshal was expressionless. "Mr. Hampson, I am not your lawyer, I am not a judge, and I'm just doing my job. All I can tell you is that you're being escorted back to the states for a tax charge. I've done this many times, and I assure you that everything will be explained to you later. You've been read your rights, correct?"

"Yes," said Hampson, looking up at him.

"And you understand the charge, correct?"

Hampson shut his eyes and put his hands on his hips while his head dropped.

"Do you understand the charge, Mr. Hampson?" The marshal's voice went up a few decibels.

Without opening his eyes, Hampson whispered slowly, "Yes, I understand."

"Unlock the cell, please, sergeant," the marshal said. The marine guard slipped a large key into the slot, turned the key, and opened the cell door. Hampson watched the marshal walk into the cell, keeping eye contact with him while he placed a briefcase on the cot. He took a pair of handcuffs from the briefcase. The marine guard watched carefully from outside the cell.

"Please place both of your hands behind your back, sir."

Hampson offered no resistance. For the second time in fourteen hours, his hands were cuffed behind his back.

"May I ask a question?" Hampson said.

"Yes sir, but I don't know if I'll be able to answer it," the marshal answered in a matter-of-fact tone.

"I just want to know what happened to my wife."

"She's already on her way back to the states. Married couples are transferred back separately in cases like this. I'm sure you understand."

Hampson did. He knew they would each be questioned separately.

He was led out of the embassy through the rear entrance to a car where another blue-suited marshal sat in the driver's seat. He watched as the first marshal signed papers handed to him by the marine guard. The marshal then opened the back door guiding Hampson into the car. Inside, Hampson heard the door shut firmly. The marshal walked around the car and sat in the seat next to him.

"Where are we going?"

"To the airport." They rode in silence.

Hampson was surprised to see them pull into a reserved space in a commercial parking lot. Both marshals got out, looking around before the driver opened Hampson's door.

"Get out, sir. Watch your head."

He swung his legs out of the car and felt the agent's hand on the top of his head as he struggled to get out of the car.

The first agent said, "We're going to unlock the cuffs from behind your back now and re-cuff them in front. Do you understand?"

"Yes, but do you have to handcuff me? I promise I won't do anything."

"Yes, sir, I'm afraid it's policy."

Hampson said nothing. He heard the sound of the cuff around his left hand being unlocked and felt hands around both of his wrists as his hands were positioned in front of him. He watched as one of the marshals slid the open end of the cuffs through the belt around Hampson's waist, re-cuffing his left wrist, preventing him from raising his hands. Since Hampson was wearing a suit, he was surprised when the first agent handed him the gray sweater he had been carrying.

"What's this for?" he asked.

"It's to cover your wrists so that no one will know you're in handcuffs. It'll just look like we're three business men walking to our plane."

After Hampson covered his wrists he said, "Thank you, I really do appreciate your thoughtfulness," offering a weak smile.

"We don't want to scare any of the passengers in the terminal," Marshal Vensel replied.

Hampson suddenly appreciated the situation in which he found himself.

The three of them walked into the terminal. Hampson stood silently while the marshals showed paperwork to the security personnel at the metal detectors. They were allowed to walk around them. When they reached the gate, one marshal waited in line with the other passengers. When he got to the front of the line, he handed the papers to the ticket agent, who read them, and handed them back. He nodded after glancing at Hampson. The marshal put the papers into his breast pocket and walked back toward Hampson. Between the two U.S. marshals, he walked to the door marked Gate 12. Vensel showed the gate agent the same paperwork, and the agent opened the door to the gateway before announcing boarding instructions for the rest of the passengers. Once aboard, a flight attendant asked for the paperwork, and said, "Thirty six A, B, and C. The last row." She didn't look at Hampson. He walked awkwardly between the two marshals to the back of the plane.

He sat in the middle seat with his hands cuffed in front of him, the gray sweater still over them. He could tell by the way a few of the passengers glanced in his direction that they knew he was a prisoner and that the men to his left and right were U.S. marshals escorting him back to the United States.

About two hours into the flight, Hampson turned to the agent who was sitting in the aisle seat, reading the airline magazine. "I have to use the bathroom," he said. Without looking up from the magazine, the marshal said, "Can't it wait until we land?"

"No," Hampson said softly.

The agent looked at him. "Okay, but I've got to go with you."

The marshal looked up the aisle and stood up. When Hampson started to get up, the marshal said, "Sit down until I come back for you." He did as he was told and watched as the marshal talked to one of the flight attendants. About thirty seconds later, after assuring himself no other passengers were in line waiting to use the lavatory, he came back. "Okay, come with me," he said, and Hampson got up and walked into the aisle in front of the marshal. The lavatory on his left said VACANT in the little slot over the doorknob, so he pushed opened the door and walked in. As he reached to close the door, Marshal Vensel stepped into the cramped space behind him. Vensel locked the door from the inside.

"Is this really necessary?" Hampson asked.

"I'm afraid so. Procedures."

"Christ," Hampson said as he pulled down the zipper on his trousers and turned toward the toilet bowl. "This is embarrassing. Don't you think this is taking things a bit too far?"

"Listen, Hampson, this isn't exactly a picnic for me either!"

Hampson had trouble starting his urine. He finally did, though, and as he was relieving himself, it occurred to him that he hadn't had anyone watch him urinate since he was about six years old—a long, long time ago.

When he was ready to leave, he turned in the cramped space, brushing against the marshal, who was having trouble unlocking the door. It finally opened, and Hampson walked out in front of his guard and back to his seat. He tried not to make eye contact with a surprised woman who had been waiting for the rest room. They walked back to their seats in the last row.

The long plane ride seemed endless to Hampson. Humiliated, he wondered what to expect next.

# Chapter Forty–Three

Friday morning, October the Thirteenth, Malcolm Karl, special agent in charge at the FBI's Baltimore office, was introduced to Gilbert Autry at the firm's office downtown. Almost exactly what Autry expected, Karl *looked* like an FBI agent. He was of average height with a thick neck and close crew cut, was obviously in superb condition and could clearly take care of himself. When he put on his eyeglasses and spoke, though, his appearance and demeanor became that of an intellectual.

"So what do I have to do?" Autry asked.

"Nothing much," Karl answered. "All you really have to do is agree to let McGuire work from this office. You've got to swear to keep all of your conversations confidential."

"Why work out of here? Don't get me wrong, I'm more than happy to cooperate, but wouldn't it be easier for Pat to work out of your office?"

"That's a good question, Mr. Autry," Karl responded. "I'm going to be frank with you; even with all our resources, we don't know what they know. We don't know where Ms. Davies is, nor Poupore and, for all we know, you're all being watched." As Karl spoke, he noted Autry's rapt attention. "We discussed this at length at our office and we all find it's better this way. Who knows, Rita or her sister or even Poupore or Lovelady may try to reach Pat, and we want him here with one of our people just in case. Am I making any sense?"

Autry nodded.

"I'll leave you alone then and get to work with McGuire now, if you don't mind."

"Fine."

As Karl left the room, Autry had to pull in his urge to get himself involved. He knew his efforts and hard work had made him financially prosperous and an admired professional but, like many men his age, he secretly wished he had spent at least some of his time, particularly when he was young, doing something exciting.

Autry felt he had never tested himself physically. His career was successful and rewarding, but he wanted so much to be able to say that he was a veteran or that he had volunteered as a local firefighter, or had done something exhilarating and adventuresome—maybe even dangerous. He envied Pat and was even somewhat jealous of his own son because of their football experiences and Pat's Marine background.

Gilbert Autry first viewed the situation as an opportunity but, as a professional, he knew better than to become overly-involved and he wouldn't interfere. He would let them deal directly with Pat and Russell; he quietly accepted that he wouldn't do anything unless asked. Part of him hoped he would become involved.

Pat had the call-forwarding button on his telephone engaged and his office door closed so they wouldn't be interrupted. "Okay," Agent Karl said, "this is what we want you to do."

Malcolm Karl told Pat that he was to listen to the tape carefully. He was to note airlines and flight numbers and cross-reference each alias used for air travel and room reservations with the conspirator present at the meeting. He was also asked to try to identify the voices, as scientists in the FBI lab, working on voice-identification tasks later on, would need all the help they could get.

The FBI had already made arrangements with the airlines and hotels involved. After Pat's work with the tape was finished, he would be working with another agent and the air carriers and resorts. They would be getting copies of tickets and hotel confirmations, evidence of who made the reservations, and other information. Signatures on all the documents would need to be analyzed by handwriting experts to prove that the individuals under suspicion were actually at the price-fixing meetings.

When his work was completed and reviewed, a judge would be approached. If everything went right, the data should present sufficient grounds for the judge to issue subpoenas for the bank records, time and attendance information, and other evidence deemed important to close the case.

"One more thing," Karl said, pulling a piece of paper from his suit pocket. "This is a list of emergency telephone and beeper numbers for my staff and I. Any one of us can be reached any time, day or night. If you are ever in danger, you know how to get us, and we'll get help to you immediately. Do you understand?"

"Sure," Pat said as he took the paper from Karl, glanced at it and put it in the pocket of his appointment book.

He long ago accepted the fact that what he was doing was dangerous, particularly after his football injury, but as he glanced at the emergency numbers, the gravity of the situation sobered him and again he thought of the extreme danger Rita might be facing.

He had spoken precious little about his feelings for Rita with anyone except Russell and his parents, and even with them he never shared that they were falling in love. He and Rita had never even discussed it themselves, but he knew as did she, that their relationship was headed for an inescapable conclusion. The way they looked into each other's eyes and the surge of electricity they each felt when they touched were unmistakable. Pat had never experienced these emotions with Lynn.

He missed Rita terribly and would do anything to get her back safely, no matter what it took.

Karl had been observing Pat and knew that, for the moment, he was lost in thought. He somehow knew when to continue, and he did.

"Don't forget," Karl said, "if you hear from Miss Davies or her sister, you give them these numbers too. Convince them that they're in danger. I hope I'm wrong, but it's possible that Lovelady and the others are trying to get to them also."

"And you don't have enough on Lovelady now to make a move?"

"There's no way right now. Like I said, we ran everything by the judge. She's still not convinced we have enough. You do your job, and then we'll have what we need. Patience pays off in this work."

"Malcolm, I'm sorry, but we're not talking just money and a cash scam here! Everyone in this office has had to deal with Bob Ramsey's murder, and to me that's enough!" Pat was discouraged and he spoke his feelings with conviction and without apology.

Karl didn't interrupt, letting Pat vent his frustrations. When Pat had finished, Karl removed his glasses and looked Pat directly in the eye. "Pat, in this work you have to remember one thing, and that is the fact that our laws aren't designed to punish guilty people; they're intended to protect innocent people. As frustrating as it gets at times, we try never to forget that."

Pausing respectfully, Pat smiled, realizing Karl was right and everyone was doing all they could. "So, how long do you think it'll take for you to find Rita and her sister?" he asked.

"No way to tell. She's slick, I have to tell you. We'll find her, but when is anybody's guess." Karl could see the look of frustration and anxiety on Pat's face. "Don't worry, we'll find her, Pat."

Pat just nodded as Karl left the office. Pat momentarily thought again about the hazards Rita might be facing and the feelings he had for her. He quickly went to work.

That afternoon, Bob Ramsey's widow answered a knock on her door. When she opened the door, she was disconcerted to see the neighborhood postman.

"Hi Jimmie, how are you today?" he asked with an understanding and compassionate smile on his face.

"I'm fine, Steve, is there a problem?"

"Oh, no," he said cheerfully, "I just need you to sign for this letter."

"What is it?" Since her husband's death, she hadn't received anything but bad news and she didn't know if she could cope with any more. The letter she had signed for from the insurance company had been the last straw. The lack of coverage her husband had on his life, and the required waiting period in a homicide case had been almost more than she could handle.

"I really don't know, but you have to sign for it." He handed her a yellow form. She scribbled her name and handed it back to the letter carrier. He ripped off the original receipt, and gave a copy of the form and the letter to her. He wished her a pleasant day and left.

Jimmie Ramsey sat down at the kitchen table, put on her reading glasses, and took a deep breath. The return address designated the sender to be United Federal Bank. The bank had a Baltimore address. "Please don't be more bad news," she silently prayed, as she tore open the envelope. She began to read:

*Dear Mrs. Ramsey:*

*By way of introduction, my name is Connie Wick. I am a bank officer with the trust department of United Federal Bank. I represent one of the bank's clients who wishes to remain anonymous.*

*Our client has taken an interest in your plight, since the unfortunate circumstances surrounding the death of your husband. The client has deposited a large sum of money with our trust department. Our instructions are to arrange a meeting with you at our headquarters in Baltimore to discuss executing the client's instructions.*

*Briefly, you will receive a monthly stipend from the corpus of the trust fund to assist you and your family with the ordinary and necessary expenses of maintaining your home, providing adequate care for your children and so forth. Additionally, the client has instructed us to provide for continuation of formal education for both you and your children, in the form of tuition payments, room and board expenses, etc.*

*At your earliest opportunity, please contact me at the telephone number noted on this letterhead, so we can proceed accordingly.*

> *Cordially,*
> *Connie Wick*
> *Trust Officer*

Jimmie Ramsey read the letter several times before taking off her glasses to wipe her eyes.

# Chapter Forty-Four

With the time change from Madrid to New York, this Friday the Thirteenth was beginning to feel to Hampson like the longest ever. Dusk was settling in oranges and muddy yellows over the New York sky when Hampson, accompanied by U.S. Marshals, landed at the John F. Kennedy Airport. They stayed in their seats until all of the other passengers had deplaned, then Hampson began his long, humiliating trek through the terminal.

Flanked on both sides by the marshals, they passed the few passengers still standing in the gate seating area, obviously talking to friends and relatives. His embarrassment escalated as everyone stopped talking, staring as they passed. Finally, they reached the center of the terminal and stood next to a door that had **Airport Security** imprinted in large letters on it. One of the marshals said, "Okay, Hampson, stop right here." The agent knocked on the door, and it opened almost immediately. A tall, muscular man in a green suit filled the doorway, smiling.

"Hi Mike, how have you been?" he asked, ignoring Hampson.

"Just great, Chris," Vensel answered. "How about yourself?"

"Couldn't be better. Is this our man?" He turned toward Hampson.

"That's him."

"Any problems I should be aware of?"

"No. He's a pussy cat."

Hampson felt his face flush red at the remark.

Still looking at Hampson, the burly man said, "I'm Agent Howe with the FBI, Hampson. I'll be taking you from here."

"Where are we going, and what am I being charged with?" Hampson asked.

"We're going to Metropolitan Correctional Center in New York City. I'm not at liberty to discuss anything else. They'll explain everything to you once we get there," he said, turning back to Vensel

"Got paperwork for me, Jim?"

Vensel reached into his breast pocket, pulling out the handcuff key and some papers. He handed them to the FBI agent. "Here you go," he said. "You know where to sign."

Agent Howe took the papers, glanced over them, and signed in two places. He folded one copy and put it in his briefcase, giving the other copy to the marshal.

"Okay, Chris, he's all yours," Vensel said. "Have a safe ride up to the Center."

"Take it easy, Jim," Howe said smiling. As he turned to look at his prisoner, his expression changed instantly.

"Listen, Hampson, you walk on my left side through the airport, and keep your hands covered with that sweater. We don't want to upset anyone. Understand?"

"Yes," Hampson said, with frustration in his voice. He had spotted a phone on the desk in the office. He wanted desperately to call Poupore, but the opportunity passed as he was ushered through the doorway. He doubted they would have let him make the call anyhow.

As they walked through the terminal, Hampson tried to act naturally but felt conspicuous. To his surprise, no one paid any attention to him, not even making eye contact. He and the FBI agent looked like the hundreds of other hurrying businessmen. They left through the two exit doors of the main terminal entrance, and Hampson stopped without resisting when the agent took his arm, tugging on it lightly.

"Stop here," he ordered. They stood in the fading New York sunshine for a few minutes without speaking until a red Ford Explorer pulled up to the curb. It was unmarked. A blonde woman stepped out of the car and came directly to Howe.

"Any trouble, Chris?" she asked.

"Nope, routine. Are we ready?" he answered.

"All set. Let's go, then." She opened the rear door of the Explorer near the curb on the passenger side. Howe led Hampson to the car, giving him the familiar, "watch your head" admonition. He then walked around the car, opened the driver's side rear door, and got in.

The driver pulled out into traffic toward the Long Island Expressway, heading for lower Manhattan.

They passed a full half-hour of bumper-to-bumper traffic in absolute silence. Hampson became more and more anxious. He wanted to shout out loud. He wasn't used to being treated this way; usually he called the shots. When he couldn't stand the tension anymore, he broke the silence. "Listen, could someone tell me what's going on here?"

Agent Howe took off his sunglasses, turning toward him. "Listen," he said, "we're not permitted to talk with prisoners. Understand?"

Hampson felt incredulous. How could this be happening to him? The agent was still looking at him, obviously waiting for an answer. After a few seconds, he nodded with resignation.

A few minutes later, the driver pulled into a narrow alleyway around a large, imposing building with the words *Metropolitan Corrections Center* imprinted above the doorway. If you hadn't known about the Center, it could easily have been missed.

Hampson could see the bridge connecting the center to the Courthouse and City Hall. They were in the middle of New York's Police Plaza.

They pulled the car around the back to a sign: **GATE 1.** The tall, chain-link fence gate, with razor ribbon glistening on the top, opened. The car moved toward another closed gate, about twenty feet ahead. Hampson heard clanking behind him and turned his head to see the first gate closing. Once it was closed, Agent Howe opened his door and walked around the back of the car to open Hampson's door.

"Get out," he said, and Hampson swung his legs, lowered his head, and stood up. Howe motioned toward a small, locked, door-sized gate beside the large gate. Two uniformed federal corrections officers were inside. Silently, the FBI agent took papers from his briefcase and handed them through the fence. The first officer looked through the papers, noted the appropriate signatures, and handed them to his partner. He removed a key ring from his belt and sifted the keys through his fingers until he found one for the padlock. The lock popped, and he swung the gate open.

"Thanks, Chris," he said, adding, "Anything we should be aware of?"

"Routine for this place."

"Okay, Hampson, come with us." Hampson passed through the gate, and the corrections officer immediately swung it shut and locked it.

"Where are we going, and when is someone going to tell me what's going on?"

"We're taking you to processing and classification. They'll tell you everything. Let's go."

The three headed toward a sign saying **PROCESSING**. As they walked, he heard the Explorer backing out of the gate and the gate closing again behind it.

Inside the processing room, he was fingerprinted and photographed, front and side. Hampson was told to put all valuables into a box. With no choice but to cooperate, and without hesitating, Hampson removed watch and rings, putting them and his wallet into the box. The officer noted the items on a form on his clipboard and handed the clipboard to Hampson. "Sign."

Hampson's valuables were handed to another officer standing behind the counter under a sign that said **Prisoner Inventory**.

Hampson's gut wrenched when he was told that he would be strip-searched, and the sobering fact struck him that the really harrowing scene of the nightmare he was living was about to start. The very thought of standing naked before another man was offensive. He looked around at the men. For the most part, he conjectured not a highly educated bunch. He wondered what they did all day and whether they enjoyed their jobs. What would make a man become a corrections officer? He wondered if he could trust any of them.

Lost in thought, he jolted back to reality when he heard an officer call his name aloud to get his attention. "Hampson! Turn your pockets inside out." He complied, and a peso fell face down on the concrete floor. One of the officers picked it up and it was included with the rest of his personal effects. After handing over Hampson's coin to the inventory officer the correctional officer ordered Hampson to follow them to another room. Walking down the hall between the two correctional officers, Hampson's arms started trembling uncontrollably when he saw a grey door, badly in need of sanding and repainting, with a sign above it that simply said, **SEARCH ROOM**. The door had no windows.

One of the officers unlocked the door lock with a key from the ring on his belt and opened the door. The other officer led Hampson in by his upper arm. The room itself was painted a dull shade of white and, like the door, it had no windows. The fluorescent tubes in the recessed lighting fixture in the ceiling emitted a kind of light that Hampson hated so much he refused to have this type of lighting in his home, as it seemed to almost emphasize skin imperfections. His vanity could not allow that. Other than a simple wooden chair, a small table, a railing attached to the wall, and a shower nozzle protruding from the ceiling in the corner, the room was barren. The floor was cold concrete.

"Okay, now everything off."

"Right here? Now?" he said, still not quite believing that he was living this nightmare. Both officers put on rubber gloves.

Alarmed, as he pulled off his clothes, he saw that the man in front of him held a flashlight. His mind raced. He wanted to make a phone call, but here he stood, taking off all of his clothes in front of a man with a flashlight. One of the officers put his clothes on the table.

Once he had shed his clothes, the second officer started to check through them. Systematic and unemotional, he seemed to have searched clothes all his life. He squeezed and shook out every part of every piece of clothing.

The first man asked Hampson to assume a spread-eagle position and lean against the wall. From that moment, he tried to disassociate himself from the ordeal. He closed his eyes, trying to breathe deeply, hoping to relax. He replayed the details of the vacation he had been planning. He tried to picture the beach, the white sand, the pure green-blue water, and Linda wind-surfing.

Time seemed to stand still. He opened his eyes quickly when the officer asked him to run his fingers through his hair. He did as he was told, and then the officer also checked his hair. Hampson was asked to open his mouth wide, move his tongue, pull his upper and lower cheeks away from his teeth. He was ordered to turn around. He closed his eyes again as the officer checked his back and chest down to his waistline, his fingernails, and his armpits. The worst was yet to come, and Hampson knew it.

One of the officers sat on the chair and, still shining the flashlight on him, examined his buttocks and groin areas as he was standing. Though the officer didn't touch him, Hampson felt violated. He forgot about the beach and thought about this man. Who was he? How dare he? Why did he, Jim Hampson, once head of the National Tobacco Federation, once head of a group of highly educated, prestigious directors have to submit to this?

"Bend forward, grab the railing with one hand and spread the cheeks of your buttocks with the other, Mr. Hampson." The officer interrupted his thoughts.

Then, the flashlight focused on his groin area and in between his legs. He was asked to lift his private parts. Except for asking him to help with the search by bending and lifting, the officer never spoke.

The search over, the officer directed him to the shower, standing within a few feet of him the whole time. When he was finished, he was told to wait, they had to spray him for lice. Once again he tried to dissociate his mind from his body during the humiliating ordeal.

When they were finished, at last the officer returned his underclothes. He was asked his clothes and shoes sizes and was handed an orange jump suit marked L, folded neatly, and a pair of new, white tennis shoes. The clothes he had left on the table were now with his personal items also.

Hampson put on the jump suit with **MCC New York** written in gold letters on the back and pulled on the tennis shoes. He could hear the men talking, but all he could make out were the last two words, "Follow me." He moved with resignation. He felt ashamed, humiliated, and angry. But he knew that this was not the time to protest.

They walked down a short hallway, stopping at a door marked **Classification**. The officer knocked. A male voice from behind the door, responded, "Come in." The corrections officer opened the door, and Hampson saw a man in a gray suit working at his desk. He didn't look up when the door opened. Hampson hated waiting. He had fired highly paid professional people for keeping him waiting.

After a few minutes, the man looked up. "Hampson, I'm the classification officer here, have a seat." When Hampson sat the man continued, "I see that you have no past record. Is that true?"

"Yes, that is true."

"Good. Now I'd like to ask you a few questions from this screening questionnaire." The classification officer held up the questionnaire so Hampson could see the heading.

"You'll be getting a thorough physical when the doctor comes in this week. For now, we just want to make sure that you don't have any immediate needs.

"Mr. Hampson, are you on any medications now?"

Hampson answered his question directly and without emotion, holding his head slightly to the side and looking down.

"No, no medications," he said.

"Are you depressed?"

He jerked his head upright, "What do you mean, depressed?"

"Have you ever thought about suicide?"

Hampson nearly smiled. But he answered in a monotone, "No, never."

The officer nodded as he jotted down short notes on the form.

The screening process took about ten minutes.

"Do you think that you'll have any problems getting along with other inmates?"

"No, why should I?"

"I don't know, only you can answer that. Do you think that there might be anyone in here who might have a grudge against you?"

"Not that I'm aware of."

"Okay then, I'm going to classify you with general population."

"What does that mean?"

"It means that you'll be staying in Cellblock B. You'll eat in the cafeteria with everyone else, exercise with everyone else, relax with everyone else, and shower with everyone else."

Hampson paused before speaking. The meeting in the safety of this office was ending, and soon he would be walking into the jail. *"With everyone else"*—that was the phrase bothering him. He felt his stomach sink, and he needed some kind of reassurance.

"Listen, uh," he said, "I've heard stories. Am I going to be safe?"

The officer squinted when he said, "We try our best to keep that sort of thing under control, but I'm not going to tell you that it doesn't happen. There are a lot more of you than there are of us, and we can't watch everybody all the time."

Hampson swallowed hard. "What next?"

"You'll be taken to your cell."

"When will I find out what's going on?"

"Tomorrow. You'll meet with an attorney who will explain everything."

Before he could ask any more questions, the man pushed a button on his desk and the door behind Hampson opened. Another corrections officer walked in. "Yes?" he said.

"Cellblock B. General population for now."

The corrections officer touched Hampson's upper arm, when Hampson spoke to the classifications officer again. "Listen, I think . . ."

"Not now, Hampson," he said, cutting him off, as he pulled a file from the side of his desk drawer. He paused to look up. "You know I'd love to chat, but I'm afraid I have work to do."

Hampson felt the officer tug at his arm again, and he walked with him to the end of the corridor to a metal door. Another officer met them at the door.

"Whatcha got?"

"Cellblock B, general population," he said. The other man pushed a button and the door to Hampson's right opened. The officer waved him through, and he heard the door clank shut behind him.

He had never been inside a jail before. He felt scared. He felt he would suddenly start trembling again as the inmates in the hall of Cellblock B turned to look at him.

Hampson saw row after row of bars lining the corridor. A few cell doors were open; others were closed. As the officer walked him down the cellblock, he tried to look straight ahead, but he couldn't help glancing from side to side. Some cells were empty; some contained one prisoner, and some two. Most of the prisoners were either reading or sleeping. The prison echoed with a dull roar of television sets, radios, and conversations, yet everyone seemed to stop what they were doing to stare at him as he passed—the New Guy.

Some of the cells were just what he expected—Playboy and Penthouse nude centerfolds taped to the cell walls. Most weren't what he was expecting at all, being meticulously clean and neat. Some held rows and rows of paperback books and several had crucifixes and quotes from the Bible on the walls. Hampson hoped his cell would fall in one of the last three groups.

His knees were shaking and he had to stiffen his body and take short, quick breaths as they walked the entire length of the cellblock, stopping in front of the last cell on the left.

"Well, Hampson, you're in luck for someone just checking in," the corrections officer said.

"What do you mean?" he asked.

"You've got a private room. At least for now." Hampson looked into an empty cell and back at the officer.

"Go on in, Hampson."

He forced himself to walk into the cell, and the officer closed and locked the cell door behind him. From the center of the small space, he turned to ask, "When do I talk to an attorney?"

"Listen, you'll know everything you need to know tomorrow. Why are you in a hurry anyway? You got a hot date tonight or something?" The officer chuckled, and without waiting for Hampson to respond, he walked away.

He turned back slowly, taking stock of his new situation. He guessed that the cell was about ten to twelve feet long and about eight feet wide. On his left were bunk beds, each about the size of a cot. Instead of the metal frame he was expecting, the two beds were concrete and permanently attached to the wall. They were unmade, with a pillow, two folded sheets, and a brown blanket at the bottom of each. In the right-hand corner of the cell was a toilet with no lid, also attached to the wall. This was next to a sink with a metal, scratched mirror over it. The only other item was a recessed light in the ceiling. Almost immediately the same officer unlocked the door, walked in and took the bedding off the top bunk.

"Why did you take that?" Hampson asked, but the guard just looked at him like he had been asked the dumbest question he'd ever heard. The officer relocked the cell, not bothering to answer when the obvious reason suddenly occurred to Hampson—suicide.

He sat down on the bottom bunk. He put his face in his hands, trying to gather his thoughts, thinking about all that had happened, about his wife, the money, and the scam. Who could have tipped off the FBI? He sat alone, thinking for a long, long time.

At about 8:00 PM, he guessed, the same officer strolled up to his cell. "You hungry, Hampson?"

"Not particularly."

"Suit yourself then," the officer said. "You won't eat again 'till tomorrow morning."

He was glad he decided not to eat—he needed the time to think.

# Chapter Forty-Five

Unused to the constant drone of the noisy life that surrounded him, Hampson lay awake for most of the night. His mind, numb with tiredness, still churned as he contemplated what lay ahead. Finally, around 4:00 AM, the halls became still, and Hampson lay quiet in a dreamless but troubled sleep.

"Hey! Are you Hampson?" Daylight streamed down the hall. A corrections officer stood outside his cell.

"Yes." He pulled himself up to look. As he rose to a sitting position, he realized he hadn't even attempted to convince the officer that his name was Sanchez.

"Come with me," the officer unlocked and opened the cell.

"Where are we going?" Hampson pushed his fingers through his uncombed hair.

"Your attorney wants to talk to you."

"My attorney? I haven't even spoken to my attorney yet. What's he doing here?"

"He's your appointed attorney."

"I want to talk to my own lawyer." His voice rose; he had to start fighting back. "When do I get to talk to him?"

"Look, talk about it with the lawyer. They make a lot more money than I do and, if you don't want to talk to him, fine. You stay here, and I'll tell him to go away. If you want to talk to somebody, you've got to come with me now. Understand?"

Hampson sighed. "Okay," he said, following the officer between the same long row of cells he had passed the day before. They went through the same security checkpoint, stopping in front of a wooden door marked **CONFERENCE ROOM 2**.

Without knocking, the officer opened the door, silently gesturing Hampson into the room. Hampson saw an overweight man in a rumpled suit reading a file. The collar of his white shirt was visibly soiled, the top button of the shirt wasn't fastened and the loosened purple tie was a loud ugly print. Without looking up, the man motioned for Hampson to sit in the chair across the table from him.

Hampson watched impatiently as the man read page-after-page of the file. He fidgeted, feeling tired and realizing now that he was hungry. Finally, the man closed the file and put it on the table.

He studied Hampson for a few moments and finally said, "Well, Mr. Hampson—looks like you and your wife are in a whole heap of trouble."

"Who are you?" Hampson asked.

"Zietz, Lou Zietz. I'm your court-appointed attorney."

"I want my own attorney," Hampson said, "and what the hell is going on here?"

"You can have your own attorney if you want. Just let me know any time. Hey, you're not going to hurt my feelings. But, look man, it's Saturday, and until you get settled, I'm all you've got."

Attorney Lou Zietz's suit was definitely out-of-style, he was overweight, had an untrimmed mustache and needed a haircut but, somehow, his face was pleasing, even attractive.

"What am I being charged with?" As Hampson began to feel more awake, he was regaining his old assertiveness.

Zietz opened the file before answering. Raising his head, he met Hampson's eyes. "Income tax evasion," he said calmly.

"Income tax evasion?" Hampson was surprised. He had expected to hear something else.

"Yeah. Tax evasion."

"Bull shit! You people don't go through all this for a tax charge."

"*Those* people, you mean," Zietz said. "Don't forget that I'm your attorney for now.

"You're right, they don't go through all this for a routine tax case. Tax evasion was just an excuse to extradite you back here. They've got you here, and now they've got time to process the other charges they'll be laying on you."

"Like what?" Hampson wondered just how much they knew.

Zietz picked up the file again. "Well," he said, "seems like a whole lot of money is missing from the National Tobacco Federation."

Hampson looked surprised at what he had just heard, considering what he had against the others. *How could they risk it?* he thought.

"And that's not all."

"What else?"

"Murder."

"Murder! Whose?" Hampson's voice shrilled.

"It seems a fellow by the name of Ramsey bought it, and the Feds think you may have had something to do with it."

"Bob Ramsey is dead?" Hampson asked with sincere surprise. Zietz studied his reaction before answering.

"Yeah. Gunned down right in front of his office. You knew him, didn't you?"

Hampson put his head in his hands, trying to take it all in. At last, he said, "Mr. Zietz, this is all a bit too much for me right now. I need some time to think and then talk with my own attorney. What do I do now?"

"As your attorney right now, I have to tell you that you're up to your ass in alligators, and you'd better start some serious thinking about draining the swamp. You've got 'till Monday morning to decide who's going to represent you. I'll see you Monday at ten. Okay?"

Hesitatingly, Hampson nodded.

Zietz stood up. "An officer will take you to your cell. Here's my card." Hampson looked at the card and then at the attorney.

"Mr. Zietz," he said.

"Yes?"

"Two things."

"Yeah."

"Where is my wife?"

"It's my understanding that she's in a women's area of the center here, facing charges of her own, specifically being an accomplice to you. What else?"

"Can I make phone calls?"

"Yes. The officers will take care of that."

Hampson heard the door behind him open. A corrections officer said, "Okay, Hampson, time's up. Come with me."

"By the way," Zietz said, closing his briefcase.

"Yes?" Hampson replied.

"I understand from your wife's attorney that she doesn't have any idea what happened to the money. Just something for you to think about until Monday."

# Chapter Forty-Six

Two hours later, Hampson stood at a long bank of telephones, waiting his turn. When a phone became free, he quickly dialed an operator who placed his call.

"Law office," he heard a female voice say.

"I have a collect call for Mr. Ralph Poupore," the operator said. "It's from Mr. Jim Hampson. Will you accept charges?"

"Just a moment, operator, and I'll check. He usually doesn't take calls on Saturdays."

Hampson heard the operator say thank you and a click as she left the line.

"Jim! Is that you?" It was Poupore's voice.

"Of course it's me! Who the hell else would call you using my name!"

"Are you calling from Spain?" Poupore asked.

"No, New York City—the Metropolitan Corrections Center!" Hampson answered gruffly.

"What! What happened?"

"If I knew, I wouldn't be in this goddamned mess, and I wouldn't be calling you! Listen, I don't have much time. I need your help."

"Of course! Anything."

"First, you've got to get me out of here. Do whatever you have to do."

"Jim, I hate to say this, but you're talking to the wrong guy."

"What do you mean? You're my lawyer, for Christ's sake!" Hampson's voice was rising, and the inmate on the telephone next to him gave him an angry look.

"I'm your lawyer, Jim, but I don't do any criminal work! You know what kind of work I do."

"Shit," Hampson said. "What the hell am I supposed to do?"

"Listen, don't get upset. I'll get the right person for you. Stay there and I'll have someone contact you as soon as I can."

"Stay there!" Hampson said, mimicking Poupore. "Of course I'll be here! How in the hell can I go anywhere! Who're you going to call?"

"A lawyer by the name of Heinrich—John Heinrich. He's expensive but all he does is criminal law, and he's good. I'll call him at home right away and don't worry, he'll get you out. If anybody can do it, John can. Let's just hope we can get him at home today."

"Okay, you better! Tell him the attorney they appointed to me says I've got to get this resolved by Monday."

"What's your number?"

Hampson looked at the number slot on the phone, frowning. "Listen, some son-of-a-bitch has scratched out the number! I'll just have to call him. What's his number?"

Poupore gave Hampson the number, which he quickly committed to memory.

"Heinrich, right?" he asked.

"Right, John Heinrich."

"Call him now, and tell him I'll be calling collect in about five minutes. Understand?"

"Okay, Jim, and don't worry, he's good."

"He'd better be," Hampson said, as he hung up the phone.

Poupore hung up, smiling. He sat for a moment, then picked up the phone and dialed a number.

"Hello, Heinrich residence." The phone was answered on the first ring.

"Hello, Ann? Ralph Poupore. Sorry to bother you at home, but is John in, please?"

"Sure, Ralph, he won't mind. Just a minute."

Poupore was still smiling when he heard Heinrich say, "Ralph?"

"Hi, John. Listen, I just got off the phone with the guy I told you about."

"He called, huh?"

"Sure, I knew he would. You didn't doubt my word, did you?" he asked, laughing.

"You're a piece of work, Poupore. You didn't give out my personal number to another inmate, did you?"

"No, of course not."

"What would you like for me to do for you then?"

"He'll be calling you collect from the Metropolitan Correctional Center in New York. He's the only one I gave your number to. Don't worry, he certainly can't afford you now."

"Jim Hampson, right?"

"You got it."

After waiting again in line to place his second phone call, Hampson dialed Heinrich's number. In a few seconds, the connection was completed, and Heinrich answered, accepting charges.

"Jim Hampson?"

"Yes, this is Hampson."

"This is John Heinrich. Ralph Poupore told me that you needed help. Tell me what's going on."

"This is confidential?"

"Of course."

"Listen, my wife and I have been charged with tax evasion."

"Is that it? No problem."

"No, that's not all," Hampson answered.

"What else."

"They also said I'm under suspicion for embezzlement and a murder I don't know anything about."

Hampson heard a whistle come through the phone.

"Can you help me?"

"Sure, but it's going to be expensive."

"How much?"

"I don't know how much until I know more about the case, but at least fifteen K."

Hampson thought before answering. "And you're sure you can help me?"

"As sure as I can be. Obviously one can never be *absolutely* sure about these things, but let's just say I've been very successful in the past."

"Okay. When can I see you?"

"I can drive up there tomorrow."

Hampson breathed a sigh of relief.

"Great."

"One thing," Heinrich said.

"Anything."

"I need ten now. I'm sure you understand."

"What! I don't know how I can get it to you now!"

"Wait a minute, Hampson. Poupore told me to get you out of there and that money wouldn't be a problem!"

"I can't explain now. I'll tell you all about it when I see you."

"Sorry. No tickee, no washee. We're both in business here, and I'm a busy man. Now do we have a deal or not?"

Hampson closed his eyes and said, with desperation in his voice, "Mr. Heinrich, I need your help. If you come up here and help me, I'll double your fee when all of this is worked out. Please help me, I don't know who else to turn to!"

Immediately, Hampson heard Heinrich say, "I'm sorry for the misunderstanding, Mr. Hampson, but I'm afraid I can't help you."

"Mr. Heinrich, I . . ."

"Good day, Mr. Hampson," Heinrich said and hung up the phone.

Hampson heard the click and dropped the receiver. He stood by the phone a few seconds, staring at nothing, when an officer said, "Time's up, Hampson."

"Can I make one more call?"

"If I let you make another one now, you don't get any telephone privileges tomorrow."

"I know."

"Well, it's your dime and it's your time. Five minutes," he said, and walked away.

Hampson made another collect call to Poupore. Only this time, Poupore's secretary said that he was unavailable—out of the office—he was gone for the weekend and wouldn't return for a few days.

Hampson hung up the telephone and was taken back to his cell. Sitting on his cot, locked in a tiny bare cell, he thought, again, about how, just three days earlier, he had been heading to the bank to withdraw money for a vacation.

Poupore was at his desk when he heard the telephone buzz.

"Yes?"

"Mr. Poupore, Mr. Heinrich on line two."

"Fine. Did our friend call?" he asked the receptionist.

"Yes. I told him that you had already left, as you asked me to."

"Thank you," Poupore said, pushing in line two.

"John?"

"Yes."

"And?"

"Seems our friend is having a little difficulty coming up with the down payment."

Both men laughed.

"Okay, my man," Poupore said. "Thanks, let me return the favor for you sometime."

"It's been a pleasure, Mr. Poupore."

"Likewise, Mr. Heinrich."

On that note, they both hung up.

"Let's see," Poupore said aloud to himself, stretching back in his chair. "If all goes well, should be about a week 'till he calls again. Two at the most."

He walked over to an impressive-looking diploma on the opposite wall, admired it for a second, took it off the wall and placed it on the carpet against his desk. He muttered the combination under his breath, as he turned the dial on his wall safe. He took out the white metal box Hampson had given him months before, and smiled again, patting the still-intact seal.

"Fifty thousand," he thought to himself. For the first time, he was genuinely curious about what else was in that box.

"Two weeks at most," he thought again to himself. He returned the box to the safe, locked it and replaced the diploma, carefully straightening it.

Jim Hampson spent a long weekend waiting for Monday to come.

# Chapter Forty-Seven

The following Monday. . .

"You've got a visitor, Hampson," a corrections officer opened his cell door.

"Who is it?" he knew it had to be Lou Zietz.

"Your attorney. Follow me."

They arrived at the conference room, and Zietz rose from the table. He wore the same brown suit and the same tie.

"Hey, you made it through the weekend!" Zietz said, a slight smile on his lips.

"Don't you have any other clothes?" Hampson asked.

"Don't you?" Zietz shot back wryly with a half-smile, looking at Hampson's prison jump suit.

"Touché!" Hampson said with a sarcastic smile as he sat down opposite Zietz

"Well, have you decided who will have the privilege of representing you?"

Frustrated, Hampson looked away and then back at Zietz. "I guess it's you for now."

"I'm honored." Zietz's sarcasm equaled Hampson's frustration.

After a few seconds of awkward silence, Zietz said, "Let's cut the shit, Hampson. We don't have much time. Now tell me everything you know."

"This is privileged conversation?"

"Of course."

"Tell me what you know, first." Hampson was fishing. He didn't want to reveal anything the authorities didn't already know and Zietz had not yet earned his confidence.

"Fair enough," Zietz looked Hampson straight in the eye. "You've been charged with income tax evasion."

"Who's the plaintiff?" Hampson asked.

"The U.S. government, of course."

"I don't understand. I've covered my tracks pretty well. Where did they get their information?"

"Somebody squealed," Zietz answered.

"Who was it?"

"Don't know. Whoever it was had damn good proof, and they were granted anonymity. Any idea who it could be?"

Hampson thought. "There can be only one person."

"Who's that?" Zietz asked this time.

"Robert Ramsey."

"The same guy who was killed?" Zietz asked, trying to piece together the puzzle.

"Yes," Hampson said, adding, "but I swear to God I didn't have anything to do with it. I didn't know anything about it until you told me a couple of days ago." Hampson then told Zietz about Ramsey's role in skimming cash.

Zietz leaned toward Hampson, looking him in his eyes. "I'm your attorney. You've got to tell me everything."

"I will. I swear, I don't know a thing about what happened to Ramsey."

"What about the money, then?"

Hampson sighed. "Okay. I'll tell you everything."

Hampson began his story. He told him about the secret price-fixing meetings, about the slush funds that Ramsey helped him set up, about embezzling the money from the Federation, and how he got identification from Poupore before leaving for Spain. He told him about his affair with Rita Davies and her role in setting up the meetings. He told him that everything had gone according to plan, until he and his wife were picked up by the Spanish police and extradited back.

"So where is the money now?"

"I swear I don't know. All I know is that I went to the bank to make a withdrawal, and they told me that my wife had closed out our accounts. I don't know what in hell happened to the money. What do *you* know?"

"Your wife said she doesn't know anything about it either. Are you sure you're being up front with me?"

"Of course! What do I have to gain by lying?"

"What makes you think your wife closed out the accounts?"

"The bank made copies of her identification for their files. They showed it to me. It was Linda, damn it!"

"Are you absolutely positive?"

"Yes, I swear," Hampson said. "If Linda didn't do it, I don't have any idea what's going on. What am I facing, and what can I do?"

Zietz waited a few seconds before answering. "They've probably got you nailed on the tax evasion through bank records. That's how they got you here. And because they've got you under wraps, they have all the time in the world to piece together the embezzlement, and maybe even tie you into Ramsey's murder."

"How much time could I be facing on the tax charge?"

"Six to eight, probably, unless you cooperate with them."

"How?"

"By telling them where the money is."

Hampson took another deep breath. "I can't. I swear I don't know what happened to it." He inhaled very deeply and looked blankly at the ceiling, frustrated.

"It's six to eight then, unless you have something to give them." Zietz paused, studying Hampson. "And there ain't nothin' anybody can do to help you; high-priced lawyers or lawyers like me. That's just the way it is."

Hampson took another deep breath, resting his forehead in his hand. He looked up suddenly.

"There is something."

"What?"

"Just in case something went wrong along the way, I bought myself a little insurance policy."

"What did you do?"

"I taped the price-fixing meetings."

"You what?" Zietz's voice and face both told of his surprise.

"You heard me. I taped all the meetings. Not only that, but I made notes of where the meetings were, airline flight numbers, aliases of everyone there, check numbers, amounts of cash payments—everything." He told Zietz how easy it had been to tape record the meetings.

"Where are the tapes now?"

"In a safe place."

"Where?"

"In due time."

"What do you want in return for the tapes?"

"I've got to think about it. Don't do anything until I see you tomorrow, and I'll tell you what I want."

"Same time, same place," Zietz picked up a telephone, calling for an officer to take Hampson back to his cell.

Alone in his cell, Hampson tried to think who it was that might have turned state's evidence on him; Ramsey knew about the unreported cash, but now he was dead. Who murdered him and why? Poupore could have surmised what was going on, but did he have any proof? Would he turn in his own client, particularly considering he was threatened? Lovelady and the others knew, but why would they implicate themselves? How about the other accountants, what could they know? Did Rita know more than he told her? Did Linda?

His imagination leaped; the possibilities and connections seemed endless.

# Chapter Forty–Eight

The next day, Hampson met with Zietz again in Conference Room 2. Without exchanging pleasantries, Zietz said, "Well?"

"I'm ready to deal," Hampson said.

"Shoot."

"I want you to contact the head guy for me here in the New York district—the U.S. Attorney. Tell him I've got all they'll need to crack one of the biggest price-fixing scams ever. You can tell them who I am. They'll know me, believe me, and tell them everything I've told you."

Zietz shook his head. "Look, Hampson, I don't have a lot of experience at that level, you know." He sat back in his chair, with his arms behind his neck.

"Don't worry about it. Once you tell them who I am and what I've got, they'll be ready to talk. They've been trying to find out something on that tobacco group for years. I know what I'm talking about."

"And what do you want out of it?"

"I want out of here. I'll plead no contest to the tax-evasion case and the embezzlement. I'm not worried about Ramsey's murder, because I didn't have anything to do with it. Christ, I wasn't even in the country."

"Is that it?"

"One more thing."

"What?"

"I want to be put in the witness-protection program."

"That's all?"

"That's all."

"What about your wife?

"Fuck her."

Hampson's answer shocked Zietz.

"What?" he asked incredulously.

"You heard me, fuck her. She transferred the money, not me, and I wouldn't be surprised if she's the one who squealed on me and already made her own deal. She can go to hell, as far as I'm concerned."

Zietz was dumfounded.

Finally, Zietz put his arms on the table and leaned in. "Well, Hampson, you're the boss."

"What now?"

"I'll contact the U.S. Attorney's office today, and you'll hear from me as soon as I know something."

"You just tell them what I told you. They'll be interested."

Hampson stood up and knocked on the door behind him. A few seconds later, it was opened, and Hampson said to the officer, "You can take me back to my cell now."

As Hampson was being led back to his cell, Zietz walked the short distance to the Federal Building, across the bridge from the Metropolitan Corrections Center.

Hampson lay on his bunk, a smile crossing his face for the first time since his ordeal had begun. He congratulated himself for having the foresight to plan a little insurance policy.

Later that evening, as he was trying to get to sleep, he heard footsteps coming toward his cell. "Hampson?" a corrections officer asked. "I've got a message from your attorney."

"What is it?"

"He said to tell you that they're interested, and to be ready to meet with him and a rep from the U.S. Attorney's office Friday morning."

"I knew they'd be interested," Hampson thought to himself, smiling as he fell asleep.

# Chapter Forty-Nine

Friday morning, Jim Hampson walked back to his cell after morning exercise. He was combing his hair when an officer, accompanied by a stocky man with fading blond hair, dressed in a pinstriped suit, appeared at the cell door.

"Hampson?" the latter asked.

"Yes."

"My name is Travisono." Travisono's perfect posture made him appear taller than his actual stature.

"Are you from the U.S. Attorney's office?"

"No, I'm the warden here. Some people are waiting for you, and I'm going to join your little party, if you don't mind. It's not every day that the Assistant U.S. Attorney wants to see one of our prisoners."

"And if I mind?" Hampson asked.

"I'm going to sit in anyway," replied the warden, smiling.

Hampson and Travisano made their way through wide prison hallways to a large conference room. Several men sat around a long mahogany conference table. Hampson saw his attorney sitting next to a smaller, studious-looking man, wearing round granny glasses. Zietz stood up first.

"Mornin', Tony," he said to the warden, extending his hand. "Good to see you again."

"Lou," the warden said, extending his own hand.

"Bob, I think you know Mr. Thomas Mehl, the Assistant U.S. Attorney."

The warden extended his hand again. "Yes, good to have you here, Tom."

While the Assistant U.S. Attorney and the warden exchanged pleasantries, Hampson unobtrusively shifted his weight from one foot to the other. An exciting new game was beginning.

Zietz introduced Mehl to Hampson, but when Hampson offered his hand, Mehl didn't move. Hampson didn't appreciate the slight, but swallowed his pride and dropped his hand, saying nothing. It was the first awkward moment.

"Let's get on with this," Mehl said, and Hampson found a chair across from his attorney. He sat up tall in his chair, maintaining the attitude of a man who held all the cards in a very high-stakes game.

"First, I'll bring everyone up-to-date." Zietz said, looking around the room, but nodding toward the warden. He reviewed the basic facts about the tax-evasion charges, the missing eleven million dollars, and Hampson's possible involvement in the murder of Ramsey.

Then he said, "After discussing certain facts with my client, we would like to make a proposal to the government."

"And what exactly do you propose?" Mehl asked.

"First, I want to caution everyone that this conversation is confidential. Does everyone agree?" Zietz looked around the table, as the others nodded in agreement.

"Okay. My client has indicated that he will plead no contest to the tax evasion and embezzlement charges in exchange for certain privileges. He will cooperate with the government by providing evidence that may implicate several other notable individuals in what may be one of the largest price-fixing arrangements in the world."

The warden's eyes widened, and he slipped out of his role of observer by asking, "What arrangement?"

"Fixing the prices of tobacco on the world market," the Assistant U.S. Attorney answered. The warden looked at Mehl and then at Hampson. Travisono was astonished, but he fought to maintain his professional composure.

Zietz continued, telling them about the secret meetings. He indicated that he and his client knew the government had been suspicious for some time about the possibility of price-fixing, but that it had been unable to uncover any evidence of substance.

He took a drink of water before going on. "In any event, my client says that he has concrete proof of the involvement of every individual participating in the price-fixing arrangement." He explained about Hampson's secret tapes.

The warden again asked a question. "Have you heard the tapes yet?"

"No, not yet," Zietz answered. "My client says he'll turn them over as soon as an acceptable agreement has been made."

"What's he proposing?" Mehl asked.

"Very little, in exchange for what he claims to have," Zietz said, with a confidence that surprised Hampson. "All he wants is the charges against him to be dropped, and he requests that he be set up in the witness protection program with enough cash to live on."

"What happened to the eleven mill and the murder charge?" Mehl asked again.

"My client couldn't have been involved in the murder; we know he was out of the country," Zietz answered. "He says that he doesn't know what happened to the cash, and I believe him."

"Why?"

"He passed a polygraph test, and I understand you have already seen the results. We all realize it's not admissible as evidence in court, but he voluntarily took it and he did pass, and we feel that's important." He waited a moment before adding, "Are there any more questions?"

"Where are the tapes now?" the warden asked.

"My client has indicated that he will apprise us of the location of the tapes, once both he and I are assured that an agreement has been met."

The warden nodded and looked toward the Assistant U.S. Attorney. After several moments of silence, Mehl spoke. "Mr. Zietz, I have discussed this situation at length with the U.S. Attorney for this district and with the Deputy Attorney General's office in Washington and," he said, switching his glance for the first time to Hampson, "I think I have an acceptable proposal to offer."

The room was absolutely silent. Hampson hung on every word. Mehl continued, "The Attorney General would like very much to be instrumental in breaking up this price-fixing group. He has discussed it with the President, who agreed with the proposal I'm offering here on their behalf."

He looked back at Zietz.

"In exchange for providing the government with evidence in the form of the tapes and other records that Mr. Hampson claims to have, if the evidence is conclusive, the government is prepared to drop the charges and to terminate the investigation of Hampson's involvement with Ramsey's murder."

Is this offer acceptable to your client, Mr. Zietz?"

Zietz questioned Hampson—with a glance. He nodded slightly in agreement. He then looked back at Mehl and said, "Your offer is acceptable to my client."

"There are a couple of caveats that I must place on the table though," Mehl continued.

"And they are?" Zietz asked.

"First, we don't believe the story about what happened to the money. Despite what the lie detector results were, we think Hampson knows where the money is. With that in mind, we will very carefully monitor Hampson's finances in the future. Under the Witness Protection Program, we will follow his every move, and if the money ever shows up, all bets are off. Understand?"

Zietz looked at Hampson, "Jim?"

"I'm telling you all, I don't know where the money is. If it shows up somehow, I'll advise the government. No problem."

"Fine," Mehl continued. "The other caveat is that these tapes must have all the information on them that you say they have. Understand?"

Hampson answered, "They do. They are everything I said they are. You'll have everything you need to prove your case."

"I don't know if I'm being clear," Mehl said. "The Attorney General has gone out on a limb with the President. Both of them want to close this deal and take credit for exposing the scam, particularly considering the current attitude toward smoking, but they don't want to be embarrassed by coming up short after a deal has been cut.

"Let me put it another way; if those tapes aren't exactly what you say they are, you are going to stay in prison for most of your life. We'll stretch out the tax charge and ensure that you're sentenced to the max. And while you sit in your cell, we'll continue investigating the embezzlement charge and link you to it, I assure you, and we will process charges just before the statute of limitation expires. And because it appears that you won't be able to make restitution to the association—because you don't seem to know where the money is—you'll be in a rather poor position to make any kind of deal. Understand?"

Hampson started to answer, but Mehl interrupted. "But we're not finished yet. We'll be working with the Maryland authorities on tying you into Ramsey's murder at the same time, and, we'll have all the time in the world with that because there is no statute of limitations on homicide." He paused to let his words sink in before continuing.

"Before you agree to a deal, do you understand what you'll be facing, if you don't have what you say you have, Hampson?"

"I'm absolutely confident that you'll get what you're expecting with the tapes, and we have a deal."

"Then it appears we are all in agreement, gentlemen," Zietz said, starting to put his papers together.

"Not quite yet," Mehl said.

Zietz stopped. "What else?"

Mehl addressed Hampson. "We want to know where the tapes are now and how we're going to get them."

Hampson looked at Mehl and then at Zietz, who nodded.

"Mr. Mehl, after I recorded each meeting, I put them in a bank safe deposit box."

"Did anyone else have access to the box?"

"Just my secretary, Rita Davies. As I said, she helped me arrange the meetings."

"Go on."

"Anyway, before I left for the Las Vegas meeting, I stopped at the bank and got the tapes. Obviously, I didn't tell anyone, particularly Davies, under the circumstances."

"What did you do with the tapes?"

"I gave them to my attorney for safe keeping, and we have an arrangement."

"Who is he and what is the arrangement?"

"His name is Ralph Poupore and he has an office in Baltimore. After I picked up the tapes from the bank, I went directly to his office. They were never out of my sight."

"Go on."

"I never even told Poupore what they were. I personally put the tapes in a metal box, sealed it, and gave it to him for safe keeping."

"What's in it for Poupore?" he asked curiously.

"Before sealing the box, I took a sum of cash and put it in the box. I marked on the envelope that the cash was his property and that he was entitled to it under certain circumstances."

"Which were?"

"If I were ever harmed, he was to take the box to the Justice Department, explain the situation, and keep the money. If nothing happened to me over several years, I was going to pick up the box when it was safe to do so, get the tapes, and give him his money."

"That's it?"

"Only one more thing."

"What?"

"If the situation arose that I currently find myself in, he would be instructed to deliver the box. The seal would be broken in your presence, I would get the tapes to hand over to you, and he would get the money. Simple."

Zietz, Mehl, and Travisono all looked at each other. The setup was masterful. "I see," Mehl said, not wishing to acknowledge Hampson's thoroughness.

Hampson smiled smugly before saying, "And under the circumstances, I think I'm entitled to a minor caveat of my own."

"Which is?" Mehl asked.

"The seal. If the seal on the box is broken before I open it, all bets are off. Fair?"

The Assistant U.S. Attorney nodded at Zietz, who said, "I think that's a fair request. If the seal has been broken, there's no way my client would know whether or not the tapes have been tampered with."

Mehl sat back in his chair. His eyes moved toward the wall as he was thinking. Then, he turned toward the warden. "Tony, what do you think?"

He answered without hesitation. "I think it's reasonable."

Mehl turned back to Zietz. "Okay. That's fair, but you understand that my boss has to bless it?"

"Of course," Zietz answered.

"One last thing," Mehl said, addressing Hampson.

"Yeah?" asked Hampson.

"After all this, these tapes had better be exactly what you say they are."

"They are; they were never out of my possession."

Mehl stared at Hampson a few seconds before speaking. "All right, then," he said, "I am prepared to report to the Attorney General that everything is a go, and we have a deal. He has the final say." Mehl said his good-byes and walked out of the room.

Hampson spoke first.

"Well?" he asked both the warden and his attorney.

"You heard the man," Zietz answered. "I interpreted it as being 'Don't call us, we'll call you.'"

# Chapter Fifty

Three days later. . .

"Where in the hell have you been?" Hampson asked Zietz, as the corrections officer closed the door to the conference room.

"What do you expect, Hampson?" Zietz answered with a question of his own. "You're *not* my only client!"

The two men stared at each other for a few moments before Zietz said, "Now calm down, we've got a lot to go over."

Zietz put his briefcase on the table, opened it and pulled out several papers and a yellow legal pad for notes. Before he closed the briefcase, Hampson said, "Look, I'm sorry. You don't know how long three days in here are."

Zietz shot an impatient look. "Now, you look, I don't have time to be worrying about hurting your feelings. I've been working hard, and I've got a lot more to do." His tone betrayed his growing weariness.

Hampson wanted to shake this little man. He wanted action and he wanted it fast. But he saw that Lou Zietz was the only thing standing between him and a life behind bars. Zietz was a long shot but, at least, he was a shot. He softened his tone. "Look, I'm sorry," he said, "where do we stand?"

"It's a go," Zietz said, not bothering to build any suspense. "I heard from the Assistant U.S. Attorney late last night."

Hampson took a deep breath in relief, exhaling slowly.

"Thank God," he said.

"Don't thank God yet," Zietz said. "We still have a lot to do.

"Mehl said that he, and possibly the U.S. Attorney from the eastern district of New York would be here next Thursday to hear the tapes. They're working closely with the antitrust division in Washington on your case. He said the President was anxious to close the deal on the scam and to get some good news for a change."

"That's great," Hampson said.

"Anyway, the paperwork has all been taken care of. The warden has been told that you'll be released the same day. Is that good enough for you?" he asked, his dark brown eyes twinkling below bangs of dark hair in need of cutting.

"What do you think?" He was almost gleeful. "Of course, it's satisfactory!"

Zietz took off his glasses, put them on the table, and searched Hampson's face. "Look," he said. "For your own sake, you've got to come straight with me here. Are you *positive* that you have what you say you have?"

"Of course," Hampson answered. "I put the tapes in the safety box *myself*, I marked each tape *myself*, I took them out of the box *myself*, and handed them to my attorney. Then, I sealed the box, and both of us signed the seal. The only way those tapes aren't exactly what I said they are, would be if the seal has been broken, and Poupore has too much to lose by breaking the seal. Besides, he doesn't even know exactly what's in the box! Why do you people keep asking me this?"

"Because, Hampson," Zietz said, trying to be patient, "the AG doesn't like to make deals to begin with, and he definitely doesn't want to go to the President and be embarrassed in the end. You still have a choice. You can say the deal is off, and you'll probably get out in about three years or so on the tax charge. If you're telling me the truth, and I believe you are, I don't think they have enough to tie you into the murder. Understand?"

"Understood. And what's my other choice?"

"Go forward with the deal, obviously," Zietz said, adding, "but I want you to remember what Mehl said. If those tapes aren't exactly what you said they are, the shit is going to hit the fan in a big way, and they'll arrange for you to spend most, if not all, of your life in prison. Now do you understand where you are?"

"Yes!" Hampson said. "For the last time, yes! Look, I've still got one last ace in the hole."

"What's that?" Zietz asked.

"The seal. If the seal is broken, I can still back out of the deal and then I'm looking at only about three years, right?"

"Right."

"And if the seal isn't broken, we can go on with the deal. Poupore gets his money, they get their tapes, and I get out of here next week. The way I see it, it's a win-win for me!"

"Okay, as long as you understand, it's your choice."

"Come on, Zietz. Can we please go on!"

"Well," Zietz sighed to himself, "it looks like all we have to do is to contact Poupore and tell him to show up here next week with your box." He then gave Hampson the instructions that Poupore would need in order to enter the prison with the box.

When he had finished, Hampson said, "Okay, counselor, just show me to a phone."

Hampson hadn't noticed it before, but Zietz pointed to a telephone on a small table in the corner of the conference room. Hampson made his collect call to Baltimore. "Poupore here."

"Will you accept a collect call from Jim Hampson?"

"Sure, why not?" Poupore answered, smiling.

A few seconds later, Poupore said, "Jim, how are you? I've been worried sick!"

"Cut the shit, Poupore. Just listen."

"Sure, Jim, of course."

"I don't care what you've got planned for next Thursday, but whatever it is, your plans have been canceled. You're going to get that box you've been holding for me and drive it up to the Metropolitan Correctional Center. Understand?"

"Jim, I think you're being a little unreasonable, I . . ."

Hampson cut him off.

"Shut up and just listen. If your ass isn't here with that box next Thursday morning, your little fake ID business is going to blow up in your face, because I'll have no problem telling anyone who'll listen all about it. I've got nothing to lose. Am I being clear?"

After a few moments, "Yes."

"Okay then. Drive up here with the box next Thursday morning. Ask for the warden's office, and tell them who you are."

"Okay."

"It's important to ask for the warden's office. They'll be waiting for you. That's the only way you'll ever get in with that box."

"I understand. How about the envelope inside with my name on it?" Poupore asked.

"I've made a deal. The box will be opened in your presence, and as long as the seal hasn't been broken, you'll get your envelope."

"I see," Poupore said.

"Poupore?"

"Yeah?"

"Can I assume the seal is intact?"

"You can, and it is."

"Good," Hampson said. He hung up the phone and turned to Zietz.

"I hate to say this," Zietz said, "but I'm impressed. You've really done your homework, haven't you?"

Hampson just smiled. "I'll see you next Thursday morning."

Zietz called for a corrections officer. As Hampson was being led out of the room, he turned around.

"One more thing," he said.

"What's that?"

"Don't forget to bring a cassette player with you next week to play the tapes."

"I won't. I'll even buy a new one."

# Chapter Fifty–One

The next Thursday morning at eight o'clock, Hampson was led down the cellblock for the biggest meeting of his life. His spirits were high; he felt good. Soon, he would be leaving this place forever. He was surprised when they didn't stop at the usual conference room.

"Where are we going?" he asked.

"Warden's office," the officer answered. Without continuing the conversation, he led Hampson through a series of secured doors. After a few more minutes, they stopped at a dark wooden door with a bronze plaque: **WARDEN'S OFFICE**. The officer knocked on the door softly.

"Come in."

Hampson noticed everything in the paneled room: the large wooden desk with several flags behind it, one wall covered with pictures and plaques, a leather sofa with a large coffee table in front of it, and several chairs arranged around the table.

Zietz sat in the office alone. Hampson noticed he was wearing an unfamiliar gray suit and had gotten his hair cut.

"New suit?" Hampson asked.

"Yeah. It's not every day I get to be part of a history-making meeting with the Deputy Attorney General."

"The Deputy Attorney General!" Hampson raised his eyebrows.

"That's what I've been told. The antitrust division in Washington is under his charge, and I guess he's interested. Now sit down, you're making me nervous, and I'm nervous enough already."

"Where is everybody?"

"Warden Travisono is on his way to the front gate to meet Poupore. He told me that the Deputy Attorney General, the U.S. Attorney, Mehl, and several secret service agents are in a special room waiting for us."

Hampson felt his anticipation and excitement growing. He was in his element again. "The warden will bring Poupore here to his office first, where they'll turn the box over to you. Assuming that you're satisfied the seal hasn't been broken and you don't want to back out of the deal, we'll all be escorted to the room where they're waiting, and you'll open the box in their presence. You'll give the envelope to Poupore, and then we'll all listen to the tapes. If they're satisfied, you'll be out of here this afternoon."

Hampson smiled.

"Did you bring the cassette player?"

"Right here," Zietz pointed under his chair. I bought it last week and I've used it several times to learn how to work it."

Hampson smiled.

About fifteen minutes later, the door opened. Warden Travisono, followed by Poupore, came into the office. Poupore was holding the white metal box with both hands. Hampson and Zietz stood up, and the warden introduced the two attorneys. Each nodded without speaking.

Travisono then turned and said, "Hampson, your guest is here."

Poupore reached out to shake hands with Hampson. "I can't tell you how good it is to see you, Jim. Sorry you and John Heinrich couldn't work out an arrangement."

Hampson put his hands on his hips and said, "Cut the fucking shit, Poupore! I don't know what the hell your involvement with Heinrich was, but spare the conversation, will you!" Seeing this man again, with his constant, sneering smile put a temporary damper on Hampson's high spirits. He would have to think of a way to hurt him, after he was back in circulation.

Poupore smiled slightly, remaining silent.

"Is this the box you were talking about?" Zietz asked.

Poupore gave the box to Hampson, who looked it over carefully, checking to see that the seal was intact and the signature authentic.

"This is it."

"Are you sure?"

"Positive."

"Do you still want to go on?"

"Yes, I'm certain."

He was instructed to return the box to Poupore.

Zietz nodded to the warden who was standing behind his desk with his hand on the phone. In a few moments, he lifted the receiver and said, "Carol, would you please tell the Attorney General's party that we're ready?"

Soon, a knock was heard on the warden's door. "Come in," he said.

A corrections officer led in two men wearing dark blue suits. The officer closed the door and stayed in the room.

"Gentlemen, I'm Agent Greene," one of them said. "I hate to inconvenience you, but I'm afraid we'll have to check you all for weapons before we take you into the meeting. I hope you understand." Everyone, including the warden, was searched.

During the search, Zietz mentioned that he had a cassette recorder that would be taken into the meeting. An agent opened it, checking it thoroughly.

"Okay, please follow me," said Greene. He led the small group out of the room and down the hall. The other secret service agent was the last to leave, following the group.

They stopped at the door marked **PAROLE BOARD HEARING ROOM**. The first agent knocked six times on the door. It opened immediately and the group filed into the room.

Hampson recognized the Deputy Attorney General seated at the head of the table. As they entered the room, the Deputy Attorney General stood up, followed at once by the U.S. Attorney, who Hampson also recognized, and by Mehl and the other three secret service agents. Everyone was still standing as Assistant U.S. Attorney Mehl made the introductions.

The warden and attorneys shook hands with the Deputy Attorney General.

When Travisono introduced him, Hampson fully expected a cordial greeting and moved toward him. But one of the secret service agents stepped forward, blocking his path. Ignoring the incident, the Deputy Attorney General said, "Please sit down everyone, so that we can continue. Mr. Mehl?" Hampson swallowed the indignity, not easily, but felt he could stand anything a little while longer. Soon, it would all be over.

The Assistant U.S. Attorney remained standing. "Gentlemen, I think everyone is aware of the details, and I must remind you that this meeting is confidential.

"Before we begin, is the prisoner certain that Mr. Ralph Poupore, who has just been introduced, is the individual who has been custodian of the box in question?"

Hampson looked at Poupore, at Zietz, and finally at Mehl before answering. "I am certain."

"Mr. Poupore," Mehl continued, "has anyone besides yourself been in possession of the box?"

"They have not," Poupore answered.

"And is the seal intact?"

"It is."

"Fine. Then would you please hand the box directly to the prisoner?"

Poupore walked over to Hampson, and once again handed him the box.

"Please sit down, Mr. Poupore," Mehl directed.

All eyes were on Hampson, as he held the box.

"Mr. Hampson, is that the box you told us about?" Mehl asked.

"It is."

"Are you certain?"

"I am."

"Is the seal still intact?"

Hampson examined the seal carefully, again turning the box in his hands nervously.

"It is," Hampson finally said.

"Are you certain?"

"I am."

"Is the signature on the seal authentic?"

Hampson looked at the seal again. "It is, and I'm certain."

"Fine, please have a seat," Mehl directed. Hampson sat down next to his counsel.

"Before the seal is broken and the box is opened, would you please tell us what is in the box?"

"Several cassette tapes and an envelope."

"What is on the tapes?"

"Details of secret meetings and recordings of the meetings themselves."

"And what is in the envelope?"

"Cash."

"Who is the owner of the cash?"

"Ralph Poupore. The writing on the envelope indicates such."

"Fine. Are you aware that you are not obligated to proceed further."

"I am."

"Do you still wish to proceed, knowing the consequences?"

"I do."

"Are you certain?"

"I am."

Mehl then walked from his seat next to the Assistant Attorney General, and stood next to Hampson. He took a small penknife from his pocket, opened it and handed it to Hampson.

"Would you break the seal and open the box in our presence, please?" No one spoke.

Hampson felt the sweat on his palms and felt his heart racing. He carefully used the tip of the knife to cut the seal and handed the knife back to Mehl.

Hampson looked first at Zietz and then at the box. His thumb moved the small tab to the right and he opened the lid. He closed his eyes for a full second, then peered into the box.

Hampson was visibly relieved—the tapes and the envelope were there. He then glanced up at Mehl standing beside him.

"Would you describe to everyone what is in the box, please?" Mehl asked, peering into the box himself.

"Several cassette tapes and an envelope with writing on it," Hampson said.

"What does the writing say?"

"Property of Ralph Poupore."

"And are the envelope and its contents the property of Mr. Ralph Poupore?"

"Yes."

Mehl looked at his boss who was listening intently. "Do I have your permission to give Mr. Poupore his property, so that we can proceed, sir?"

The U.S. Attorney nodded yes.

"Counselor?" he looked at Zietz.

"Yes," Zietz said.

"Mr. Hampson."

Hampson looked up at Mehl, "Yes."

"Remove the envelope from the box, please."

Hampson took the envelope in his right hand.

"Mr. Poupore, would you take possession of your property, please?"

Poupore walked across the room, and Hampson handed him the envelope. Without opening it, Poupore put it in the breast pocket of his suit coat and sat down.

The room was silent.

"Mr. Hampson," Mehl said, "are the tapes the same tapes you placed in the box?"

"They are."

"And how do you know this?"

"I recognize the brand name of the cassettes. The tape on each cassette noting the location of each meeting is written in my handwriting. I'm positive that these are the original tapes." As Hampson finished speaking, the Deputy Attorney General leaned forward in his chair and placed his elbows on the table, listening intently.

Mehl then looked at the box and asked, "Shall I have the prisoner play the tapes, sir?"

Without looking at Mehl, the deputy AG said, "Yes, please."

Zietz walked around the table and handed Hampson the audiocassette player, which Hampson placed on the table in front of him.

Finally, Mehl said, "Would you please play one of the tapes for us now, Mr. Hampson?"

"Any particular one?" Hampson was fingering the tops of the tapes as he asked.

"Yes," Mehl answered, "let's start with the Colorado meeting."

Hampson carefully removed one tape at a time from the box, until he found the one that said COLORADO, KEYSTONE RESORT.

"Now?" he asked.

"Now," the deputy U.S. Attorney replied.

Hampson pushed in the STOP/EJECT button, and the cassette door opened. He looked at the tape's directional arrows on the player and the tape, aligned the tape, placed it into the cassette player and closed the door. He took a deep breath. The rest of his life was hanging on these tapes. He pressed the PLAY button.

Nothing. His heart jumped.

He pushed the STOP/EJECT button again, took out the tape, and looked at the directional arrows again. He carefully placed the tape back into the machine, snapping the door closed. And, again, he pushed the PLAY button.

Nothing. Now, his heart was pumping fast, and his breathing was shallow.

He shot a panicked look at Zietz. Everyone else in the room was looking at the exchange of glances between the two.

"Is this the right type of player for the cassette?" Hampson asked Zietz.

"Yes, I'm positive. That's a standard audiocassette, and it should play on this machine. I don't understand the problem."

Zietz started to walk around the table again to try his hand at the player when the warden said, "May I say something?" he asked, looking toward the head of the table.

"Of course." The Assistant U.S. Attorney was now sitting back in his chair with his arms folded.

"There probably aren't any batteries in the machine. I think you need to plug it into an electrical outlet."

Zietz shook his head, obviously embarrassed. "Of course," he said, "You're right, I didn't put batteries in it." This time, he reached across the table for the machine and fumbled with the door on the back of the cassette player. It finally opened, and he pulled out an electrical cord and glanced around the room looking for an outlet. He found one on the wall directly across from where he was sitting. After plugging it in, he checked for the little red light on the front of the machine. It was on.

"That was the problem," he said, looking at the Deputy Attorney General again. "I'm sorry, sir, I'm very nervous."

Once again, Hampson put the cassette into the machine, closed the door and took another deep breath. Now it would begin. Soon he would be a free man.

He pressed the PLAY button.

To his relief, he saw the tape spool begin to turn and, in a few seconds, he heard tape hiss come from the speakers.

He looked toward his attorney and smiled. No one was speaking.

A few more seconds passed, and he heard a single guitar chord come from the speakers, and then familiar voices. *It's been a hard day's night, and I've been working like a dog. It's been a hard day's night, I should be sleeping like a log.*

Startled, he quickly pushed the STOP/EJECT button, looking up to see confused faces. Hampson spoke first. "It must be a lead in for the tape that I didn't know about." He looked calm to everyone in the room, but his heart was pounding. "Let me fast forward this for a few seconds," and he pushed the FF button. After a few seconds, he pushed in the STOP/EJECT button again, and the machine stopped. He had no idea what was happening. He was a man who never prayed, but he said a silent, "Please, God."

He cautiously pushed PLAY. The same familiar voices came from the speaker. *He's a real nowhere man, sitting in his nowhere land, making all his nowhere plans for nobody.* He pushed in the STOP/EJECT button again, but he now had a strange look on his face. "Oh, my God, what in the hell is this," he thought. The others in the room were staring at him intently.

"I must have marked the wrong tape," he said, remembering he gave a copy of the Colorado meeting to the others in Las Vegas and thinking there must be a mix-up, he tried to calm himself down. His hand shaking, he took the cassette from the machine and placed it on the table. Without asking anyone which one he should play next, he pulled another tape from the box. The tape on the label read, *MAUI, HAWAII*, in his handwriting. He put that cassette into the machine and closed the door.

He pushed the PLAY button again.

Again, they listened to tape hiss and again they heard the same familiar voices, Help, I need somebody. *Help, not just anybody. Help, you know I need someone. Hel---lp.*" A few guitar notes could be heard before Hampson pushed the STOP/EJECT button, stopping the machine.

He started to talk and looked confused, "I don't . . .," but the Deputy Attorney General stood up, cutting him off.

"What's going on here?" he asked. "You got me over here to listen to Beatles music!" There was agitation in his voice as he looked around the room for an answer. No one dared make eye contact with him. They were, instead, staring at Hampson.

Hampson looked around the room with a desperate look and, without saying another word, played another cassette marked NEW ORLEANS.

Tape hiss again. Hampson's hands visibly shook while he waited and prayed for the tape of the New Orleans meeting to start.

*"I'm a loser. I'm a loser. And I'm not what I appear to be. Of all the love . . ."* Hampson hit the STOP/EJECT button and stood up.

"I don't understand," he said. "I swear I . . ."

The Deputy Attorney General interrupted him again. "I don't know what in the hell you're trying to pull here, Hampson, but I'm not amused! Now listen, you had everyone convinced that you had what I needed to put a lock on the tobacco deal. Now I've got to go back and explain this to the Attorney General and to the President." His voice began to rise.

Without asking for permission, Hampson took the PALM SPRINGS tape from the box. His chest heaved, and he had a desperate look on his face as he put the tape into the machine. Again, he pushed PLAY. Immediately, the same voices came from the speakers. *"Oh, Lovely Rita, meter maid, where would I be without you."* Without turning the machine off, Hampson picked it up with both hands and lifted it over his head. Alarm filled the room as the men began to rise. A secret service agent lunged toward him, as Hampson smashed the machine on the floor.

Shattered bits of black plastic and metal scattered across the room. Hampson began to sob, and the men began to settle down, realizing he was harmless and humiliated.

As Hampson wept, Zietz couldn't help but feel embarrassed for his client. Not knowing what to do, he wondered what would happen next. Every eye in the room focused on the sobbing Hampson.

Silently, the Deputy Attorney General stood up and walked over to the prisoner. Mehl and the U.S. Attorney sat in tense silence as the secret service agents rose to the ready. Zietz was surprised how detached and unemotional his voice was, as the Attorney General spoke to Hampson for the last time. "Now, you listen to me, Hampson, and listen carefully because I'm in no mood to repeat myself. After this little episode, you're in here for most of the rest of your life, if I have anything to do with it." He suddenly slammed his fist on the table, startling everyone and causing them to jump. "And I'm telling you, I do and I will!" His voice was still calm.

He and his entourage left the room, as did Ralph Poupore, and the warden closed the door gently, turning to look at his prisoner. "I've been here a long time, Hampson, and if there is one person I would not want to piss off, it's the guy who just left," he said calmly.

Hampson's eyes looked like those of a deer facing oncoming traffic. He whispered, but his voice rose to a scream as he spoke. "That bitch. That fucking bitch! She switched the fucking tapes!" He then kicked the broken cassette player.

He looked at his attorney, still shrieking, "What do I do now?"

Zietz surprised himself with his calm response. "Don't look at me, it's up to your host, here," and he looked at the warden, who was still at the door.

Without a hint of emotion, the warden addressed the two corrections officers still in the room. "Take the prisoner back to his cell. We'll deal with him later.

Hampson looked at his attorney again. "What can I do? Help me! I don't know what she did with the tapes or how to get them! What can I do?"

"There's still the money," Zietz said. "Tell us where the money is, and maybe we can help, but without the tapes or the money, you're up shit's creek without a paddle."

"I don't know where the fucking money is!" he screamed as two officers grabbed him by both arms. "You've got to help me!" he pleaded as they led him out of the room.

At the door, he turned back to Zietz. "Zietz, you're my attorney for God's sake! Do something, will you?" Zietz just shrugged his shoulders, as the officers led him back to his cell.

Zietz and the warden stared at each other, listening to Hampson's voice screaming, as it trailed off. When they couldn't hear him anymore, Zietz finally said, "Tony, I'm sorry, but he had me convinced he was telling the truth."

"Don't feel bad, Lou, he had everybody convinced."

"Quite a story, huh?"

"Quite a day," said the warden.

As Zietz shook Travisono's hand, the warden asked, "Do you think we'll ever know the truth, Lou?" Zietz just shrugged.

Sitting in his car in the parking lot, Ralph Poupore wrote down everything he had observed, before driving to his Baltimore office.

It was quite a day for everyone, but especially for Jim Hampson.

# Chapter Fifty–Two

Thursday evening, October 26th. . .

"Right on time, Andy!" Lovelady, in a jovial mood, remarked to Lombardo as they met outside Ruth's Chris Steak House in Annapolis. Both men smiled as they shook hands, but Lombardo's grip was strong and unnecessarily rough.

Lombardo said cheerfully, "It's good to see you, Dave. Except for our short conversation last week, I don't think we've spoken since the Ramsey incident." Lombardo held on to Lovelady's hand a little too long, and Lovelady wanted to draw back. As he spoke, it suddenly became frighteningly apparent to Lovelady that the man grasping his hand had absolutely no qualms about murdering anyone. Lovelady got queasy as Lombardo discussed it casually.

When Lombardo finally dropped his hand, he reached for the restaurant door, allowing Lovelady to go in first. When they were both inside, Lovelady whispered, "I made the reservation under the name of Jeff Greene, just in case." By the look on Lombardo's face, he knew he didn't have to tell him. "Just don't use a credit card, Dave." Lombardo winked.

As they were waiting for the hostess to seat them, Lovelady thought about the conversation he had had with Lombardo earlier, when he suddenly started calling him "Dave". Lovelady would have preferred the more formal "Mr. Lovelady", considering the amount of money Lombardo was being paid. He decided he would discuss it later in the evening.

The hostess quickly found their reservations and escorted them to a corner booth. Lovelady was glad she had chosen a secluded spot.

As they were settling in their seats, a waiter approached and asked if they would like something from the bar before ordering.

"I think I'd like a vodka martini straight up, please," Lovelady said, as he was eyeing the entrees on the menu.

"And you, sir?"

"Iced tea, please," Lombardo replied.

"Very good, gentlemen, I'll get your beverages and come back for your order shortly."

As the waiter was walking away, Lombardo said, "I make it a rule never to drink during business hours."

Lovelady became more uncomfortable.

After their orders had been taken, they discussed business. Lombardo began, "So, you are in need of my services again?"

Taking a sip of his martini, Lovelady said, "Yes. Let me fill you in." He folded his hands confidently on the table, consciously trying to reassert his authority as the architect of any plans that were to be made. "The bottom line is that we still don't have a clue where those fucking tapes are; we don't know where Hampson is, and the Federation's money was transferred to Switzerland. I was hoping Ramsey's death might scare whoever has the tapes, but nothing."

He took another sip of his drink. "I had a long conversation with my people and brought them up to date right before I spoke to you."

Lovelady filled Lombardo in on everything that had been discussed. Awkward silences punctuated Lovelady's monologue. Lombardo stared at Lovelady without blinking, never speaking or reacting. Lovelady felt he was experiencing something of what Ramsey must have felt during that last meeting in the Federation's offices.

"So, there you have it. Hampson's secretary, Davies, has split and my people have directed me to get her and McGuire out of the picture."

Lombardo finally moved. "So, what do you want me to do?" he said coldly.

Lovelady inhaled deeply. "We need you to get rid of them."

"When?"

"ASAP, of course."

"No problem," he said. "McGuire should be easy, he's local, but I'm going to need some information on Davies."

Lovelady pulled an envelope from his inside breast pocket, handing it across the table. "This is all we have on Davies from her personnel file, along with what little I could find out about McGuire. You'll see that Davies is from Texas, so my guess is that's where she went, but I can't be sure. She shouldn't be too hard to track down though; as you can see, she's listed a sister to contact in case of an emergency."

Lombardo put the envelope on the seat beside him without opening it.

"There is one problem, though, that we haven't discussed."

"What's that?"

"These have got to look like accidents. The police are still investigating Ramsey's murder and the money problem, and my people feel that another murder, much less two, will have them on us like stink on shit."

"Your people are right," Lombardo said calmly.

"Can you do it?"

"Sure, but it's going to be expensive. Accidents are tough to pull off, and I might need some out-of-town help with Davies."

"Do you have the contacts?"

Lovelady was immediately sorry he had asked. Lombardo abruptly pulled back in his seat, folding his arms defiantly across his chest and looking to his left. Turning back toward Lovelady, he looked up, closed his eyes briefly and took a breath, as he tried to maintain his patience.

"Dave, don't worry over my business," he remarked through clenched jaws. At that moment, to Lovelady's relief, their waiter approached with a tray of food.

The waiter placed plates of steaming food in front of each of them, cautioning them to be careful of the hot plates. When he was satisfied with the presentation, he said, "Will there be anything else at this time, gentlemen?"

"Yes," Lombardo said, "I'd like a glass of your house red, please."

Surprised to hear him order wine, Lovelady realized that Lombardo was adjourning the business part of the evening. Lovelady had never had control of the meeting.

"Join me, Dave? They've got an unusually good wine selection here." Lombardo's tone switched as he asked the question, and his expression was warm and engaging. This man's mood- swings baffled Lovelady.

"Yes, I believe I will," Lovelady said to the waiter. He hoped Lombardo didn't realize that he was almost afraid not to.

After the waiter left, Lombardo put both of his palms on the table, and leaned toward Lovelady. "And don't forget, Dave, from this point on, don't call me, I'll call you," he said smiling.

For the remainder of dinner, Lombardo conversed in a lively, intelligent manner about politics and the upcoming presidential election. He seemed genuinely interested in drawing out Lovelady's opinion of whether the incumbent could be defeated. Lovelady was surprised at the depth of Lombardo's knowledge.

Lovelady couldn't relax until the evening was finally over.

During the drive home, his thoughts were preoccupied with doubts about his decision to continue to use Lombardo.

# Chapter Fifty–Three

It was Friday, October 27th, and Lovelady snacked on candy corn as he worked at his desk in the National Tobacco Federation's offices. The telephone rang. "Yes," he said, swallowing a mouthful of candy, but still absorbed in a NTF contract he was reading.

His secretary said, "Mr. Lovelady, your eleven o'clock appointment is here. Shall I show him in?"

Lovelady looked at his watch. It was exactly eleven A.M. "Yes," he said, sliding the contract into the center of his desk.

He stood up when his secretary led in a tall man, whose forced smile exposed teeth the color of a smog-filled sky. Lovelady held out his right hand, "Dave Lovelady," he said. The visitor looked at him for a moment, "Ralph Poupore. I'm grateful you made time to see me." Poupore handed Lovelady one of his cards.

"Have a seat, Mr. Poupore," Lovelady pointed to a chair across from his desk. "Susan, please shut the door."

Lovelady sat down, elbows on his desk, hands clasped, leaning forward slightly.

"I must say you were very persistent in getting this appointment, Mr. Poupore. But I don't have much time, so what can I do for you?"

"I think it's what I can do for you, Mr. Lovelady," Poupore said.

Lovelady's expression turned from one of strained patience at the intrusion to irritation at Poupore's glib response. Accurately assessing Lovelady's reaction, Poupore got to the point.

"Mr. Lovelady, you may have an interest in one of my former clients and some other people we have in common."

"Who?" Lovelady's irritation turned to curiosity.

"Jim Hampson for one."

Lovelady's eyebrows rose on hearing the unexpected name. He sat upright, looking at Poupore intently. "What do you know about Hampson?"

"Everything," Poupore answered calmly and confidently.

"Who else?"

"A woman by the name of Rita Davies and two young accountants by the names of McGuire and Autry."

Lovelady's expression was serious.

"Should I continue then?" Poupore asked, already knowing the answer.

"What else do you know?"

"I think I may also have a missing piece-or-two of a puzzle you're probably anxious to finish."

"What puzzle?"

Poupore leaned forward, looking Lovelady directly in the eyes before answering. "You wouldn't be searching for several audio cassette tapes and a whole lot of money, would you?" His voice was composed.

Lovelady leaned back in his chair, never losing eye contact. He calmly reached for the telephone on the corner of his desk and pushed in a button.

"Yes, Mr. Lovelady?"

"Susan, please cancel all my appointments for the rest of the day."

"Yes, sir, I'll take care of that right away."

Lovelady hung up the telephone. "Okay, you have my attention. Tell me what you know."

"Not quite yet. We have to agree on a few things first."

"What?"

"First, compensation."

"For what?"

"For what I know and you don't."

"How much?"

"Fifty thousand dollars."

Lovelady considered the audacity of this man and his request, but he knew he desperately needed those tapes. It didn't take him long to surmise that Poupore had thought about his cards very carefully and was ready to show his hand. "Done. What else do we need to agree on?"

"That I'll be included in whatever happens next, and that I'll be compensated for my participation."

"Tell me what you know."

An hour later, Poupore had almost finished his story. "Jim 's gonna be sittin' still for quite some time. I don't think he's going to be getting too far with this court-appointed fellow, Zietz."

"So, you were in the room when Hampson played the tapes for the government attorneys?"

"The whole time."

"And all that was on the tape was Beatles music?"

"That's it."

Lovelady laughed out loud. "Would I have loved to have seen his face. That son-of-a-bitch was so cock-sure he had all his bases covered."

Lovelady had Poupore describe various aspects of that scene before continuing.

"So Rita Davies has the tapes and the money then?"

"I don't think there's any doubt about it." Poupore's voice was confident.

Lovelady thought for a second. He picked up the telephone and dialed a number.

"Lombardo here," he heard.

"This is Dave Lovelady."

"Yes, Dave."

"We have to meet. There's been a little change of plans, and my guess is there's a lot more work in it for you. Interested?"

"Sure."

"I want you to meet with me and a friend of mine tonight."

"Where?"

"How about the Red Sage here in town?"

"When."

"Eight."

"I'll be there."

Lovelady redirected his attention to Poupore. "You and I and an associate of mine are going to meet at eight tonight at the Red Sage."

Poupore smiled broadly. "See you then."

"There is one more thing." Lovelady said.

"And that is?"

"How do I know I can trust you? After all, you've already double-crossed your own client."

Poupore chuckled softly. "Mr. Lovelady, if I read the situation correctly, and I think I do, then you don't have any choice."

Lovelady just acknowledged the remark with a slight nod—Poupore was right and he knew it.

The Red Sage restaurant had been artfully decorated with spider webs and skeletons, for an early Halloween celebration. Customers costumed as ghouls and witches, streamed in to sit at the bar. The small group in the corner booth ignored the festivities. By nine-thirty that evening, Dave Lovelady, Ralph Poupore, and Andy Lombardo were reviewing their plan for the final time. Lovelady had Rita's personnel file open in front of him.

"So the bottom line is, nobody has any idea where she is, where the tapes are, or where the money is," Lombardo established. "And all we've got on her is her sister in Texas?"

Lovelady and Poupore nodded.

"Let me take a look at her personnel file."

Lovelady slid Rita Davies's personnel file across the table to Lombardo.

He read carefully the section where Rita wrote her sister Lisa Herrera's name, address, and telephone number, as her emergency contact. "This says she lives in Irving, Texas. Where's that?"

"Irving's just outside of Dallas. In fact, it's between Dallas and the Dallas-Fort Worth Airport."

"Do you know if she's still there?"

"No. We tried to call her earlier today at the number Davies noted, but all we got is a recording that says her number had been disconnected."

Lombardo took a deep breath and sat back in his chair. "Let me tell you what I think we should do."

"Go on."

"First, forget about McGuire for now, we can always handle him later. Davies is our immediate concern and we've got to move real fast. You can bet the feds are looking for Davies, too, and who knows what they know. The way I see it, the first one who finds Davies wins, and the fastest way to Davies is through her sister. She'll know where Davies is, and if she doesn't feel up to sharing her whereabouts with us, I'll convince the information out of her—I guarantee it."

Lovelady felt as if he were experiencing deja vu. As Lombardo detailed his methods of "convincing," Lovelady tried to push back his natural, human responses—he tried to bury his feelings of fear and revulsion, the same feelings he had felt the evening they had dinner together in Annapolis. Tonight they were accepting the leadership of a monster. Lombardo was again in charge, and both Lovelady and now Poupore, who sat quietly throughout the evening, tacitly accepted it.

"So what do we do now?" Poupore finally asked, dizzy with the excitement of participating in a high-stakes adventure. His eyes, alternating contact between each of his dinner companions, settled on Lombardo for the answer.

"Your friend here," Lombardo nodded toward Lovelady, "will deliver a cash down payment to me early in the morning. I'll call you, Ralph, later tonight with our flight information. We'll meet at the Baltimore Airport early and we should be in Dallas before noon. And you're sure that, by tomorrow morning, you can come up with the fake IDs we'll need for the trip, Ralph?"

"No problem. In fact my people are already working on it. I'll have them with me."

Lombardo nodded.

"What if Herrera's not there?" Poupore asked.

Lombardo looked toward Poupore, replying gently, "If she's not there, Ralph, and she probably won't be, we'll just have to find her. Don't worry, we'll find a way." The considerate tone of Lombardo's answer once again bewildered Lovelady.

Unceremoniously, Lombardo scooted his chair back and stood. The meeting was over.

Even though he hired and was paying Lombardo, Lovelady had to summon up his courage before speaking. "There is one more thing, Andy."

"What's that?" Lombardo sounded agitated.

"At Ruth's Chris you said you may need some help." He swallowed hard and found it difficult to look Lombardo in the eye. "If you do, who are you going to get? I've got to tell my people."

Lombardo sat back down. The apologetic tone of his voice confused Lovelady and Poupore, once again. "You're absolutely right, Dave, and I'm sorry I didn't tell you before." He told them of the secret network that existed among people who were in Lombardo's type of work. Lovelady and Poupore sat and listened, fascinated by what they were being told.

"So," Lombardo continued, "don't worry, if I need help, and I don't think I will, I have the contacts."

"Who are they?"

"I can't tell you under the circumstances, I'm sure you understand." Again, his personality was completely unpredictable. "If I do need help, I'll tell you then, of course, but right now I have to protect identities. Anything else?"

Both of them knew better than to press the matter, even with Lombardo's current demeanor.

"Okay then." Lombardo once again stood.

"Lovelady, I'll see you at six A.M. Have the money. I'll see you, Ralph, at the airport."

Lombardo took two steps and stopped momentarily, and then turned around and faced Poupore.

"By the way Ralph, remind me some time to tell you what happened to someone who double-crossed me. I think you'll find it particularly interesting."

On hearing these words, the blood drained from Poupore's face making him appear so pale one would think he lived in a cave and never saw the sun.

Lombardo didn't waste time shaking hands or saying goodbye just turned back around and he left the restaurant alone. Lovelady and Poupore watched as he walked through the restaurant, smiling at customers' Halloween costumes and exchanging pleasantries with the staff.

Both Lovelady and Poupore had been humbled by Lombardo's lack of deference. They sat in silence. Poupore broke the quiet. "Something about that guy gives me the feeling he could eat a person for dinner and not think twice about it."

Lovelady continued staring at nothing. "Yeah, he seems pretty nasty. But he'll get the job done."

# Chapter Fifty-Four

"Dave, United is *the* way to go—not only are they efficient, but their ticket agents are always the most charming and lovely." Turning back to the agent at the ticket counter, Lombardo cocked his head to the side and smiled, "Thank you for taking such good care of us, darlin'. It's always nice to see a face as pretty as yours this early in the morning."

Lovelady, using false identification Poupore had delivered earlier, picked up his first-class ticket to Dallas and placed it in his inside jacket pocket. The three headed down the wide hall toward another carrier. Lombardo insisted that they also buy tickets to Los Angeles on another airline. If someone were attempting to trace their movements, multiple locations would make it much more difficult and time-consuming to find them. The flights, like everything else, were paid for in cash, as credit cards and checks were too simple to trace.

Before boarding the Dallas flight, Lombardo directed the other two not to discuss the plan they had carefully calculated the night before. He suspected they might already be the targets of an investigation.

They settled into their seats in the first-class cabin. About an hour into the flight, Lovelady watched Lombardo charm the flight attendant.

The airliner's wheels touched the hot tarmac of the Dallas-Fort Worth Airport exactly on time at 11:45 A.M. Poupore and Lovelady walked to the car rental booth, while Lombardo retrieved the lone piece of luggage he had checked. They leased a green Lincoln Town Car, and all three were written into the contract as drivers, once again using the false identification Poupore had provided. Lombardo picked up a map of the area and asked the counter clerk for directions to Irving, while Lovelady completed the car rental agreement.

They located their car and Poupore slid into the driver's seat as Lombardo climbed into the front passenger's seat. Lovelady settled into the back.

Poupore took the second Irving exit off the interstate. At the bottom of the ramp, he asked, "Which way?"

"Go right. I see a restaurant down there. We need to go over are a few things." Poupore eased the Town Car onto the lot. At Lombardo's direction, he parked under a tree, as far away from the restaurant as possible.

The parking lot reflected the sweltering Texas sun. As Lombardo opened the restaurant door, they were met by a refreshing blast of cold air. Lombardo asked for a secluded booth and, as they sat, the host gave each of them a luncheon menu.

"Good, beer's on tap. I'm thirsty," Poupore said, glancing down the menu. Looking up, he was stunned to see Lombardo glaring at him.

"What's your problem?" Poupore foolishly chuckled. Feeling the coldness in Lombardo's stare, he suddenly turned solemn, like a young boy facing a father with a wide, leather belt.

Poupore did not underestimate the gravity of his flaw. Lombardo didn't blink as long seconds passed before he acknowledged the question.

"Now you pay attention, because I don't want to waste any more time with this," he was eyeing Poupore, but glanced briefly at Lovelady, "and this goes for both of you. This is business, and professionals do *not* drink during business hours. I'm going to assume this is the final time I'll find it necessary to bring this up. Before we go on, let's get this straight—I'm in charge here. I tell both of you what to do during this phase of the operation, and your job is to do what I tell you." He sat upright, folding his arms across his chest. "Understood?"

Both Poupore and Lovelady felt their hearts racing and nodded in agreement. Poupore wondered if getting involved wasn't a very big mistake and if the money was going to be worth it.

Lombardo continued, but his tone was now calm and rational, as though the episode had never occurred. "I found Davies' sister's street on the map. Ralph, you drive, and I'll sit in the back with Dave on the way over. The bag in the trunk has three pistols and ammunition in it. Can each of you handle a piece?"

Poupore and Lovelady each had kept a weapon in his home for protection. They were comfortable carrying one and knew how to use it, should the need arise.

"Good," Lombardo said when they were finished. "Let's go. You two settle up and I'll meet you at the car. Let me have the keys, Ralph." Poupore didn't ask why; he did as he was told.

After paying the bill, Lovelady and Poupore walked together toward the car. Lombardo had the trunk open and was waiting for them. Lombardo's baggage was open, exposing three pistols, shoulder holsters, boxes of ammunition, a wallet, and an audiocassette. He explained that the wallet had another set of identification papers for himself. He just smiled at them and said, "You'll see," when Lovelady asked about the cassette tape.

**316**

"I've already scoped this place out, and no one can see us here. Take off your jackets, and slip on the shoulder holsters before we leave." Afterward, they climbed into their assigned places in the car, and Lombardo made a right out of the lot.

"All right," Lombardo said coolly, as he studied the map. "Go about two miles down this road, and make a left onto Marksworth Road." Poupore pushed in the trip odometer button, glancing at it occasionally as he drove. The mileage read one-point-nine miles, when he saw the Marksworth Road sign and he turned.

"Now, in about a mile make a right onto Pleasant Plains Drive. That's her street." Once again the mileage was almost exact.

"Pull over. All *right*, here's where the fun starts and we earn our money," Lombardo uttered. Poupore wondered if he mistook the gleeful tone in Lombardo's voice. "Her address is ten-twenty. We're in front of ten-oh-two, so the house should be right in the middle of the block.

"Ralph, I want you to pull up as close as you can get to the house. You stay in the car with the motor running. Dave and I will go in and check things out. Let's move."

Lovelady felt as though his heart would pound out of his chest, as he counted the house numbers to himself. Ten-fourteen. Ten-sixteen. Ten-eighteen. Ten-twenty was a modest, well-kept, brick rancher. The car rolled to a stop directly in front.

"Shit!" Lovelady said. "A fucking FOR SALE sign! She's gone." Despite his apprehension, he couldn't conceal the frustration.

"Maybe not. Let's check it out. Come on." Lombardo's voice displayed no emotion. He and Lovelady got out, and the two of them walked across the green lawn to the door, while Poupore stayed with the car. Lovelady took in the surroundings with an experienced eye, before knocking on the door. There was no sound from inside. "She's been gone a while."

"How can you tell?"

"See that FOR SALE sign on the lawn?"

"Yeah."

"Look how high the grass is around the posts sticking in the ground. If she were still here she'd trim it back to make the house look better from the road. The real estate company must be paying some neighborhood kid to mow it."

"What now?"

"Come with me."

Lovelady followed him to the car where Poupore was waiting apprehensively.

"She's not here. You can turn off the engine." Without offering any facts, Lombardo started walking to the house next door and once again,

Lovelady followed. Lombardo struck the door gently and waited. Almost at once, the door was opened by an elderly man wearing black over-the-calf socks, Bermuda shorts and a white dress shirt buttoned up to his neck.

"Sir, I can't tell you how sorry I am to disturb you, but I'm hoping you can help me." Lombardo stated.

"Yes?"

"We're trying to locate the owners of the house next door that's for sale. Do you know them?"

"Oh yes, a young lady named Lisa Herrera used to live there. We knew her, of course, but she's gone. I woke up one morning, and there was a FOR SALE sign on the lawn. Strangest thing. She used to come over to visit with my wife and me once in a while. Nice girl. We're disappointed she didn't come over to say good-bye. We're worried about her. Do you know her?"

"No, we just wanted to talk to the owner to see if we could get a better deal, before contacting the real estate agent. You know."

"I really wish I could help you, but we don't have any idea where she is. We tried to call her, but her phone's disconnected. Are you interested in the house?"

"Might be. Listen, we don't want to bother you. Have a good day, sir."

Lombardo reached his hand toward the gentleman's hand and squeezed it gently before turning away.

"Just a minute," the man said.

"Yes?"

"If I give you our names and phone number, would you see that Lisa gets it, if you track her down. We're both worried about her, and we'd like her to get in touch with us. Would you mind?"

"Certainly not, it would be our pleasure."

As the neighbor left to write the note, Lovelady, once again, marveled at Lombardo's ability to be gracious and charming one moment, and to inspire terror the next. Lombardo smiled broadly as he took the note, folded it neatly, and put it in his wallet. He assured the elderly man that Lisa would get the message, if at all possible.

"Tell Lisa that Floyd and Rose are concerned."

"What's your last name Floyd?"

"Martin. Floyd and Rose Martin."

"I will, Floyd. I promise."

"Do you have time to come in for a glass of iced tea? It's awfully hot, and my wife and I don't get much company anymore, since Lisa left."

"We would love to, but we just can't right now." Lombardo grinned again. "I'll tell you what, I'll take you up on your offer if we find we're interested in the house. Deal?"

Floyd smiled back. "Deal. And I hope you end up buying the house, you seem real nice."

"Thank you, Floyd, and I'm sorry we don't have time to meet your wife. It'll have to wait until next time."

As they walked back to the car, Lombardo said, "What a nice man. Reminds me a little of my own father." They got into the back seat.

"So what do we do now?" Lovelady asked.

"Just a minute." As he spoke, Lovelady noticed that Lombardo was studying the note with Martin's address and phone number.

"You just never know when this type of information can come in handy." Lombardo said, as he refolded the note and put it back in his wallet. Poupore, still sitting in the driver's seat, fully appreciated the potential value of what Lombardo was doing.

Lovelady summoned up the courage to be more forceful. "Andy, what do we do now? We have nothing to go on. No address, no telephone number, no nothing!"

Lombardo replied in a surprisingly considerate tone. "I know you're frustrated, Dave, but we haven't really even started to look for her yet. To be perfectly honest, I would have been dumbfounded if she were stupid enough to still be here. I'm certain Davies set her up somewhere else with another name and everything else. We'll find her."

"How, for Christ's sake?" Lovelady was becoming pessimistic about the chances of finding Rita and the tapes before the feds did. Lovelady felt his own life might be in peril if he didn't get the tapes first, knowing he had forced his leadership on the other conspirators. He had been the one to suggest that McGuire had to get off the audit. He had been the one responsible for Ramsey's murder. He had to solve the problem and, if he didn't, he knew that there would be a price to pay, as he had warned Bob Ramsey.

Lombardo sensed Lovelady's desperation. Realizing his own role in finding the tapes quickly, if he expected to get paid, he squeezed Lovelady's shoulder. "Look, we've got to get to work. I know we could find out where the sister is fast, if we put pressure on the real estate agency handling the sale. But that could get messy, and I have another idea."

"What?" Even in his current state, Lovelady didn't want to ask him what 'messy' meant.

Lombardo had noticed a teenage boy wearing baggy blue jeans, a black t-shirt with no sleeves and a baseball cap facing backwards, riding a bicycle. He was delivering newspapers. Lombardo pushed in a lever and the window came down. "Son, do you think you can help us?"

The boy walked his bike over to the car. "What do you want?" Poupore thought the question to be flippant.

"You know the area pretty well, don't you?"

In a sarcastic tone, he answered "No, I'm only delivering papers here for my health."

Lombardo didn't react to the affront. "We just need to know where the post office is that services this street."

"Make a U-turn and turn left at the end of the street. The post office is about three miles down on the right. You can't miss it."

"Thank you." Without saying a word, the boy resumed his paper route.

"Smart ass." Poupore said.

"Ralph," Lombardo said, "You can't sweat the small stuff. Let's go. We've got more important things to do."

Poupore drove off, found the post office easily, and parked the car directly across the street. Lombardo watched people go in and come out for a few minutes. "Okay, I've seen enough. Let's go."

"Where?"

"First, we need to find a room for the night. I noticed one of those suites hotels on the way. Let's check in there, and I'll tell you what happens next."

Using aliases and paying cash in advance, they checked in. After each had unpacked, they met in Lombardo's suite.

As they gathered around the dining room table drinking coffee, Lombardo briefed them. The plan was brilliant. Once again, Lovelady was confident and he was pleased he had selected Lombardo, despite his mood swings and heavy-handed ways.

"All right. You two drop me off at the mall. I'll get a cab back here. You know what to do at the post office, right?"

They both nodded yes.

At four-thirty they dropped Lombardo off at the mall entrance and continued to the post office. Lombardo went into a department store and headed for the shoe department. Joking and flirting amiably with a young salesperson, he tried out various styles, finally settling on a pair of expensive, black leather loafers. Lombardo paid in cash and the clerk wrapped up his purchase and handed it to him with a warm smile. Lombardo winked at her as he left.

Strolling through the mall, he stopped at an office supply store and bought a roll of brown paper, scissors, tape, and a black marking pen. He then bought three cellular telephones, arranging for three separate numbers.

Lombardo enjoyed an ice cream cone and walked slowly around the shopping center before hailing a cab to take him back to the hotel. On the way, he had the driver stop at a store, where he bought some expensive beer, spirits, cheese, cold cuts and crackers.

By eight that evening they were once again gathered around the table in Lombardo's room. Lovelady was talking. "We were watching them from across the street, and someone locked the door right at five. About fifteen minutes later, everyone had left and the lot was empty."

Lombardo was expressionless, absorbing every detail. "Go on."

"Anyhow, a couple of people drove up to mail some letters, but, other than that, there wasn't any activity until a big white U.S. Mail step-van pulled into the lot—right about five-thirty."

"What happened?"

"The driver pulled around back to the loading dock. He was in there for around fifteen minutes or so. He locked up, and we followed him just like you told us. He drove for about ten minutes, and then stopped at the same restaurant we were in today. I guess he had dinner. He was in there a good half-hour. Anyway, he left and kept going in the same direction.

"About twenty minutes later, he pulled into a big post office, and that's the last we saw of him. We did find out that he went to the area postal distribution center, where they separate the mail from the local branches and ship it out. After that, we came straight back here."

Lombardo shook his head. "Good job. It looks like everything's a go for tomorrow." He stood up, went to the closet, and came back with the three cellular telephones. He gave one each to Lovelady and Poupore. "I want each of us to each have a phone. If we're ever separated, we can always get in touch with each other. Let's memorize our numbers; nothing gets written down."

Lovelady and Poupore were impressed with the details.

Lombardo stood and walked over to the refrigerator. "Now, what can I get you two to drink? I went out and got some good beer and liquor." As he spoke, he rubbed his hands and smiled freely, reminding Lovelady of the maitre d' at a fine restaurant that he frequented in Washington. What would you like? It's been a long day, and we've worked hard."

Lovelady and Poupore exchanged glances, surprised and not expecting this invitation. "Uh, I'll take a gin-and-tonic," hastened Poupore.

"I think I'll join you, Ralph," added Lovelady. "Thanks, Andy."

"Actually, that does sound refreshing," replied Lombardo, mixing himself one as well. As he completed the drinks, he placed them on a tray. Deftly lifting the tray with one hand, he picked up a plate of aged blue cheese and crackers with the other.

The men moved to the living area as Lombardo placed the refreshments on the coffee table.

"So who's been keeping up on the elections here?" started Lombardo. The men started to relax, as they speculated on the hotly-contested race. Lovelady found himself laughing out loud, as Lombardo repeated a political joke from late night television.

Abruptly, Lombardo got out of his chair. "Look, you two have a good time. Make yourselves at home. I've got to leave, and I probably won't be back until late."

"Where are you going?" Lovelady asked, unable to hold his curiosity.

"I've got a date."

"With whom?" Poupore asked, perplexed.

"The young lady who sold me these shoes. She said she'd pick me up at nine, and I've got to go."

Before he closed the door, he said, "Don't forget, all work and no play and all that." He was grinning. "And be out of my room by midnight, in case I get lucky." He raised his eyebrows and exchanged playful glances with both of them, "And I usually am!

"You two work too hard. Learn to relax."

# *Chapter Fifty–Five*

Pat soon learned Charlene Hackman was a true professional, skilled at locating passengers and hotel guests traveling under assumed names. She got results. Pat found her pleasant manner and sense-of-humor a relief, under the tense circumstances.

Hackman quickly reviewed tickets and hotel documents, discovering similarities in handwriting of passengers and hotel guests, though different names were used, and she seemed to have a best friend at every airline and hotel. Pat stood back, amazed, as she teased and cajoled her contacts. Zipping through the most tangled airline bureaucracy, she emerged from every phone call with another critical piece of information about Rita or the conspirators.

Her prompt results buoyed Pat's confidence. While the conspirators' destination was the same, the airports they left from were predictable. Pat was able to use Agent Hackman's information to identify each of them— the headquarters of the companies they represented were always located close to the airports she identified.

"How's it going, buddy?" Russell stuck his head through Pat's office door. Pat McGuire was diligently working.

Pat looked up from the papers spread out on his desk. "Great—Agent Hackman and I have been making a lot of progress."

"What are you doing?"

"Well, I've finished identifying the voices on the meeting tape and the aliases have been matched to the voices. We've been able to track down almost everything."

"So, what is the next step?"

"Once Hackman finishes tracking down airline tickets and hotel receipts and matching them to signatures, points of origin and things like that, we hope we'll have enough for a grand jury and judge to make arrests and subpoena records."

"Any word about Rita?"

Pat's exuberance dimmed. "Not a thing—I'm hoping Agent Hackman can help."

"They'll find her Pat, don't worry."

Pat shook his head forlornly and tried to smile. After a moment he said, "Shut the door will you, Russell. I have to tell you something."

He shut the door and sat down. "Go for it."

Pat scrunched his face. "Russell, Malcolm tells me that, in his experience, anything can happen in this game and I need a favor."

"Anything."

"I've already talked to Edie, and I asked her to give you my mail when I'm out of the office. What I want you to do is to go through it when I'm not here, before you do anything else. If you come across anything suspicious, I want you to call me or Malcolm Karl right away."

Pat pulled out a sheet of paper and handed it to Russell. "Here's where you can reach Malcolm or any of his people. He's already assured me that they know who you are, and you can reach them any time of the day or night. I'll be sure to give you my itinerary and phone numbers, so you can get me any time I leave the office."

Russell eyed the papers and nodded.

Pat went back to work.

In Irving, Texas, Andy Lombardo had just returned to his room, after working out in the hotel gym. After his shave and shower, he put his old shoes in the shoebox the Nordstrom's clerk had given him. He carefully wrapped the box in the brown paper he had purchased the day before and taped it tightly. He then used the marking pen to address the box:

**Ms. Lisa Herrera**
**1020 Pleasant Plains Dr.**
**Irving, Texas 20711**

Diagonally across the box he wrote neatly:

**Please Forward**

He took the hotel elevator down to the lobby level and approached a clean-cut looking young bellman, standing by the door. His nametag said MIKE.

"Good morning sir, do you need a taxi or anything?"

"No, Mike," Lombardo said, "I need a favor."

"Yes, sir?"

"How would you like to earn a quick fifty?" Lombardo discreetly pulled a crisp new bill out of his wallet, so the bellman could see it.

The young man eyed him curiously, "What do I have to do?"

"Just take this to the post office down the street and mail it for me. That's it."

Mike eyed the fifty in Lombardo's hand. Thinking someone could be watching, he said, "Sir, they'll be happy to take your box at the front desk."

"I appreciate your loyalty, Mike, I really do, but this is very important to me, and I can't take any risks that this isn't mailed today. Just take it down to the post office. They'll weigh it and take care of it from that point. I can't imagine it costing any more than around three dollars. Here's another ten. You keep the difference. Deal?"

Mike looked at his watch. "I'm due for a break anyway."

As the bellman was driving to the post office, Lombardo joined Lovelady and Poupore in the hotel restaurant for breakfast. After eating, they went back to Lombardo's room to talk about the plan for that evening. On the way to the room, Lombardo passed the bellman, who gave him a thumbs-up sign.

At five o'clock that evening, the three of them waited in the rental car across the street from the post office. Like the night before, the building and lot were vacant by five-fifteen.

Ten minutes later, a white Post Office van with blue and red markings, pulled into the lot and stopped at the loading dock. They watched every movement intently. Twenty minutes later, the van pulled out of the lot, driving in the same direction as the night before. The Town Car followed the van, about two-hundred feet behind. Cresting a rise in the road, the postal vehicle headed toward the same restaurant where the driver had eaten dinner the night before.

"Come on, baby, pull in." Lovelady was almost whispering.

"He'll pull in, Dave," Lombardo said. "People are creatures of habit." On cue, the postal driver pulled onto the restaurant lot and Lombardo winked toward Lovelady. They stopped the car several spaces behind the van and watched the short, slightly-built driver get out, lock the vehicle, and walk toward the restaurant. After he was in, they parked the car in the space next to the van, opposite the driver's side, and waited. Half-an-hour later, they saw the driver open the front door of the restaurant and step out into the still-fierce Texas heat, though the sun had begun to set. The driver, wearing a USPS baseball cap, blue USPS shirt and short khaki trousers, stretched and ambled slowly toward his truck.

Just before the driver inserted his key into the door lock, Lombardo looking frazzled came around from the other side of the van-with a map in his hand. "Sir! Sir, can you help us? We're not from around here. It seems we've gotten ourselves lost!" he said, convincingly apologetic.

"Sure," the driver said, anxious to help. "Where are you trying to go?"

Lombardo walked up to him, opened the map, and spread it across the hood of the van, pointing to a particular area on the map.

"We're trying to find this street."

The driver put on his glasses and glanced down. There was a yellow post-it note stuck to the map. The driver read:

**Walk with me to the other side of the van.**

"What is this?" the driver asked, appearing confused.

Lombardo smiled.

"Do as you're told, and you won't get hurt. Do anything stupid and you will." Lombardo's tone was gruff, but he was still smiling amiably. They walked together to the other side of the van, where Lovelady and Poupore were waiting. Lovelady had his pistol at his side.

Seeing the pistol, the startled driver took a step back and raised both hands over his head.

"Listen, I'm not the John Wayne type. Whatever you want, it's yours. Just don't hurt me."

"Good. You learn real fast. Now just open the van and get inside." The driver was fumbling with his keys and had trouble inserting one in the lock. Finally he managed to open the door. He stepped into the van, Lombardo followed him, slammed the door shut and looked into the passenger mirror. Poupore and Lovelady were climbing into the Town Car.

Lombardo addressed the postman: "I'll drive. Just give me your hat." There was no resistance. Lombardo adjusted the hat to his head, he sat in the driver's seat, started the motor and made a left out of the driveway.

"Where are you taking me?" The driver was shaking, and his voice trembled with fear. "Mister, I don't want any trouble, I'm just a mailman." The man was now crying.

"Just do what you're told." As Lombardo drove, he checked the rear-view mirror often, making sure Poupore and Lovelady were still following. They had been driving about fifteen minutes, when Lombardo noticed a NO OUTLET sign. He turned right and pulled onto a pockmarked, gravel road, which came to an abrupt end at the edge of a creek, about three-quarters of a mile from the main road. Lombardo stopped the van and turned off the motor.

It was very dark. The only sound was the din of crickets and frogs in the woods lining the road. Lombardo was motionless and the postman was sobbing. About a minute later, the headlight beams of the Town Car interrupted the darkness. Poupore parked it directly behind the van and turned off the lights. There was now total darkness.

"How do you turn on the inside lights?"

"The switch by your left hand. What are you going to do with me?"

Lombardo switched on the van's interior lights. He turned toward the postal driver—his eyes were swollen from crying and mucous was dripping from his nose. Lovelady and Poupore got into the van; both of them were startled by the driver's appearance.

"What do you want from me? We don't carry any money, and if you find any it's yours." The driver was terrified. The warm dampness of urine trickled down his legs.

"Where do you keep the parcels?"

"There, in two bags by the door." He pointed to two large white bags. "Everything else is letter mail."

"Open them."

The driver scurried over to the sacks, opened them, and spilled their contents onto the truck floor. Immediately, Lombardo noticed the box he had wrapped in brown paper and had given to the hotel bellman earlier. He picked it up, smiled and looked at his accomplices. "Bingo!" Just under his 'Please Forward' notation was a yellow sticker with the forwarding address:

*2321 Earleen Drive*
*Cape Girardeau, MO 63701*

"Here it is fellows. Just like I said."

The driver closed his eyes in relief, thankful his captors had found what they came for.

Lovelady looked at the driver. "What's your name?" Lombardo's voice was steady, even friendly.

"Kenneth. Kenneth Aud."

"Give me your shirt, Ken."

Again, offering no resistance, the driver took off the shirt and handed it to Lombardo. "Here. Anything you want. Please don't hurt me." He was shaking uncontrollably.

Lombardo took the shirt, placed it across his left shoulder and reached into his jacket, removing the pistol from the holster. Seeing the weapon, Kenneth Aud crossed himself, clasped his hands, and looked upward. With desperation, he prayed, "Hail Mary, full of grace, the Lord is with thee. Blessed art thou among women, and blessed is the fruit of thy womb, Jesus." His voice became louder. Words came out faster. "Holy Mary, Mother of God . . ." Lombardo waved the gun in front of his face before lowering his arm and gently squeezing the trigger with his index finger. The pistol exploded. A deafening noise bounced off the walls of the van, echoing in the woods surrounding the truck. The forest became silent, the frogs and crickets must have sensed a dangerous invasion to their territory.

The bullet had struck the driver just above his left eye, and had torn out a large piece of his skull as it came out the back. The deadly projectile shattered the windshield before expending itself and dropping into the creek. The inside of the windshield was splattered with flesh. The driver's body came to rest in the stepwell at a grotesque, unnatural angle. Bright red blood covered the passenger door and the driver's face was unrecognizable. Lombardo put the pistol back into the holster and turned.

Neither Lovelady nor Poupore had ever witnessed anything like this in their lives. Their faces, whiter than ash, betrayed their shock. Lovelady was leaning on the inside of the truck with his eyes closed. He was mouthing the words, "Oh my God, Oh my God. Oh my God." Poupore somehow found his way out of the truck and was throwing up next to the Town Car.

Knowing enough to let them have their privacy until they collected themselves, Lombardo left them alone. He recovered his parcel, putting it into the Town Car trunk with the driver's shirt and hat.

Lovelady and Poupore were now like robots and each got into the back seat. Although their faces didn't resemble each other at all, their expressions were identical. As they sat in silence, they didn't even notice that Lombardo had slipped the mail truck into neutral and easily stepped out of the vehicle, as it started its slow roll down a slight embankment before coming to rest in a ditch. Lombardo watched the truck's final journey before turning and walking back to the car. He had a satisfied smile on his face.

Lombardo drove back off the abandoned trail toward the street. He didn't turn the headlights on until they reached the main road. No words were spoken.

They had been riding for about ten minutes when Lovelady finally spoke. "Was that necessary?" He was surprised he said anything.

Lombardo's reply was similar to a professor responding to a pupil. "Rule number one: *Never* drink during business hours. Rule number two: *Never* leave a witness who can identify you."

Lombardo continued to drive until they crossed a bridge. He brought the car to an abrupt stop, immediately on the other side, surprising both Lovelady and Poupore. He turned his head toward the back seat. "Out of the car, Poupore."

Poupore was paralyzed with fear, too frightened to speak or to offer resistance. Lovelady sat silent and motionless, picturing what could happen next. Poupore did as he was told and stood by the side of the road. He was praying that one of the passing cars would be a police cruiser and stop.

Lombardo got out, went to the rear of the car, and opened the trunk. He tore off the brown paper with Rita's sister's address, folded it, and put it in his pocket. He handed the box to Poupore. Poupore still couldn't speak. "Take off your shoes and put these on. You have vomit all over your shoes."

Poupore looked at his feet and saw the foul liquid on his shoes. He took them off, sliding on the shoes that were handed to him. Lombardo was much bigger than Poupore, and the new shoes slid on easily. "Now throw yours into the bushes." Poupore did as he was told and got back into the car, sitting next to the still-quiet Lovelady, who was almost catatonic.

"That's much better. I couldn't take that stench any more."

Lombardo continued to drive in the Texas darkness. They passed a TRUCK STOP 1 MILE road sign, and he followed a truck onto the parking lot. He drove slowly around the parked trucks, stopped next to one loaded with loose field corn, turned out the lights, walked briskly over, and quickly threw his pistol into the trailer. It vanished into the loose corn.

Lombardo returned to the car, and before driving away, said, "Rule number one: *Never* drink during business hours. Rule number two: *Never* leave a witness who can identify you. Rule number three: *Always* get rid of the murder weapon as soon as possible." He chuckled. "That truck had Nebraska tags. God knows how long it'll take them to find that pistol, if they do at all."

He eased the car into the interstate traffic and reached down to turn on the radio. He continued to push in the SEARCH button until he found a classical music station. He hummed along until the piece ended. "Oh, I love Bartok, don't you?" They listened to two more compositions. After each concluded and before their titles were announced, Lombardo named the melody, the composer, and the orchestra. They continued their drive toward the Dallas-Fort Worth airport, listening to classical music. No one spoke, until Lombardo, in a reluctant tone, said, "Dave, there's something I have to get off my chest."

Lovelady didn't answer, but made eye contact with Lombardo in the rear-view mirror instead. He had a quizzical look.

"I hate to bring this up, but your language leaves something to be desired."

"My language?"

"Yeah. I've noticed that you curse a lot."

"I curse a lot. What are you talking about?"

"Cursing offends me. Now, you might take this as an affront, but I want to tell you something." His tone was now that of a parent who had caught his teenager with cigarettes. "When you curse, all you are doing is announcing to the world that you have a limited vocabulary and that you have difficulty expressing yourself. Understand what I'm trying to say?"

Lovelady didn't respond, but continued the eye contact through the mirror. "When you said the F-word when you saw the FOR SALE sign, what you were telling me was that my sensitivities didn't matter. That offended me, Dave. I wouldn't think much of myself if I didn't say something about it. I hope you understand."

Lovelady did understand. He was having a one-sided conversation with a madman—and a smart and controlling one, at that.

"One last thing, and then I promise I'll let it go."

"Yeah?"

"It's your temper. I can't help but notice that you have a temper. Dave," he hesitated, "when you said the F-word, you lost your temper. Let me tell you my philosophy on temper." Lombardo didn't hesitate this time. "It's a sign of weakness, Dave—a big road sign that you've let the situation control you. When you do that, you've weakened your own position. Know what I mean, Dave?"

Lovelady shook his head in affirmation. He understood more clearly: his every move, and that of Poupore's, was in the hands of a polite, educated, refined, and sophisticated killer.

The Dallas-Fort Worth Airport finally came into view to Poupore's and Lovelady's relief. Lombardo followed the RENTAL CAR RETURN signs. Settling up with the attendant, they took the shuttle bus to the terminal. They followed Lombardo into a travel agency, where they learned that the closest major airport to Cape Girardeau, Missouri, was Saint Louis. They purchased first-class tickets and reserved two rental cars at the Saint Louis Airport.


As the three men settled into the first-class cabin, Lovelady felt the weight of his involvement sink in deep. He replayed, in his mind, his evening with Lombardo at the restaurant. *I knew he was off! —This man doesn't know his place. When am I going to learn to listen to my instincts? We'll never make it out of this shit!* Looking out the window, he rubbed his forehead.

Lovelady could sense Poupore's nervousness and discomfort too. Until today, their involvement had been only an adventure.

Lovelady tried to push back the scene that kept replaying itself in his mind—the terrified expression on that driver's face as he said his prayers, before Lombardo pulled the trigger; the man's head exploding in front of his eyes. No, no, he pushed it back down, further, further back, into the recesses of his brain. Approving McGuire's football accident and Ramsey's murder were different—he hadn't *been* there. He had *been* there tonight. He had seen it, and he was part of it.

Lovelady tried to resign himself to the situation he had created. Everything he had, everything he had worked for, his very destiny was now entirely in the hands of Andy Lombardo, and everything was happening so fast.

Lovelady suspected that Lombardo's fourth rule might involve Poupore and him, if they didn't continue to go along. There was no way out now.

Lovelady recognized that Andy Lombardo wasn't just a hired gun. He wasn't just a murderer. He wasn't just violent and brutal. He was a psychopath, born without the conscience gene.

# Chapter Fifty-Six

Agent Charlene Hackman and Pat had made a great team, and Pat was almost euphoric with their progress in identifying the conspirators but reality struck hard when Charlene told him how little she had uncovered about Rita's travels. She told him the truth: "Tracking down people on domestic flights staying in American-owned hotels is one thing, but international travel is something else altogether. Your friend has carefully covered her tracks. Pat, it's going to take us a long time to find her."

"Can you tell me what you do know?"

"Sure."

She was positive that Rita had been a passenger on the flights to Spain and Switzerland as, unknown to Rita, she was on the planes herself, but Charlene was unable to trace her precisely after she had left the plane abruptly in Zurich. Her ticket back to the United States had never been used. Two days after landing in Switzerland, a Linda Hampson had purchased a one-way fare to Ireland, and she had definitely used the ticket. "It gets even more interesting. On the same day, a Rita Davies bought a one-way ticket to Rio, with a two-day layover in Jamaica and, once again, both tickets were used."

She saw the perplexed look on Pat's face. "What are you trying to tell me?"

"What I'm saying, Pat, is that she could be in Ireland, Rio, Jamaica, or even someplace else. That's all we have at this point, and it's going to take us quite a while to locate her."

He looked even more confused. "I don't understand. Why would it be so difficult to find her?"

"Pat, these are foreign countries. If this were the United States, we'd have more power to make airlines and hotels cooperate. We can't *make* foreign countries do anything, under this set of circumstances. I'm sorry to have to tell you this, but you're going to have to be realistic about our chances."

The gleeful mood Pat was experiencing on the progress on the conspirators had turned to concern and frustration, as Charlene Hackman bluntly told him about Rita. He frowned, "How could she be on two flights at once?"

"Obviously she can't, and that's in our favor."

"So what do you think?"

She hesitated. "I've told you everything I know. I've talked it over with Malcolm, and I'll tell you what we think so far." She hesitated again. "We haven't been able to prove this, so this is just a theory, okay? We think that the names might be just a coincidence. Another passenger traveling the same day could have had the same name as one of her identities."

Pat looked her directly in the eye. "Charlene, where do *you* really think she is?"

"I think she's in Rio." She didn't hesitate before answering.

"Why?"

"Well, *I* think she took a few days in Jamaica to rest, which is understandable under the circumstances. Then I think she went on to Rio. It'll be even harder to find her in South America."

"Why?"

"Both Ireland and Jamaica are relatively small. Of the three potential areas, it would be easiest to find her in either of these places because she can only go so far. If she made it to Rio though, she could easily rent a car and be anywhere in South or Central America—or even Mexico. Pat, if she did that, I doubt if we'll ever find her."

The words hit like a thunderbolt. Now Pat understood. He inhaled deeply and sighed.

She reached across the table and put her hand on his. "Pat, we'll never give up looking for her, and I'm telling you that we're not going to waste any time. Our people are already in both Rio and Ireland. At this point, we're not going to waste our time with Jamaica. She probably wouldn't have gone there—it's *too* small."

"Okay, if that's all we've got, that's all we've got." He managed a weak smile. "Listen, I'm supposed to call Malcolm Karl. Do you need anything from him?"

"Nope, I'm fine. I'm going back to work. I want to get this thing resolved."

Pat tried to sound professional, composed, and optimistic with Karl. "You wouldn't believe the progress we're making on one end of this, Malcolm." He told him how they had systematically connected each of the accessories to the airports near their company headquarters.

"You and Charlene are doing a great job, Pat! Keep calling so I'm apprised at least once a day." He hesitated momentarily before continuing and changed his tone from one of encouragement to one of concern. " Pat, look, there's something else I have to go over with you."

"Sure, what's up?"

Karl hesitated before continuing. "We've made some progress tracking down the guy who took you out in the football game."

Pat sat up straight in his chair. His attention was riveted. "You have?" This was the first time anyone had brought the subject up since his injury.

"Yeah, we have, and that's not all." Karl didn't let Pat interfere before finishing what he had to say. "We're pretty sure it's the same guy who carried out Ramsey's homicide. I didn't want to tell you anything until I was certain."

Pat was dumbstruck, hanging on to every word.

"We're pretty sure it's a local creep by the name of Andy Lombardo. He's our number-one suspect in a good number of hits, but I have to tell you, he's one cool customer. We've tailed him, we've tapped his phone, we've done everything imaginable, but we can never get anything on him. He's sharp, and I have to tell you something else."

"What?"

"I'll be up front with you—this is one bad actor. He's brutal. He appears to have absolutely no conscience whatsoever, and he's extremely bright. He covers his tracks well—no witnesses, no paper placing him anywhere, no murder weapons, no nothing. And I mean nothing." Pat sensed the frustration in Karl's voice. "I'm telling you to be careful. We haven't seen him around town, and we're pretty sure that he's with Lovelady and Poupore."

As Karl continued, Pat appeared to be under a spell. This traumatic episode firmly placed in the past, it was difficult to think about it again and to digest all the new information. Pat was completely at a loss.

"I don't have time to go into all the details, but the circumstances surrounding Ramsey's murder are very similar to other cases in which Lombardo is a suspect and that has to be more than coincidence."

Karl took a sip of water.

"When we combine this with Lombardo's physical description and the description of the guy who hurt you, I think you can see how we've come to this conclusion."

As Pat was processing what he had just been told, Karl interrupted, "So this is where we are now—Poupore and Lovelady are unaccounted for and so, to the best of our knowledge, is Lombardo." He took another sip of water. "Pat we think the three of them are after Rita."

Though strongly disinclined, Pat realized that he had to come to grips with the fact that he might never see Rita again. He didn't know if he could cope with that uncertainty.

"Well, I have to give you one thing, Malcolm."

"What?"

"When you say you're going to be up front with me, I'll know you're not kidding."

Karl had suggested that Pat keep Russell involved, so when Pat finished with Karl he cradled the phone to his neck and punched in Russell's extension. Russell reacted with surprise and concern, as Pat relayed to him the details of the conversation.

"Do you think we can tell my father?" Russell asked after Pat informed him of the details.

"Malcolm said it was okay, but he preferred not telling anyone else in the office."

"Good. Dad hasn't said anything, but I know he's dying of curiosity. Hey, so nothing in the mail yet?"

"Nope. Just routine stuff, and, believe me, I've been looking. Edie's looking out for me, too. Listen, I've got to go back to work. I'll talk to you later on. Just remember what Karl said about Lombardo. If you happen to run across him, no macho shit, understand? Call Karl."

"Pat, I've been called a lot of names in my life, but stupid hasn't been one of them. This isn't a football game, and I know I'm out of my league. Don't forget, this Lombardo character almost took off my arm in the Glen Burnie game, even before you got hurt. I was no match for him then, and I'm sure I'm no match for him now—he's probably armed now and I'm not! You have nothing to worry about on my end."

After they finished, Pat briefed Agent Hackman in his office. Neither said much as they resumed their work.

Lombardo, Lovelady and Poupore approached their rental cars, parked side-by-side in the Saint Louis Airport lot. They all agreed that the best route was the interstate highway, south for about a hundred miles to Cape Girardeau, situated on a bend of the Mississippi River.

Lombardo took the lead, and the other two followed. They took the first Cape Girardeau exit, stopping at the bottom of the ramp. Lombardo put his car in park, jumped out quickly, and walked up to Lovelady and Poupore. "Follow me. Let's stop at some restaurant, get a bite to eat, and go over the plan one more time." They nodded.

Ten minutes later, they were sitting at a table at a local restaurant. Lombardo ate his lunch, and ordered dessert and coffee. Poupore and Lovelady just picked at their food. The events of the night before were still too fresh in their minds.

After the waiter took their plates, Lombardo took out a plain white envelope from his jacket pocket. He wrote down Rita's sister's name and Earleen Drive address on the face. On the upper left-hand corner, he wrote Floyd and Rose Martin's names and their address in Texas.

Lombardo was talking. "Okay then. Ralph, when we get back to the cars, you give me your weapon. Dave still has his in case anything comes down, but I don't think it will. I'm going to pull my car into her driveway and do my thing. I'll call one of you on the cell phone from inside the house. You two know what you have to do then?"

They both nodded yes.

"Then I'll meet you by the cars in about five minutes."

Lovelady and Poupore went to the cars to wait, too jittery to chat. Lombardo thanked the hostess for the directions to Earleen Drive she wrote down for him. After paying the bill, he went into the men's room, and slipped on a plain blue shirt and the postal hat he had taken from the murdered driver in Texas. Seeing Lombardo walk toward them with the postal hat on, Lovelady felt his heart pounding and sweat seeped through the back of his shirt, thinking about the plan that was about to be put into action.

"Earleen Drive is only a few minutes from here, but I'll need to make a stop first. Just follow me."

Poupore and Lovelady followed Lombardo for about three blocks. Lombardo made a quick turn into a lot with a small bank of stores. He parked in front of a hardware store, and Poupore pulled in a couple of spaces down.

A few minutes later, Lombardo emerged with a large brown bag and walked over to the other car. Poupore rolled his window down. "Don't forget, you two wait around the corner until I call you. Clear?" He didn't wait for an answer, and he slipped his pistol into the right pocket of his trousers.

Carefully following the directions given to him at the restaurant, Lombardo easily found Earleen drive. The neighborhood impressed him as very quiet and very middle-class. It directly bordered an obviously upper-class neighborhood with much larger homes. Before turning onto the street, he waited for the second car to pull up behind him and stop. He turned right; 2321 was the second house on the right. He pulled onto the concrete driveway and parked the car between the doors of the two-car garage. Putting on the blue USPS baseball cap, he grabbed the letter, walked to the front door, and knocked. A female voice came from inside the house, "Who is it?"

"Postman."

"Back again?"

"Yes, ma'am—certified mail."

The door opened slightly and Lisa Herrera peeked outside. Relieved to see a uniformed postal employee, she asked, "Who is it for? I'm not expecting anything."

He casually looked at the letter and read, as if he seeing it for the first time. "Let's see, it's for Lisa Herrera at this address. Are you Miss Herrera?"

She thought her heart might stop when she heard the sound of her own name. She and Rita had been so careful and thorough about arranging for pseudonyms. "Who is it from?" She hoped her voice sounded composed. She was straining to read the return address herself.

"Let's see," he said again. "Looks like it's from a Floyd and Rose Martin in Irving, Texas." He was squinting, pretending he was having difficulty reading without glasses.

A sigh of relief came over her immediately, and she thought to herself, *Floyd and Rose. Dear old Floyd and Rose. If anyone would find out where she was, it would be them.* She smiled at the postman. "Yes, I'll sign for it."

He handed the letter across to her. "Where do I sign?"

"I have the form right here." He reached into his right pocket and took out his pistol. He pointed it straight at her, careful to hide his motions, in the event a neighbor might be watching.

In one graceful motion, he pushed his right shoulder against the partially-opened door, set the pistol on the safe position, and slid the weapon back into his pocket.

She backed away and started to run toward the back door when, with one quick sweep of his right leg, he tripped her, and she fell to the carpeted floor. She tried desperately to get up, but the weight of his body was already on her back and she was helpless against him. Before she could yell for help, he had shoved a handkerchief into her mouth. She tried, but she couldn't get the material out of her mouth before he brought both of her hands behind her back, holding both wrists with his left hand.

Dragging her across the room, Lombardo bumped Lisa's head against a chair and blood slowly trickled from a small cut over her left eye. Spotting an electrical cord plugged into a wall outlet, Lombardo yanked. In rodeo fashion, he used the cord to tie her hands behind her back and to her ankles. She tried to use her tongue to get the handkerchief out of her mouth. Deftly, he grabbed a kitchen towel and used it to hold the gag in place, fastening it behind her head.

As she lay helpless, Lombardo walked to the front door and closed it. He reached for the cellular telephone in his back pocket and dialed. Lovelady answered, "Dave here." Despite his state of mind, Lovelady remembered the order to never use last names over the phone.

"You two can come on in now. Leave the car where it is." Lovelady and Poupore did as they were told, walking nervously. They entered the house, locked the door and saw Lisa Herrera as she lay curled in a humiliating position.

Rita Davies' sister did not have Rita's blond curls; her hair was long and auburn—but their faces were almost identical. In some way, Lovelady couldn't help feeling that he, Poupore, and now the woman on the kitchen floor were all, in different ways, captives of Andy Lombardo.

Lombardo started giving orders. "Ralph, get the bag of hardware and my luggage out of my car. Dave, help me get her up. They lifted her by her shoulders. Her body was arched backwards, and they had to support her until Poupore came back with the bag.

"There's a pair of wire cutters in the bag. Take it out and cut this extension cord so she can stand up straight." Poupore cut the cord and she immediately recoiled to a more natural position, with hands and feet still tied. "Set her on the chair, and hold her steady."

While they held her, Lombardo's facility with rope and duct tape resulted in the complete immobilization of Lisa. She couldn't move and she couldn't make a sound. Her eyes were wide with fear—she was too stunned to cry.

Lombardo barked out more orders. "Ralph, go around the house. Shut every blind and curtain and make sure every door and window is locked. Dave, you come with me."

Grabbing the bolt cutters, Lombardo led Lovelady through a kitchen door leading to the garage and Herrera's car. "Pop the hood." Lombardo used the bolt cutters to sever both battery cables and each spark plug wire.

Noticing an antenna on the rear window, Lombardo cut the wires connecting the car phone to the antenna and battery.

They went back to the kitchen as Poupore came down the hall, finished with the blinds and curtains. Lombardo went to the wall telephone, activating his cellular phone, and dialed the number on the telephone cradle. A moment later, three telephones were ringing. He traced the rings to the den, master bedroom, and kitchen. Using wire cutters, he cut each wire leading to the telephone jacks and severed the electrical and connecting wires on the answering machine next to the bedroom phone.

Returning to the kitchen, Lombardo slid a kitchen chair across from his bound captive. Lovelady and Poupore, leaning against the opposite wall, watched and listened intently.

Lombardo's voice was slow, calm, and deliberate as he spoke to Lisa Herrera. "Do you have a cellular phone? Just blink your right eye if you do." She blinked.

Lombardo looked around and saw a purse on the kitchen counter. "Is it in your purse?" Once again, she blinked. He pulled the cellular telephone out of the purse, removed the battery, and put it into his pocket. He then opened the phone, set the bow-shaped instrument on the floor, and stepped on it, breaking it into two pieces. "Well, it appears that you are totally cut-off from the outside world, wouldn't you agree?"

He hesitated for a few long moments so that she could fully realize how desperate her situation was. Poupore and Lovelady, still watching the unfolding drama, were as silent as Lombardo's new, helpless captive.

He continued. "You can make this real easy for all of us or *really* difficult for just you. It's totally up to you, and I really don't care." He paused again.

"We don't have much time, so I'll get right to the point. We want your sister, we want the tapes, and we want the money. Simple?" Lovelady and Poupore stood mesmerized. "Now, I'm going to take the gag off, and you're going to tell us where she is. Understand?" She tried to shake her head up-and-down.

"Good girl. Dave, take off the gag." He untied the knot and removed the kitchen towel. As soon as he did, she spat out the gag and inhaled deeply to get oxygen into her lungs. When she caught her breath, Lombardo continued. "Okay, then. You understand my proposition. Where is she?"

She looked at him with contempt in her eyes and voice. "I don't know where she is, and I wouldn't tell you if I did. My sister hasn't done anything wrong, and neither have I. Why can't you people let us alone?"

Lombardo looked disgusted. "Oh please! What do you take us for? Dave, gag her again. This time use the tape." In a few moments her mouth was taped shut. "Like I said, we don't have time for this, and I'm only going to give you one more chance. I want you to *believe* me, when I tell you that I've got ways to make you talk."

He smiled menacingly and looked at the other two. "Would you listen to me! I sound like Lon Chaney playing some Nazi talking to a prisoner in a World War Two movie. 'Vee haff vays to make you talk.'" He pounded the table for effect, looked at them, and laughed. Poupore and Lombardo forced stiff grins across their faces.

Pulling items from the paper bag, Lombardo slowly and carefully laid a knife, wire cutters and bolt cutters on the kitchen table. He reached for his luggage and took out an audiocassette tape.

Lombardo's tone became deadly serious. "I'm going to play this for you and, after you listen, I'm going to ask you again about your sister. I made this tape especially for another client of mine. The client needed some information this couple had, and the client had difficulty getting it from them. That's where I came in.

"I had both of them tied up exactly like you are right now, around the kitchen table and everything, and, like you, they stupidly tried to resist. They didn't want to listen to reason and they exhausted my patience. I put a cassette player with this tape in it on the table, and I hit the record button. I'm sure you get the setting."

Lombardo walked over to the stereo system in the living room, put in the cassette, and pushed PLAY. Lovelady and Poupore were both visibly apprehensive about what they were going to hear remembering Lombardo in action in Texas with the pitiful mailman. Andy Lombardo's voice came through the speakers:

*I've lost my patience with both of you, so now let me tell you what I'm going to do. You've noticed that I've placed a few instruments on the table? One is a hunting knife, one is a wire cutter, and the other is a bolt cutter. First, I'm going to flip a coin. Heads it's you, Steve, and tails it's you, Judy."*

A coin could be heard bouncing on the table.

*It's tails. Congratulations, Judy. Steve, I want you to watch and listen closely. First, I'll take the gag out of her mouth, so you can get the full effect. Then, while you watch and listen, I'm going to use the wire cutters to cut off the tip of the middle finger of her right hand. Then it's your turn. I'm going to tape her mouth shut again and remove your tape, while she watches me take the hunting knife and cut off your middle finger at the first joint. You can probably guess what I'm going to do with the bolt cutters.*

*They could hear him rip the tape off the terrified woman's mouth. She was pleading with him.*

*Please don't! I'll tell you everything! Please don't! I'll do anything!*

*A second later they heard the scream.*

*Ahhhhhhhhhhhhhhh . . . . . . . . . . . . . . . . . . . . . . . . .*

They had never heard anything like her scream.
**"STOP!"** it was Poupore. "I can't take this any more!" He ran over to the stereo and turned it off. He was almost hyperventilating and thought sure he was going to vomit again. This wasn't a canned movie scream. This scream couldn't possibly have been acting. It was real, and it was harrowing.

Lombardo winked at Lovelady, whose left leg was shaking uncontrollably. "You should have left it on, Ralph, you're going to miss the best parts." Lovelady looked at Rita's sister. Petrified, she was defenseless in the chair.

"Take the tape off her mouth, Dave." Lovelady tried to calm himself and fumbled as he tore off the duct tape. Numb with panic, Lisa did not flinch at the pain the tape caused.

Her voice quivered and the expression in her eyes was desperate, as she begged Lombardo not to hurt her. She promised to tell them anything they wanted to know. Lovelady stiffened in anger, feeling he wanted to help her, but aware that he was as helpless against Lombardo as she. No one noticed that Poupore had made his way to the bathroom and was splashing cold water on his face.

"I thought you'd see it my way. Now, like I said, we don't have much time here. Where is she?"

"Jamaica. All I have is her telephone number and address. It's in that little purple phone book on the counter under 'R'. Please believe me!"

"I'm going to call her, and let's just say it had better be her voice on the line."

"It will be. Please call her."

He picked up the book and turned to the 'R' page. On the top of the page she had written:

**RITA**
**5214 IDLE HOURS COURT**
**RUNAWAY BAY, 9, JAMAICA**
**(876) 741-1814**

He recognized the area code as Jamaica's and he knew Lisa was telling the truth. He dialed the number. "Dave, you would recognize her voice. If it sounds like Rita, just hang up." He handed the receiver to Lovelady, who put the instrument up to his ear.

"Hello," he heard. It was Rita. Lovelady nodded his head and pushed the OFF button, disconnecting the call.

"We're rounding third and heading for home, boys. We've got her right where we want her. Those tapes will be in our hands in no time."

Lovelady felt a sudden surge of confidence. His empathy for Lisa seemed to evaporate. For the first time in a long, long time, Lovelady felt glad he had chosen Lombardo. Yes, he got the job done. The end was finally in sight.

Lombardo looked at Lovelady and bit his lower lip in thought. He walked to Lisa, who was watching his every move, and very gently put the duct tape gag across her mouth. "Why don't we go outside where we can talk in private?" He followed Lombardo onto the wooden deck where they sat on patio chairs. A composed Poupore, who had returned to the kitchen, saw them on the deck and joined them. Lisa strained to listen to the conversation, despite her situation.

Lombardo's voice was gentle and as he spoke, it was obvious he had given the situation a lot of thought.

"This is what I think we should do." he said, alternating eye contact between the two men. They hung on every word.

"I'm leaving you two here with the sister, and I'm going to Jamaica alone to find Rita."

Lombardo went on to tell them that the first priority was to find Rita in Jamaica, as she was the irreplaceable key to the tapes and the money.

Time was of the essence because they could be sure government authorities were just as anxious to find her.

He explained how important it was to keep Lisa as a hostage, as they may have trouble with Rita in Jamaica. They needed Lisa and they needed her alive to "bargain" with Rita, as Lombardo chose to phrase it.

"The problem is," Lombardo continued, "when we get what we need from Davies, we no longer need Lisa here," he glanced toward the helpless woman in the kitchen, "and you remember my rule about not leaving any witness who could identify you."

He let them think for a moment about the desperate mailman.

Lovelady summoned up his courage to speak, but before one word was spoken, Lombardo anticipated the question and answered it. "Look Dave, it's best for me to go alone. If the authorities are in Jamaica, they'll be looking for you two and probably not me. It will be much easier for me to get in unnoticed."

Both Lovelady and Poupore nodded in agreement.

"But," Lombardo said, taking a deep breath and almost sighing before he continued, "you know it's up to you two to take care of the sister later."

Their eyes widened simultaneously as the words sunk in.

"You can do it, I have confidence in you." Lombardo's voice was now that of a football coach building up the confidence of a substitute, and the tactic worked.

"I'm going back to the Saint Louis Airport right away, by myself, and take the first plane to Jamaica."

"Dave, I don't think I . . ." It was Poupore, and Lombardo cut him off immediately by pounding his right fist hard on the table, startling both of them as well as the imprisoned Lisa. He reached across the table, and grabbed Poupore by the collar.

"Now, you listen to me." His voice was almost a whisper. "I don't have time to babysit you two any longer. Are you going to get the job done or not? I really don't care because, I promise you, I'll get my money even if we terminate this operation right now." He let go of Poupore, crossed his arms across his chest and slowly turned his head toward Lovelady. He smiled at Lovelady's expression of helplessness.

His smile broadened. "So, Dave, what have you decided? We're wasting valuable time here, you know."

Lovelady knew he had no choice and simply nodded his head up-and-down slowly.

"All right then, I'm leaving now. I'll call you after I get what I'm going to Jamaica for and take care of Rita.

"When I give you the word, you've got to get rid of our little hostage in the kitchen, Dave." He nodded toward the bound and helpless Lisa. His next words made the hair on the back of their necks stand up, "If you don't take care of the sister, I'm going to have to take care of you."

Lovelady knew he meant it.

Lombardo continued, " After I leave, you can make her a little more comfortable, but that's all. Everyone stays in the house—don't do anything to draw attention to the house. One of you two has to be awake at all times to watch her and cover the phones, in case I need you for something."

Without warning and without wasting any more time, Lombardo walked out the front door. He quickly glanced around the neighborhood and, when he was satisfied he wasn't being watched, he calmly walked to his rental car and drove north to the St. Louis Airport.

Lovelady and Poupore sat across from each other and neither said a word. They were mentally preparing for the grizzly task facing them.

# Chapter Fifty–Seven

Lisa was recalling another unthinkable incident—the burglarizing of her apartment—that had left her feeling violated and fearful. Every time she had opened that apartment door, she remembered and eventually she moved somewhere else. She couldn't have imagined anything worse than that incident.

But this was worse—*much* worse. Shackled, held captive in her own home, and threatened with unimaginable atrocities, Lisa felt hopeless. These men hadn't stolen anything material; they had stolen her dignity. She didn't feel violated this time, she felt *defiled*.

After being terrorized by the audiotape, Lisa was left bound in the kitchen for the next several hours. The two men moved alternately from her deck to her bedroom, and she could hear only muffled voices. She imagined what they must be discussing—what tactics Lombardo would use once he got to Jamaica and what they would eventually do to her and Rita.

The only time she spoke was when she had to use the bathroom. Poupore unfastened her and let her use the hall washroom, as it had only one door and no windows. Before letting her in the small bathroom, he removed everything but the toilet paper. Sharp objects and medications were removed, as well as towels. He needed her alive, in case there were problems in Jamaica. She felt humiliated as he waited outside the closed door for her to finish.

When they were ready to sleep, they tied her down on the living room sofa. Poupore fastened her wrists and ankles, and tied her legs to a leg of the heavy sofa. She was trapped, and she accepted it. She had never been more uncomfortable and scared, but she was alive. She ached, she was tired and she couldn't sleep. But, she *could* think.

Lisa felt she had let Rita down, and now Rita's life was also in jeopardy. Maybe she *should* have gone with Rita. Rita had wanted her to come along, but Lisa didn't think she could live life on the run, particularly in another country. Rita was generous; she had provided her with more- than-enough money to live on—Lisa had never had to ask. Finally, Lisa fell into a troubled sleep.

When she opened her eyes, it was morning. Her two captors were having coffee in her kitchen. She never asked for any food, and no one offered her any.

The day dragged on. Lovelady and Poupore were bored but tense, knowing the hour of Lombardo's unimaginable task would soon come. Lisa kept absolutely silent, refusing to eat when they did offer her food. Around noon she finally broke her silence.

"Can I go out and get the paper and the mail? I can see the paper on the driveway, and the mail should be here by now."

Lovelady and Poupore looked at each other, not sure of what to do. She sensed their hesitation. "Look, I'm not going anywhere, and I'm not stupid. There're two of you and one of me. Obviously, I can't drive the car, and where would I go if I did run away?"

She let them think about what she said. "I overheard what that guy said about not drawing any attention to the house. I think a paper staying on the driveway looks suspicious, if no one gets it."

She was thinking as fast as she could, and decided on one of the excuses she had come up with during her long night. "I don't want to get hurt and I want to cooperate with you." She continued, "Look, the guy across the street is a cop and he can't take his eyes off me. He makes any excuse to come over here, even if it's just to give me the paper or the mail. I'm telling you, he's going to see that paper and bring it over. Don't forget he's a cop and, if he does come over, I can't go to the door looking like I do or he'll start asking questions. It would really look strange if one of you were seen coming in-and-out of the house. Look, I'll even take off my shoes. Even if I did try to run away, I couldn't outrun you in bare feet. Wouldn't you like to read the paper anyway?" She was desperate to get to the mailbox.

They knew she was right. She couldn't go anywhere and the boredom was too much for Lovelady and Poupore to stand.

Without saying anything, Lovelady got up and untied the constraints. She stood up, rubbing her wrists and ankles to revive her circulation.

"Okay, go ahead, but I'll be watching you from the window."

She slipped off her shoes and walked out the front door. He was watching her closely from inside the house. She walked to the paper, picked it up, and glanced casually at the front page, before going to the mailbox. She opened the mailbox, leaned over, and peered inside. It was empty. As she had practiced many times before, she positioned her body just right and deftly reached in with her right hand, so that her movements couldn't be seen from inside the house. She pulled down an envelope that she had taped to the top of the mailbox the first day she moved into this house, as she and Rita had discussed so many times before, when planning what to do in a desperate situation. She left the envelope in the mailbox, shut the mailbox door and walked back to the house with the paper.

"No mail?" Lovelady asked, as he took the paper.

"No. And it's usually here by now." Her heart was racing.

Once again, he tied her hands and feet, but not as tightly as before. He didn't keep her on the hard kitchen chair, but let her rest on the sofa, watching her tensely. She was silently praying he wouldn't go to the mailbox and that the postman would stop.

She held her breath when she heard the postal jeep drive up. "Please stop," she silently prayed. To her relief, the driver stopped, opened the mailbox and noticed the large blue and white EXPRESS MAIL postal envelope in the box. He removed it and read the note that was attached: *"Mr. Overton: I had an emergency and had to leave before I could take this down to the post office. I've already filled out the information on the address form and enclosed $30 to cover the postage. This is really critical. Thanks for taking care of this for me."*

The driver looked at the envelope. She had checked off the 'Next Day Delivery' box on the form. Her name and address were noted as sender in the FROM section. The letter was addressed to Patrick McGuire, in care of Autry, Martin & Ramsey CPA firm's offices in Baltimore, Maryland. The letter carrier placed the letter on the seat beside him and drove off. Within two hours, the letter was on a plane en route to the Baltimore Post Office.

# Chapter Fifty-Eight

It was eleven the next morning, when Russell Autry burst into the conference room. Pat and Charlene, startled, looked up from their work. "Pat, Edie buzzed me because she couldn't find you! There's a postman with a priority mail envelope for you up front and I think it's what you're looking for. You need to sign for it."

"Let's go," Pat said. Could this be the one break they had prayed for?

They rushed to the receptionist area, where the postman was making small talk with Edie. "Are you Mr. McGuire?"

"Yes, I am."

"Just need your signature, sir."

"Where do I sign?"

The postman pointed to the signature box on the form and Pat scribbled his name. The postman took it back, ripped off his copy, and gave the parcel to Pat. Pat was too excited to notice that Edie, Russell, and Charlene Hackman all stood next to him.

"Who's the sender, Pat?" Russell asked.

He looked at the FROM box and glanced up. "Oh my God!" he exclaimed softly. "It's Rita's sister!" Pat wanted to be discreet, but he was having difficulty containing his excitement. "Russell, call your dad. We'll look at it together in the conference room." Good or bad, he wanted to share this moment with the people who had been so supportive of him.

Edie called for relief at the front desk as Russell called his father. Pat and Charlene headed down to the conference room to wait for the others. Relieved to find it empty, Pat turned on the lights. He sat down at the long table, nervously turning the envelope in his hands. Charlene sat quietly waiting for the others.

Russell and his father came in, Edie followed. Pat made eye contact with each of them before pulling the tab on the back of the envelope. Inside was a single sheet of white paper. He read the note out loud:

*Dear Pat:*

*If you get this note, something is dreadfully wrong, and I'm not in a position to explain what's going on, other than to say that, in all likelihood, either Rita or I, or maybe even both of us, are in danger.*

*We think this is all you have to know:*

RITA DAVIES
5214 IDLE HOURS COURT
RUNAWAY BAY, 9, JAMAICA
(876) 741-1814 (this is a cell phone)

*You got this letter because I couldn't contact you:*

*LISA HERRERA*
*1232 EARLEEN DR.*
*CAPE GIRARDEAU, MO 63701*
*(573) 533-9557 (this is just a regular telephone)*
*(573) 533-2733 (this is my cell phone)*

*God bless you and good luck. You're all we've got.*

*Lisa*

Pat looked at Charlene. "Well?"

"We have to call Malcolm. Right now." She picked up the conference room telephone and called Malcolm Karl.

"Karl here."

"Malcolm we've got a break in the Davies case. Pat just got an express mail letter from her sister in Missouri."

"Read it to me."

Malcolm listened to the message and, without hesitating he said, "Stay where you are. I'll be right there. Don't do anything until I get there."

It seemed much longer to everyone, particularly Pat and Charlene, but Malcolm Karl was in the conference room in less than thirty minutes.

"Okay, here's where we are. We tried to contact the sister in Missouri, but there's no answer on either telephone. The phone company says there's nothing wrong with the lines, but no one picks up. We'll keep trying. We tried to call Miss Davies in Jamaica, but there is some problem with the connection, and we just get a recording telling us to try later."

He paused to catch his breath. "I've already contacted our office in Missouri, and we have a team of people headed to Cape Girardeau right now. They'll keep us up to date."

He looked around the room. "There's an aircraft waiting at Andrews Air Force Base to take me, Charlene, and Pat to Montego Bay airport in Jamaica. I've got another team headed there right now from Miami. They're going to meet us there." He looked at Gilbert Autry. "Mr. Autry, can we continue to count on you?"

"Of course. What can we do?"

"We need you to arrange to have someone here twenty-four-hours a day to monitor the phones and, of course, to watch the mail. This is their only point of contact, and I want someone here if Davies or her sister calls." He pulled a piece of paper out of his jacket pocket. "You can get us at this number anytime, and please don't hesitate to call, even if you're not sure it's important. Okay with you?"

He shook his head yes, glad to be involved.

"Let's go then; we have a marked car waiting downstairs to get us to Andrews."

They left the building in the marked police car that waited directly in front of the door. The officer switched on the cruiser's emergency lights, and they sped through the streets of Baltimore toward Andrews Air Force Base in Camp Springs, Maryland.

As the car's siren wailed its way through traffic, Karl gave directions from his cellular telephone to his deputies in Baltimore and brought the Miami office up-to-date. The gate sentry was waiting for them as they pulled into Andrews Air Force Base's North Gate. A military police car, its emergency lights flashing, and a **FOLLOW ME** sign affixed to the trunk escorted them to hanger number three, where the jet was waiting. As two MPs opened an AU-THORIZED VEHICLES ONLY gate, they drove directly onto the tarmac to the waiting plane. Ten minutes later, having cleared District of Columbia air space, they were headed south toward Jamaica, when Karl turned to Pat.

"Pat, I'm going to try to reach Rita. If I make the connection, I'm going to hand the phone to you. I want you to talk to her first, so she knows we're for real. Then hand the phone to me, and I'll take over."

As he carefully dialed her number, Pat and Charlene held their breath. Pat closed his eyes and said a silent prayer: "Please God, let her answer and be safe." As he opened his eyes, Karl was handing him the instrument. "Pat, it's ringing!"

He took the phone, and listened. "One ring. Two rings. Three. Come on, Rita, pick it up. Four." He had a frustrated look on his face when, suddenly, he heard Rita's voice.

"Hello."

"Is this Rita?"

"Yes. Who is this?"

"Rita, it's Pat! Pat McGuire!"

"Oh, my God! Is it really you? How did you get my number?" she asked, too excited to realize the obvious answer.

"Rita, listen, I don't have time to explain now but I'm in an airplane headed for Jamaica. I'm going to hand the phone to Agent Karl of the FBI, and I want you to listen to him." He handed the phone to Karl.

"Miss Davies?"

"Yes, this is she, what's wrong?"

"Miss Davies, I'm with the Federal Bureau of Investigation. Please listen to me, and do exactly what I tell you to do. We believe someone, who may already be on the island, has been hired to get those tapes. Your life could be in serious danger, and we don't have any time to spare. First, where are you now?"

"I'm in my car outside a grocery store."

"Do you still live at the Idle Hours Court address?"

"Yes."

"Don't go back there for anything. Is there any hotel near you?"

"Yes, there's one."

"What's the name of it?"

"The Villa on the Beach." Karl noted the hotel name on a piece of paper.

"I want you to go there right now. Check yourself into a room under another name. I want you to use the name Charlene Hackman. We'll call the hotel as soon as we're off to make arrangements. Do you understand?"

"Yes. Charlene Hackman." She committed the name to memory.

"Correct. Go to that hotel right now, and don't leave until someone calls you from the FBI. I don't want to frighten you, but this is very serious. Do you understand?"

"Yes. I'll go as soon as we hang up." She suddenly realized that the only way they could have reached her was through the letter her sister had taped to the top of the mailbox. She knew that her sister must be in trouble. "How is Lisa?"

Karl didn't hesitate. "I'll be honest with you. We don't know. We just got her letter and tried to contact her, but we haven't been able to so far. Our people are on the way to her right now and, I promise you, as soon as we know anything, you'll know. Okay?"

"Okay."

"Go to that hotel right now. Don't stop at the house or anywhere else, and don't leave until one of our people contacts you. We should be there within three hours."

"Can I talk to Pat?"

"I'm sorry, but no. We have to go, but we'll be there as soon as humanly possible. I'm going to disconnect now." He pushed the OFF button and turned to Pat and Charlene. Pat was sure this was the first time he had ever seen Karl smile. "She's going to be okay."

Pat was beside himself. After all this time and worry, she was safe. He had never felt better.

At about the same time, Andy Lombardo's flight was touching down at the Kingston Airport. During the flight, he had written down every possible scenario that he could imagine and planned how he would handle each different set of circumstances.

Lombardo got his baggage and arranged for a rental car and a mobile phone. After getting directions to Runaway Bay, he put his luggage in the trunk and headed out. He stopped briefly in a beautiful, secluded picnic area.

Getting out of the car, Lombardo inhaled a breath of moist Jamaican air. He popped the trunk, opened the suitcase, inserted a fully loaded clip into the pistol's grip and put his shoulder holster on under his suit jacket. The only other items he had taken with him were also in the suitcase: a pair of handcuffs and false credentials identifying him as Agent Robert Diehl of the United States Federal Bureau of Investigation.

# Chapter Fifty-Nine

Forty minutes later, Andy Lombardo stopped at a gas station just beyond a sign that read RUNAWAY BAY 2 KM. He topped off the car's tank, even though the fuel gauge indicated he had used less than a quarter tank to get to his destination. Striking up a conversation with the attendant, he got directions to Idle Hours Court.

Runaway Bay was larger than Lombardo had expected. Driving through the center of town, he noticed it had a small shopping area, several restaurants, a bank, and an apartment building. Several hotels and bed-and-breakfasts outlined the perimeter of a peaceful cove.

He found Idle Hours Court and drove slowly, looking for a mailbox with 5214 painted on the side. He parked the car directly in front of the house, leaving the key in the ignition. He carefully surveyed the surrounding area and, after assuring himself that he was not being watched, he cautiously walked to the front door.

He had his FBI identification in his left hand as he tapped solidly on the teak door and listened for any movement from inside the house. After hearing none, he knocked again, more forcefully this time. There was no response. He put the credentials back into his jacket pocket and walked to the rear of the house, hoping Rita might be relaxing on the beach. The beach was deserted.

Lombardo walked completely around the house, again confirming that it was vacant, before he got back into the car and drove to a remote restaurant he had noticed on the other side of the town, FRASER'S VE-RANDA. He parked the car in the shade of the far corner of the gravel lot, and from an inside pocket of his jacket, took out a pen and small pad of paper.

Neatly folding his jacket, he returned it to the back seat and picked up the mobile phone. Before dialing Rita's number, he reviewed, in his mind, each possible scenario that he had so carefully rehearsed on the plane. To sound convincing to Rita, he knew he would have to pick each word with tweezers before he spoke. He dialed her number and heard the connection. She answered after the first ring.

"Hello."

"Is this Rita Davies?"

"Yes. This is Rita, who is this?"

He knew precisely what to say. "Miss Davies, this is Agent Diehl of the FBI." He listened to her response closely, knowing it would guide the direction of their conversation.

"Is Pat with you?"

He processed what he had just heard and wrote the word 'Pat' on the pad. "No. Not yet." Thinking quickly he continued. "Where are you right now?"

"I'm at the hotel like Agent Karl told me. Are you in the lobby?"

He quickly wrote 'Karl' and the word 'hotel' with question marks beside the words, before proceeding with the dialogue. He guessed that the authorities had already contacted her and he knew he had to act fast. "Are you alone?"

"Yes. No one else has called me but you and Karl."

He understood the current situation and he knew exactly what to say next. "Agent Karl has assigned me to make the first contact. I want you to do exactly what I tell you to do. We have people watching the hotel, and we're concerned you may have been seen going in. Do you know where the Fraser's Veranda restaurant is?"

"Yes."

"I'm calling you from there right now, and I want to meet with you here. I want you to go down to the lobby and take a cab here. Don't use your car. Understand?"

"Yes. When do you want to meet with me?"

"Right away. You'll see a white Oldsmobile Cutlass in the far corner of the lot. I'll be standing next to the car and I'm wearing a gray suit. Have the driver drive directly to my car, in case you're being followed. Do you understand?"

"Yes. I'm leaving right now."

He heard her hang up and smiled to himself. He was almost there. He knew he would have the tapes and the money within his grasp shortly. Timing was perfect; he was one-step ahead of the authorities once again, and he knew precisely what to do.

Less than ten minutes later, Rita Davies was sitting in a taxi, nervously giving the driver directions to the restaurant. She was jittery about what would eventually happen to her. Knowing she was an unwitting accomplice, she comforted herself because of her faith in the justice system. Placed in a desperate position, people take desperate action and, at least, she would be safe. She prayed for her sister.

The jet carrying Pat McGuire, Malcolm Karl, and Charlene Hackman received clearance to land at Montego Bay Airport. The pilot brought the aircraft to a stop and shut down the engines. Two vehicles pulled up to the parked plane: one carried two FBI agents and the other, a marked Jamaican police car, carried two uniformed officers. The officers in the police car were part of a special squad used for emergencies and, unlike patrolmen, they were armed.

McGuire, Karl, and Hackman were hustled down the plane's steps and ushered into the unmarked car. The police cruiser turned on its lights, and the unmarked car followed its escort to The Villa on the Beach Hotel in Runaway Bay.

Rita's thoughts were interrupted when she saw the FRASER'S VERANDA sign. The taxi driver pulled up to the front door. She looked around and saw a man in a gray suit standing beside a white Oldsmobile in the far corner of the parking lot. She asked the driver to take her to the Oldsmobile. As she got out and paid the driver, she noticed with relief the calm, serious demeanor of the man next to the Oldsmobile. "Agent Diehl?"

He pulled his FBI identification from his jacket pocket, flipped it open, and held it so she could read it. After she glanced at it and made eye contact with him, he put it back in his pocket. "Miss Davies, I'm glad you were able to get here so quickly. Did you notice anything unusual at the hotel or on the drive over here?"

"No. Nothing. Listen, have you found out anything about my sister yet?"

Once again, he was thinking fast. "No, not yet. Karl told me that he has people on the way to Missouri right now but, other than that, I don't know anything." He was glad she asked this particular question, and she seemed satisfied with his response.

"Miss Davies, I want you to listen to me. We both know how serious this situation is. We'll need to get you out of Jamaica and back to the states right away. We've arranged for an airplane out of the Kingston airport, but we have to take care of two things immediately and I'm sure you know what they are."

"The tapes and the money, I'm sure."

"First, where are the tapes, Miss Davies? Our people need them to close in on these conspirators. We know they want the tapes just as badly. Listen, this is very serious. They may have people here right now looking for you, and these people won't stop at anything to find you. We can't waste any time and it's possible that we're being watched right now." He reached out and gently squeezed her shoulders.

She looked at him and saw the sincerity and concern in his face. She closed her eyes and told him, "I knew it was just a matter of time. I hope you all understand why I did what I did. I'm not a bad person, I was concerned for my life. Please believe me!" Her eyes were now wide open, and she waited for his reaction.

He touched her shoulders gently once again. "Miss Davies, I'm not the judge, and I can't give you legal advice, but I can tell you that the more you cooperate, the more favorably you'll be treated in court. I *can* promise you that." His voice was compassionate and seemingly sincere. "We'll get you out of here safely and do all we can for your sister, but you have to tell me now. We can't wait. Every second is precious."

She took a deep breath and exhaled. "The tapes are in a safe deposit box at a bank—near where I used to live in Maryland. The key is in a safe deposit box at a bank here in town."

He asked her questions about the name and address of the bank, writing the information down on the pad of paper. As he was writing, he continued to ask her questions. "Are you the only person with access to the safe deposit box?"

"Yes."

"We're going to have to go to the bank right away and get the key. Is the money at this bank too?" He continued to write as she answered.

"No. The money is still in Switzerland, and all of the paperwork is in another safe deposit box at another bank here in Jamaica."

Lombardo continued writing notes.

"All of the money is still in the Swiss account?"

"Most of it. I arranged to use some of it to help that poor murdered accountant's widow back home, I needed some, of course, and I sent some to my sister in Missouri but, other than that, the money is in the Swiss bank." She paused, giving him time to catch up on writing what she had told him. "All of the paperwork for the money still in Switzerland is in that safe deposit box too."

He continued writing and said, "What are the names of the banks?"

"Queen's Bank and the Duke of Windsor Bank, right here in Runaway Bay."

"Do you have the safe deposit keys with you?"

"Yes. They're on my key ring in my purse."

"We're going to have to go to the banks right now and get everything. Then we'll get you out of here and you'll be safe. Let's go." He started to walk around the car to open the passenger door.

"Mr. Diehl, I'm embarrassed, but you're going to have to give me a minute."

"Miss Davies, we don't have any time to spare."

"I know, but I have to use the ladies room. I promise I'll only be a few moments. Can you wait for me at the entrance? I promise I'll be right back."

Lombardo was irritated, but had enough presence of mind not to break character. "Of course. I'll finish writing my report and pull the car around."

Meanwhile, unknown to Lombardo and the others, FBI agents and the Missouri State Police SWAT team had taken crucial positions around the house in Cape Girardeau, Missouri where agents had successfully identified the automobile parked on the road as a rental car. Neighbors, whose homes were being used as vantagepoints, had cooperated fully. The officials were waiting for just the right moment to move in.

As Rita was walking into the restaurant to use the ladies' room, the two-vehicle police caravan pulled into the entrance of The Villa on the Beach Hotel. They entered the lobby and the startled clerk asked if there was a problem.

"Please ring Charlene Hackman's room. This is an emergency," Malcolm Karl said, holding out his FBI identification for the clerk.

The desk clerk entered some information into his computer and watched the screen. A moment later he said, "Here—you can use this phone."

He handed a telephone across the counter to Karl. Several long seconds passed. "There's no answer!" He handed the instrument back to the clerk. "We'll need you to let us into her room. This is an emergency."

"I don't have authority to do that. I have to get my manager." Before anyone could react, the manager came out of his office, attracted by the commotion in the lobby.

"What seems to be the problem?"

Karl answered. "We don't have time to explain now, but we're the people who called you earlier about having Charlene Hackman check into this hotel. This is a police emergency and we need immediate access to Charlene Hackman's room."

Pat's anxiety was building by the minute. He felt relief when the manager didn't bother asking for identification. "Jacques, what's her room number, please?"

"Room two-fourteen."

"Follow me."

Pat, three FBI agents, and two uniformed Jamaican police officers followed the manager to the room, where he opened the door with his master key. Before entering, Karl pulled the manager back and said, "Let me go in first."

Karl stood by the side of the door, swung it open with his left hand, and cautiously peered inside. He entered with his weapon in his right hand, in the FIRE position pointed toward the ceiling. "Everyone stay here." Sensing no movement, he entered the room in a crouch, looking quickly into the bathroom, before entering the sleeping room. The room was unoccupied. "You can all come in now, it's empty." Everyone rushed into the room. Karl put his weapon on SAFE and put it back into his holster.

"What do we do now?" Pat asked.

Without wasting time to explain, Karl used his mobile phone to dial the number for Rita's cellular telephone.

Uncharacteristically, Karl tapped his foot, saying, "Come on, answer. Come on, Rita."

Rita was washing up in the ladies' room of Fraser's Veranda restaurant when her cellular telephone rang, startling her and the woman standing next to her. Pushing in the PHONE button, she put the instrument to her ear. "Hello?"

On the other end of the line, Malcolm Karl was visibly relieved. "I've got her," he said.

Pat and Charlene Hackman began to relax again. He continued, "Miss Davies, this is Agent Karl. Where are you? We asked you not to leave the hotel until we got there!"

The woman standing next to Rita noticed the confused look on her face. "What do you mean? I'm with Agent Diehl at the restaurant, just like I was told."

This time Karl was confused and looked around the room. "Do we have an Agent Diehl involved?" One of the agents who met them at the airport said, "No. Never heard of him, and I would know."

Karl continued, "Rita, what does this man look like?"

"He's very big, short blond hair, and wearing a gray suit. He showed me his identification!"

Karl responded quickly, "Listen to me closely, Rita. That man is not one of our agents, and he may be dangerous. Do whatever you have to do to stall and protect yourself. We're on our way. Lock the door, and don't hang up! What's the name of the restaurant?"

"Fraser's Veranda!"

Lombardo had moved the car to the front of the restaurant. Rita wasn't waiting for him at the door. Annoyance and suspicion began to pulse through him. Moving quickly, he walked into the restaurant and approached the bartender. The bartender smiled and said, "What can I get for you?"

"Did you see a blonde woman come in a few minutes ago?" Lombardo asked.

"Yeah. She went into the ladies' room." He pointed to the rear of the restaurant. The woman who had been standing next to Rita was coming out. Lombardo approached her.

"Ma'am did you notice a blonde woman in the restroom?"

She smiled. "Yes. She's on her telephone."

Lombardo reacted immediately. He walked over to the ladies' room and pushed on the door. It was locked from the inside. He drew up his right leg and kicked the door with all his might, but it didn't open.

On the phone, Karl heard Rita scream when she heard the door kicked.

The bartender's eyes grew wide as he watched Lombardo continue to kick the door. He picked up the phone on the bar and dialed for police. It seemed to take too long for someone to answer. He continued to hear Rita's screams. Frightened patrons rushed to the front door. Finally, a voice said, "Police, fire, or ambulance?"

"Police!" he shouted. "Hurry!"

Another voice asked, "What is the problem sir?"

"I'm calling you from the Fraser's Veranda Restaurant in Runaway Bay, and I think I'm witnessing some kind of kidnapping or something. Hurry!"

In a very calm voice, the dispatcher said, "We'll have a unit there shortly."

On his sixth kick, the jamb shattered, sending splinters into the air. The door swung open on its hinges, bouncing off the sink that was next to the door. Lombardo went in, but the small bathroom appeared empty. Looking for feet and seeing none under the two stalls he kicked in the first stall. It gave easily, but was empty.

He kicked in the door to the second stall. Rita stood on the toilet, terrified, with the telephone up to her ear. She was screaming into the phone, when he grabbed it out of her hand, threw it to the floor and shattered it.

Rita was no physical match for Lombardo's strength. He took one of her wrists and drew it behind her back. He reached into his pocket, pulled out handcuffs and quickly had Rita's hands cuffed. Rita screamed and struggled desperately, but he grabbed her hard around her right arm and dragged her out of the room.

Meanwhile, his expression troubled, Karl ordered, "Let's move!"

As they ran down the stairs to the lobby, the Jamaican officers described to Karl the route they would follow to Fraser's Veranda. Moments later, the agents' car was speeding toward Runaway Bay, behind a cruiser with flashing emergency lights and a wailing siren.

Lombardo dragged Rita, helpless, through the restaurant, noticing that the restaurant's panicked customers and bartender had run outside. The bartender and the restaurant's patrons were huddled paralyzed behind the restaurant, as Lombardo pulled Rita across the threshold toward his car.

The whine of a far-off siren became louder and, seconds later, a lone police car skidded to a stop in the parking lot. An unarmed Jamaican officer ran toward Lombardo, who had managed to force the struggling Rita into the back seat of his rented Oldsmobile.

"What's going on here?"

Lombardo stood outside the car as the officer approached. The officer started to back away as Lombardo reached into his pocket, but recovered when Lombardo flashed identification papers, which the officer recognized as an FBI badge and identification.

"What's happening here?" he asked, more calmly.

Lombardo was breathing hard, but his voice was under control. "Listen, we've been working undercover. She's a fugitive that we've suspected in some terrorism. Do you know where Queen's Bank is?"

The officer appeared confused.

"Listen, I'll explain everything later; I could use an escort to get to Queen's Bank right now! There may be a bomb in her safe deposit box! This is an emergency." Lombardo was hoping Queen's Bank had the information on the money, *his* highest priority.

The officer composed himself, sensing the urgency of the moment. "Follow me. I'll have you there in five minutes."

Running back to his cruiser, he turned on the emergency lights, and pulled back onto the street. Lombardo followed him closely, noticing the officer was driving with one hand and holding his radio with the other. Lombardo knew he didn't have much time left.

Rita sobbed futilely as they followed the police car with the blaring siren. Four minutes later they pulled up to the bank. The lights of the police cruiser continued to flash as the officer ran up the bank's steps and opened the door. Lombardo dragged Rita into the bank. In the lobby, there were only two customers. Seeing the uniformed police officer and the screaming woman in handcuffs, the customers ran out of the bank, followed by most of the bank employees.

The manager, shocked to see Rita in handcuffs, looked to the officer for an explanation, and didn't reply to Rita's desperate pleadings for help.

"This man," he pointed to Lombardo, " is with a U.S. crime agency—the FBI—and the woman is a fugitive. They suspect she may have placed an explosive device in her safe deposit box. Do you recognize her?" the officer asked.

"Yes. She's one of our customers! I see her in here about once a week."

Lombardo took over. "We don't have time to explain right now, but we were tipped she has placed a bomb in her safe deposit box. Open the vault right now."

The startled bank manager ran back to his office, returning with keys in his hand. He opened the barred door leading to the vault and, after several turns of the safe's locking mechanism, the vault door opened, exposing the safe deposit boxes. He led Lombardo and Rita into the vault, while the officer waited outside at Lombardo's direction.

While Lombardo, the bank manager, and Rita were in the vault, the officer used his radio to contact his shift commander to request assistance from the explosives unit and to get direction on what he should do next.

"Listen to me! You've got to help me! This man wants to kill me!" Rita was still screaming in desperation, as Lombardo dumped the contents of her purse onto the floor. He picked up the key ring and gave it to the manager.

"It's one of these."

The man fumbled with the keys, settling on one. "This is one of our keys. Box 192."

"Open it. Hurry."

Speedily, he opened the thick, stainless-steel door, and Lombardo could see a metal box inside. "Get out, I'll take it from here. Shut the vault door, but don't lock it, in case this thing goes off!"

The manager quickly got out, leaving them alone in the vault. Lombardo pulled out a grey metal box, set it on a table and opened it. A small brown envelope, holding a single key, was inside. "Is this the key to the safe deposit box in Maryland where the tapes are?'

"Yes," she answered sobbing, "just like I told you."

Lombardo was irritated with himself that he didn't ask her first which bank had the key to the tapes and which bank had the Swiss bank documents. He put the key into his pocket.

He dragged Rita out of the vault and the bank manager came over.

"Do you know where the Duke of Windsor bank is?"

"Of course. It's on Ocean View Drive."

"How do I get there?"

As the manager was explaining, Lombardo realized it was not far from the restaurant where he had met Rita. At first he was upset with himself that he hadn't had the presence of mind to go there first, but quickly he decided it was fortunate, as he was sure authorities would be on their way to this bank very soon, and he would pass them going in the opposite direction.

"Was there anything in the vault?"

Lombardo answered quickly, "There is a device in there, and I think I disarmed it, but we'd better lock the vault just in case." The frightened man started toward the vault door.

Lombardo turned and saw that the police officer had his radio up to his ear. The officer's expression was troubled, as finally he understood the situation.

Lombardo pushed his hostage away, quickly drew his weapon, pointed it at the officer and fired. The projectile struck him directly in the middle of his chest, and he fell backwards over a wooden railing. Turning, Lombardo pointed the pistol toward the bank manager, who was now locking himself in the vault. The heavy door thudded shut before Lombardo could make his move. Grabbing Rita, Lombardo pulled her outside to his car, ignoring the screaming onlookers and shoved her into the passenger's seat.

Driving toward the second bank, he watched his speed to avoid attracting unnecessary attention.

Pat McGuire, the FBI agents, and their Jamaican police escort pulled into the parking lot of the Fraser's Veranda restaurant. The crowd of patrons had gathered at the entrance.

Karl and the FBI agent who had been driving got out, as did one of the uniformed officers from the Jamaican police vehicle. The bartender immediately came forward and, explained excitedly what had happened.

"No, sir. They're gone. They followed the officer who responded when I called. I heard him say she was a fugitive. He seemed to be some sort of undercover officer from the States."

He told them that he had no idea where they were headed, but the man and woman were in a white Oldsmobile. Things happened too fast for him to get the license number.

The bartender was interrupted as the officer's partner called from the car. "Mervyn—headquarters! You're wanted on the radio. Come—it's the Commander."

Karl followed Officer Mervyn Alleyne to his car. Once the officer had concluded his conversation with the commander, he spoke quickly with Karl and climbed back into his cruiser. Karl and his driver followed suit.

As they pulled out to follow the cruiser, Karl briefed the others. "A Jamaican officer was hit at Queen's Bank in Runaway Bay! A witness said a white male had a woman hostage—they left in a white car! Sounds like our man."

Once again, they were following their escort, this time toward Queen's Bank. McGuire and Karl were in the back seat and Hackman sat in front with the driver. Pat's heart pounded with adrenaline. He prayed for Rita's safety. Other sirens sounded in the distance. He was sure they were also headed for the bank.

Lombardo smiled as the marked police car, lights flashing, passed him, headed in the opposite direction. Once again, he was one step ahead of the authorities. He had the key to the tapes, he had the woman they were looking for, soon he would have the money, and *they* were headed in the wrong direction.

Rita knew her time was almost up. Lombardo needed her to get to the money, but that was all. She knew she would end up like that poor policeman when Lombardo no longer needed her. She cried out as the police car passed, feeling helpless with her hands cuffed behind her. Another police car followed and then an ambulance sped by.

All at once, she realized what she had to do. She had to try something. Anything.

She heard another siren. Vehicles pulled off the side of the road as a police cruiser passed. The cars that had let the police pass eased back onto the road. They were approaching in the opposite lane.

Accepting immediate action as her only hope, Rita leaned her back against the passenger door, lifted her right leg and, with her foot, pushed the bottom spoke of the steering wheel with all her might. Lombardo was caught completely by surprise.

The car veered sharply across the lane of the oncoming traffic, and headed toward a deep drainage-ditch bordering the shoulder of the road. Lombardo tried to turn the wheel back to his left but Rita kicked furiously at his hands and the steering wheel, as he attempted to regain control.

She felt a tremendous impact and heard glass breaking, as the car spun out of control. Fruit tumbled from the pick-up truck that had crossed their path, as it spun in the opposite direction.

The truck had smashed the car on the driver's side. The force of the impact pushed the Oldsmobile sideways down the road where it finally stopped, about a hundred feet from the point of impact. The collision had shattered all the windows.

A deep gash was evident in Lombardo's forehead, and his right arm seemed to be injured. While he was writhing in pain, Rita took advantage of his confusion. From behind her back, she lifted the passenger door handle. Managing to work her way out of the car, she slammed the door shut with her foot.

Glass shards and fruit covered the road, and steam poured from the truck's ruptured radiator. The dazed men who had been in the truck had gotten out and were yelling unintelligibly. They stopped when they saw the strange, handcuffed woman running down the road.

The adrenaline surging through her body pushed Rita's legs as fast as they could go, as she ran in the direction that the police cars had been headed, hoping another would pass by and see her. Her hands still bound behind her back, Rita ran clumsily. Gasping for breath and sweating profusely, she knew she couldn't stop running. There was no time to turn her head to see whether her captor had gotten out of the car and was pursuing her.

Lombardo had managed to slide over to the passenger seat and get out of the vehicle. The men from the truck started to approach him, but stopped when they saw the blood covering his face. He pulled a gun from under his jacket, pointing it toward them. He shouted that he was a police officer and ordered them not to follow, as he started running after Rita.

Holding the gun in the palm of his left hand, Lombardo cradled his right arm close to his body with his left forearm. Though hampered by his injury, he was closing the distance between himself and Rita. Blood now soaked his shirt, and Lombardo could feel himself becoming woozy, as he watched Rita disappear over the crest of a small hill.

Pat, the FBI agents, and their police escort were speeding toward the bank when they saw the accident. They saw the smashed pickup truck first. Several people were gathered around, talking with animated gestures. As they passed the scene, Pat shouted, "It's a white Oldsmobile!" The driver skidded to a halt, as the police cruiser in front of them continued on.

Car doors opened. Spectators yelled, pointing in the direction where Rita and Lombardo were running. The agents' car resumed the chase.

The officers in the police car had not noticed the white Oldsmobile or that the agents' car had come to a stop. Continuing on, it sped toward the bank. Neither its driver, concentrating on driving at high speed, nor the officer in the passenger's seat, who had turned around and was still looking in the direction of the accident, noticed that they had passed a figure in a gray suit running in the same direction. Cresting the hill, all four wheels of the police car left the ground. The car landed hard on the downward slope of the hill, and the impact of the landing caused the passenger to hit his head hard against the roof, stunning him briefly as the driver tried desperately not to lose control of the vehicle. Neither policeman saw Rita jumping up and down, trying to get their attention as they passed her and they continued toward the bank. Lombardo had already started down the opposite side of the hill when he saw Rita, doubled over, fighting for enough breath to continue her sprint. He let his injured arm drop painfully to his side as he extended his left arm toward her and fired. Not seeing him, Rita stood up to catch her breath. She had started to run again when she heard the strange, cracking sound. She turned to her left and saw Lombardo in a crouch, pointing his weapon toward her. Instinctively, she continued running, praying out loud that she wouldn't fall. Her weaving gait and the fact that Lombardo was right-handed caused him to miss his first shot.

Lombardo, kneeling with his shooting arm still extended, waited for her silhouette to cross the sights of his weapon. Pat's car then flew over the same ridge. It, too, bounced off the asphalt of the hill's descending grade. Its passengers closed their eyes and tensed to absorb the impact. The car bounced off the road twice, passing Rita and Lombardo. As they sped off, Lombardo closed the distance between him and Rita.

As they drove, Pat thought he noticed something in the car's side mirror. He turned to look out the rear window. "It's them!" he screamed. The driver quickly glanced in the rear view mirror, and saw the two figures on the side of the road, a man and a woman. He slammed on the brakes, expertly bringing the car to a skidding stop. Putting the car in reverse and draping his left arm around the passenger's seat, he backed up as fast as the car would go. Passing Rita, he turned the steering wheel quickly. This time, the car skidded to a halt between Rita and her pursuer. "Get down!" he yelled the moment he saw the gun, and everyone obeyed.

Lombardo had a bead on the driver and fired off one round. The bullet pierced the driver's window, entering his right shoulder and lodged in his neck. Yelling in pain, the agent slumped unconscious across the seat, his head coming to rest on Hackman's hip. Lombardo fired off another shot, piercing a window and just missing Karl. Then he moved to position himself at the back of the car, making escape impossible for its occupants.

Lombardo, now directly behind the car, was shooting into the car's exposed fuel tank, knowing that, eventually, one of the rounds would cause a spark, exploding the car. Pat and the agents, trapped, crouched down on the floor of the car.

Pat closed his eyes tightly, preparing for the explosion. His heart surged and, for an instant, he envisioned his parents. This picture vanished from his mind as the car seemed to vibrate from the impact of Lombardo's bullets.

Time seemed to freeze as more shots from Lombardo's weapon rang out. Pat winced as bullets pierced the trunk and fuel tank of the car.

Still crouched in the back seat, Pat couldn't see that Agent Hackman had somehow crawled over the wounded agent, without exposing herself to Lombardo's barrage. She put the transmission in reverse and turned the steering wheel, pressed the accelerator with her hand and the car rolled backwards at an angle. Praying she had correctly judged the movement of the car, she pulled her hand from the accelerator and pushed hard on the brake, stopping the car. Quickly, she reached up and slid the transmission into PARK. The excitement and her movements had her completely out of breath. She inhaled as deeply as she could and yelled, "I've got the car facing the shooter; open the doors to use them for cover and get out."

Hackman, in front, drew her weapon, opened the door and got out, using the door for a shield. At the same time Karl opened the door behind the driver and did the same. As soon as he was out of the car he ordered, "Stay in the car and stay down McGuire, you're not armed."

Pat did as he was told, feeling useless as he crouched on the floor.

Despite his wounds, Lombardo's experience provided him with the presence of mind to position himself behind a tree so as to make himself invisible to the agents protecting themselves behind the open car doors. He knew they would have to coordinate their next move and he used the time to reload his weapon.

Karl, the agent in charge of the operation, called out to Hackman, behind the front door. "Help should be here any second. Just stay down and wait." At that very moment, Lombardo fired at the exposed feet below the opened front door, and the bullet struck Hackman directly in her ankle. Racked with pain, she somehow crawled to the back of the vehicle and screamed, "Karl, I'm hit! I can't help you."

Watching the unfolding drama from his vantagepoint, Lombardo heard the remark. He moved to his right, unseen by Karl, still behind the rear door. Soon Karl, exposed and unprotected, would be in full view of Lombardo, as he continued to move right.

Lombardo continued stalking and soon Karl's profile was fully exposed to him. He was drawing up his weapon to fire but saw Karl, in a crouch, retreat to the back of the car to check on Hackman.

Without hesitation, Lombardo seized the moment. Unseen, he ran to the car, and dove into the driver's seat pushing aside the wounded agent. He immediately pulled the transmission into drive and smacked the accelerator to the floor. The car roared forward, fishtailing, leaving the stunned Karl and the wounded Hackman behind. Karl fired off five shots, but the bullets harmlessly pierced the trunk. Lombardo steered the speeding car in the direction Rita had been running and didn't notice that Pat McGuire was still on the floor in the back seat.

Pat's mind was racing. He hadn't seen a thing and had no way of knowing who was driving. He lifted his head, trying not to make a sound until he could see the driver. He had never prayed like he was praying, while slowly getting off the floor. *Please let the driver be one of the agents or a Jamaican police officer! Please!*

Slowly, ever so slowly, his head rose over the back of the front seat.

His eyes widened as he saw the driver's profile. *It can't be!* he thought. But it was and he had no doubt. The driver was the same person who had injured him a couple of years earlier in the football game. Despite the circumstances, Pat remembered what Karl had said about his being "one bad actor."

McGuire didn't know what to do; Lombardo was concentrating on the road, searching for Rita. Cresting a small hill he saw her halfway up the slope on the other side bent over and gasping for breath. Lombardo pulled up directly behind her and slammed the vehicle into PARK. Pat had the element of surprise as he threw his right arm around Lombardo's neck and screamed for Rita to continue running. Rita, exhausted, couldn't move.

Pat was squeezing Lombardo's neck with all his might but Lombardo's training didn't fail him. Despite his injured arm, he managed to get his feet up to the dashboard, coil his legs and push off, catapulting his body over the front seat and on top of Pat. While they were struggling Lombardo pulled his pistol from his shoulder holster. Pat let go of Lombardo's neck and grabbed his wrist with both hands. Despite his injury, Lombardo was much stronger than Pat and used the leverage of being on top of him to his advantage. Pat was using all his might to push the barrel of the weapon away from him but watched it continue to move in the direction of his face until, mercifully, two hands grabbed Lombardo by the shoulders and he was dragged out of the car.

"Thank you, God; thank you, God," Pat mumbled almost unintelligibly, as he lay on the back seat catching his breath.

His relief was momentary for almost immediately he felt hands reach under his armpits and he was pulled from the car. Before he could react or gain his footing, he found himself face down on the shoulder of the road with a heavy knee digging into the small of his back. He had no energy left to offer any resistance to having his hands handcuffed behind his back by a Jamaican police officer.

"What are you doing?" he screamed. He flipped over onto his back and saw Lombardo pointing his pistol at him, while two uniformed Jamaican police officers stood at his side. On his left, he saw Rita on her stomach, hands shackled behind her.

"Stop him! Stop him!" Rita screamed, "He's the man you're after!"

Lombardo still had the weapon pointed toward Pat. The confusion reflected in the faces of the officers was real.

"I'm with the Federal Bureau of Investigation in the United States," Lombardo said, "and this man and woman are wanted for drug-trafficking." The officers were obviously confused until Lombardo said, "One of you reach into my coat pocket and you'll find my identification." The officers looked at each other and one nervously reached into Lombardo's jacket and removed a black leather object. He unfolded it and saw the badge and FBI identification with Lombardo's picture on it. They both examined it and slipped it back into Lombardo's pocket.

"What can we do to help, Agent Diehl?" one of them asked.

Lombardo was thinking fast. "Look in the car—I've got a seriously wounded agent that I have to get to a hospital right now or he'll die." One of them ran over to the car, looked in and nodded to his partner. Lombardo directed, "You two stay here and guard my prisoners. I'm taking him to the hospital. Our people should be here any second to take over."

Pat and Rita were pleading for the policemen not to believe him, but Lombardo got into the driver's seat and drove off, leaving Pat and Rita in the custody of Jamaican police.

Hackman was lying on the road as Karl and Jamaican police wrapped her shattered ankle with a towel and elevated it. Once she was stabilized, Karl again took charge and directed the Jamaican police to follow his orders. He jumped into a marked police cruiser and told the driver to follow the same direction Lombardo had taken when he commandeered the vehicle.

Light flashing and siren wailing, a caravan of Jamaican police cars sped down the usually lazy road. Karl soon saw the lone police car at the side of the road and an officer waving frantically for them to stop. In his hurry to get to Rita and Lombardo, Karl didn't realize that the black Lincoln Lombardo had hijacked wasn't at the scene.

The driver pulled over, stopped behind the police car and turned off the siren. Karl jumped out and the officer ran up to him. "We have your prisoners on the ground." Karl drew his weapon and followed the officer. He couldn't believe it when he saw Pat and Rita with their hands cuffed behind them, on the ground "Oh, no," Karl said, "you've got the wrong people!" Karl closed his eyes and tipped his head toward the sky.

The police officer's face displayed a strange mixture of pride, confidence and total disorientation. "What do you mean the wrong people? The man who was fighting with this man was with you! He showed us his identification! Isn't Agent Diehl with you?"

Karl opened his eyes and immediately processed what happened. Lombardo got away.

Or did he?

Forgoing apologies or explanations, Karl had Pat and Rita's handcuffs removed. Rita went right to Pat and he hugged her tightly, while he explained to Karl what had happened in the car. Karl thought quickly and had the officer get on his radio to describe the armed and dangerous man who had fled the scene of the accident in a stolen vehicle, the direction he was last seen taking, and that he had a seriously-wounded American law enforcement official as a hostage.

While the officer was on the radio, several other marked cars, with lights flashing, had pulled up behind the cars at the scene. The senior officer in charge ran up to Karl, who quickly explained the situation. Shortly, the commander had all the cars driving off in every conceivable direction, in hopes of finding the fleeing black Lincoln. Orders were given to place the airports on alert to look for Lombardo and news flashes were soon broadcast.

As Karl was coordinating all of this with the commander, the whine of two approaching helicopters was heard. Unknown to Pat and Rita, the police had closed the road and set up landing zones for the aircraft. As they watched, the helicopter settled down on the road, with their rotors still turning. An officer ran to each aircraft, boarded it and, within seconds, the helicopters were once again airborne. They flew off in opposite directions, searching desperately for the fleeing Lincoln.

As Karl was walking to Pat and Rita, still huddled together, the ambulance that had picked up agent Charlene Hackman passed by, heading for the hospital emergency room.

Pat looked down at Rita, who was hugging him as hard as she could. She was totally exhausted; sweat matted her hair down and her face was streaked with dirt and makeup. Still, Pat thought she was the most beautiful woman he had ever seen. He thanked God she was unharmed and they were together at last.

Karl ushered them into a police cruiser and they were on the way to the hospital.

While Rita was still being evaluated, Karl, other American law enforcement officials and Jamaican authorities met with Pat in a private room.

They recorded the conversation with Pat and, for the next hour-and-a-half, he told them everything he could possible recollect about Lombardo. Karl was immediately on the phone updating his colleagues, and the Jamaican police commander did the same.

Within ten minutes of Pat's concluding his interview, Rita, her medical evaluation completed, was led into the room for her interview. Pat was asked to sit in, in the event Rita's talk might spark other facts that Pat had forgotten.

Rita told them everything. When she told them about the tapes and the money, Karl immediately had the bank where the tapes were located in Maryland notified. In addition, all of the documentation for the money in the Swiss account, still in the safe deposit box at the second bank, was now in Karl's hands.

Rita was given a sedative before leaving the hospital. Less than an hour later, they all boarded the jet that was still on the tarmac of the Montego Bay airport. Before they cleared Jamaican air space, Rita—mentally and physically exhausted—had fallen asleep in Pat's arms. She did not wake up until they landed in Washington, DC.

Pat stayed awake during the trip, as the gravity of his experience wouldn't allow him to rest. Karl was on the telephone the entire time trying desperately to obtain information on Rita's sister, Hackman's condition and the whereabouts of Lombardo and the wounded agent. When the plane landed, Karl had no further news.

# Chapter Sixty

Lovelady had made coffee and was sitting at the kitchen table. The clink, clink of his spoon in his coffee cup was the only sound in the house. Lisa, her hands bound in front of her, was in the hall bathroom, guarded by Poupore standing outside the closed door.

The strain of waiting to hear from Lombardo had taken a toll on both of them. They should have heard something from him by now. Lovelady had tried to contact Lombardo in Jamaica several times during the night, but never connected.

Lovelady was watching the green digits in the kitchen microwave clock, seven fifty-five. He silently accepted that Lombardo had failed. He heard the bathroom door open, turned and saw Poupore taking Lisa back to the sofa. Concentrating on what to do next, he got up and walked to the front window, peeking outside through a narrow slit in the curtain, when his eyes widened immediately. "Jesus Christ, there are cops everywhere!" he screamed, when he saw the street in front of the house filled with police cars, lights flashing. Officers were quickly taking cover behind their cars, pointing rifles toward the house.

Poupore ran to the window. "Out the back! Now!" Lovelady ordered. They ran for the back door, but it appeared to detonate off its hinges toward them, pushed by four police officers manning a battering ram. The men holding the battering ram fell to the floor, and four other officers outfitted with full protective clothing ran across their backs into the house.

All four of the officers had their rifles pointed at Lovelady and Poupore, who were now standing stunned in the kitchen. One of the officers screamed, "Hands in the air! Now!" Lovelady and Poupore did as they were told and offered no resistance as they were handcuffed. In police cruisers, they were soon being rushed to the county jail to be questioned separately.

As soon as the house was declared safe, two female paramedics and two female police officers ran to the bathroom where they could hear Lisa sobbing. In less than five minutes, she was carried to a waiting ambulance, sedated and taken to a nearby hospital for evaluation and questioning. Her ordeal was over.

Pat, Malcolm Karl and other authorities gathered in the boardroom of the hospital at Andrews Air Force Base in Camp Springs, Maryland. Pat and Rita had been admitted in order to receive more complete medical exams than time afforded them in Jamaica. Pat had survived the experience remarkably well, but Rita, now in a private room, was heavily sedated.

As they were talking, an Air Force nurse, looking very serious, walked into the room, asking for Agent Karl.

"I'm Karl."

"You have a phone call, sir. Please come with me."

Karl looked at the others, held his hands in front of him and crossed his fingers before leaving with the nurse. He returned in less than five minutes.

Pat and the others could tell from the look on his face that at least some of the news he had to tell them was bad.

He sat down and took a deep breath before beginning.

"I just got off the phone with our people in Baltimore and I'll tell you everything I know." The room was totally silent and no one interrupted him as he continued.

"First, Rita's sister Lisa is okay." Pat felt a surge of relief on hearing the words, but he wouldn't allow his face to reflect it, knowing Karl had more to tell.

"They stormed the house and captured Lovelady and Poupore without resistance. Lisa went through quite an ordeal, but she's fine and they're flying her here now."

No one spoke for a long minute, still deferring to Karl.

Karl hesitated again and inhaled deeply before continuing. "And now the bad news." He put his hand to his forehead and looked down, not wanting to make any eye contact.

"They found the car Lombardo drove off in. The driver who got hit didn't make it." Pat had never seen the always business-like Karl show emotion, but when he looked up, his eyes were glassy. "We worked together for years and he was a good man." Pat could see the other agents were also reacting to the news.

Karl continued, "The doctors said he could have made it, but Lombardo shot him again before abandoning the car." He pulled a handkerchief from his pocket and wiped his eyes. After composing himself, he continued. "And somehow Lombardo got away. Everyone did all they could, but somehow he got away."

One of the other agents walked over to Karl. He put his hand on Karl's shoulder and squeezed gently. "Malcolm, I think it's a good idea if you come with me." Karl followed him out of the room, leaving Pat with the others.

Pat didn't have any reason to, but he felt a little embarrassed being among them at that moment. Sensing his discomfort, one of the agents explained, "It's hard to describe, but we're all like brothers here."

Pat knew exactly how they felt. Somehow he managed an appropriate grin, "I know what a brotherhood is and I know how you feel. I was a Marine." They all smiled weakly.

"Can I tell Rita?"

"Of course, you go right ahead." Pat left the room leaving the agents alone to grieve in private.

After checking at the nurses' station, Pat walked slowly to Rita's room.

Rita lay quietly, staring out at the hospital parking lot. Despite having been medicated, sleep eluded her, as she worried about her sister's plight.

"Rita?"

"Hey, Pat—come on in," she offered tiredly, pushing her hair back from her eyes and pulling herself up a bit.

Pat sat carefully on the edge of her bed and took her hand. Gently, he told her. "Good news—Lisa's fine, Rita. Agents are with her in Missouri, and she's just fine. Karl just heard."

Rita covered her face and leaned toward Pat, as her tears of relief and exhaustion began to flow. "Oh, thank God—I've been so scared for her. I don't know what I would have done if anything had happened to her! I put her in so much danger!"

Pat held her close and let her cry. "Come here, sweetheart, everything's going to be alright," he said softly. Rita relaxed in his arms. Finally, the ordeal was really over. Rita felt she was where she belonged, as Pat cradled her warmly and gently kissed the back of her neck.

For a moment, Pat held her where he could see her face and tenderly brushed the hair from her eyes. "And Rita, the nurse told me I can stay right here in that chair next to your bed all night," he said.

Rita smiled and patted on the bed with her left hand. Pat took off his shoes, climbed into her bed and pulled up the sheet, covering them both. They held each other tightly all night long.

He decided to tell her everything else in the morning.

# Chapter Sixty–One

The next day at 3:00 P.M.:

A car carrying four armed FBI agents pulled up to the entrance of the Tobacco Exports International Headquarters Building. They went directly to the receptionist's desk. "May I help you gentlemen?" he asked with a smile.

One of them pulled his identification from his pocket, showed it to the man behind the counter, and said, "We're with the FBI. Is Mr. Kerry Barber in?"

The young man tried to stay cool as he picked up his phone. "Just a moment. I'll check."

Before he could connect the call, the agent interrupted him sternly: "Just ask if he is in, please. Don't say anything about our being here." The receptionist registered the agent's serious tone.

"Yes, sir." He pushed in a button. "Christy, is Mr. Barber in the office today?" He continued to make eye contact with the agents. "Thank you. Yes, he's in all day."

"Thank you. We need you to take us to his office, please."

"Follow me."

As they walked through the office, the receptionist attempted to be businesslike. He knew all of the employees who saw them must be wondering why the receptionist, who was always at the front desk, was leading four very serious-looking strangers through the office. Arriving at the executive office wing, they stopped at a desk where a secretary was working outside a closed office door. The brass plate on the door read:

## KERRY BARBER
## CHIEF EXECUTIVE OFFICER

"Christy, these gentlemen are here to see Mr. Barber. Gentlemen, this is Christy Nolen, Mr. Barber's personal administrative assistant."

She looked up and smiled. "I'm sorry, Mr. Barber is in a meeting now. He asked not to be disturbed. Would you care to make an appointment?"

"No, ma'am." The agent was once again taking out his identification. Showing it to her he said, "We're with the FBI, and we need to see Mr. Barber immediately."

"I'm sorry, but he asked not to be disturbed. He's conducting a very important meeting. I'm sure you understand." She smiled again.

Wasting no time, the agent said, "Ma'am, we have a warrant for his arrest. Please tell him we are here."

"I'll tell him you're here." She picked up her telephone and pushed in a button.

"Mr. Barber, there are some gentlemen out here who say they have to see you." After a moment: "I understand, sir, but they said they're with the FBI." She continued to hold the phone up to her ear, and a few seconds later she said, "I understand." She hung up the phone and looked up. "I'm sorry, gentlemen, but Mr. Barber says you'll have to make an appointment."

The agents all looked at her for a second. Understanding the helplessness of her position, they walked the few steps to the closed door, opened it, and entered the room.

Startled faces looked up. Barber, seated at the head, spoke angrily, "What is the meaning of this!"

"Are you Kerry Barber?"

"Yes, I am. Who are you?"

"We're with the FBI. We would like a word with you in private." Barber's wide-eyed guests all glanced at each other.

"You'll have to make an appointment. This is an important meeting!" Seeing the four agents, Barber knew he was facing the unimaginable.

Continuing his feigned outrage, he protested, "You'll have to leave my office. I'm a very busy man, and I refuse to discuss any matters with you or anyone else without my attorney present! Now get out!"

The lead agent gave Barber a long, icy stare before continuing. "Mr. Barber, I have a warrant for your arrest. You'll have to come with us."

"I told you already! I'm not going anywhere!"

Taking papers from his pocket, the agent said, "You don't have any choice, sir, you have to come with us." As he was talking, one agent walked to Barber's side, and the other two stood on each side of the door. All three pulled their jackets back to expose their shoulder holsters, and stood with their hands on their hips. "It will be easier on everyone concerned if you just come quietly. Everything will be explained to you later."

"I want to speak with my attorney!"

"We understand, sir, but we can't let you talk to him here. Please come with us now. You'll have plenty of time to talk to him later."

Barber slid his chair back and started to leave the room. The agent grabbed his right arm, and in a matter of moments, his hands were shackled behind him. One of the agents read him the words of the Miranda ruling, and soon he was being led down the halls of his own offices.

Employees stared. Humiliated, Barber soon found himself sitting between two FBI agents, being driven to his arraignment.

At precisely the same time, this scene was being replayed in the offices of the other conspirators. The conspiracy to secretly fix the prices of tobacco and to jeopardize Latin markets was over.

# Chapter Sixty–Two

$\mathsf{T}$he following week . . .

Malcolm Karl had arranged for Rita and her sister to meet with the District Attorney in his office in downtown Washington, D.C, at the J. Edgar Hoover Federal Building. Pat and Charlene Hackman, who had a cast that ran from her toes to her knee, joined them. They were seated in a private conference room, and the district attorney explained that the meeting was going to be tape-recorded.

After the formal introductions, Karl started the discussion. He explained, in great detail, how Jim Hampson, in his position as the Chief Executive Officer, had participated in and, in fact, orchestrated the clandestine price-fixing meetings. He illustrated how Hampson had used Rita as an unknowing accomplice. He indicated that her sole involvement had been to order plane tickets and book hotel rooms for the conspirators all at Hampson's direction. Karl used charts to show links among the individuals involved in the price fixing arrangement. He pointed out that these men were all now in custody, due in large part to Rita's safeguarding the original tapes of the meetings.

Karl showed how it was understandable—indeed, even prudent—for Rita to fear for her life after Ramsey's murder. Lovelady had been systematically checking the files for leads regarding others involved with Hampson. The District Attorney listened closely to the details of Rita's experiences while transferring the money from Spain back to Switzerland. Finally, when Karl had finished, the DA addressed Rita, who had been sitting nervously between Pat and Lisa.

"Miss Davies, I must say, I'm impressed with what you and Mr. McGuire were able to do on your own before our involvement. Under the circumstances, I can see how you didn't know whom to trust." He tried to force a compassionate smile. "But—I'm sure you know we have a serious problem, and you know what it is."

"Sir?"

"The money. It's a fact that you took money that wasn't yours. I can't ignore that under the law. Do you understand?"

She sighed. "Yes, sir, I do. I would like to say something, though."

"Go on."

"I had no intention of keeping the money. I would like for you to check with the bank. They will concur that the only disbursements have been for small amounts of money to support my sister and me. Please think about the position I was in. My life and my sister's life were both in danger, and there was no way we could support ourselves on what we had, and getting a job was impossible. The bank will confirm that I made an arrangement that if anything happened to me, the money would be automatically transferred back to the federation. When I was in Spain and Switzerland, I was desperate and didn't know what to do, but I never had any intention of keeping the money. Please believe me—when I thought it was safe to do so, I planned to contact the authorities through Pat and return the money voluntarily."

The District Attorney raised his eyebrows.

Before he could say anything, Malcolm Karl said, "What she says is true. We've already checked with the bank."

He shook his head approvingly.

"The bank did substantiate one other item relating to the money."

"What was that?"

"A sum of money was set aside to support Ramsey's widow and children. Other than that, everything she said is true." He paused, "Don't forget, without those tapes we could have never moved in on the price-fixing scam in the first place. The judge who finally issued the warrants wouldn't let us move in with just a copy of a single tape. She needed all the tapes—and not just copies, but the originals."

The District Attorney was tapping the eraser of his pencil on the table, deep in thought.

"May I say something else?" Karl asked.

"Of course."

"Miss Davies couldn't have been more cooperative. The tapes were what she said they would be, and *she* took the initiative and turned over the bank's paperwork to us, permitting the transfer of money back to the federation from the Swiss bank. This has been done."

"So the money has been returned already!"

"Yes, it has. In fact, we've met with the federation's board of directors. They're satisfied to have the money back and relieved the situation is over. In fact, I understand they voted to continue the trust fund that Rita had set up to support Ramsey's wife and children, even though they had the right to rescind the agreement.

"One final thing."

"Go on."

"The federation's board also voted not to pursue any action against Miss Davies or any of the accomplices."

The District Attorney continued to ponder, occasionally glancing at the report. "Miss Davies, I have a question."

"Yes, sir."

"How in the world were you able to be in several places at the same time? I can't help but be curious."

"Sir? I don't understand."

"I was reading Agent Hackman's portion of the report and it said that Rita Davies and her alias of Linda Sanchez had simultaneously paid for and used tickets to Ireland, Jamaica and Rio. How were you able to do that? You covered your tracks so well it would have taken us forever to find you, if your sister hadn't sent that letter to Mr. McGuire."

Rita relaxed a bit and smiled. "It was really very simple." Everyone was looking at her, but particularly Charlene Hackman, who had been trying to track her down before the letter arrived. "When I was in Switzerland, I was concerned that Jim would somehow track me down. I had to do something to make it difficult for him to find me. I made friends with the Swiss bank's representative; her name is Heidi. I gave her my real identification and passport, and I bought her a one-way ticket to Ireland. I gave her enough money for a short holiday and a return ticket in her own name. That way, the records showed the ticket was used. I contacted her several weeks later from Jamaica, and she just mailed me my identification.

"In the meantime, I bought a one-way ticket to Rio—with a layover in Jamaica. I went to Jamaica on Sanchez's ID. When I landed, I made arrangements with the airlines to extend the layover to two days. While I was there, I met a young woman and, essentially, made the same offer to her that I did to Heidi. I gave her some money, too, and she went on vacation in Rio, using Linda Sanchez's documents. She returned to Jamaica using her own identification and gave me Linda's papers when she returned."

Pat, the FBI agents, and the District Attorney sat in stunned silence as she finished the story. After several long minutes of thought, the attorney looked around the table. "Correct me if I'm wrong. It appears to me that you were an innocent accomplice to Hampson and his role in coordinating the price fixing meetings. It seems that you have never benefited from your participation personally."

Everyone in the room hung on the DA's words, knowing Rita's future was in the hands of this attorney. He continued, "I can understand how his deception toward you led you to switch tapes without his knowledge, leading to a whole series of events that you had no control over. I can also understand how you feared for your life and your sister's, after the accountant was murdered." He paused, "I would have been frightened, too, under the circumstances. I can't say I blame you for taking action to protect yourself."

He glanced at the FBI report for the final time. "As a direct result of your actions, Jim Hampson and his wife are now awaiting trial for their roles in the conspiracy, for embezzling a large sum of money, for fleeing the country, obstructing justice, possessing false identification, and so on."

He took a sip of water and continued. "As if that's not enough, safeguarding the tapes provided us the key ingredient we needed to close in on one of the largest price-fixing scams of its kind, the participants of which, I understand, have been arraigned, and we have a whole list of things to pin on Hampson's attorney and Lovelady." He looked at her and smiled.

"And it's all due to the fact that Hampson lied to you when he said he was going to take you with him, isn't it?"

She smiled weakly, nodding.

Continuing to look at his notes, the District Attorney asked one final question. "Am I correct then to gather that the only missing link in this chain of events is the man who eluded us in Jamaica? The one who shot that unfortunate agent and wounded agent Hackman here?"

"Yes." He paused, "We tried everything we could and we haven't given up, but the bottom line is, he got away."

The District Attorney and everyone in the room knew that Karl summarized the situation with the mysterious and elusive Andy Lombardo with that one statement.

The District Attorney stood up, gathering his papers. He looked at Rita for the last time. "It appears to me that, since the money has been returned and the injured party is satisfied with the recovery and has declined to pursue any further action, that you're not guilty of any crimes, Miss Davies. You and your sister are free to go."

Cheers of joy erupted from the usually reserved FBI agents. Everyone burst from their chairs, applauding, slapping each other's backs, and shaking hands with the District Attorney. When the emotion subsided, Pat walked over to Rita.

No one seemed self-conscious watching Pat McGuire and Rita Davies as they kissed.

> *"Heaven hath no rage like love to hatred turned,*
> *Nor hell a fury like a woman scorned."*
> —William Congreve
> "The Mourning Bride"